"A seductive, brooding tale of dark love. Victoria Holt, move over!"
—Bertrice Small, Author of The Last Heiress

A SHOCKING DISCOVERY

Sara's heart pounded in her breast, thudded against her ribs. Pressed up against the crack in the door, she held her breath in anticipation. The heavy footfalls coming closer were not those of a servant, certainly, who were well-skilled at moving without making a sound. No, these footfalls had no care for discretion, their owner weary and borne-down. When he passed, she gasped in spite of herself. It was Dr. Breeden!

What was this? The doctor's rooms were on the second floor, not the third. Sara waited until he disappeared in the shadows of the landing below, before stepping into the corridor again. No candlelight flooded the hallway from the chamber he had vacated now, only a thin sliver of light seeped out from under the door. She crept toward it.

Hot blood surged into her temples. The flush of it narrowed her eyes. She would not knock. Grasping the knob, she threw the door open…and stopped dead in her tracks, teetering on the threshold of a well-appointed sitting room. The man inside stood beside the hearth, naked to the waist, a brandy snifter in his hand. His left shoulder was wrapped in heavy bandages. He spun to face her, and the look in his eyes—half horror, half pain-laced rage—would have sent her fleeing if she weren't rooted to the spot.

"Step inside and close the door," said her husband.

DAWN THOMPSON

THE RAVENCLIFF BRIDE

LOVE SPELL   NEW YORK CITY

In memory of my father, George Wellington Thompson.

LOVE SPELL®

September 2005

Published by

Dorchester Publishing Co., Inc.
200 Madison Avenue
New York, NY 10016

ISBN 0-505-52653-0

Visit us on the web at www.dorchesterpub.com.

THE RAVENCLIFF BRIDE

One

The coast of Cornwall, 1815

"Please, sir, I beg you, have the driver slow the coach!" Sara cried. "We shall tip over at this pace." Clinging to its hand strap, she held her bonnet on her head as the carriage sped toward the summit with horses at full gallop. Since they passed through the spiked iron gates at the bottom of the approach to Ravencliff, they'd been traveling at breakneck speed through the darkness as though the hounds of hell were nipping at the horses' hooves.

"We need to maintain such a pace on this steep incline," her companion replied. "Take ease, my dear, the coachman knows what he's about."

Peering out the window at the sheer-faced drop to the rocky shoreline below, Sara doubted that. The road—if one could call it that—didn't appear wide enough for another coach to pass. There was no shoulder. All that separated them from the edge of the bluff was the remains of a low, stacked stone fence on the sea side, while a high wall of

1

granite looming over the road on the other seemed to nudge them toward impending calamity.

The sound of loose pebbles and crumbling earth raining down over the rocks as they streaked along all but stopped her heart. Below, towering white-capped combers pounded the strand, the echo of their thunder amplified by a cottony fog ghosting in off the water with the turn of the tide. Chased by the risen wind, it climbed the cliff and crept across the road, obscuring Sara's view through gaps in the broken fence. She shuddered. If she couldn't see, how could the coachman?

Its wheel struck a rut, and the coach listed, hesitating. The road was pockmarked with such. But the crack of the driver's whip and guttural shouts to the horses soon set it in motion again, every spring and seam in the dilapidated equipage groaning under the strain.

Sara sank back against the cold leather squabs and shut her eyes, certain that at any moment the post chaise would topple over the edge—coachman, groom, horses, and all. As if he'd read her thoughts, her gentleman traveling companion gave a throaty chuckle.

"We are almost there, Baroness Walraven," he said. "But for the fog, you'd be able to see Ravencliff once we round the next bend. Have no fear, I shall deliver you to your bridegroom all of a piece, you have my word."

Baroness Walraven. Her heart leapt at the sound of it. She must be mad—marrying a man she hadn't even met.

"You aren't having second thoughts?" he said. "It's a bit too late for that now, my dear."

"I've been having 'second thoughts' since you came to me with this bizarre proposal, Mr. Mallory."

Again, Mallory chuckled. "In that case, you should have voiced them before accompanying me all the way to Scotland to finalize it," he said. "There's nothing to be done now."

"That is what puzzles me," Sara returned. "If the baron

was so anxious to marry me—'to our mutual betterment,' I believe it was you said—how is it that he couldn't come in person? Why did he send you, his *steward*, as proxy? That's insulting. Even under these peculiar circumstances."

"I'm crushed," the man said, feigning heartbreak, "And we made such a handsome couple, too."

"What if I don't suit the baron?" Sara said, ignoring his flirtatious wink. Wasn't her traveling companion full of himself, though? He was handsome, and he knew it—fair-haired and fashionable, impeccably dressed, and cultured; the second son of a baronet, to hear him tell it. She wasn't impressed.

"Oh, I wouldn't worry about that," he replied, sliding familiar eyes the length of her. They were the color of steel, and just as cold. "But if by some unlikely happenstance such should be the case," he went on, "I'll be only too happy to oblige you. I thoroughly enjoyed our . . . nuptials."

Sara wasn't about to dignify that remark with an answer, yet he was right: What was done was done. And there was no doubt that he looked down upon her for consenting to such an arrangement.

Had the nodcock forgotten where he'd come to make the baron's offer? After six months in the Fleet debtor's prison, she'd have considered a marriage proposal from the Devil himself to buy herself free. Would her bridegroom look down upon her for it, too? She shuddered to wonder.

How the mysterious baron had heard of her predicament puzzled her, although she'd been told that oftentimes benefactors would offer for the inmates of such places as the Fleet. That hers was an offer of marriage and not something more indelicate should have been a comfort, she supposed; but it wasn't. The plain fact was, she had consented to wed a man she'd never even seen—by proxy out of the country, mind—and let a total stranger deliver her to him in this inhospitable place in exchange for payment of her debt. The exact details of the arrangement were yet to be disclosed. She knew nothing about the baron at all, except that their fathers had served together in India, and that they were evidently close friends in those days. He had stressed that point, she imagined, in order to put her at ease. Somehow it hadn't. Aside from Mallory's insistence that all proprieties would be strictly observed, and the baron's well-written proposal that was too good to resist tucked away in her reticule, she had no idea what lay in store. It couldn't be worse than the hellish nightmare she'd just come from . . . could it?

"Will the baron be in residence to greet us, at least, Mr. Mallory?" she asked.

"Why don't you call me Alex, my dear," he replied. "We shall be seeing quite a bit of each other, you know. I'm often at the manor. I keep rooms there . . . for when I'm not abroad on estate business." He gave another chuckle. "You'll likely see more of me than you will of your husband, truth to tell. He keeps to himself, does Nicholas—always has done. You can take me at my word on that. We go back a long way, Nicholas and I, since our school days actually."

"Then, why—"

"You will have to take the whys and wherefores up with him, my dear," he interrupted. "I am not at liberty to disclose his objectives."

"You haven't answered my first question, *Mr. Mallory*," she said, making sure he didn't miss her rejection of his offer to put them on a first-name basis. "Is his lordship in residence now?"

He consulted his pocket watch. "Oh, he's in residence," he replied. "Whether he's available or not, I really couldn't say." He tucked the watch away again inside his waistcoat. "But *I* shan't be. Once I've delivered you to the manor, I'm off to London for a sennight to collect his houseguest, and to give you two some time to yourselves."

Sara hadn't missed the seductive implications in his tone, and said no more; the less discourse with this individual the better. She'd seen too many like him in the Fleet. She tugged her spencer into shape, and ordered her traveling dress of dove-gray twill. It had gone limp in the bone-chilling dampness that had run her through like a javelin since they sighted the sea. Though the coach windows were closed, she tasted the salt on her lips. The fog still blocked her view, but that was no hardship; it spared her the sight of the restless sea rolling up the coast below, creaming over the rocky shingle, and topping off the tide pools that filled the coves. This would have been a breathtaking sight by day. In the dark, it was a fearsome thing.

"Look," Mallory said, pointing, as the chaise careened around yet another turn. "*Ravencliff*. You see? We have arrived."

Sara's breath caught. The sight knit the bones rigid in her spine. The house was in darkness, a huge, rambling structure steeped in fog to its turrets, looming three stories high above the courtyard. It was crowned with a pair of carved stone ravens, set like gargoyles in the eaves. It looked deserted. All at once, the dissipating mist drifted inland, as though the carriage had dispersed it by tooling into the drive, and she gasped again: Rising from the sheer-faced seawall, Ravencliff Manor looked as though it had been hewn from the rockbound cliff it crouched upon.

The coachman reined the horses in, locked the brake, and climbed down to set the steps. The mist had soaked him through from his wide-brimmed hat to the red traveling shawl he wore beneath his coat—the only splotch of color in the vicinity, glistening in the light of the coach lamps. Meanwhile the groom, likewise drenched, hopped off the dickey behind, and began unloading luggage from the boot.

"Not those," Mallory spoke up, exiting the chaise, as the man began to unstrap the two portmanteaus on top. "They are mine. I'm not staying." He offered Sara his hand, and she stepped down into swirling mist that all but hid the Welsh blue stone crunching underfoot. "Come along, my dear," he said. "Unless I miss my guess that's a flaw brewing, and I want to be on level ground again before it hits."

"A *flaw*?" she questioned.

"That's what the locals call the wicked storms that plague this coast, especially now, in spring. You'll not want to venture out in one. The winds will blow you right over the cliff, a mere wisp of a girl like yourself. You'd best keep away from the edge even in fair weather."

They had reached the entrance, and Mallory banged the brass knocker. After a moment the door opened and they were greeted by an aging butler and two wigged footmen dressed in blue and gold livery. Mallory ushered her over the threshold, and raised her gloved hand to his lips.

"Forgive my want of conduct, running off like this," he said, returning her hand to her dutifully kissed, "but all good things must come to an end. You're quite safe in the custody of Smythe here, Baroness Walraven. He will see to your every need. It has indeed been my pleasure, but now I must away."

Sketching a bow, he bounded down the steps and disappeared back inside the coach, whose wheels were rolling over the blue stone drive before he'd settled once more against the squabs.

Footmen rushed past to fetch Sara's luggage. There wasn't much: one portmanteau and a small valise containing necessities bought in London. The rest was to be provided at Ravencliff. Once they'd been brought inside, the butler shut the door and slid the bolt.

"Take Baroness Walraven's bags up to the tapestry suite," he charged the footmen. He turned to Sara. "If you will follow me, madam," he said, "Baron Walraven awaits you in the study."

So, he was in residence. She almost wished he weren't. What would he think of her in her damp, clinging traveling costume? She tried to tuck the wet tendrils of hair plastered to her cheeks underneath her bonnet, but it was no use; there were just too many. To her surprise, since it had seemed so dark from outside, candles set in branches on marble tables and in wall sconces lit the Great Hall, and each of the corridors they traveled. They did little to chase the gloom. There was a palpable presence of sorrow in the house, in the stale, musty air, and in the melancholy echo of their footfalls on the terrazzo floors.

Just for a second, Sara thought she heard the patter of dog's feet padding along behind. She turned, but there was nothing there, and after a moment, she turned back to find the butler watching.

"Is something amiss, madam?" he inquired.

"I thought I heard a dog," she said, feeling foolish now that, as far as she could see, the corridor behind was vacant.

"The house groans with age now and again," he said, resuming his pace. "You'll hear all sorts of peculiar noises, especially when the wind picks up. It's naught to worry over."

When they reached the study door, Smythe knocked, but there was no response at first. It wasn't until the butler paused a moment and knocked a second time that the Baron bade them enter, and then the butler ushered her into a large room, walled in books. Dark draperies were drawn at the windows. But for a branch of candles on a stand beside the wing chair Nicholas Walraven occupied, and a feeble fire burning in the hearth, the room was steeped in shadow. Sara flinched as the door snapped shut behind her in the butler's hand. The Baron set the tome he'd been perusing aside and surged to his feet, taking her measure.

Alexander Mallory had provided her with a description of her bridegroom, but he hadn't prepared her for the reality of the man. She assessed him to be in his mid-thirties, a striking figure, tall and slender, though well muscled. The Egyptian cotton shirt he wore tucked into skintight black pantaloons was open at the neck, giving a glimpse of chest hair beneath which matched the hair—as black as his namesake, the raven—waving about his earlobes, and falling in a rakish manner across his broad brow. The deep-set eyes beneath, dilated in the darkness, shone like obsidian. They had the power to hypnotize.

"Please be seated," he said, gesturing toward a Chippendale chair on the opposite side of the Aubusson carpet. "This needn't be awkward unless you make it so."

"Forgive me for staring," Sara said, sinking into the offered chair. "I didn't expect—I mean to say . . . Mr. Mallory didn't exactly prepare me for . . . all this." What had really tied her tongue was why such a man as this needed to resort to such outrageous lengths to get a wife.

"Have you eaten?" he asked. His deep voice resonated through her body, striking chords in places hitherto untouched in such a manner, and she shifted uneasily in the chair.

"I have, sir," she replied, "at the coaching station inn on Bodmin Moor."

"Would you like a glass of sherry, or perhaps something . . . stronger, to warm you?"

"No, thank you," she said. "I do not take strong spirits."

Walraven did not resume his seat. Instead, he strolled to the desk, and leaned against it, half-sitting on the edge with one well-turned thigh draped over the side in a casual pose. His polished Hessian boots gleamed in the candle glow, and the flickering firelight cast shadows that played about the deep cleft in his chin. No; Alexander Mallory had not done the man justice at all.

"Naturally, you have questions," he said in that throaty baritone that had such a shocking effect upon her. "To save time, how much has Alex told you?"

"Only that your offer was an honorable one; that all proprieties would be strictly observed; that the arrangement was to our . . . mutual betterment, and that you would provide the details once I arrived."

"Did he give you my missive?"

"Yes," Sara said, studying her folded hands in her lap.

Her heart skipped its rhythm. His eyes had picked up red glints from the fire. They were burning toward her like live coals. She couldn't meet them. "A most gracious invitation, Baron Walraven," she murmured.

"That won't do," he said. "You shall call me Nicholas, and I shall call you Sara when we are alone—commencing now. You shall need to get used to doing so. You are Sara Ponsonby no longer. We are husband and wife, and you must present that image. The private familiarity will help you adjust to that. On state occasions, you are Baroness Walraven, of course, more informally, Sara Walraven, which is how you will sign your documents. Is this clear to you?"

"Y-yes, Bar—Nicholas." His name did not roll off her tongue. It was all too new.

"Very well," he said. "Would you remove your bonnet, please?"

Sara was hoping he wouldn't ask her to do that, not until she'd had time to order herself. Hot blood rushed to her temples. Blushing was her most grievous fault, the curse of her fair-skinned heritage. She didn't need a mirror to tell her she was blushing now. Her cheeks were on fire. The heat rising from them narrowed her eyes.

"Please," he repeated, prompting her with a hand gesture. Sara removed the bonnet, and he arched his brow. "I see you are no slave to fashion," he observed.

"Sir?"

"Your hair," he said. "You haven't cropped it after the current craze."

"With so much upon me of late, I've hardly had time to think of fashion," she returned. Was her reply too snappish? She feared so, but it was too late now.

"I shall be brief," he said, shifting position, and the conversation along with it. "I am in need of a companion—only that. Someone to preside over my gatherings, and appear with me in public . . . on occasion, in order to deter predatory females, and keep the *ton* from continually trying to snare me into the marriage mart. If I have a wife . . . well, I think you get the point."

"Is that why you don't come to Town for the Seasons?" she couldn't help inquiring. It didn't ring true. If all he wanted was a hostess, he could have taken a mistress.

He hesitated. "That is . . . one of the reasons," he said. "My motives need not concern you—only my needs. Suffice it to say that I couldn't hire someone for the position, and have her reside here under the same roof with me without a breach of propriety. Since the woman of my choice would have to live here, she would have to become my wife. She had to be attractive, cultured, and above reproach. You possess all of those qualities. She also had to agree to the arrangement, as you have done on the strength of my missive alone, without full knowledge of the . . . conditions. That was paramount. It proves trust, and trust is vital. When I was made aware of your . . . situation, it seemed to me that we might strike a mutually beneficial bargain. I am glad that you have chosen to accept it. You will want for nothing. There are a few simple house rules that I must ask you to follow, but I shall come back to that."

Sara stared into those all-seeing obsidian eyes that seemed to penetrate her soul. The firelight still shone red in them. It was an odd business, and though he'd answered many of her questions, there was still one that needed to be addressed, and she didn't know how to ask it.

"Is something unclear?" he asked, as though he'd read her thoughts. "Oh, yes, of course," he hastened to add, convincing her that he did indeed possess such powers. "Your duties do not include sharing my bed. I have no desire to perpetuate my line. I hope that shan't be . . . a problem? I thought, under the circumstances, it might be somewhat of a relief."

"N-no, not a problem," Sara said. She hadn't considered the possibility of children, or the lack of them. His bluntness shocked her, and she avoided the issue. "There is one other thing that has puzzled me from the start, though," she said, with as much aplomb as she could muster. "Why did you send Mr. Mallory to London to fetch me, and why a proxy wedding, when such things aren't even possible in England? Why didn't you come yourself? I should think that would have been simpler than having me trek all the way to Scotland with a total stranger to have it done."

"That is not 'one thing,' Sara; it is three things," he said. "And all three encroach upon *motive*. However, I will allow it this once. Let us just say that . . . preexisting situations here on the coast prevented me from leaving it—even to marry." Striding to the bell pull, he yanked it, and turned back to her. "I've rung for Mrs. Bromley, my housekeeper. She will show you to your rooms, and introduce you to Nell, your abigail. Her quarters adjoin your suite."

"Thank you, Nicholas," Sara murmured.

"You will join me for meals," he continued. "Breakfast and nuncheon are served in the breakfast room. The evening meal is served in the dining hall. The servants will direct you."

"You said something earlier about . . . house rules," she reminded him.

"Yes," he said, "I was just coming to that. You will be given a complete tour of Ravencliff tomorrow. Please do not go off exploring on your own. The house is very old. Much of it is in disrepair, and you could do yourself a mischief. Please do not go out to the seawall unescorted. The Cornish winds are notorious. They have been known to blow strapping men off cliffs, and gales come up suddenly. We are on the verge of one right now. Though there are stairs hewn in the rock, do not go down to the strand. Those stairs were carved there centuries ago, and used by smugglers. This coast is rife with cairns and caves and passageways, none of them safe. Riptides are common here, and you could be cut off in seconds. Finally, what occurs within these walls *stays* within these walls. I expect you to be discreet. Do not carry tales. If you have a question, or a concern, do not burden the

Dawn Thompson

servants or Alex. Come directly to me. Do we have an understanding?"

"Yes, Nicholas," Sara replied, rising as he came closer.

"Good," he said. "I want this to be a pleasant association . . . for the both of us."

How he towered over her. Those riveting eyes, wreathed with dark lashes any woman would envy, were even more alarming in close proximity. They were hooded now, devouring her in the candlelight, making her heart race. He smelled clean, of the sea, with traces of tobacco, and brandy drunk recently. Combined with his own—almost feral—essence, the effect was intoxicating. She drank him in deeply, extending her hand.

He took a step back, breaking the spell. "Forgive me," he murmured, "I do not like to be touched."

A light knock at the study door made an end to the awkward situation, but not to her embarrassment, and she dropped the hand to her side.

"Come!" he called.

The door came open, and a plump, rosy-cheeked woman entered wearing crisp black twill, and a starched lawn cap and apron.

"Please see Baroness Walraven to her apartments, Mrs. Bromley," he said, "and have Nell attend her. See that all her needs are met."

"Yes, sir," the housekeeper responded, sketching a curtsy.

He turned to Sara. "It's late," he said. "You must be exhausted. I will expect you at breakfast. If you have further questions, I will address them then. Good night, Sara."

He dismissed her with a cursory bow, turned, and strolled to the hearth, his obsidian gaze fixed on the sparks shooting up from a fallen log in the grate. She had questions—so many questions, but there would be no answers then. The strange interview was over, and she followed the housekeeper into the corridor.

He'd made it clear that their marriage would be in name

only. He'd addressed that head-on, and she'd received it with mixed emotions. While she had been worried about sharing a bed for the first time with a virtual stranger, she was more disappointed than relieved that this wasn't to be part of the arrangement. Why would the man not want an heir? Come to that, why didn't he even want to be touched? Alexander Mallory had seized her hand earlier, and pressed it to his lips before it was offered; Nicholas, who was albeit technically her *husband,* had stressed that she was to present a wifely image, yet he'd refused such an innocent gesture of goodwill as taking it to seal their bargain.

Perhaps she'd been too hasty. Nicholas Walraven was a mystery, but there was nothing hidden in her situation. It was common knowledge that her father, wounded in battle and knighted for valor after serving under Wellington on the Peninsula, had died heavily in debt leaving her encumbered. Nicholas had paid a staggering sum to free her—far more than he would have had to settle on the daughter of one of his peers. Why; with so many well-to-pass prospects to choose from, had he made her the subject of his quest? It couldn't just be because their fathers once served together on foreign soil. He wasn't even born then. There had to be more to it than that, but what could it be?

She didn't believe his feeble explanation for marriage, either. He did imply that there was more to that. Why hadn't he explained? Why had a proxy wedding been necessary? Why hadn't he choosen to get to know her before making his offer? What had seemed an answer to her prayers in the beginning was now taking on darker dimensions. The worst of it was the way this strange, enigmatic man impacted her in the physical sense. That was most frightening of all.

"The tapestry suite, my lady," Mrs. Bromley said, jarring her back to the moment.

The windows rattled in their lead casings when the housekeeper threw the door open, and she waddled through the foyer that separated the rooms to draw the bedchamber draperies. Still, drafts snaked their way over the floor, ruffling the hem of Sara's damp traveling costume. Outside, the flaw was in full swing. Rain pelted the panes, driven by gusts that moaned like human voices, and the roar of the sea rolling up the cliff chilled her to the marrow. She had scarcely crossed the threshold when another sound bled into the rest and gave her heart a tumble: a plaintive, wolf-like howl echoing along the corridor. It rooted Sara to the spot.

"I knew there was a dog!" she cried.

"The wind, my lady, only the wind," said the housekeeper, shutting the door to the hall. "It howls through these old halls in a flaw somethin' terrible."

"That was no wind," Sara insisted. "I ought to know a dog's howl when I hear one. We had kennels once, fine hunting hounds . . . and horses." She spoke haltingly, remembering. She'd had to sell them all, and still it wasn't enough to satisfy the debt. Mist blurred her vision. She blinked it back. How she missed her beloved hounds. Losing them had wounded her heart. She would never forget the confused look of betrayal in their eyes, their whines and whimpers as their new master took them away—a cruel master, compared to the cosseting they were accustomed to at her hands. She couldn't think about that now else she dissolve in the threatening tears.

A maid burst through the door of the adjoining sitting room, face as white as milk.

"Ah! There y' are," Mrs. Bromley said. "Have ya readied my lady's hip bath?"

"Y-yes, mum," the girl replied, sketching a curtsy.

A stern look from the housekeeper softened the maid's expression, and she offered a feeble smile in Sara's direction, though her owlish eyes were still riveted to the door as though she expected someone to come crashing through it.

"Good," said the housekeeper, turning to Sara. "This is Nell, my lady, your abigail. She's a feared o' storms, but she serves this house well, and she'll serve you likewise." She glanced at the maid. "Well? Set out madam's nightdress, then help her ta bathe and make ready for bed. It's past eleven, and mornin' comes quick in this house."

"Y-yes, mum," the girl mewed.

"The clothes the master ordered sent are all hung in the armoire," the housekeeper explained, "your unmentionables are in the chiffonier. Whatever's lackin' will be brought from Truro, you've only ta make a list so's I can go myself, or send one o' the maids."

"I'm sure everything is more than acceptable," Sara responded. Compared to the state Mallory had found her in at the Fleet, anything would be an improvement.

Glancing around at the tapestries hung on the walls, it was easy to see how the suite got its name. But she was too distracted to do them justice. She was straining her ears in anticipation of another howl from the dog no one seemed to want to acknowledge. There was no sound now but the true wind driving the rain, slamming against the mullioned panes, and moaning about the pilasters.

Sara shuddered, moving on toward the dressing room, where her bath awaited. Having set an ecru gown and wrapper on the bed, Nell turned to follow, when Mrs. Bromley caught the maid's arm, drew her aside, and whispered something to her. It was obvious that whatever was being said was not for Sara's ears, and Sara left them to it, anxious to take advantage of the bath before it grew cold.

The water was strewn with crushed rosemary and mint, and Sara let it envelop her, while Nell sprinkled a few drops of rose oil into the mix. The effect was rapturous, and she groaned as the mingled scents threaded through her nostrils, and the precious oil silkened her skin.

"We'll have real rose petals soon now," the maid said. "They're late this year, too many flaws. You'll know when they're bloomin'. The wind spreads the scent all through the house."

"That wasn't the wind before, was it, Nell?" Sara asked.

"It *was* a dog, wasn't it—and you heard it too, didn't you?"

"I don't know what ya mean, my lady," the girl said. "All I heard was the wind. I'm scared o' it—ever since it took the north turret roof clean off, and blew it over that cliff out there. The master had it fixed, but that don't matter. It'll only go again. You're fortunate he didn't put you in one o' the turret suites. You'd be wakin' up in the ocean."

Sara would have no answers from the mousy little maid, and she was too tired to argue. The heavenly bath had relaxed her enough to sleep, and she let Nell help her into the gown, and brush out her hair.

"Such a fine color, my lady," the girl observed. "It shines like spun gold in the candlelight. Most o' the ladies are cuttin' their hair off these days."

"Do you think I should?" Sara queried, recalling Nicholas's remark earlier. She still wasn't sure if he'd meant it as a compliment or a criticism.

"Oh, I wouldn't venture ta say, my lady," the maid returned. "That'll be up ta you."

The decision would have to wait; the turned-down fourposter looked inviting, and Sara dismissed Nell, snuffed out the candles, and climbed beneath the counterpane and crisp linen sheets. The chamber faced the sea, and the westerly wind blowing off the water slammed full bent against that section of the house. The draperies—heavy though they were—trembled against the panes, and drafts teased the fire in the hearth, throwing tall auburn shadows against the tapestries on the wall. Sara shut her eyes. Lulled by the rhythm of the breakers rolling up the coast, she'd just begun to doze, when a strange noise rose above the voice of the storm, a scratching sound at the door.

She swung her feet over the side of the bed, but hesitated before she stepped down. *Rats! Of course there would be rats this close to the sea.* She shuddered. There were rats in the Fleet—big, ugly, hairy black creatures, with long, skinny tails. More times than she cared to recall, she'd awakened to one crawling over her legs in the night . . . in the dark. Gooseflesh puckered her scalp, and she sucked in her breath, remembering.

The noise came again, and a crippling chill gripped her spine. It wasn't coming from inside the chamber. Something outside was scratching at the door, and she tiptoed closer, listening. She held her breath. This was no rat scratching at the paneling. It was something . . . larger.

For a moment there was silence. "Who's there?" she said, waiting. There was no reply, but then she didn't expect there to be. This was not a human sound. It came again. This time there was a whimper, and her clenched posture relaxed. *The dog. Of course!*

Sliding the bolt, she eased the door open, and froze on the threshold. She gasped again, come face to face with what looked like a large black wolf. Surely not! It was a dog that *looked* like a wolf. It had to be. There were no more wolves in England.

For a moment, the creature stood gazing at her, its eyes glowing blood red in the firelight. Then it turned and padded away, disappearing in the shadows that collected about the second-floor landing.

Two

The storm was still raging when Sara woke at dawn. She hadn't had much sleep. It had been some time before she drifted off after her nocturnal visitor disappeared, and though she'd lain wide-eyed in the mahogany four-poster waiting until the wee hours for the scratching to resume, the animal had not returned. Deep in the night, the howl had come again, from some other part of the house—one long, mournful wail, the way a dog ... or a *wolf*, bayed at the moon. But there was no moon. Even if there had been no storm, there wouldn't have been; it was moon dark.

She was still groggy when Nell came to help her dress and order her hair. From the selection that was provided in the armoire, Sara chose a high-waisted sprigged muslin frock with touches of blue that complemented her hair and eyes. Nell had just finished adding ribbons to Sara's upswept coiffure, when Mrs. Bromley arrived to escort her down to the breakfast room.

Liveried footmen presided over an array of breakfast entrees set out in silver chafing dishes on the sideboard.

Nicholas was already filling his plate. Aside from a polite "good morning," Sara refrained from conversation as she helped herself to a modest portion of baked eggs and sausage, and a warm, fragrant cheese biscuit.

The table was set before a bay window that overlooked the courtyard. Sara and her new husband were seated at opposite ends, while a footman poured the coffee. But for the storm, the window would have offered a spectacular view of the garden. Instead, the well-manicured lawn was strewn with beheaded blooms, like confetti littering the ground. All but obscured by the rain sliding down the panes in sheets, the scene more closely resembled a spoiled watercolor.

"I presume you slept well," said Nicholas, breaking the awkward silence between them.

"Actually, I didn't," she responded. "I had a visitor last night."

"Oh?" he said, dosing her with that riveting obsidian stare. It was even more alarming in daylight, but the effect it had on her was the same. It made her blood race, and her heart begin to pound.

"A dog," she said, "a black and silver dog that looked like a wolf. The odd thing is, no one will admit that there is a dog in residence."

"That would be Nero," Nicholas said, around a swallow from his cup. "He isn't supposed to have the run of the house. He belongs below stairs. The staff is supposed to keep him there, which is probably one of the reasons they denied him. Another, more pointed reason is that I instructed them not to call your attention to the animal. I do not want him made a pet of." An exasperated frown knitted his brows. His nostrils flared, and his taut jaw muscles began to tick. "I shall speak to Smythe," he said. "He shan't bother you again."

"Oh, but he was no bother," she said. "He's a beautiful animal. I love dogs. We had so many wonderful hounds at home. I had to sell them. That was the worst of it for me. What breed of dog is Nero? He looks so like pictures I've seen of a *wolf* . . . something about the eyes."

"I have no idea," her husband replied, making short work of his sausage. How fine and white his teeth were. A pity he never smiled. "He walked out of the woods on the other side of the drive one day after a flaw, and the servants took pity on him. You know what happens once you feed an animal."

"Please don't punish him on my account," Sara said.

"What makes you think I would punish him?" he said, his fork suspended.

"I . . . don't, that is to say . . . I . . ."

"Yes?"

"That look in your eyes just now," she said. "I get the impression that you aren't too fond of dogs." He seemed almost angry, and she didn't know how to regain her footing on what seemed unsteady ground. This was no way to begin, and she wished she hadn't brought the topic up.

He said no more. After dosing her with that articulate stare for longer than she cared to suffer it, he speared the last piece of sausage on his plate with a punishing stab of his fork, and resumed his meal.

"My rooms are quite beautiful," she said, aiming for neutral ground. The conversation needed a new direction.

"I'm glad you approve," he replied, troubling his eggs with his fork. "There are a few reproductions, but most of the tapestries are very old. My father was a collector."

"I haven't had an opportunity to appreciate them as yet," she admitted. "I shall do so after breakfast."

He shook his head. "After breakfast, Mrs. Bromley will give you a tour of the house," he said. "You are free to make yourself at home here, of course, but as I told you last evening, there are certain areas that are unsafe. Pay close attention to her directives."

"I shall, of course," she said, concentrating on her food.

He had almost cleaned his plate, and was lingering over a second cup of coffee waiting for her to catch up. He was a gentleman, if nothing else. His etiquette was without flaw.

"My wardrobe is exquisite, Nicholas," she said. He appeared to have mellowed somewhat, and a few well-placed compliments couldn't hurt.

"I have jewelry for you as well," he replied, over the rim of his coffee cup.

"Oh, that isn't necessary," she protested.

"Yes, it is. You must dress and look the part, Sara, and if there is anything lacking in what's been provided thus far, you have only to bring it to my attention."

"I'm sure you've omitted nothing, but . . ."

"But what?"

"Mrs. Bromley said that if anything has been overlooked, she or one of the maids would fetch it from Truro—"

"Yes."

Sara hesitated. "Am I not permitted to shop on my own?"

"Not unchaperoned," he said, torturing her with those eyes again. "It's neither safe nor appropriate. Aside from the issue of propriety, Cornwall is rife with cutpurses and brigands, and I can spare no male escort to attend you. We are short-staffed here. It would be more convenient for the servants to deal with your needs. They make regular trips for supplies."

"I see."

"I don't think that you do," he said. "You are not a prisoner here, Sara, if that's what you're thinking. But you are Baroness Walraven now, and you must behave accordingly."

Sara didn't much care for the "behave." He had an arrogant streak, this paradox she'd married, but that could wait. It was only their second conversation, and she'd already managed to anger him once. One thing was certain. If Nero paid her any more nocturnal visits, she'd keep it to herself. She wouldn't put it past Nicholas Walraven to chain him up, or otherwise chastise the poor animal—or the servants either, for that matter—and she would not put any of them to the hazard.

"I doubt there'll be need to send anyone for anything, Nicholas," she said. "I'm sure you've overlooked nothing."

He studied her for a moment, and then went back to the remnants of his meal, giving her a chance to do likewise since she still couldn't meet his eyes. She watched the way the muscles stretched the cotton fabric taut across his biceps and shoulders, admired the way his jet-black hair fell across his brow in soft, glossy waves, feeling them with her eyes, since she wasn't likely to get the chance to do so otherwise. He was too far away for her to inhale his scent, but that didn't matter; it was still with her. It had been all night. His angular features—the shape of the jaw and the ledge of his smooth brow were signs of strength; but the eyes beneath, for all their glower, possessed a facet of something vulnerable and sad. She knew it well. She'd seen it in her own.

Having finished eating, he looked up from his coffee cup and caught her out. Hot blood rushed to her cheeks, and her fork rattled against her plate as she tried to set it down. Her heart skipped a beat. She was physically attracted to this man. That couldn't be. She couldn't let it be. There was no hope of anything physical between them—he'd made that quite plain. She would have to guard herself. Such a one-sided attraction could mean only heartbreak, and she'd had her fill of that.

"Is something amiss?" he asked.

"N-no," she replied, "It's just . . . all this seems unreal somehow. A sennight ago I was eating moldy bread, and some anonymous, maggoty swill that passed for stew; was dodging rats, and foul, unsavory jackanapes in that place . . . and now this. You must be patient with me. It will take time to adjust."

"You weren't . . . harmed?" he said, his brows knitted in a frown that cast his eyes deep in shadow.

"No, not physically," she said. "But keeping abreast of the dangers was a challenge." That hadn't changed. There could well be more danger right here at Ravencliff than there ever was in the Fleet—rats and rogues notwithstanding.

"Have you any pressing questions before we adjourn?" he said.

Sara opened her mouth to speak, but thought better of it, causing his eyebrow to lift. She had many questions, and more kept cropping up, but this was not the time to voice them. She wondered if there would ever be a time. He studied her in his inimitable manner for a moment, before folding his serviette and setting it beside his plate.

"Very well," he said. "I shall summon Mrs. Bromley to show you around the manor. After your tour, do take a moment to look at the tapestries. I think you will find them . . . consoling."

That would have to wait. A silent command passed to the butler only moments earlier brought the housekeeper before they'd risen from the table. After sketching a dutiful bow, Nicholas strode out of the room and disappeared in the shadows that lurked everywhere—day and night—in the old house.

Mrs. Bromley was an excellent tour guide. In less than an hour, they'd visited the dining hall, morning room, several sitting rooms, the parlor, library, and music room on the first floor. While pointing out a green baize-covered door beside the grand staircase as they started to climb, the housekeeper didn't offer Sara access to the servants' quarters that it marked; it was inappropriate, and a breach of household etiquette for the master or mistress of the house to venture below stairs.

The second floor was comprised of bedchambers and suites of rooms like her own. Each followed a theme as well, and but for poking her head in for the purpose of identification, the tour of these was brief. When Sara started toward the third-floor landing, the housekeeper held her back.

"Ya can't go up there, my lady," she said. "That part o' the house is restricted—it ain't safe ta go poking around up there. Storm damage has weakened the upper part o' the house over time, and the master don't want ya goin' up and comin' ta harm. His suite is the only one in use up there anyway. The rest has been shut up since his father died. The whole third floor will come down one day—granite rock or no—you mark my words. Why, the master's chamber is the only turret suite on the sea side up there that ain't lost its roof ta the gales."

"Why on earth would he want rooms in such a dangerous place with so many fine chambers down here on the second floor to choose from?" Sara asked, thinking out loud.

"I dunno, my lady, he's a creature o' habit, the master is. He's had rooms up there since I come here twenty-four years ago, when he was a lad o' twelve. He likes ta keep ta himself."

"How old is the house, Mrs. Bromley?"

"Ta hear him tell, they carved it outta the cliff out there. Built it outta the same rock around the time the Normans come, at least its roots go back that far—maybe farther, for all I know. It's changed over time, o'course. It started out as a keep, then over the years it become a monastery, an abbey, and a priory, amongst other things at different times. More rock was quarried as time went by, rooms was added, outbuildings and stables and stacked stone fences went up, until it come to be what it is now, and has been for the last two hundred years—Ravencliff Manor. Except for storm damage repairs, o' course."

"It must have a fascinating history if it's stood here since before the Norman Conquest," Sara said, trying to imagine.

"There's books in the library that'll tell ya a lot more than I ever could."

"I shall make it a point to avail myself," Sara replied.

"Yes, my lady. Now, there's plenty o' time before nuncheon

for a lie-down," the housekeeper offered. "Ya won't be disturbed. Nell will come ta fetch ya when 'tis time."

"Thank you, Mrs. Bromley. I think I shall," Sara said—but she wasn't planning on napping. Nicholas's comment about the tapestries had intrigued her. His use of the word "consoling" in particular piqued her interest, and she dismissed the housekeeper and made her way back to her bedchamber.

The storm was still flinging sheets of rain at the windows. Whipped by the wind, the cascading ripples obscured the view. It was just as well. All was dark and depressing. Somehow, Sara couldn't imagine what the place would be like in bright sunlight. The shadow-steeped manor seemed at home in dirty weather.

There was a fire in the hearth, throwing pulsating warmth at the drafts that seeped through the very walls where the tapestries hung. The tapestries shuddered, attracting her attention, and she took up a candle branch and began her inspection. The periods represented varied from medieval, to pastoral, to Renaissance. A common palette threaded through the lot—muted shades of green and cinnamon brown, sand, claret, burgundy, cream, and various shades of blue. The theme was the same: *the hunt*. Dogs and horses surrounded her, among them the works of Detti, Oudry, and Bernard Van Orley. Each was more magnificent than the rest, but the most magnificent of all hung beside the bed: a breathtaking rendering of Diana the Huntress with her noble hounds.

The candle branch trembled in Sara's hand. Was this strange man she'd married a saint or the Devil? He seemed so austere, and now this tender consolation. He had surrounded her with the animals she'd loved and lost. He'd assigned her that suite before she ever arrived. He'd *known*. What else did he know? Her eyes misted with tears; the tapestries blurred before them. She blinked her sorrow back and moved on to her sitting room, which was likewise decorated. An exquisite medieval piece depicting a unicorn hunt caught her eye, and she fingered the hounds worked at the bottom. All around the room unicorns and horses pranced, and dogs cavorted. The storm forgotten, Sara moved from wall to wall, and room to room of her spacious suite, drinking it all in to the last detail.

Three

Sara couldn't wait for Nell to come and collect her for the noon meal so she could thank Nicholas for his thoughtfulness, but the breakfast room was vacant when she reached it. Her husband didn't come down to dinner that evening, either, and she faced his absence with mixed emotions. On the one hand, she was anxious to use the tapestries as a means of easing the tension—the awkward strain mounting between them from the very first. Something in his voice, in his furtive glances had put her on her guard, made her wish she possessed more experience with men. It was almost as if those eyes said one thing and his lips another. The man seemed full of contradiction. On the other hand, she was glad of his absence in that it gave her more time to marshal courage enough to address the issues that had nagged her since she entered Ravencliff Manor. She hadn't fooled him. He knew she had questions. He was about as eager to answer them as she was to ask.

Mrs. Bromley wasn't able to tell her why Nicholas hadn't made an appearance at nuncheon or dinner, only that he often skipped meals, and that she shouldn't take it to heart.

Whatever the reason, Sara felt it was rude. He should have sent his apologies, and she had half a mind to march into his study and tell him so. That was where she presumed him to be, since she saw a sliver of candlelight showing under the study door when she came down to dinner.

After the meal, she decided to do just that, but the study door was ajar, and the candles had been extinguished—recently, judging by the strong odor of smoke and tallow in the musty air. Gripping the doorknob she eased it open a little wider and peered inside. The fire in the hearth had died to glowing embers, casting just enough light to show her that the room was empty. Nicholas's Hessians stood beside the wing chair, and what looked like some of his clothing lay in a heap on the floor. The boots were caked with mud, and the clothing looked wet. Had he been out in the storm? What were his clothes doing here—had he left them for the servants to collect? Was he accustomed to changing in the study? Her breath caught. He could be coming back! Cold chills gripped her at the thought of being found there, and she repositioned the door just as she'd found it. Glancing up and down the corridor, she searched the shadows, but nothing moved, and she hurried toward the grand staircase and went straight to her suite.

Entering through the little foyer, she turned right, and opened the door to her bedchamber, where Nell had turned down the bed and was laying out her ecru silk nightgown and wrapper.

"Oh, la, my lady!" the abigail said. "Ya look like ya just seen a ghost!"

"Nothing of the kind," Sara responded. "I took the stairs too quickly after eating."

"If you say so, my lady."

"How long have you been in service here, Nell?" Sara asked.

"Long enough ta know the tales o' ghosts are *true*," said the maid, casting a furtive glance about the room.

"I haven't heard any such tales."

"You will. Just ask any o' the servants, they'll tell ya. There's strange goin's-on in this old house, my lady, you'll see."

Sara didn't dispute that for a minute, though she wasn't prepared to subscribe to ghosts. As far as she was concerned, the enigmatic Baron Nicholas Walraven was at the bottom of the "strange goings-on" at Ravencliff, and that was more frightening than ghosts.

It was still early, and she wasn't tired, but she did want to be alone to order her thoughts. That meant dismissing Nell. She let the maid help her change and brush out her shoulder-length hair before the vanity mirror in the dressing room, then bade her good night. Snuffing out the dressing room candles, she stepped back over the threshold into her bed-chamber only to pull up short before Nero, sitting on his haunches in the middle of the Aubusson carpet, watching her, his eyes like mirrors glowing red in the firelight.

"Nero?" she breathed. "You frightened me. How did you get in here?" She took a cautious step closer, but the animal made no hostile move, and she ventured nearer still. "You shouldn't be here, you know, but I shan't tell." Squatting down to his level, she reached to stroke his shaggy black coat. "You're soaking wet!" she discovered. "Have you been out in the storm, too? So that's why the master's clothes were all wet. He was out looking for you, wasn't he? And you've escaped him. Well he mustn't find you here. He knows you visited me last night, and it's the first place he'll look." She surged to her feet and started toward the foyer. "Well, come on, then."

Nero hesitated, then stood and padded toward her. Sara gasped again, taking a good look at the animal—at the long, corded legs, and slender, barrel-chested body; at the way he held his head, and the way the strange eyes staring at her picked up the firelight. It was impossible to tell their true color.

"You do have wolf in you, don't you?" she murmured. "If I didn't know better . . ."

The door to the corridor was ajar. She could have sworn she'd closed it earlier. She opened it wider, but the animal stood his ground. He had a lean, hungry look about him. Whatever the conditions of his residence, Sara was certain he wasn't happy with them. He was obviously lonely, too, to seek her out—a total stranger—and she wondered when he'd had his last meal.

"Don't they feed you, Nero?" she said. She hadn't finished everything on her plate at dinner, and she wished now that she'd thought to tuck something into her serviette for him, since she'd been hoping he'd return. "I have nothing for you now," she said, "but the next time you visit me I shall . . . I promise. Now, you need to go back to the servants' quarters before someone catches you out. Go!" she charged, shooing him away with a hand gesture. But he stood his ground, staring up at her with those penetrating red-fire eyes.

What a soulful expression for a dog. Of course, he couldn't understand what she was saying, but she was certain he would respond to her tone. She knew how to gentle dogs, and horses, too, come to that, but this dog was . . . different. He seemed to understand every word.

"What am I to do with you?" she scolded. "You cannot stay here. One bark, one howl, and we are found out. Then I shall be called to task, and God alone knows what will happen to you."

Still Nero stood his ground, and Sara poked her head out into the corridor. Candle sconces dotted the walls, but only half were lit. She looked both ways. The hallway was deserted, and she pulled her wrapper close around her against the drafts, and stepped over the threshold.

"I suppose I could walk you down to the servants' quarters," she said. "It isn't that far. The door is doubtless closed, and you won't be able to get below stairs otherwise, will you? Is that what you're trying to say, Nero? What I want to know is how you got out. There must be another entrance. I don't suppose you'll show me, will you, boy?" The animal made no move to comply. He nuzzled her hand with his cold, wet nose, and followed her into the corridor.

"Yes, I love you, too, you poor wretched creature," she soothed, ruffling his shaggy coat. "Well, come on, then, we shall have to do this quickly."

Nero padded along beside her. His nails made no sound here the way they did in the downstairs hall, where there was no carpet. She could detect his step just the same. They had nearly reached the landing, when he bolted and streaked on ahead of her.

"*Nero!*" she cried out, as loud as she dared. There was a dreadful echo in the house, amplified by the storm, and voices carried. "Come back here!" Still the animal ran on toward the landing, and disappeared in the shadows.

Sara lost sight of him before she reached the staircase, and she hurried down to the first-floor landing, but the green baize door that led below was closed, as she knew it would be, and Nero was nowhere in sight. Why hadn't she brought a candle branch? The halls beyond the servants' quarters door were black as coal tar pitch. She ventured halfway down one, calling to Nero in hoarse whispers, but there was no sign of him, and she turned back when she nearly fell over a settle. It was no use; he was on his own. Why hadn't he waited for her—or answered her call? He seemed such an intelligent animal. She was so sure he understood her.

When she reached the green door, she tried the knob. It was locked. There was nothing she could do for Nero now even if she did find him. Unless one of the servants had let him in when he came down, he was abroad for the night, and she prayed Nicholas wouldn't find him.

There was nothing to be done but go back to her suite, and she started toward the landing, only to pull up short, her hand frozen to the newel post. Nicholas was descending from the third-floor stairwell barefoot, wearing a burgundy satin dressing gown. It gapped in front, exposing a patch of dark hair that diminished to a narrow line, like an arrow disappearing beneath the sash. As he rounded the bend, she glimpsed a well-turned thigh, and very nearly something more. He was naked underneath. Her breath caught in a strangled gasp, and her hand flew to her lips—but not in time to keep the sound from escaping.

He stopped three steps above her, and cinched his dressing gown in ruthlessly. His hair was tousled and wet, tumbled over his brow, and his eyes were hooded dark things that drove hers away. He didn't speak directly, and when she braved another look, she saw that he was taking her measure. She was standing beneath one of the sconces. Glancing down, she realized that her gown was transparent in the candlelight. He could see *everything*, and she tugged her wrapper closed in front with both hands.

"May I be of assistance to you, Sara?" he said, stepping down to the landing.

"N-no, thank you," she replied. "I was just going up." Did that sound as ridiculous to him as it did to her, considering her attire? He was so close. How he towered over her. His scent overwhelmed her, his own unique essence, freshened with the tang of sea salt, of the wind, and the rain. She was right; he *had* been outside, and he'd probably come down to collect the clothes he'd left behind earlier, not wanting to muddy the house.

"You oughtn't be down here unsupervised until you're familiar with the house," he said, stopping her in her tracks. "These corridors aren't used after the dining hall is cleared, and they're sparsely lit at this hour."

" '*Unsupervised*'?" she said.

"Yes. I can't have you blundering into danger in the dark."

"I don't 'blunder,' my lord," she snapped. First *behave*, and now *unsupervised*? The man was certainly no study in diplomacy. "Your choice of words can sometimes be unfortunate, I'm finding out."

" 'Nicholas,' " he corrected her. "I'm sorry if my vocabulary offends you, but I've never been the sort to mince words. There are dangers in this old house. Loose boards, rusty nails"—he pointed at her bare feet—"heavy old furniture to stub those pretty toes on. Browse all you want in daylight, when you can see the pitfalls, but please, do not go knocking about after dark . . . *unescorted*, if the word better suits your sensibilities. We don't have a surgeon in residence, and the nearest one is on Bodmin Moor. Why are you down here?"

She'd been hoping he wouldn't ask that question. She would not betray Nero—never that, though it was all she could do to keep from calling her husband to account over the condition of the animal. Only wolves had such a spare look about them, not dogs. She'd seen pictures of such creatures in books in her father's library. Nero could have walked right off the pages.

"I . . . I couldn't sleep, and I came down to . . . to fetch a book from the library," she said, her reverie having prompted the excuse.

"Didn't Mrs. Bromley take you on a tour of the house? The library is in the south wing, next to the salon."

"Y-yes, she did. I must have lost my way, and I'd just given up. We toured so many rooms, and it all looks so different at night."

"Exactly my point," he said. "Can you find your way back to your rooms?"

"Of course," she snapped, beginning to climb, but his deep voice spun her around again.

"Sara, we need to talk," he said.

"*Now?*" she breathed, raking him from head to toe in wide-eyed astonishment.

"No, not now," he responded, his lips curled in the closest thing to a smile she'd seen yet, albeit an exasperated one. "It's clear to me that we need to expand our dialogue of last evening. We touched on the house rules, but what we need to establish . . . are the *ground rules*. I shan't be taking breakfast in the morning, but if you will join me after nuncheon in the study we can talk privately. I'd rather not have the servants privy to our conversation."

"You're sure you will be coming down to nuncheon tomorrow, Nicholas?" she said, recalling his rude absence at table all day.

"Ah! My apologies," he said. "What kept me from joining you at nuncheon and dinner today came up quite suddenly, and couldn't be avoided. That may happen from time to time. I should have sent my regrets. Please forgive my want of conduct. I shall try to be more chivalrous in future."

"After nuncheon, then . . . in the study," she agreed. "Good night, Nicholas."

"Good night, Sara."

He moved on then, but the deep, sensuous echo of his voice lived after him, tampering with her balance. So did the image of that lean, corded, lightly furred body half-exposed in the candlelight. How handsome he was, mussed by the gale, this strange man she'd married. His scent was still with her, all around her—in her. Breathing deeply, she drank her fill. Yes. She was attracted to this man, but he did not want her in that way. What he did want was still unclear. Maybe tomorrow, he would answer her questions. Maybe tomorrow, she would be brave enough to ask them. Right now, as she approached her suite, she prayed that she wouldn't find Nero crouching on his haunches in her foyer. Thank God, it was vacant.

Four

Sara heard the howl again in the dead of night. It wrenched her from a sound sleep, and she went to the door, but there was no sign of Nero in the deserted hallway. Had she dreamed it? No. It was much too intense, so plaintive and sad it tugged at her heartstrings. She had bonded with the creature and, if anything were to happen to him, the heart he'd wrapped himself around would break all over again, just when it had begun to mend. Nero's unexpected presence in her life eased the loneliness in her strange situation: to be married to a husband who wasn't a husband, who showed not the slightest affection—who didn't even want to be *touched*. How could she bear to lose the dog's comforting presence now?

She did not mention Nero at nuncheon. The meal was passed for the most part in silence, though she didn't miss Nicholas's articulate eyes studying her from the opposite end of the table. There it was again—that look. She hadn't imagined it. There was something unspoken in those eyes— something veiled, though acute, as if he were struggling with some inner demon. That hypnotic stare seemed alarmingly soft and intense, seductive and cold all at once. How could that be? But it was. If only she could read it.

The storm had finally spent itself in the night. By dawn, the rain had stopped, and the wind had died to a sighing murmur. Though the sea rolling up the coast below still had a fearsome voice, it had ceased climbing the house's ancient curtain wall and flinging spindrift high into the air, clear to the carved stone ravens at the pinnacle. The sun was another matter. Dark brooding clouds still hung heavy on the horizon, adding to the gloomy mood of the day, and Sara watched Nicholas stir the fire to life in the study hearth in a vain attempt to chase off the dampness that permeated the old house. She noticed, too, that the wet clothes and muddy boots were gone.

"You needn't look so grim," he said, surging to his full height after the chore. "You have nothing to fear from me, Sara. This isn't the Inquisition, you know. I'm in hopes that when we leave this room today, we shall have a better understanding of each other, nothing more."

"I'm not afraid of you, Nicholas," she said. It was half-truth. She was very afraid of her attraction to this man, because it wasn't returned. "You've been most generous, and you've saved me from a nightmarish existence, for which I am exceedingly grateful. It's just that your motives are . . . unclear."

"My motives are *suspect*, you mean."

"If you prefer."

"I see. You have questions. Let us begin with those then, shall we?" He took his seat on the edge of the desk as he had during their first interview. Chairs were wasted on this man.

Sara folded her hands in her lap, trying not to wrinkle the blue dimity frock she'd chosen for the occasion. She'd been hoping he would be the one to begin. This was going to be difficult.

"Very well," she said. "Forgive me, but you do not look the

sort of man who has to choose a bride from the debtors' prison. With so many lovely young ladies in the offing this Season, why me?"

"I am not interested in empty-headed debutantes, who parade themselves in Town as bait for husbands. They may as well be on the block at Tattersall's."

"Or could it be that you thought someone liberated from the Fleet would bow and scrape to your every whim?"

"That is insulting, not only to me, but to yourself."

"What, then? You must admit that at best all this is bizarre."

He hesitated. "All right," he said. "If I am to be completely truthful, I will admit that you are partly right. I did hope that someone in my debt might be more inclined to put up with my . . . idiosyncrasies, but I shan't let that damn me. I told you what I was looking for in a wife. That I found her in the Fleet and not at Almack's matters not. I have found her—end of issue. I assume there's more?"

"Yes," Sara said, with as much confidence as she could muster. "I find it hard to accept that you do not want an heir." She had come this far—too far to stop now. "A handsome, prosperous aristocrat such as yourself, a man with property and wealth to leave after him, surely needs someone to leave it to."

Again he hesitated. "My reasons are . . . private, Sara," he said.

"But we are *married*, Nicholas."

"Married people do keep some things to themselves, and this is not your usual marriage. You need to accept that."

"I can accept anything I can understand," she sallied, "and I do not understand this! It is beyond my comprehension. Will you allow me to be blunt?"

He ground out a low chuckle. There was no humor in it. "I'm sure you will be, whether I 'allow' you or not."

"It is unfortunate that you force me to take the initiative in this conversation. It offends me and I shan't forgive you for it, I'm sure, when you could so easily spare me. You asked for my questions, my lord—"

"Indeed, I did," he flashed, "but I made no promise to answer them. Don't let that deter you, however. Speak your mind."

"All right, since you insist. Do you . . . prefer the company of men?" she blurted. There! It was out. Maybe the key to conversing with this man was to let anger mouth the words.

He did laugh, then—rich, deep, throaty laughter that resonated through her body like the shuddering vibration of a snare drum, right down to her toes. It was the first time she'd seen him laugh, and it thrilled her, despite the sarcasm.

"If it were only that simple," he said on the wane of it. "No, Sara," he said. "I do not 'prefer the company of men.' "

"What then? It isn't just the matter of an heir. You have no interest in . . . in sharing your bed with—"

"I haven't said I have no interest," he interrupted her. "I said it shan't be part of our arrangement."

"Don't mince words with me, Nicholas. The result is the same. Am I unsatisfactory in some way? Am I not what you expected? Is my hair too long, considering the current fashion? Do you have a mistress? *What?* For pity sake, it's only natural that I would be curious about such things. I need to be clear upon what to expect from this union. I am amazed that you haven't explained yourself without my having to embarrass myself by dragging it out of you like this."

He slid off the desk with a sinuous motion more animal than human, and took a step nearer. That strange look had come again into his eyes. For a moment, she was certain he was going to take hold of her, and she leaped from the chair and put it between them.

His posture collapsed, and he raked his hair back from his brow. It glistened with sweat. "No, Sara," he said, "you are most definitely not unsatisfactory, and I have no mistress. You weren't plucked from the Fleet at random, either. I won't have you thinking so. I thought I made it clear in my proposal that our fathers were long-standing friends. I was hoping it would ease your mind to know that there was some sort of a link between us, even a tenuous one."

"You did mention it, yes, but how would you even know of it? All that would have been before you were born."

"Quite so. My father kept journals of his war adventures. They came into my hands, along with all his other effects after Mother passed on. Colonel Ponsonby, your father, was mentioned quite often. He and Father were together in India at the beginning of the British Occupation, and on one occasion, he saved Father's life out there. But that is a tale . . . for another time. When I heard of your misfortune, I realized who you were, and took the liberty of engineering your rescue. If I had known before the fact, you never would have seen the inside of Fleet Prison. So you see, I knew what I was getting before it was gotten. There is no . . . ulterior motive here, unless you want to count my doing something that I knew would please Father, albeit posthumously, as ulterior." Jamming his fisted hands into his pockets, he strolled back to the desk. "I'm not prepared to go into detail in regard to my not wanting an heir, but this much I will tell you: There is a defect in the blood that I do not wish to pass on to future generations. It is best that the Walraven line end with me."

"*Madness?*" she breathed. That would explain a lot. He had just canceled all of her other suspicions—shot them all down with a word.

"No, not madness. Please don't look at me like that. I told you, you have nothing to fear from me, Sara. I assure you, I'm as sane as you are."

"Nicholas . . . there are ways of preventing the conception of children," she murmured. It was the hardest, most intimate thing she'd had to say to this man yet, and the look in his eyes once the words left her lips was so devastating, it drove hers away.

"I'm aware of that," he said, ". . . but I prefer to take no chances. You will just have to respect my wishes in this regard . . . and my privacy. I'm sorry."

Sara was silent apace. Though he'd answered some of her questions, she was more confused now than ever. Since she'd had her doubts, she was somewhat relieved that he did know something of her family background from a personal source, other than what Alexander Mallory had obviously unearthed during his investigation of her. He was hedging on the rest, however, and that troubled her.

"Now, if there's nothing else, I have a few questions of my own," he said.

"Nicholas, wait," she said. "Is it because you do not trust me that you choose not to confide your reasons?"

"No, Sara, it is because I do not trust *myself*," he said. "If I don't leave myself open to argument, I shan't be tempted to compromise my integrity in the matter. It's best that the issue is dropped here and now, and I really must get on with this. I don't mean to be rude, but the house and grounds have suffered in the storm, and I must assess the damage before repair work can commence."

"I'm sorry," Sara murmured. "Do continue."

"Very well," he said. Squaring his posture, he began to pace before the hearth—slow, measured steps, as if he were trying to calm himself. "Have you had a chance to examine the tapestries yet?"

"Oh, yes," she cried, "I meant to tell you earlier. They are 'consoling,' just as you said. It was very thoughtful of you. Selling my dogs was no less painful than if I'd been forced to part with my childr—my next of kin," she amended. It wouldn't do to bring up children again. "Our preseason spring hunts were the sporting event of the parish in Yorkshire. Everyone looked forward to them. Those tapestries took me home again. I miss the animals so dreadfully."

"I'm glad you're pleased," he said. "Alex is bringing several more when he returns from London. What did you think of my steward? Did he behave himself, or did you have to put him in his place? I noticed that he hadn't convinced you to call him by his given name. Knowing Alex, that's telling."

"May I speak frankly?"

"I hoped that you would," he responded.

"I did not have to put him in his place. I simply kept him in it."

"Bravo!" he erupted, breaking his stride momentarily. "Alex wouldn't be Alex if he didn't try. He's more than just my steward, Sara. We've been friends since we were breeched. We were at school together . . . until it was decided that I continue my studies here at Ravencliff, with a tutor. His mother died when he was born, and my mother took pity upon him before she passed. Being the second son, he was often ignored. His father's estate was close by, and he used to spend his holidays here, exploring this old house with me. After he went off to Oxford, I didn't see much of him for a time. He got into one scrape after another at school, and was finally sent down. His brother married, and took his bride to America, and his father died shortly thereafter. It was then that I took Alex on as my steward. He'd frittered away his inheritance until he hadn't a feather to fly with, and taken to drowning his sorrows in flirtations and *Blue Ruin*. So, you see, I'm fully aware of his shortcomings. As long as they do not interfere with his situation here, I've been content to overlook them . . . until now, because he's been a good friend, and a good steward, but I shan't stand for any disrespect toward you. I want that clearly understood."

"I didn't much care for his forward manner, and I ignored it," Sara said. "I believe we understand each other."

"Good, I'm glad," he replied, resuming his pacing. "I shall have a word with him as well. Once he knows his place, he usually stays in it. If there should be a problem, however—no matter how slight—I expect you to come to me at once. Is that clear?"

"Yes, Nicholas, but I assure you there shan't be."

"As to your hair, you may do with it as you please," he continued. "But I will be very disappointed if you cut it. It is lovely, and becoming, and quite a novelty in times like these when fashion rules, and the frivolous weak-willed bow to it."

"I hadn't planned to cut it. I just wanted to be sure you approved."

"Good," he replied. "Now then, about the ground rules I spoke of last evening . . . I've already told you that I do not want you prowling about after dark, and you are aware of my reasons. As to your . . . obligations as Baroness Walraven, they shall be simple, and untaxing, as I outlined when you arrived. I shall have a houseguest soon, and you shall be put to the test, I'm afraid. I'm sure you won't disappoint me. Much depends upon it. Next, in regard to our . . . intimate relationship, there shan't be one. You are a young and . . . vital woman, Sara. I am not insensitive to that, and since I sense . . . disappointment over this aspect of our arrangement, you have my permission to take a lover—so long as you are discreet, that is, and so long as it isn't Alex Mallory, which is why I asked your opinion of him earlier. That would be awkward, since he has no family, and resides here when he isn't off on business for me."

Sara's breath caught in her throat. That was the last thing she would have expected him to say, and for once in her twenty-three years, she was speechless.

"Other issues may come up," he said, "and we shall address them if and when they do, but these are the most important, and they are unequivocal." He stopped prowling the hearthstone like a predator midstride, and faced her. "Do we have an understanding?"

"Y-yes, Nicholas," she said low-voiced. She wanted to scream out: *I don't want a lover. You are my husband. I want you to want me*, but her throat closed over the words, and it was all she could do to choke back her tears.

"Oh, and one more thing," he said. "Do not get too attached to Nero. Keep your distance. I have . . . plans for him, and if they come to fruition, he may be leaving us soon, which is why it was my wish that you not even know of his existence. I wouldn't want you to suffer any more separation angst than you already have over another animal, especially one of mine."

"It isn't because . . . because . . . I came to his defense?"

"No, it is not," he said. "You needn't go on. You didn't fool me last night with your 'book from the library' tale. You're an intelligent woman. I cannot imagine having to tell you twice where any room in this house is after you'd been shown. I knew why you came downstairs. You were . . . involved with that animal in some way. That was fairly obvious, and that's not why I've brought it up. My plans for Nero were formed long before you ever came here, Sara. There's nothing you can do to change them, and if you knew what they were, you wouldn't want to. I don't know what's put it into your head that I mean to harm that animal, but I assure you I do not. I simply do not want you to form an attachment that you will later regret. This, too, I must insist upon as one of the ground rules . . . probably the most important one. And now, if you will excuse me, I really must be about house business."

He streaked past her then, his fists still jammed in his pockets, and disappeared in the shadows of the corridor outside.

His abrupt departure was jarring, but welcome. She barely made it to her suite before the tears came. How could he offer her a lover so casually? Did he think so little of her? Why hadn't she spoken out? Why hadn't she at the very least let him know the suggestion was repugnant to her? His words had stalled her brain. What must he think, that she was no better than the two-thirds of society who embraced the taking of lovers and mistresses as a viable way of life? It wasn't that he proposed such a thing that had stricken her so. It was that he seemed to think she would accept such an arrangement.

Sara flung herself across the bed and sobbed her heart dry. He was going to take Nero away. What terrible fate did he have in store for that poor animal? She wouldn't bear it. It was already too late not to become attached. *I'll hide Nero away before I'll let Nicholas harm him*, she decided, pounding the feather-down pillow. What was happening to her? She was never a watering pot—not once during all the horrid debasement in that odious prison had she shed a single tear.

She had nearly cried herself to sleep, when Nell came to help her dress for dinner. One look in the cheval glass was enough to make her beg off. Her eyes were puffy and red, nearly swollen shut, and her fair skin was covered with blotches. It always happened when she cried, which was one of the reasons she so seldom indulged. She certainly couldn't go downstairs looking like that. She didn't bother to send her regrets. Nicholas probably wouldn't be dining anyway, if his past behavior were any example. She wasn't hungry, but she opted for a tray in her suite anyway. Were she to refuse and call attention to her distress, it might prompt a visit from Nicholas, and she'd had quite enough of him for one day.

When the food arrived, she managed to eat most of it. Afterward, she had Nell prepare her for bed, and dismissed her for the evening; the mousy little abigail had set her sights on one of the hall boys, and was only too willing to oblige. It was too early to sleep. Sara couldn't even if she'd wanted to—not with so many troubled thoughts rattling around in her brain. But she could climb between the sheets and try to order those thoughts.

Despite Nicholas's insistence, she would not discourage Nero. Who knew but that she was the only friend he had at Ravencliff. She'd saved some of her dinner, tucked it away in her serviette, just in case, and she cracked the door—not enough to be noticed, just enough for his paw or snout to brush against and gain him entrance. She'd scarcely climbed into bed, when the knock came, but it wasn't the animal's familiar scratching that sat her bolt upright in the bed, and it wasn't Nero who crossed the threshold. It was Nicholas.

A cry on her lips, Sara leaped from the bed, turned her back, and shrugged on her wrapper before she faced him. Meanwhile, he stood arms akimbo, a striking figure in his black pantaloons and Hessians, black cutaway tailcoat of superfine, and burgundy brocade waistcoat. An expertly tied neck cloth over modest shirt points challenged the jet-black hair curling about his earlobes. It offset the cleft in his uptilted chin.

"Are you in the habit of crashing into ladies' bedchambers unannounced?" she snapped, feeling ridiculous for having said it, since it was his house, and they were technically husband and wife.

"I did knock, and the door was open, Sara," he responded. "Perhaps Nell—"

"No," she interrupted. She would not have the blame fall to Nell for something the girl had no part in. "I came in rather . . . quickly earlier. I thought I'd pulled it to. Evidently not, but that doesn't matter. It was hardly flung wide, and as you can see, I am not dressed for entertaining. I was about to retire."

"Hmmm," he growled, his eyebrow arched. The hooded obsidian eyes beneath, flashing red in the firelight, were raking her familiarly, and her heart began to pound. "Why didn't you come down to dinner, are you unwell?"

"*Unwell?*" she snapped. "No, Nicholas, I am not 'unwell,' I am unhappy!"

"You've been crying," he observed. "Those blotches there . . . do they often occur when you cry? Mrs. Bromley is a skilled herbalist. I shall have her concoct a remedy."

45

"Don't worry," Sara snapped. "I shan't spoil my appearance and embarrass you before your guests. I do not cry often, only when I'm angry."

"I've been too blunt," he said, his posture deflated.

"*Blunt?*" she shrilled. "My dear man, 'blunt' is not the half of it. If you hadn't been such a coward and stormed off earlier, before I'd had half a chance to recover from your insensitive . . . insulting—my God, there is no word to describe your benighted *ground rules*—I'd have told you just exactly what I think of you *and* them!"

"Sara—"

"No!" she cried. "No, Nicholas. How could you stand there and tell me to take a *lover?* Is that what you think you've bought in me—someone who will jump into another man's bed at the snap of your fingers . . . an ornament to host your gatherings and afterward foist off on someone else to take her pleasures? There are names for women like that, and you do not have to marry them. *I* am not one. How *dare* you!"

"I have not 'bought' you," he murmured.

"Oh? You've heard nothing past that, have you? And just what would you call it, then?"

"Certainly not 'bought,' not in the way you put it," he defended. "*Redeemed*, is how I see it . . . how I wanted you to see it. And I didn't mean to disrespect you," he went on, searching the ceiling for composure. Were those tears misting those magnificent eyes? Remorse certainly hadn't put them there. He was cold and unfeeling, this strange man she'd married. Nonetheless, his thick, dark lashes were wet from blinking them back when he met her gaze again. "I was merely trying to offer you an alternative solution to a . . . sensitive situation that cannot be helped," he said. "I am sorry if I have offended you, but do not damn me for it. I shan't retract my suggestion, and you shouldn't reject it out of hand. Do not be too quick to decline. Marriage is forever.

As time goes by, you may be glad you've left that door open, Sara."

He sketched a bow and then left her, striding out without a backward glance. His scent was all around her, spread by the heat of the hearth, and by the drafts that seemed to come from nowhere and everywhere. She heard the door latch click in the foyer. After a moment, she rushed there and opened it again, leaving it just as she had before. Nicholas wouldn't be returning, but Nero might, and she climbed back into bed to wait.

Five

Nicholas Walraven prowled the edge of the cliff in the darkness. The sighing wind had risen again, teasing his multicaped greatcoat: lifting the hem of it, playing with the collars, like the fingers of a curious child. It was still moon dark, and but for an occasional glimpse of whitecaps riding the breast of the water below, the night was black as ink. He needed no moon or stars to light his travels there. He knew every rock, every derelict weed and blade of grass bent low between them in the storm, by heart. This was the only place he felt safe, the only constant in his life that never disappointed, this precipice that welcomed him. He haunted it often—fair weather and foul, he went to it for comfort, like a child to its mother's breast, like a lover to his mistress—but it couldn't stop the nightmare. Nothing could.

His valet would be preparing his bath now—a cold bath. Again. It wouldn't chase the madness, for that is what it was. Sara had named it, by God! A madness in the blood, and he cursed his father for it. He must have been mad to think this marriage of convenience would work, to think he could live like other men lived, have what other men had. It was a mistake, and if he were to pace the seawall until kingdom come, it wouldn't be put right. He would have to do that himself, and he would have to do it soon. He'd come to that conclusion when he first clapped eyes on Sara, Baroness Walraven, nee Ponsonby, the beautiful, innocent creature he'd plucked out of live coals only to cast into a raging fire . . . *but how to put it right?* She'd already gotten under his skin. He didn't dare keep her, and he couldn't bear to send her away. He couldn't tell her, either, and chance exposure. His was a well-kept secret. He couldn't compromise that. The repercussions would be catastrophic. Not even Alex Mallory knew, only Mills—his valet, his confidante, protector, and friend, just as he'd been Nicholas's father's before him. But Nicholas had already cast into the water the pebble that would damn him. The ripples had begun, and there was no way to stop them from spreading.

He glanced up toward Sara's windows. They were dark. She was asleep. Finally. It was safe to go back now, but back to what—a cold bath and an empty bed, or the madness again? That was the other constant, the unpredictable constant, the one over which he had no control.

His bath was waiting, just as he knew it would be, and Mills was ready to help him into it. The straight-backed, white-haired valet of indeterminable age stood beside the chiffonier in the master suite dressing room. It was heaped with towels, and littered with herbal jars. Beside them, Nicholas's nightly cordial waited, brewed of skullcap, linden, and hops sweetened with honey. It was supposed to keep him calm, and bring natural sleep. Its effectiveness was questionable, considering the events of the last two days.

Cold though the water was, the strong, pungent aroma of crushed rue, and the sweet evergreen pleasantness of rosemary, wafted toward him from the tub. Purging inside and out: that was the regimen. Gypsy remedies eons old. He'd thought they might be working . . . until Sara.

"You're going to catch your death out on that cliff, my

lord," the valet predicted, helping him out of his damp clothing. "It's penetrated you to the skin." He clicked his tongue, laying the clothes aside.

Nicholas held his breath as he submerged himself in the water. He should be steeled against it by now. Somehow, he never was, and doubted he ever would be. Calm and cold, he had to stay calm and cold. *How,* when even the faintest image of Sara ghosting across his memory brought his sex to life, the icy water notwithstanding? It soon warmed to his body heat, to the fever in his blood, the blood that caused the madness that wasn't madness, at least not the stark, staring variety. *That* could be cured, and if not, mindless oblivion would be release. There was no release from this breed of madness. That was what it was: a *breed*—his erect manhood and raised hackles were proof positive of it. If this could be from the mere thought of her, what would happen if they were to touch? He'd nearly scourged his traitorous body raw, before Mills snatched the sponge.

"Here!" the valet cried. "You'll have no skin left on you, my lord."

"Pain is the other deterrent, old boy—that, and death."

"Don't talk nonsense," the valet scolded, dumping a pitcher of water over his head. "We're making strides."

"We *were* making strides," Nicholas corrected, shaking himself like a wet dog. "That's why I thought the arrangement might work. I was a fool."

The valet wagged his head, dodging the spray. "You were warned, my lord."

"You know why this . . . marriage had to be," said Nicholas. "People were beginning to talk, and the *on-dits* were getting back to me *even here*, entombed as I am in this drafty old mausoleum. Each time Alex returns, there are more rumors. The *ton* is rife with them—an eligible bachelor, titled, with lands and wealth, personable enough to appeal to the catch of the Season in Town . . . in seclusion in the wilds of Cornwall. You know how many invitations to fêtes, *fête champêtre*, routs and balls and teas I've refused. The missives arrive daily, and the Season hasn't yet begun. I shudder to wonder what will be when it does, and I cannot go abroad again. It's too dangerous. I will surely be found out. Hah! Sara asked if I were a sodomite—not in those words, of course, she was most diplomatic, but that was the gist of it. You know I cannot take her to my bed as I am, and that was what she imagined to be the reason. What am I going to do, Mills? I can't let her stay, and I can't let her leave—not now, not *ever*. It's only a matter of time before she finds me out."

"You've grown fond of her," Mills said, "—and so soon."

"Worse than that," said Nicholas. "The feeling is mutual. It's more than I dared hope for, and more than I can stand. She is everything I ever wanted—golden, and fair—eyes like Highland bluebells. I saw them once . . . when I was a child. Was I ever a child, Mills?"

"Ahhh, my lord," the valet crooned. "You mustn't take on so. You know what it will lead to. Perhaps once Mr. Mallory returns with your houseguest—"

"Ahhh, yes, the good Dr. Breeden, who will surely think I'm addled, some crackpot who's read his treatise and means to exploit or discredit it, and Alex mustn't know. I've gone to great lengths to keep it from him, as you well know. That would be dangerous. You're going to have to help me there."

"Haven't I always, my lord?"

"Yes, old boy, you have, but this is different here and now. Things are unpredictable. *I* am unpredictable, and Alex is on the prowl."

"For my lady?" the valet breathed, his steely eyes come open wide.

"She says she has it in hand, but I know Alex, and you know me. If I didn't need him here to handle the affairs I dare not leave this place to see to . . ."

"I will help you however needs must, my lord, that goes without saying," the valet responded. "But . . . if I may be so bold as to inquire, what excuse have you given Mr. Mallory for fetching the esteemed Dr. Breeden from London?"

"To assess my bothersome anemia, which we both know is nonexistent, and to enjoy the hospitality of Ravencliff—a working holiday, if you will. He'll be with us a fortnight . . . if all goes well."

The valet hesitated. "As it is now, your . . . condition is between us," he reminded him. "The more who know—"

"What other choice have I, Mills?" Nicholas cut in. "Dr. Breeden is my last hope. I have read his papers. His credentials recommend him to my 'condition.' If he cannot help me, I cannot be helped."

"What then, my lord?"

"God knows. The old man's in his grave, and I am damned with the legacy he's left me."

"It wasn't his fault, my lord."

"Don't you think I know that?" Nicholas snapped. "The knowledge doesn't make it any easier to live with. He should have done as I am doing—embrace celibacy—but no, he would have his damnable heir."

"I'm worried that this doctor will not be discreet, my lord."

"I will make certain he will before I confide in him, old boy. His oath subjects him to doctor-patient privilege. He would have to keep my confidence. To break it would ruin him professionally. I think I'm safe enough."

"But *this*, my lord!"

" 'This' is why the man was chosen, Mills. We shall just have to wait and see."

The valet was silent apace. "Have you told my lady of the doctor's visit?" he said at last.

"It never really came up, what with all the rest," Nicholas said. "I'm glad it didn't. The woman is curious to a fault, she wouldn't have let that go—a doctor living in with all the other strangeness hereabout? Take my word for it, old boy, she'd have pounced upon that like a tigress. I'm just not prepared to deal with a barrage of questions over my health at the moment. She knows we are to have a houseguest, nothing more."

"What will you ever tell her, my lord?"

"I will tell her the same as I have told Alex, now let that be the end of it."

The valet said no more, and Nicholas sank into the herb-scented water to his neck, raking his wet hair out of his eyes. Mulling over the day's blunders, he let his breath out on a long sigh. He hadn't meant to hurt Sara, but maybe it was best that he'd been abrupt. Better to arouse her anger than her ardor. Better to keep her at arm's distance, for both their sakes. Still, it went against his nature to be boorish. It offended his sensibilities—opposed every principle that knitted him together as a gentleman—to be the cause of a lady's tears. He hated himself for it, and yet he would probably do it again. It was his only defense mechanism against betraying himself, against exposing his heart—and hers—to hope when there was none to be had.

Mills was watching him, the faithful servant. How did he deserve such a loyal friend and mentor? It certainly hadn't been easy for the valet in such a place as Ravencliff, where the walls had ears, and it was up to Mills to see that nothing untoward occurred within the others' hearing. This was why they never discussed it openly, why they never spoke a word out loud that could be interpreted—even here in the sanctuary of his third-floor suite so far removed from the rest in residence. This was why, when they did speak as they did now, their speech was for the most part encrypted. The valet had never once slipped up in all the years he'd served. How he had ever managed that was a mystery, and a miracle. Nicholas made a mental note then and there to have his conversations with Dr. Breeden out of the house altogether.

However discreet the man was, he wouldn't be equal to such as that.

"Get me out of this, will you, Mills?" Nicholas charged, surging to his feet. Water ran in rivulets the length of his body, and sloshed out onto the floor, puddling on the parquetry. Moving with the agility of a man half his age, Mills spread a thick white towel on the floor for him to step on, and Nicholas climbed out of the tub. The valet bundled him in towels, and Nicholas rubbed himself dry, bruising the herbs that clung to his skin, spreading their scent, grinding their soothing oils into his pores before brushing them away, with no less a scourging than he'd inflicted with the sponge earlier.

"Will you want a fresh toilette, or shall I fetch your dressing gown, my lord?"

"The dressing gown, Mills," Nicholas responded. "I'm done for the day—exhausted."

"Yes, my lord," said the valet, shuffling into the bedchamber. Nicholas was still scrubbing himself with the towels when Mills returned, and the servant took them from him and helped him into the dressing gown. "Your cordial, my lord," the valet reminded, snatching it from a silver salver on the chiffonier.

"Ahhh, yes, mustn't forget the deuced cordial," Nicholas said, cinching his sash with rough hands. He took the offered glass, and flopped in the wing chair beside the hearth, while Mills collected the towels and mopped up the puddles. "I actually gave her permission to take a lover," he said. He needed absolution for that, and Mills had always been ready to give it. Not this time. The valet stopped mopping midstroke, and met Nicholas's gaze slack-jawed.

"*My lord!*" he breathed. "Surely, you *didn't?*"

"Oh, but I did," Nicholas said, tossing back the cordial. He grimaced. It tasted bitter despite the honey.

"Whatever did she say to that?" the valet inquired.

"It put her in quite a taking," said Nicholas, toying with the empty glass. "To say that she pinned my ears back over it is a mild assessment. But she wouldn't let it go, and I didn't know what else to suggest."

"You can hardly blame her for ringing a peal over your head, my lord. I've had but a glimpse, and even *I* can see that she's quite well to pass—a diamond of the first water, to be sure."

It wasn't the reply Nicholas wanted to hear, and he breathed a ragged sigh, setting the empty glass down on the candlestand beside his chair. The valet's reproachful eyes turned his own away; he could bear anything but this dear man's disapproval. It wrenched his gut as though an unseen hand had fisted in it.

"What would you have suggested?" he asked.

"I'm sure I don't know, my lord," the valet said. "But certainly not *that*. It's a wonder she didn't crack a vase over your head. What could you have been thinking?"

"I was thinking, Mills, that I owe her the freedom to take her pleasures where she wishes, since I cannot offer her connubial bliss. I thought it was the least I could do."

"And how would you have felt if she took you up on it, my lord?"

"I can't think about that now, Mills, else this whole blasted ritual here be wasted."

"Mmm," the valet hummed, resuming his chore.

"That door's not closed, Mills. It could still happen, and if it does, I could neither accept it with an open mind anymore, nor in good conscience could I put a stop to it. I haven't the right."

The valet collected the wet towels, and got to his feet. "What if you were to tell her outright, my lord?" he said.

"You *know* I cannot do that," said Nicholas. "She'd run screaming from the house, you can bet your blunt upon it, old boy."

"But if . . . as you say, the feeling is mutual . . ."

"There's something else," Nicholas said, getting to his feet, "something I haven't told you."

"Yes, my lord?"

"She's formed an attachment for Nero."

"Oh, my lord!" Mills cried. "You cannot allow—"

"It's already happened."

"But you can put a stop to it—*you must!*"

"I don't know that I can," Nicholas mused. "It's gone too far, and I don't know that I even want to."

The valet opened and closed his mouth three times before the words came. "We need to talk, my lord," he said, clearly struggling, "About Nero, that is. There have been . . . murmurings below stairs."

"Murmurings, Mills?"

The valet nodded. "You know how the staff feels about Nero. Up until now the chatter has been harmless enough, but you must take care. There's been talk of . . . *doing him to death.*"

Nicholas vaulted erect in the chair. "The insolent gudgeons! How dare they plot my murder under my own roof?"

"Not your murder, my lord . . . *Nero's* murder. I know how close you are to the . . . er . . . situation, but you must remember that. They would never—"

"Yes. Yes, I know, Mills, but still, to take it upon themselves to plot to harm—*to kill*—anything of mine? I pay these layabouts' wages. How do they dare!"

"I know, my lord, and I certainly shan't defend them, but you know how they feel about the animal's sudden comings and goings. They are simple folk, and it frightens them."

"Nero has not once *ever* caused anyone in this household harm," Nicholas said, with raised voice. "And his comings and goings cannot be helped, you know that."

"Shhh, my lord, someone will hear! You know how superstitious the help are in this house. I knew this would overset you, but do not rail at me for telling it."

"I'm not railing at you, Mills, I'm railing at circumstance. How long has this been going on?"

"The matter has just recently come to my attention—certainly long enough for concern, my lord. I have been keeping a close eye upon things, believe me."

"Damn and blast! You should have come to me sooner."

"Please, my lord, do not overset yourself. You know the risks. I was hoping I could quell the insurrection, but I have not been able. I did not want to burden you with this as things are here now . . . with my lady just arriving and all, but there was nothing for it. You must be careful what Nero eats when he's . . . abroad, my lord. There has been talk of putting out some of the arsenic the grooms use to poison the rats in the stables."

"Bloody hell!" Nicholas hollered, vaulting out of the chair. "Who is behind this . . . this 'insurrection'? I want his name! By God, he won't see another sun rise over this estate. He's sacked—now—tonight."

"You cannot sack the whole lot below, my lord."

"I want his name, Mills," Nicholas said, the words thrumming with dangerous calm.

The valet hesitated. "Peters is the one whose voice is loudest, my lord, but he scarcely had to convince the rest. They were ripe for it."

"Peters, you say? I should have guessed." Nicholas began to pace the length of the carpet. "This is awkward. The little blighter's formed a *tendre* for Nell. I've just made her my lady's abigail, and Peters is the hall boy up there. I do not need a disgruntled lady's maid on my hands here now, and that's just what will be if I sack the boy. There's no one suitable below stairs to replace the girl. Ha! I know what this stems from. Nero caught the lad asleep at his post and had to wake him . . . rather abruptly. Don't look at me like that, Mills! Nero only frightened the bufflehead."

The valet's bushy eyebrow lifted, and his mouth crimped at the corners. "Evidently, my lord," he pronounced.

"Yes, well, you just leave Peters to me. He gets a reprieve . . . for the moment. You had it just so. I cannot have chaos here now, as things are with my lady and Breeden coming."

"Yes, my lord."

Nicholas dosed the valet with a withering stare. "Peters is not off the hook, Mills," he said. "Not by a long shot. You've put me in an impossible position here."

"*I*, my lord?" the valet blurted.

"If I confront him, he will know you've told me, won't he? What use will you be as my eyes and ears below stairs then, hm? Without you to keep an eye out for rat poison and the like, what will become of me? I shudder to wonder. You've tied my hands quite nicely, old boy."

"Yes, my lord," the valet said, forlorn. Again, his jaw worked, forming words that would not come directly. "If I may be so bold," he said at last, "what you said earlier troubles me. It's hardly prudent to allow my lady to become attached to Nero."

"*Allow?*" Nicholas blurted. "How can I not allow it, Mills? How can I deny her a pet to cosset? Think what she's just come from, what she must have suffered in that place. She has no one—nothing but the shallow arrangement I have offered her. She is lonely. I never anticipated how lonely, and I cannot give her the affection she craves. I want her to be happy here. What harm to let her fuss over Nero if it eases her loss, and her loneliness? I should think it's a small enough consolation on my part under the circumstances. I have nothing else to offer."

"You aren't thinking clearly, my lord!" the valet said. "What if Dr. Breeden succeeds, and Nero leaves us?"

"I've already warned her of that possibility. If it happens, she will get over it."

"And . . . if it doesn't, my lord?"

"We shall tread that path when we come to it."

Six

Sara woke at first light, even though she'd lain awake until well after midnight in anticipation of a visit from Nero. He did not come, and she awoke disappointed, despite the cheery sunlight streaming in at the window and trapping dust motes that danced along the shaft as though they had a purpose. Nell had crept in, opened the draperies, lit the fire, and crept out again without waking her—a most excellent servant.

Sara yawned and stretched and dropped her feet over the side of the bed, before it all came trickling back—her confrontation with Nicholas. How would she ever face him at breakfast? She surged to her feet and squared her posture. She would face him all right, and give him exactly what he wanted: a hostess. She would submerge herself into that occupation, not hide in her rooms, sulking in corners. She would treat her residence as employment, and avoid the man as much as possible. That had to be, if she were to keep her sanity, but first she would establish a few ground rules of her own.

She had already plucked from the armoire a peach-colored muslin frock with a Mechlin lace insert that masked the décolleté, when Nell arrived to help her dress. The dampness had transformed her wavy hair into a mass of tendrils and ringlets, which the abigail fashioned into a high cascade threaded through with peach grosgrain ribbons. After several attempts to tame the tendrils about her face, Nell threw her hands up in defeat. They would have to stay. It didn't matter. Sara wasn't trying to impress a husband. She wasn't a wife, she was an employee—with a unique advantage. It didn't matter if he approved of her appearance or not. He could hardly sack her.

Breakfast was informal as usual. She was already seated in the breakfast room, enjoying a plate of Scotch eggs, which were small, hardboiled, and encased in sausage meat, and a serving of baked tomatoes, when Nicholas strode into the room. He greeted her with a bow, and began filling his own plate. He wore no vest or frock coat over his dove-gray pantaloons and Egyptian cotton shirt, though he had tied a flawlessly engineered neck cloth in place. She studied him while his back was turned. How broad his shoulders were, how narrow his waist. The skintight pantaloons tucked into polished Hessians outlined every contour of his lean, well-muscled thighs. They left little to the imagination, but then she hardly had to imagine the physique beneath; she'd seen more than she had any right to see through his gaping dressing gown on her second night in residence. It wasn't something she was likely to forget. The strong chest, lightly furred with jet-black hair that diminished to a ribbon, arrow-straight down his flat middle, pointing to the shadow of what lay beneath the gaping gown, the glimpse of a corded thigh as he descended the stairs. The mere thought of it made her heart beat a little faster, and shot her cheeks through with a rush of hot blood. Her earlobes were on fire. He turned, and she buried her gaze in her plate.

"Sara," he said, taking his seat at the opposite end of the table, "about last night—"

"I do not wish to discuss last night, Nicholas," she interrupted. "You made your position quite plain, and I believe I have also. We can leave it at that, and get on with this, or drag it out to no practical purpose."

"Very well," he said, attacking the food on his plate.

Oh, so you don't like being silenced, Baron Walraven, she noted with smug satisfaction. *Well, you began this charade, and one should never begin something one cannot finish.* Her food had flavor again. This was the way to handle the brute, but she'd only just begun.

"I have a few 'ground rules' of my own that I should like to lay down before we go further," she said, dissecting her baked tomato.

"Not here," he said, nodding toward the footmen presiding over the buffet.

"Yes, here," she responded, leaning back while more coffee was poured into her cup. "My ground rules are quite pedestrian in nature compared to yours. They concern the servants, actually. They needn't only be aired behind closed study doors." The last was delivered dramatically, over the rim of her coffee cup.

"Sara—"

"Now then, where was I?" she intoned. "Oh yes, my ground rules. First off, if I am to hostess your affairs I shall have to have free rein to do so. That means I shall have to interview your cook in regard to the menus, Mrs. Bromley in regard to the china and linens, fresh flowers, and the like, and the footmen, of course, to be sure that things run smoothly."

"Of course," Nicholas responded, his voice thin, and dejected.

"Second to that, but no less important," she continued, "I shall need to be provided with a list of your guests' likes and dislikes, and any dietary restrictions. It's so fashionable today to boast of dietary restrictions, you know, whether they exist or not—very chic. A faulty menu would be disastrous. If you got to Town more often, and didn't send gudgeons to run your errands, you would know that."

"Sara, please—"

"Let's see . . . I shall need a place to hold my interviews," she went on, enjoying every moment of his knit brows and black looks. He was the picture of a thunderhead, or a petulant child, or both, chasing a Scotch egg around his plate with a vengeful fork. At one point she was certain it was going to take flight and attack the footman, who was giving it a wide berth attempting to fill his master's cup. This was so much better than sulking and sobbing. "The morning room, I think," she said. "Yes, the morning room will do nicely. I shall hold court there after nuncheon whenever the need arises, commencing today. You may alert the servants to expect it."

"Have you finished?" he pronounced, meanwhile dismissing the footman, who bowed out gracefully, and fled.

"Finished? Oh, no, not nearly," she replied. "You're really quite fortunate having chosen me, you know, Nicholas. Before my father's . . . misfortune put him in his grave and me in Fleet Prison, I presided over all of our gatherings—including the hunts. He was a knight, you know. Well, of course you know—*you probably know what he ate for breakfast*—and we entertained quite frequently. So, you see, I've a good deal of experience to bring to the position."

Nicholas set his fork and serviette down with practiced control, and gripped the edge of the table, like an animal about to spring. For a moment, Sara thought he was going to upend it.

"Sara, that's enough!" he seethed. "You make it sound as if you are a mere hireling. You know that isn't the case."

"It is the only 'case' that I can live with and endure. . . . *This*, Nicholas," she said, "is what you want of me, and I will

62

do it well, but I must be in complete charge of the arrangements. That is unequivocal. There cannot be more than one
set of hands mixing into it if you want things to run
smoothly. Do we have an understanding?"

"Yes," he said in defeat, snatching up his serviette again.

"Good!" she returned. "When is your houseguest arriving?"

"I shall be hosting a noted physician, Dr. Mark Breeden.
Alex is bringing him on from London. They should be arriving Thursday."

"That soon?"

"I should have told you earlier. I-I'm sorry . . . so much has
been happening . . ."

"You needn't apologize; you do it badly. Three days will
be difficult, but sufficient, I think. Is it just the doctor, or will
there be others?"

"Just the doctor."

"How long will he be staying?"

"He's on holiday, and a fortnight is planned, but that is
subject to change. Doctors of his caliber rarely get to take
their full vacations. I shall keep you apprised."

"Thank you. I shall see that a flexible menu is prepared,
with enough of a variety in the entrees and viands to allow
for restrictions, but you shall need to broach the subject with
him early on once he arrives, and inform me of anything urgent."

"Of course," he muttered, finally spearing his Scotch egg.
She wanted to cheer.

"Very well, then," she said, rising. She wasn't about to let
him eat the egg—at least not while it was still hot.

He bolted to his feet.

"You can inform Mrs. Bromley that I shall require her
presence in the morning room at two o'clock sharp this afternoon. And now if you will excuse me, Nicholas, I have
much to do beforehand. Good morning."

She was just about to cross the threshold, when he blocked

her exit. He reached toward her then retracted his hand, as though he'd nearly plunged it into the fire, and jammed it—white-knuckled and fisted—into his pocket. The other soon followed.

"Sara, I deserved some of that just now, I'll concede," he said, "but you cannot behave in that manner when my guest arrives. When *any* of my guests arrive."

"Don't worry, Nicholas," she said, brushing past him into the corridor, scattering the eavesdropping footmen. "I shall be the soul of propriety, good manners, and grace. Now, I do not mean to be rude, but you really must excuse me. I need to prepare myself to attend to house business."

Turning on her heel, she floated off and left him no less abruptly than he had left her in the study.

Nicholas didn't join her for nuncheon, which was just as well. She hadn't worked out the strategy of their next meeting yet. There hadn't been time. Before the day was gone, she'd held interviews with Mrs. Bromley; Agnes Knott, who answered only to "Cook;" and both Searl and Robbins, the two footmen who presided over meals at Ravencliff.

Mrs. Bromley made suggestions for the menus, and gave her a list of Nicholas's preferences and dislikes. The house-keeper also walked her through a room off the dining hall, where china and silver were housed in elaborate cabinets. There were breakfast, nuncheon, and dinner dishes, several different sets for each meal, one lovelier than the next, and silver to coordinate with each. Glassware was also housed here. The array was staggering. Grand parties were once held at Ravencliff, Mrs. Bromley told her. Some of the china hadn't been used in thirty years. Well, it was going to be used now, Sara vowed. Nicholas Walraven was in for a surprise.

It was nearly dusk when she returned to her suite. Nell would soon come to help her dress for dinner. She set the tablet containing her menu notes on the writing desk in her sitting room, and went to the window, studying the view through the mullioned panes. The seas were running high. White-capped combers crested far from shore; their sighing echo reached her where she stood. It was a soothing sound that could lull her to sleep if she'd let it.

Her gaze drifted toward the south. A figure was traveling the edge of the cliff in the soft semidarkness. It was Nicholas, and her heart tumbled in her breast following his long-legged stride as he paced along the seawall. There was no anger in his posture; something more akin to restless agitation moved him. This was a man wrestling with some demon yet to be named, and she longed to fly down the grand staircase, out through the great hall, over the sculptured grounds to his side, and make him tell it. This, of course, was a fantasy. She didn't even know if it were possible to access the cliff from the circular drive. It hadn't seemed so when she arrived. There had to be another entrance, one closer to the west side of the house and the sea. *I'll bet Nero knows,* she realized. *He was soaking wet when he paid his visit.* She shrugged. Since the animal had no voice to tell, she made a mental note to inquire of the servants in the morning.

She was just about to leave the window, when Nicholas took a different direction. All at once, he broke his stride and began to climb down the cliff. The means of his descent was hidden from her, but she assumed it to be the stairs hewn in the rock leading to the strand. He had warned her away from those stairs. Was it just as he'd said, that it was unsafe to climb down, or was there something down there . . . something that he didn't want her to see? She'd negotiated such descents at Dover and Lyme, and come to no harm— steep, treacherous descents, often slick from spindrift and backwash. She would do so here as well. When the time was right.

She couldn't see Nicholas any longer, and she turned away from the window. The notes she'd taken during her interviews drew her to the desk. She'd been hasty in her boast;

three days really wasn't nearly enough time to prepare for a houseguest, considering, and she began forming her notes into lists. She was still poring over them when Nell came to dress her for dinner an hour later.

"I think I shall have a tray here in my rooms," Sara said, looking up from the stack of papers her notes had become. "See to it, will you, Nell?"

"Yes, my lady. Are ya feelin' poorly, my lady?" said the abigail, studying her with knitted brows.

Sara responded by exhibiting a sheaf of papers. "No, no, I'm just bogged under with all this. We're to have a houseguest Thursday week. There are menus to be worked out, accommodations—all sorts of issues to be addressed. I fear I shall be closeted here until the gentleman's arrival."

"Yes, my lady," said the abigail. "Do ya want ta send your regrets?"

"Ah!" Sara cried, taking a piece of parchment and red sealing wax from the drawer. She scribbled a few lines, folded it, then took up a candlestick, and sealed it shut with a stamp embossed with a *W* in scrollwork. Indeed, she would send her regrets. She wouldn't make that mistake again. The last thing she wanted was another late-night visit from Nicholas Walraven. "Would you see that his lordship receives this?" she said, handing it over. "Afterward, you may do as you please. I'll dress myself for bed. I have all this to see to before I retire, and I don't want to be disturbed again tonight."

"Yes, my lady," Nell said. She sketched a curtsy, and left as quietly as she'd come in.

The dinner tray arrived soon after, and Sara set a portion of her larded pheasant aside in case Nero should pay a visit. Once the tray was collected, the draperies drawn, and the fire stoked with fresh logs for the night, she left the foyer door open a crack, and went back to the stack of papers on her desk.

It was nearly midnight when she set the lists and menus

aside, and blew out all the candles except for a branch on the stand beside her bed. She was exhausted, but she'd chosen the china to be used at breakfast, nuncheon, and dinner during the doctor's stay, and formed a workable menu plan that would cover meals for a sennight. The rest could be done at her leisure. At least she had an impressive accomplishment to submit to Nicholas in the morning. She would take it with her when she went down to breakfast. That should show Baron Nicholas Walraven just what sort of investment he'd made in purchasing a hostess. Thinking on that revived her, and she kicked off her Morocco leather slippers, and flopped on the bed to gloat over her success. She didn't mean to fall asleep there, fully dressed on top of the counterpane, but she did. Her eyelids drooped then closed, and she drifted off almost as soon as she curled on her side and relaxed.

Her sleep was deep and dreamless, yet something woke her in the wee hours, something physical. The bedding beneath her moved, and her body moved with it, displaced by whatever phenomenon wrenched her eyes open. Dazed, she blinked awake. The candles beside the bed had burned down to nubs. One had gone out altogether, and wax frosted the shafts and shackled the candle branch to the mahogany stand with globs of unsightly tallow.

Blinking back sleep, she focused her eyes on what had awoken her. There, on the foot of the bed, sat Nero, like the Sphinx, licking larded pheasant grease off his jowls with his long, pink tongue, watching her. He looked just like a statue straight out of John Nash's neoclassical Egyptian decor, so fashionable among the *ton* that season.

"Nero!" she cried. Scrabbling to his side, she threw her arms around his neck, and he rewarded her by licking her face all over. She giggled. He tasted of pheasant, and he smelled clean, of the sea. She ruffled his thick, shaggy fur, and planted a kiss on the top of his head. "I told you I'd have a treat for you the next time you came," she said, hugging him again. "I see you've found it. Did you like it, boy?"

Nero whined in reply, and nudged her with his cold, wet snout.

His red-fire eyes almost seemed human, gazing at her in the semidarkened room. Aside from the glowing embers in the hearth that had colored those deep, soulful eyes, only one candle remained lit now, casting a halo of shimmering light about the animal's body

"You've been outside," Sara whispered. "I smell the sea on your coat. I taste the salt. You know how to get out there, don't you, Nero? You'll show me, won't you? It'll be our secret."

There was such an expression of comprehension in the animal's eyes, as though he'd understood every word. The fingers of a cold chill crawled up her spine, watching the closest thing to a frown she'd ever seen on a dog's face manifest itself across Nero's broad, flat brow. It was a fleeting look that turned feral in a blink. Whining, the animal sprang off the bed, streaked through the open foyer door, and disappeared down the shadow-steeped hallway before she ever got to the threshold.

So much for the answer to her question; when she reached the corridor all that met her eyes was the faintest shudder of suggested motion that might have been Nero's bushy tail disappearing over the second-floor landing. She didn't even stop to think or collect her slippers. Moving on feet that made no sound, she raced along the carpeted hallway, flew over the landing, and ran down the grand staircase to the green baize door. Nero was nowhere in sight, and she was just about to try the knob, when it turned, and she ducked beneath the bifurcated staircase and held her breath.

The door creaked open. One of the servants was entering the main house from the servant's quarters below—a footman, or one of the hall boys. She couldn't be sure from her vantage, flattened against the wall in the shadows. Whichever, a candle branch lit his way, and she stood there, spine rigid, until the scuffling patter of his footfalls became distant, and the stairwell grew dark around her again.

Sara drew a deep, ragged breath, and slumped against the wall, but it wasn't a wall, it was a *door!* It came open, supporting her no longer, and she backpedaled trying to maintain her balance before it swung shut on her escape with a heart-stopping *click.*

Falling was her last conscious sensation.

Seven

Sara groaned awake some time later in dank, cold darkness. The hard floor beneath her was slimy with dampness, recalling Fleet Prison. She screamed at the top of her lungs for help, but all that replied was the mournful echo of her cries drifting upward. Her head was splitting with pain, and vertigo starred her vision. The swirling white pinpoints before her eyes were the only light. There was a lump on her brow. She fingered it gingerly. By the swelling, she assessed it to be impressive. It wouldn't be easy to hide. How would she explain it to Nicholas? First things first, she decided. She would have to find her way out of wherever she was to do that, and she drew herself up to her knees, and began groping the floor.

All at once something brushed her neck, and she cried out, swatting it away. It was only her Mechlin lace insert that had come loose in the fall, and she heaved a gushing sigh of relief trying to tuck it back in place. That, however, was impossible. The dress was torn at the shoulder, one of the puffed sleeves was hanging where the neck was torn, and there was nothing to tuck it into. It barely covered her breast. *That's the trouble with fashions today*, she thought ruefully. *They're made too flimsy to be serviceable.* But then, one wasn't supposed to go tumbling down stone staircases in them, was one? Which was what her fingers finally showed her—a narrow step, then above it another, and another. She staggered to her feet, climbed up, and found two more, then a wall. She felt it— every inch of it. Where was the door she'd fallen through? It wasn't there!

Panicked now, she screamed with all her might for help, but the sound echoed back at her, ringing in her ears. The wall was granite rock, impenetrable, and she slid back down to the bottom, and began searching the blackness with out-stretched arms, and hands carving circles in the damp, stale air. Several steps more and she bumped into another wall. This, too, was granite. If she could only see!

Inch by inch, she felt her way around the cubicle— scarcely larger than a closet—stumbling over what must have sufficed for a bed, and a pile of debris beside the stairs. That, she presumed to be what had broken her fall, since she'd come to in the midst of it. It had spared her a much more serious injury than the lump on her head that she'd ev-idently gotten on the way down.

On the other side of the narrow stairs, she tripped over a small chest against the wall. She felt the top of it, and her hands came away slimed with mildew, but not before she found a little drawer recessed under the carved edge. Damp-ness had all but fused it shut, and it took some time, but she finally worked it open. There was a candle, and a tinderbox inside. Did she dare hope the tinder was dry enough to burn? Praying that the little metal coffer had protected it enough, she worked the flint and anonymous flammable bits until they finally ignited and lit the candle. It was short and squat and she anchored it to the top of the chest with tallow drippings and turned to survey her prison. Her breath caught. *A priest hole*, could it be? If the house went back be-yond the Norman Conquest, it was very possible. Such things were common through the ages, and most old castles and houses had them. Ravencliff qualified in both cases.

All at once cold chills shook her body, and gripped her heart like a fist. She'd heard tales of men dying in such hidey-holes, of suffocation, and starvation—walled up inside and forgotten, sometimes deliberately. Their construction was inscrutable. The walls on this one had to be more than a foot thick. They would never hear her cries from above. Suppose no one thought to look for her here? Another glance around the room—at the heavy, undisturbed coating of mildew spread over everything—told her that it hadn't been used in some years. Did anyone even know it was here? She could only pray that they did.

She looked in dismay at her torn dress. It was filthy with dust and slime from the bleeding dampness that clung to the place. Her hands and bare arms were black with it. She was cold, and she hugged herself for warmth, searching the room with anxious eyes for something she could use as a wrapper. They finally came to rest upon a pile of old linens in the corner, and she fished out a piece of cloth that might have at one time been used as bed linen, so old it ripped when she tugged it around herself. It would have to do.

She glanced at the candle. Its flame was tall and straight. No drafts. Her heart sank. That meant no air was getting in. It also meant she had to save the candle for emergencies. There was precious little left of it as it was. Besides, she dared not leave it lit and risk burning up the oxygen, and she quickly paced off the area, and committed the dimensions of the cell and its contents to memory.

There was no use spending her energy and her lungs before daybreak. No one was abroad to hear her. All she could do was wait, and hope that the sounds of servants moving around above would tell her that dawn had broken, before she called out for help again. It couldn't be long, and she took one last look around, and snuffed out the candle.

* * *

Nicholas ate his breakfast alone in the morning. Sara didn't appear, and she hadn't sent her apologies. He was on his way up to her suite when Nell met him coming down from the second-floor landing.

"Oh, sir, I was just comin' after ya," she whined. "Somethin's happened ta the mistress. I just know it!"

"Calm yourself, Nell," he responded. "What do you mean, something's happened to her?"

"She's gone, sir. Her bed ain't been slept in, and her shoes are on the floor up there. Where could she have gone off to barefooted in the dead o' night?"

"Show me," he said, bounding up the stairs ahead.

"That mangy old dog was in there, too," the abigail said, hurrying after him. "She must'a give him somethin' ta eat from her dinner tray. The empty serviette was on the floor, all streaked with grease, it was."

Nicholas loosed a string of expletives under his breath, and burst into the tapestry suite, his breast heaving with rage. Rage was dangerous. *Anything* was dangerous here now, considering, and he took deep, slow breaths as he entered the bedchamber.

"When did you see her last, Nell?" he demanded.

"When I brought up her tray," said the abigail. "I made up the fire, and drew the drapes while she was eatin', then she said she didn't want ta be disturbed—that she'd ready herself for bed, so I left her ta her business."

"That would have been approximately what time?" he persisted.

"I dunno, seven . . . eight—about the time you sat down in the dinin' hall."

Nicholas snatched up Sara's shoes from the floor, and examined them, his brow knit in a frown.

"That's what's got me worried, too," Nell said. "She couldn't have gotten far without them slippers. She's got ta be somewhere in the house, but where? We've searched it top ta bottom, sir."

"All right, Nell," said Nicholas. "I want you to remain here in these rooms until I tell you otherwise . . . in case her ladyship returns. In that event, come and fetch me at once." He exhibited the slippers. "I'll take these," he said, "in case I find her."

"Yes, sir," she replied, straightening the rumpled bedding. "See here?" she said, brushing short black hairs tipped with silver off the tufted surface. "That dog was in here just like I said—right on her bed, he was." She clicked her tongue. "He's soiled the counterpane with grease here, too."

"Yes, well, I shall take Nero to task," Nicholas replied. "But for now leave the foyer door open. If the animal returns . . . follow him. If he was here last night, as you say, he might know where my lady has got to."

"Yes, sir," said Nell, "but, beggin' your pardon, sir, Nero . . . he ain't the kind o' dog for a fine house like this, all scruffy and wild-lookin' like he is—all skin and bones. He looks half-starved. That ain't our fault, neither. Half the time, he don't even eat what we set out for him. He's scary, he is, always sneakin' around in the shadows. I know it ain't my place ta say it, but it's not just me speakin'—it's what all o' us are sayin' below stairs. Ya ought ta get rid o' that animal."

"Yes, well, that is the plan, Nell," said Nicholas. "Hopefully, you shan't have to worry about Nero much longer . . . but for now let us see if we can't make him earn his keep, hmm?"

Try as she would, Sara couldn't hear any sounds coming from above. It was so hard to gauge the time entombed there in the darkness. Surely it must be daylight by now. She had to try something—*anything*—to free herself from the cold, dank cubicle, or go mad dwelling on what might happen if she were never found.

How long would it take to die there? The atmosphere was

close already. How much longer did she have before there was no air left to breathe? It would be a slow, horrible death, and she climbed the steps and began screaming, meanwhile pounding on the wall that once was a door, with both her fists. She soon realized the futility of that. It wasn't long before her tender skin was bruised and broken assailing the rough granite, and she groped her way back down the steps, snatched the tinderbox from the drawer in the chest, and began attacking the wall with that.

Again and again, she screamed at the top of her voice until it broke into hoarse whispers, then pounded the wall with the tinderbox until it slipped from her hands and fell to the floor below. Sara groaned in despair. She needed the tinder and flint inside the coffer to light the candle. How was she going to find it in the dark?

It all seemed so hopeless, and she sank down on the step with her head in her hands. After a moment, she caught her breath and ordered her thoughts. There had to be something she could do. Perhaps another look in the candlelight might show her something she'd overlooked before, and she groped her way down the steps and began searching the floor. When she finally found the tinderbox among the debris beside the stairs, her heart sank. It had broken open in the fall, and the flint and tinder were gone.

It was no use. Her throat was raw from screaming for help. Her head ached, the lump on her forehead was throbbing like a pulse beat, and her hands were cut and bleeding. Vertigo threatened her consciousness. How long had it been since she fell down those stairs? How long had she been unconscious afterward? If only the little cell weren't so small. If only it weren't so airtight. If only it weren't so free of drafts, which crept through every crevice in the rest of the house. Somewhere, she had heard that thrashing about would use up oxygen faster in confined spaces. It could already be too late to apply that knowledge. Exertion had sapped her strength. She could scarcely breathe, and she laid her face on the cold granite step, and shut her eyes.

"When I don't want that damnable creature, he comes quick enough," Nicholas railed, pacing the carpet in his dressing room. "Now, when it's vital . . ."

"Don't take on so, my lord," said Mills, picking up Nicholas's clothes as he shed them. "What do you think he can do that you cannot? You will find her, my lord."

"How?" Nicholas flashed, tossing his waistcoat on the floor. He untied his neck cloth, and threw it down as well. "We've searched the house from top to bottom—every deuced chamber. Good God, I even went below and searched the strand. I need Nero! But I cannot control him, can I? No, he controls *me!* Why is it always like this? Why can I never remember all of it? She hasn't been seen since the dinner hour *yesterday*, Mills. Nero hasn't surfaced since, either. That's more than twenty-four hours. If she's hurt somewhere . . ."

"You and my lady . . . argued, did you not?" said the valet, catching Nicholas's shirt before it hit the floor. "Have a care, my lord! That nearly went into the fire," he cried, adding the shirt to his burden before resuming. "Could she have . . . left Ravencliff?"

"Without her shoes, Mills? I hardly think it likely. It's a long, steep trek to the bottom of the lane, and the gate is always locked at dusk; you know that. Besides, it wasn't all that serious an argument, and Nell said Sara was working on menus for Dr. Breeden's visit when she was last seen. That hardly sounds like she was about to flee the place to me, though I cannot say I would blame her if she did. My God, I have to find her."

"Do you want your tub, my lord?"

"No cold bath tonight," Nicholas growled, flopping in the wing chair. He extended his foot. "Get me out of these damned boots."

"Perhaps a hot tub, my lord?" Mills suggested, straddling the outstretched leg.

"No," Nicholas snapped. Planting his other foot on Mills's narrow behind, he pushed, and the valet pulled off the Hessian with a grunt. "The last thing I need to do is relax."

"I'll fetch your dressing gown, my lord," the valet panted, having successfully removed the other boot. He tucked it under his arm with the rest.

"No," said Nicholas, peeling off his pantaloons, and then his drawers. "Just lay it out on the bed."

"My lord?" said the valet, slack-jawed, as Nicholas resumed his pacing, stark naked before the hearth.

"Just leave it out for me, and go to bed!" Nicholas snapped. He snatched up Sara's Morocco leather slippers from the footstool beside the fire, and studied them like a hound on the scent as he strode back and forth.

"But, my lord, what if—"

"I know where to find you if I need you, Mills," Nicholas interrupted. "Go to bed. At least one of us needs to get some sleep tonight."

Sara woke, gasping for breath in the darkness. It was the sound of scratching that roused her. *Rats! Fleet Prison!* No, not the Fleet, that would have been heaven compared to this, her tomb in the bowels of Ravencliff Manor, where no one would find her but the rats. Adrenaline surged through her. Were they inside . . . or out? Had they tumbled down with her? Without the candle, there was no way to know, and she scrabbled up the stairs again and beat on the wall, screaming at the top of what was left of her voice.

The scratching stopped. Had she imagined it? There was no sound now, and she crawled back down the steps and collapsed on the cold, slimy floor. Time meant nothing then. She'd lost track of it. Totally. She was slipping away. Strange dreams bled into her consciousness until she could no longer part them from reality. Then, there came a grating sound that echoed through her body, setting her teeth on edge, and a sudden blast of fresh air funneled in on a beam of light. It smelled of mildew and must, but, oh how blessed it was to breathe again! A hallucination; she was going mad. She had to be.

All at once strong arms lifted her, and powerful legs carried her out of the tomb. She leaned her hot face against a familiar burgundy satin dressing gown. It smelled clean, of the sea, of *him*, sensual and feral. The heart beneath it thudded against her ear in a trembling rhythm that was both soothing and frightening. Sara leaned into it, nuzzling the satin, and slept.

Eight

Nicholas was loath to put Sara down. He despaired of letting her go. Yet he knew what would be if ever he touched her as he wanted, so it had to remain impersonal between them. It had to be a businesslike arrangement. There was no other alternative.

How soft and malleable she was in his arms, how fragrant, despite her ordeal in the musty priest hole. He inhaled her scent until it filled his nostrils and his memory: rosemary and gillyflower, primeval scents of wood, of earth, with a sensual touch of the rose. He drank her in—nectar of the gods, so long denied him.

He laid her on the bed, and smoothed her sun-painted hair back from her brow. How soft it was, just as he knew it would be, as ethereal as morning cobwebs in the shaft of sunlight the dawn had flung across the counterpane. He couldn't help but touch it, feel its silkiness between his fingers. Brushing it aside, he felt the lump on her brow, where a bruise was forming. Her hands were cut and swollen, and her fine, translucent skin was streaked with filth, spread over her face, her arms—her breast, scarcely covered by the torn frock. His loins were on fire, pulsating with achy heat, his keen senses acutely attuned to the fever in his blood, heightened like those of an animal in the wild. The sexual stream flowing between them was palpable, and he wrapped the counterpane around her like a cocoon in a vain attempt to sever it, and surged to his feet when the effort failed.

"I want that bloody priest hole walled up before the sun sets!" he seethed, scarcely aware until that moment that Nell and Mills were standing close by. "Stop that whimpering, girl!" he snapped at the abigail. "Fetch the smelling salts! Have Mrs. Bromley come up here at once to assess this. There must be some nostrum or concoction she can brew with those damnable herbs of hers to minister to her lady-ship until the doctor arrives tomorrow. I want you to get her into a warm tub as soon as she comes 'round, then put her back in this bed. She stays in it, too, until I say otherwise, should you have to tie her down. Is that clear?"

"Y-yes, sir," Nell whined. Spinning on her heel, she fled the room, her black skirts dusting the woodwork.

"Come away, my lord," the valet urged, laying a gentle hand on Nicholas's rock-hard arm. "This . . . upsetment is not good for you."

Nicholas's light-headed laugh replied to that, and he shrugged the valet's hand away and cinched his dressing gown sash ruthlessly.

"Come back to your rooms, my lord. I'll prepare your bath. They will see to her. Then, when you've rested . . . when you're calm again—"

"I will never be 'calm again,' Mills," Nicholas said through clenched teeth, and diving past him, crashed through the door and disappeared in the shadows of the empty corridor.

It wasn't a dream. He carried her up the slimy steps and out of the priest hole as though she weighed no more than a handful of eiderdown. How strong he was, how tender his embrace, as if she were something fragile, subject to breakage, and yet he clasped her to him as though his very life depended upon it. She surrendered to the arms she'd fantasized holding her since she first set eyes on Nicholas Walraven, her husband who wasn't a husband. He would be. If it was the last thing she did on earth . . . he would be.

"You've got that mangy old dog to thank that we found ya," said Nell, sudsing the cobwebs and dust from her hair. The warm bathwater was heaven, silkened with oil of roses, and strewn with crushed rosemary. "Nobody set eyes on the creature for nigh on two days, then all at once this mornin' he come tearin' down them stairs sniffin' the carpet right ta the hidey-hole door, and started diggin' and scratchin' and whinin' and howlin', makin' enough of a din ta raise the dead, he was. Then he run off, and he must've woke the master, 'cause m'lord came on all out straight, barefooted—in his dressing gown, he was."

"The scratching," Sara said. It was the second time she'd mistaken the sound. "I heard the scratching. I thought it was rats."

"Well, you're outta there now, and not a minute too soon. You was scarcely breathin', shut up in that room—no more than a closet—for thirty-six hours straight. You're lucky ta be alive, my lady, and that's a fact. He's down there now the master is, with old Gibbs, the groundskeeper. They're wallin' up that priest hole, they are."

"Where is Nero now?" Sara murmured.

"I dunno, miss," said the abigail. "Nobody's seen him since. The master said he showed him where ta look, and took off like a shot. He's like that Nero is, skulkin' about, sneakin' up on folk, and disappearin' just as quick. I don't like him much, I'll own. He scares me, if ya want the truth o' it. Oh, he's never bit nobody—nothin' like that. It's just them eyes he stares at ya with. It's like they was human eyes." She shuddered. "Gives me the creeps, he does. He gives *everybody* the creeps the way he comes and goes . . . like a *ghost*." She whispered the last, and Sara suppressed a smile.

"He's no ghost, Nell, I can vouch for that," she responded. "Ghosts don't eat larded pheasant."

"I know it," Nell replied. "They don't shed, and leave hairs on counterpanes, neither. It's just how he seems is all. I'd like to give him a good bath, I would, but nobody can catch him. The master was goin' ta get rid o' him. I don't mind tellin' ya, we'd all rest a mite easier if he'd do that, but I don't know if he will now bein' that the dog's a hero and all. They ain't too happy about that below stairs."

"Oh, I hope not, Nell," Sara said. "I've grown quite fond of Nero, and I want you to leave my foyer door open a crack each night, just in case he should visit."

"If you say so, my lady, but—"

"I say so," Sara enforced. Maybe she wasn't a real wife to Nicholas Walraven, *yet*, but she knew how to run a house and keep the servants in their place.

"Yes, my lady."

"I think I've bathed long enough," said Sara. "I should like to get out now, if you would fetch my clothes."

"Oh, ya can't have your clothes, my lady. Only your nightgown."

"I beg your pardon?"

"The master's orders, my lady," said Nell. "You're ta stay in bed till he says otherwise."

"That's absurd," said Sara. "It's scarcely past the breakfast hour. I can't stay abed all day. I'm perfectly fine, Nell, just a few cuts and bruises; nothing serious."

"The master says that's for the doctor ta decide, the doctor that's comin' from London tomorrow."

"But I can't stay abed with a guest due to arrive. There are preparations to be made—my menus, the arrangements. I must see to them!"

"I'll see ta them," said Mrs. Bromley, entering with salves, a basin with a compress steeping in it, and bandage linen laid out neatly on a tray.

"But—"

"Now, now," said the housekeeper. "The master'll sack the lot o' us if you don't behave. He's left me in charge, and you're goin' ta mind, else he'll have me on the carpet. Nell will help ya outta the tub. We'll towel ya down, get ya inta your nightdress, and fluff your hair dry by the fire, while I bandage them cuts on your poor hands. Then it's inta that bed with this poultice on your brow ta take that lump ta task. I brewed the bath for it myself, from red dock and castor oil. It'll help heal the bruise, and bring down the swellin'. Then we'll bring ya a nice bowl o' oxtail soup, and toasted bread with gooseberry jam—they're full o' iron, ta put your blood back in order. We'll have ya right as rain in no time."

Nicholas made an appearance after dinner. Though Sara was expecting him, when he entered her bedchamber, her heart began to race so severely she was certain he could see it in the rapid rise and fall of her breast beneath her nightgown and wrapper. How handsome he was in skintight black pantaloons that outlined his corded legs and thighs. How broad his shoulders were in the black tailcoat of superfine, and white embroidered waistcoat that emphasized his narrow waist and broad, well-muscled chest. Her mind's eye saw what lay beneath. Hadn't she seen him nearly naked? *Twice.*

For a moment, he didn't speak. All day, she'd been dreading his visit. She'd steeled herself against the imminent lecture. She had no defense. Exactly what he'd told her would happen if she prowled the house alone had happened. She couldn't meet his black-fire eyes reflecting the hearth glow, and when he spoke, she lurched as though she'd been shot.

"How are you feeling?" he asked, strolling nearer. She did glance up then, in time to see his brow arch as he studied her swollen forehead and bandaged hands. "I was hoping much of what I saw earlier would wash away. Foolish of me."

Sara's heart sank: He was cold and distant again. But she hadn't imagined his reaction when he carried her out of that priest hole; there was warmth and gentleness and ardor in the man. There was passion in him, too. Not just the kind that rage bred, either, although he certainly had a penchant for that. A seething, smoldering passion lay just under the surface ready to explode. She hadn't mistaken the tenderness in his embrace, the rhythm of his heart shuddering against her. He *did* care. Why was he afraid to show it?

"Mrs. Bromley's remedies are quite remarkable," she said, "but it's really not as serious as it looks."

"We shall let Dr. Breeden determine that, when he arrives tomorrow," said Nicholas.

"Nell tells me that you've taken my shoes," she said. "May I have them, please?"

"Not until the doctor gives me leave to let you out of that bed," he responded.

"I have other shoes, my lord," she snapped.

" 'Nicholas,' " he corrected her. "I hope that knock on the head hasn't affected your memory. We have a bargain, remember?"

"How could I forget?"

"I shan't scold you. I should think you've learned your lesson," he said. "I've had the priest hole cemented shut, but there are other dangers in this house. You must respect my wishes and refrain from going off exploring on your own. What were you doing down there? How did you come to fall through that revolving panel?"

"That hardly matters now," she replied.

"Oh, but it does matter," he snapped. "What were you looking for? Were you chasing that animal again? I want you to tell me the truth, Sara. You needn't skulk about in this house. You have only to ask if you need assistance with anything. I've taken into account that you've come from a prison, but Ravencliff is not one. You needn't be afraid to speak your mind here. You're very good at it, as a matter of fact. There is naught to fear but the danger you put yourself in ignoring my directives."

"Your 'ground rules,' you mean," she observed.

"If you want to put it that way, yes. Don't shift the subject. Why were you down there?"

Should she tell him the truth? She was angry enough to. He was right, she had never been afraid to speak her mind . . . until she'd come to Ravencliff.

"I'm waiting," he reminded her. "It was Nero, wasn't it?"

"Not exactly," she said. "He didn't lead me down there, if that's what you're thinking. He knows his way around this house, and he's often wet, smelling of the sea. I should like to have a walk on the cliff one day. It occurred to me that he must know of another exit on the sea side, and I meant to follow him to it—"

"In the middle of the night?" he interrupted.

"Not to go out, just to find the way out."

"Did it never occur to you that any of the servants, or I myself, would have been only too glad to show you?"

"*Show me*, yes, but not allow me to venture out there on my own."

"Oh, I see."

"You really don't, but I'm too weary to explain."

"I would like you to try," he said, folding his arms across his massive chest.

"There are times when I prefer to be alone, and I take great pleasure communing with nature. You above all should understand that, what with your passion for solitude. I believe that to be your only passion." She didn't really believe it, not for a moment, but he didn't need to know that—at least, not then.

"Which proves how little you know me," he said, pacing the carpet at the foot of the bed, taking slow, deliberate strides, his fisted hands clasped beneath his coattails.

"You don't give me a chance to know you, Nicholas."

"You're avoiding the issue again," he replied. "You followed Nero. Then what?"

"He was much too quick for me. I lost him in the shadows of the corridor, and I went below to see if I could find him, when one of the footmen, I believe it was, started to open the servants' quarters door. I didn't want to be discovered there at that hour, and I ducked behind the staircase and hid in the shadows until he passed. When I leaned against the wall, I fell through."

"You could have died down there," he said. "That priest hole was built centuries ago, Sara. It hasn't been used in over a hundred years. Though I knew of it, I'd never even been down there. There are more than one in this house, as well as a maze of tunnels and hidden passageways veining the lower regions. They were used as escape routes in time of invasion, and later as a means of access for pirates and smugglers and privateers, coming and going with their plunder. I have never even seen them all. Now do you see why I didn't want you prowling about on your own? If Nero hadn't picked up your scent, I never would have found you down there."

"You won't get rid of him now, will you, Nicholas?" she pleaded.

He stopped pacing and faced her, his eyes absent and haunting.

"Nicholas . . . please?"

"I may not have a choice, Sara," he said. "One day, you may have to choose between us."

Nine

Though Dr. Breeden pronounced Sara fit enough to leave her bed, Nicholas insisted that she keep to her rooms for a few days. He needed time with the doctor alone, but Sara wasn't his only concern in that regard. Alexander Mallory was underfoot now as well, and the wily steward wasn't as easily confined.

"Forgive me for presuming upon your skills the moment you arrived, Dr. Breeden," Nicholas said across the dinner table, as the footman presented the whole steamed salmon. "It couldn't be avoided, I'm afraid. I shall give you the same advice I gave her ladyship: Please do not go ambling about on your own in this antiquity, else you fall victim of a similar peril. Ravencliff is full of surprises, not all of them pleasant."

"I am only too glad to be of service, Baron Walraven," the doctor replied, "and you needn't fear, I shall indeed step with caution."

"There's even a dungeon below," Mallory chimed in, leaning back for the footman to lay down his plate of salmon. Then to Nicholas: "Do you remember the summer we found it? God, how old were we then—just lads. The Normans were very inventive chaps. Ravencliff is filled with examples of their ingenuity." He shifted his attention to the carver's chair. "Nicholas, how did she ever . . . ?"

"She will be more careful in future," Nicholas responded, ignoring the question, meanwhile dosing the steward with a look that silenced him.

Aside from the clink of silver against china, that silence prevailed until midway through the roast saddle of mutton course. Nicholas was champing at the bit. He was so anxious to consult the doctor that his emotions had begun to flag danger. It wouldn't do to let down his guard in front of the steward, but there were some related topics that could be discussed in company, and he decided to begin with those.

"I understand that you've spent much time in India, Doctor," he began.

"I lived there for many years," said Breeden. "It was in India that I wrote the Oxford papers you alluded to in your invitation. Fascinating country."

Nicholas had no fear that the doctor would inadvertently betray him. His invitation had made clear the necessity for complete secrecy in regard to the true nature of his visit—even from Sara, and especially from Alexander Mallory.

"My father was there, as well," said Nicholas, over the rim of his wineglass. "He was part of the early occupation under Warren Hastings. When Lord North's India Bill went into effect in 1773, and Parliament gained control of the East India Company, India came under the Governor-General's control. Once that occurred, British rule in India was vigorously pursued. Hastings, the first Governor-General, was one of my father's closest friends. Father joined him there early on, in the spring of '74, and returned to England in '76, the year before I was born."

"I see," said the doctor and, from his expression, Nicholas had no doubt that he was beginning to. Dr. Mark Breeden was a man twice his age with the most articulate pair of quicksilver eyes he had ever seen. They gleamed with an in-

ner light of understanding that was both frightening and reassuring at once. They were studying him now, and he had
no doubt that they saw more than what rested on the surface. "Mustered out after just two years, you say, and at such
a critical time—during the birth pangs of the occupation?
That couldn't have been the end of his tour. Was he injured?"

"Yes, but not in combat. He was bitten by an animal—a
wolf. The wound never healed. It festered, became ulcerated,
and the ulcer spread. It poisoned his blood, and in the end it
killed him. He died not long after I was born."

"I see," said the doctor. "How tragic. And your mother?"

"My mother died when I was twelve. She never remarried;
she never recovered from the loss of Father. They were very
devoted."

"You were an only child?"

"Yes," said Nicholas. The answer seemed to trigger relief
in the doctor's expression, and now Nicholas began studying him. "Mills, my valet, was Father's valet and his batman
during his commission. He was with him in India, when the
accident occurred. He cared for him nearly until he died, and
then looked after me as a child, especially after Mother
passed. I couldn't do without him."

"Good, and . . . *loyal* servants are so hard to find these
days," said the doctor, his emphasis upon the word 'loyal'
telling that he'd read the lines between.

"Yes," said Nicholas, "you have it exactly. We will share
him during your visit, since you're traveling without a valet.
I'm sure you'll find his service satisfactory."

"I have no doubt of it," said the doctor.

"How long did you live in India, Dr. Breeden?" said Mallory, drawing both their eyes.

"Longer than I have in England," the doctor replied. "I
was born there, spent my childhood there. Then I was edu-
cated here, and returned to India to live until my mother
passed on fifteen years ago. She was half-caste, you see. My
father was a British national working for the East India Com-

pany. Religious fanatics killed him while I was here studying at Oxford."

"No wonder you are so familiar with the culture," said Mallory, raising his wine goblet.

The footmen had begun removing the table linen, and setting out the sweet wines and desserts. Again, silence prevailed until they had laid out an array of assorted jellies and creams, rum and apple pudding, and French nougat cake.

"Good heavens," said the doctor, accepting a helping of the fragrant pudding. "I shall be courting gout if this keeps up. My compliments to your cook, my lord."

"I shall convey them, Dr. Breeden," said Nicholas, "but you have the baroness to thank for the menu. She is quite skilled at the art of entertaining, as you shall see."

"A pity she couldn't join us," the doctor said. "She's really fit enough, you know. The side effects of concussion will take awhile to dissipate, but that shouldn't deter her, so long as she's careful."

"She will be joining us tomorrow evening," said Nicholas, "once I'm certain I can trust her not to overdo. This is the first time we've entertained since our marriage, and I know how important it is to her."

"You two are getting on well, I take it, then?" said Mallory.

"Of course," Nicholas responded. "Why wouldn't we be?"

The steward shrugged. "No reason," he said, finishing his cake. "I sensed a bit of . . . apprehension on her part during the trip down, that's all."

"Apprehension, Alex? How so?"

"Perhaps that is too strong a word," said Mallory, signaling for more wine. "Unease is more accurate. Prenuptial jitters, I expect. It's only natural, considering, that she should have . . . second thoughts."

The doctor was watching the exchange with not a little interest. Nicholas wished the steward hadn't brought the subject up, but knew why he had. Alexander Mallory was easily read. He was hoping things wouldn't work out between them. He was hoping to step in once the arrangement failed. Anger was Nicholas's enemy then. It raised his hackles, and when he spoke he directed his reply to the doctor.

"I married the baroness by proxy, Dr. Breeden," he said. "Alex here stood in for me since . . . circumstances beyond my control prevented me from making the trip to London for a proper wedding."

"Oh dear, have I spoken out of turn?" said Mallory, setting his serviette aside.

"Not at all," Nicholas forced. The anger was still with him. It was all he could do to keep from leaping across the table to satisfy it. He took deep, measured breaths instead.

"I wasn't aware that proxy marriages could be performed here in England any longer," said the doctor.

"They cannot," Mallory said. "We had to travel all the way to Scotland to have it done. Dreadful trip. The weather was ghastly."

"Years ago, when such things were allowed," Nicholas said, "it was simply a matter of the absent party going before the local registrar with a stand-in to finalize the union." He gave a guttural chuckle; this was just what he needed to break the tension. "Before we realized such unions were no longer possible, in the absence of a literate female stand-in, Mills was set to do the honors for me before the registrar from Truro if needs must. There is no limit to that man's devotion to House Walraven." A round of laughter followed. They had finished their dessert, and Nicholas rose from the table. "Shall we adjourn to the study for a spot of brandy, gentlemen?" he said.

"I must cry off," the steward replied. "With your permission, Nicholas, I shall pay my respects to the baroness before I retire, and make an early night of it. It's been an exhausting journey."

Nicholas hesitated. "As you wish," he returned. "Don't tire her, Alex." The thought of the steward paying a call upon Sara made him marginally uncomfortable, but there was no real harm in it. Nell would be close at hand. He knew Sara's position when it came to Alexander Mallory, and he was anxious to have a moment alone with the doctor.

"Oh, I shan't. Good evening, Nicholas . . . Dr. Breeden," he said. Sketching a bow, he left them.

Neither Nicholas nor the doctor spoke until they were inside the study behind closed doors. Once they settled down with their brandy, it was Nicholas who broke the silence between them.

"Forgive me, Dr. Breeden," he said. "In this house, we cannot converse on the topic of our . . . mutual interest. The very walls have ears, and much depends upon secrecy. Perhaps tomorrow, weather permitting, we might have a walk on the strand. The sea will keep our secrets. She has kept mine since I could stand without my knees buckling."

"Understood," said the doctor.

"I do not mean to offend, but so very much depends upon it . . . do I have your guarantee of confidentiality?"

The doctor smiled. "Of course, my lord, that goes without saying. My oath is your guarantee—but even if it weren't, if we are going where I believe we are going with this, who would believe me if I did tell? Half of England considers me a crackpot, and the remainder is quite convinced that I'm a certified bedlamite." He raised his snifter in salute. "Your secret is quite safe with me."

The last thing Sara expected when the knock came at her sitting room door was a visit from Alexander Mallory. Thanking Providence that she was still dressed, she bade him enter, and resumed her seat at the writing desk, only half facing him in an attitude that she hoped would convey the message that what he'd interrupted was far more important than he.

"I'm sorry for your mishap, my lady," he said, strolling toward the lounge. "May I sit? I shan't stay but a moment. I see that you're . . . occupied." Without waiting for an invitation, he sat with flourish, draping his arm in a casual attitude across the back of the lounge.

"Yes, I am," said Sara. "I don't mean to be rude, Mr. Mallory, but it is late, and I must finish these before I retire."

"Shouldn't you be abed?" he queried. "You took a nasty fall, so Nicholas tells me."

"I have been abed, Mr. Mallory," she snapped. "And I have the doctor's permission to resume my activities. Now I really must insist—"

"I do wish you'd relent and call me Alex," he interrupted. "We are all one happy family here."

"Yes, well, I somehow rather doubt that, Mr. Mallory. Now if you will excuse me, I do have to finish this."

"Nicholas gave me permission to come up," he drawled, "if that's what you're worrying about. He shan't come bursting through that door like the jealous husband, pistol in hand."

Oh, he gave permission, did he? That struck a chord. Did Nicholas think so little of her that he'd given the steward leave to put her in such a position? If he did, he had about as much respect for her as Mallory. Hot blood rushed to her temples. The man was a master of mixed signals.

"He has no reason to," she snapped, surging to her feet. Her frock brushed the desk and one of the menus she had been working on floated to the floor. Mallory sprang off the lounge and dove to retrieve it as she bent to the task also. Their faces were very close, both their hands vying for the parchment on the carpet. Neither would give quarter. He smelled sour, of strong liquor laced with sweet wine. The result was sickening. Was the man in his altitudes? If he wasn't, he was well on the way.

"Allow me," said the steward.

"I have it, Mr. Mallory. Please! You have outstayed your welcome. I do not know how much plainer I can possibly make it."

"'Methinks the lady doeth protest too much,'" Mallory quoted.

The delivery was an unmistakable attempt at seduction, and Sara snatched the parchment in contention from his grip, tearing it in the process, and surged to her full height in such haste that vertigo threatened her balance. Though Mrs. Bromley's herbal compresses had reduced the swelling on her brow, the bruise remained, as did the effects of the concussion. The last thing she needed was to swoon into this man's arms, and she steeled herself against it.

"You, sir, are quite foxed," she said. "You reek of liquor. While that hardly excuses your conduct, I shall make allowances—so long as you leave my suite at once!"

"You are a very desirable woman, Sara," Mallory crooned, straightening up. He tugged his waistcoat back into shape and squared his posture, looking for all the world like a strutting rooster, Sara thought. "He won't do you justice," he went on. "He's a cold fish, is Nicholas. But then, I imagine you've gathered that by now. I, on the other hand, would be worth your while." Sara floated to the door and flung it wide. Mallory raised his hands, strolling toward it. "All right, I'm going, my dear," he said. "Just remember, when you're ready for a real man, you know where to find him."

Sara slammed the door behind him and leaned against it. Should she tell Nicholas, as he'd told her to? Why, when he'd left her open to such a confrontation? Was this some sort of test? If it was, she wouldn't give him the satisfaction. He hardly deserved blind obedience. Tears stung her eyes. She refused to let them fall. What did she expect? What *could* she expect after marrying a man she'd never even seen, by proxy, then accompanying a total stranger to the hind side of nowhere to fulfill her marital obligation? How much respect would that generate—even though Nicholas was the one who'd engineered it? He'd made the proposition; all she'd done was accept it and he knew why. It was obvious what Alexander Mallory thought of the whole business. He had no way of knowing that there had been no consummation. He thought her a tart, a ladybird, no better than a whore. He never would have behaved in such a manner otherwise— drunk or sober. The man at least had the veneer of a gentleman, albeit thin and brittle, no doubt veined with the cracks of previous conquests. Well, she would not become one of them.

She examined the torn menu in her hand. The rest of it lay crumpled on the carpet where he'd left it after his seduction failed. She snatched it up and smoothed the halves out on top of the desk. She would have to copy it over, but not tonight; Nell had already reclaimed her dinner tray.

She was just about to ring for the abigail to come and prepare her for bed, when the girl appeared and helped her into her nightdress. Sara was exhausted, and she dismissed Nell, who was only too happy to slip away in search of her hall boy. It was just as well. Sara was in no humor for aimless gibble-gabble.

She produced the portion of mutton she'd saved from her dinner tray, wrapped loosely in her serviette, and set it on the rug at the foot of her bed, where she'd left it the last time in hopes of a visit from Nero, who hadn't appeared since the night of her fall. Had Nicholas gotten rid of the animal in spite of her pleadings? She couldn't bear to consider the possibility. Padding to the foyer door, she left it ajar just as she had done from the first, in case her fears were unfounded and Nero did pay a visit. Then, snuffing out the candles on the branch beside her bed, she climbed in between the sheets trying to make some sense of the situation, but her thoughts would not order themselves. They always returned to the same questions: Why had Nicholas married her if all he wanted was a hostess? What was the real reason he didn't want an heir? He was capable of heart-stopping passion. It was in him when he'd carried her out of that priest hole, when he'd held her in his arms and soothed her with such tenderness she ached for it to go on forever; how could he treat her with such total indifference after that—leave her prey to such a one as Alexander Mallory? Nicholas was drawing her in, despite her valiant resolve to put from her the feelings she could no longer deny. She'd tried to transfer some of those feelings to Nero. Now he was gone, too, and she began to doze, imagining herself wrapped in Nicholas's strong arms again, imagining the feral, salt-sea aroma drifting from his skin—or was that Nero's scent? They were similar, and why wouldn't they be, all tangled into her dream state? She loved them both, didn't she?

The arms she'd conjured held her tighter, but the scent drifting toward her nostrils was not clean, like Nicholas, like rain-washed air drifting over the sea; it was sour—fetid with brandy and vomit. Her eyes snapped open. This was no dream, it was Mallory clutching her—groping through her peach silk gown.

"I knew it was all an act, for that abigail of yours next door, no doubt. I *knew* it," he whispered close in her ear, his words slurred and halting. "She isn't in there now, is she? Nooo, and you left the door ajar for me, just as I knew you would—didn't you, 'my lady'? You won't be sorry. . . ."

Sara screamed, but the hand clamped over her mouth cut it short, while his other hand fumbled with her gown. The scream in her throat reduced now to a desperate squeal, she kicked at him, meanwhile clawing at the hand holding in her cries. When that failed, she bit down hard, and he let her go with a yowl in concert with another blood-chilling sound, a guttural snarl that froze Sara where she crouched.

It happened in a blink. Nero's silver-tipped black body sailed through the air, and his sharp teeth sank into Mallory's forearm, driving the steward off the bed to the floor with a thud that echoed. Blood spattered the counterpane. Nero was going to *kill* him! Why didn't Nell come? Was she still trysting with her hall boy?

Sara tried to scream, but fear closed her throat over the sound—fear that Nicholas would surely banish Nero now.

She couldn't let it happen. She couldn't scream and bring the servants or Nicholas himself and risk it. This was twice now that Nero had saved her.

She peered over the side of the bed. Mallory was holding his own, fending Nero off with the fallen candle branch wedged between the animal's bared teeth and his throat, but he was weakening. Sheer terror found her voice.

"Nero, *no!*" she cried. "Let him go. My God, *let him go!*"

As if released from a trance, the animal hesitated, looking her in the eyes as though he understood—just long enough for Mallory to scrabble to his feet and stagger toward the door, clutching his bleeding forearm, the blood spotting the carpet as he went.

"I'm going to kill that mangy cur!" he gritted. "You mark my words, he won't live out the night!"

Nero faced him, feet apart, hackles raised, his dilated eyes glowing red in the firelight. Baring lethal fangs, he made a short lunge toward the steward, then another, digging his nails into the carpet with each advance, blood-flecked foam dripping from his jowls. A warning snarl leaked from his curled-back lips, and then a hoarse, rattling bark, with his head held high, before he lowered it and lunged again, another snarl driving the steward through the open foyer door.

"You mark my words," Mallory shrilled. "That animal is *dead!*"

Sara knelt paralyzed in the middle of the mahogany four-poster, her hands clasped over her mouth, watching Nero turn and lift his leg, marking his territory again and again in a semicircular arch around the bed. When he'd finished, he shook himself, raised his shaggy head, and howled his plaintive howl. It ran her through like a javelin.

She opened her arms, and he leaped up on the bed and came into them, nuzzling her hair with his cold wet nose, licking the tears from her face, wagging his bushy tail as she stroked him. There was a strong metallic odor of blood about him. They were both covered with it, *Mallory's blood.* It had spattered her nightdress, and Nero's fur was streaked with it.

"I shall have to hide you here," she said. "If he doesn't kill you, Nicholas will surely banish you now. Are you hungry, boy? See there, I've saved you a treat." She pointed out the serviette on the carpet, and Nero jumped down and padded toward it, nudging the linen cloth open with his nose, while she climbed out of the bed and began righting the candle-stand. Nero had just begun to devour the mutton, when Mallory reeled back across the threshold, a pistol in his white-knuckled grip.

"Stand back!" he thundered, taking aim.

"Noooo!" Sara screamed, hurling the candle branch in her hand at him. It missed, and Nero sprang, sailing through the air. A thunderous shot rang out, flames spurted from the pistol barrel, and the air filled with the acrid scent of gunpowder. The animal yelped, and fell hard to the floor with the impact, blood running down his leg. It was only a hitch in his stride, before he scrambled to his feet again, whining in pain. He cast a glance over his shoulder at Sara, who was clutching the bedpost behind. The gleam of metal in the firelight caught her eye, and she gasped. The steward had another pistol! She saw it before Nero did.

"Run, Nero, *run!*" she shrilled, and the animal streaked through the door with Mallory staggering after him, grinding out a string of expletives. All at once another shot rang out. Another howl echoed along the corridor, then died away.

"No, Nero, *nooooo!*" she sobbed. Then there was silence.

Ten

Sara was certain she would find Nero lying dead on the hall carpet. She ran to the door and looked out into the corridor, but it was vacant; there was no sign of Mallory or the animal. Sobbing, she stepped back inside and locked the door behind her. Her heart ached for Nero. She wanted to help him, to protect him. He had drawn the steward's fire deliberately to lure him out of her suite; she was certain of it, and she flung herself across the bed and sobbed her heart dry.

It was a short indulgence. All at once frantic pounding at the door bled into her sobs. Voices were calling her name, and she climbed down from the four-poster, shrugged on her wrapper, and went to answer. When she opened the door, Nell and Mrs. Bromley burst through it, screaming at the top of their voices. Others were grouped on the threshold, and still more came, flooding the hall—in the forefront, Smythe, the butler. Several of the footmen bore lit candle branches, and there were others she had never met. Nicholas was not among them.

Glancing down, Sara realized what had so overset Nell

and the housekeeper. The gown beneath her gaping wrapper was streaked with blood, as were her face and hands. The uproar was deafening. It echoed inside her head, making her dizzy, and she held on to it in a vain attempt to forestall the vertigo.

All at once, another servant, whom she'd seen about but not met, parted the sea of gaping servants and approached her. He had a kindly face, though his eyes, like molten silver, studied her long and hard from beneath beetled brows.

"Are you harmed, my lady?" he asked. His voice sounded as though it was coming from an echo chamber. "Are you in need of the doctor?"

"N-no, not harmed," she stammered. "You are . . . ?"

"Mills, my lady," he said, "his lordship's valet. You're certain you've no need of the doctor?" His eyes lingered on her bloodstained gown.

"I . . . I'm certain," Sara replied. "The blood . . . isn't mine. It was Mr. Mallory . . . he . . . he . . ." She couldn't bring herself to say it.

"I know, my lady," said the valet. "Do you know where Mr. Mallory is now?"

"N-no," she sobbed. "Nero? Is he . . . dead? Mr. Mallory was in his altitudes. He was trying to kill Nero!"

"That deuced animal again!" the butler barked. "I might have guessed. All right, everyone back to your stations. Resume your duties. Her ladyship is unharmed."

A chorus of mumbles was the reply as the crowd thinned in obedience to Smythe's command and the servants went about their business—all but Nell, Mrs. Bromley, and Mills, who hung back.

"Where is his lordship?" Sara asked the valet.

"His lordship has been called away on urgent business, my lady," he replied. "That is why I have come . . . in his stead. Once Nell and Mrs. Bromley have put you to rights, I must insist that you lock your door and remain in your suite tonight. Mr. Mallory is still abroad in this house. Strong drink tends to make him . . . unpredictable, and his lordship would never forgive me if you were to come to harm on my watch."

"But Nero!"

"Nero can take care of himself, my lady," said the valet.

"But Mr. Mallory *shot* him, Mills. In the shoulder, I think . . . or the leg. Oh, I'm not sure! It all happened so fast. He was bleeding so. We have to find him—care for him!"

"Do not distress yourself, my lady," the valet soothed. "I shall see to Nero. I shall attend to it at once." He turned to the housekeeper. "Perhaps a cordial, Mrs. Bromley," he said, "something from your herbal stores, to help my lady rest. Once you've done, make sure you see to that door."

"But what if Nero returns?" Sara cried. "If the door is locked, he won't be able to get in. He's *injured*, Mills."

"The animal will not be returning tonight, my lady," the valet said. "He will be found and cared for, but I shall see that Smythe posts a hall boy right outside your door . . . just in case, to ease your mind."

He shuffled off, and Nell and Mrs. Bromley took Sara in hand, closing the door behind him.

Nicholas lay swathed in a bloody sheet, bare to the waist on the lounge in his dressing room, while the doctor worked with quick, skilled hands to remove the bullet from his shoulder. His pain-crazed eyes were trained on the door, and when Mills hurried through, he gave a lurch that caused the doctor's hand to slip.

"Have a care, my lord!" Breeden cried. "You've lost too much blood as it is."

Nicholas paid him no mind. "Is she harmed, Mills?" he said through clenched teeth, as the doctor resumed his probing. "Tell me she wasn't harmed! Tell me Alex didn't . . ."

"You know she wasn't harmed, my lord," said Mills, out of breath. "Nero prevented him. Have you forgotten?"

"No, I haven't 'forgotten,'" Nicholas snapped. "How

could I forget, Mills, considering? Where is the bounder now?"

"Mr. Mallory is still at large, my lord," Mills replied.

"He hasn't left the estate?"

"I would think not, my lord," said the valet. "He was drunk as a wheelbarrow, firing off pistols in the house, of all things." He hesitated. "I might point out that he was aiming at Nero, my lord . . . not at Baron Walraven."

"Well, Nero would have chomped off his cods if her ladyship hadn't begged for the man's life. Now the chore is left to me, isn't it, Mills? Alex is going to rue the hour—the very minute—he tossed back the spirits that foxed him tonight."

"It's no use if you don't lie still, my lord," the doctor complained, putting pressure on the bleeding wound with a folded linen towel. He glanced at the valet over his shoulder. "I don't suppose there's any chloroform about? I've laudanum for after, but it must be saved for that. Meanwhile, I have to put him under. The pistol ball is wedged against the bone, and I must pass close to the artery to remove it. If he should move again like he did just now . . ."

"We've no chloroform, Dr. Breeden, but Mrs. Bromley's herbal cures are legendary. The local surgeons hereabouts swear by them, and she's treated our ills with her ointments, cordials, and concoctions successfully for years. Why, just last month, a tea she brewed of dried passionflower blossoms put the head hall boy under so the groom could extract his abcessed tooth. We seldom need to summon a surgeon to Ravencliff."

"Fetch it then," said the doctor. "This is serious here."

"You cannot involve the servants!" Nicholas groaned. "No one must know—*no one!*"

"No one will, my lord," said Mills, halfway through the door. "I shall say the tincture is for Nero. It stands to reason that a dog would need to be dosed before it could be doctored—"

"Not a dog, Mills, a *wolf* masquerading as a dog."
Nicholas flashed. "You know the dose for a dog would not
nearly be potent enough to subdue Nero."

"Please leave it to me, my lord. Have I ever let you down?"
the valet said. "You know not. Now, see if you can lie still
and mind the doctor, while I attend to what needs must."

Nicholas relaxed as much as was possible under the doctor's probing knife, grinding his teeth closed against the
pain. He dared not cry out; someone might hear. In these circumstances, he had no idea when the transformation might
occur again, and no one had ever seen it but Mills. Such a situation as what was upon him now had never been put to the
test. What if the change were to happen during the opera-
tion? He hadn't broached the subject with Dr. Breeden yet.
How would the man react? What would he think? He dared
not imagine it.

This was not how it was supposed to be. The plan had
been to take the doctor out on the cliff, out of earshot of the
curious, and consult him over the situation. That could not
be now. There were too many dangers to do it in the house,
too great a risk of being overheard. Hadn't Sara nearly
knocked in the head two footmen listening at the door when
she'd exited the dining hall yesterday?

No one, least of all Sara, was going to believe the explanation he and Mills had decided upon to excuse his absence
from the house until he was recovered enough to be seen
again. The staff knew he never left Ravencliff. Alexander
Mallory knew he never left it, as well. That was the reason
for the steward's employment. What possible emergency
could it have been to drag the master away with a houseguest just come, when he couldn't even leave to wed his
bride? It was a flimsy excuse at best, but what other choice
was there? He couldn't risk being seen as he was.

What must this esteemed scholar—this renowned doctor—
think, imposed upon in such a way on his first night in resi-

Dawn Thompson

dence? First Sara, and now this! He wouldn't blame the man for fleeing back to London on the first chaise leaving the coast.

"I know the pain is devastating, my lord," Dr. Breeden said, interrupting his thoughts. "It shan't be long now. Once we have the draught, I'll have the pistol ball out in a trice."

"Pain . . . is the least . . . of my worries," Nicholas panted, writhing under the pressure of the doctor's firm hand holding back the blood flow with fresh linen towels.

"Then you have no worries, my lord," said the doctor, his quicksilver eyes like drills. "Your secret is quite safe with me. It is, after all, the reason I am come, is it not?"

Nicholas nodded. "I . . . I cannot control it," he said. "If it should happen here now . . ."

"If it should, we will deal with it," said the doctor. "Look into my eyes, and listen to my voice. Listen to the meter. Concentrate upon the words as I speak them. Repeat them in your mind, like an echo. Think of nothing else, nothing but my voice. You need to calm yourself, my lord, as I am calm. You are losing too much blood. Take deep breaths if you can. That's it—deeper . . . good. Now look to the candle flame. Don't take your eyes from it. See how it dances in the drafts? Look into its very core. I must ask you before he returns, is Mills aware?"

"Yes," said Nicholas, "but no one else, and no one else must be. If you are going to render me unconscious, that must be understood. Mills has cared for me from the onset of this nightmare when I was but a child. If I am not able, you must trust his judgments in all things."

"I understand. Do you trust me, my lord?"

Nicholas ground out a laugh. "Have I a choice?"

"We all have choices, my lord."

"All but me in this," Nicholas responded.

"We shall see," said the doctor. "We shall see."

It seemed an eternity to Nicholas before Mills returned with the passionflower tea. It was strong, but not quite strong enough to put him under altogether, as he knew it would not. He wouldn't let it. Trust was a luxury he could ill afford. Instead, he lurked on the edge of pain, dulled somewhat, but not alleviated in total. He grimaced and groaned and gritted his teeth, while the doctor dug out the lead ball, but Nicholas made no outcry, and when the doctor cauterized the wound, he lapsed into unconsciousness.

The sun was streaming through the mullioned panes in his dressing room window, laying down blinding shafts of light where dust motes danced, when he groaned awake again. He narrowed his eyes against the glare, and Mills hurried to draw the draperies. Across the way the blurry image of Dr. Breeden asleep in the wing chair came into focus—had he spent the night in the backbreaking antique? He must have done.

Nicholas groaned again. His shoulder was bound and dressed with a linen bandage slathered with an ointment. Groundsel and chickweed, by the smell of it, one of Mrs. Bromley's favorite remedies to ward off infection. He knew it well. His arm was contained in a sling, and he groaned again, shifting position.

"It's done, my lord," said Mills, moistening his parched lips. "You shall be up and about in next to no time, so long as you mind the doctor."

"Did it . . . happen again?" Nicholas murmured.

"No, my lord," said Mills, misty-eyed. "Nothing . . . untoward occurred."

Nicholas breathed a ragged sigh of relief.

"As soon as the doctor permits, we must have you to your bed, my lord," Mills said. "You cannot stay here on this hard old lounge. You will never mend."

"I cannot speak with Dr. Breeden down on the strand now, Mills. It has to be done at once, and it has to be done here out of the range of hearing of the inmates in this asylum. There is less likelihood of being overheard way back in this dressing room, than in the master bedchamber."

"I shall keep watch if needs must, my lord," said Mills. "You have got to let others do for you now. You must recover quickly. Duping the staff is one thing; my lady is quite another—she is already asking questions. Nero hasn't returned, and she is beside herself. How long do you think she will accept that you've gone traipsing off on business, with a guest in the house? And we can't keep her confined to her suite indefinitely. You know firsthand the folly of attempting that."

"Where is Alex?"

"No one has seen him since the . . . incident, my lord."

"He has been bitten, Mills. Nero took a healthy chunk out of the bounder's arm. Do you know what that means?"

"No, my lord, I do not, and neither do you. That is why Dr. Breeden has come."

"That aside, Alex is in need of medical attention. There is no doubt of it."

"Mr. Mallory is an enterprising chap, my lord. Once he sobers up—"

"Once he sobers up and realizes what he's done, God only knows what he'll do. She's going to leave that deuced door ajar in anticipation of a visit from Nero, and we'll have it all over again!"

"Whose fault is that, my lord?"

"Mine, I'll own, but admitting it by no means negates the danger. We've no time here now for fondling regrets. I must get back on my feet."

"Then rest there, and mind," said the doctor, turning both their heads. He stretched, and got up stiffly, limping to the lounge. Laying his hand on Nicholas's brow, he frowned. "You've a fever. Bilberry or black currant juice should do the trick. Could you consult your housekeeper, Mills? 'Tisn't serious—unless, of course, it goes untreated."

"I shall go at once," said Mills.

"Bilberry or black currant juice for a *dog?*" Nicholas put in. "They will never credit that."

The doctor nodded. "Why not?" he said. "Injured dogs suffer from fevers, too. And bring some clear broth, while you're at it, Mills. You shall have to pilfer what food you can scrounge from the kitchen once his lordship is recovered enough to take it, but for now the broth will do."

"Yes, Dr. Breeden."

"See if anyone has news of Alex," said Nicholas. "Check with Watts in the stables. See if he might have taken a coach, or one of the horses. I shan't rest until I know where the bastard is."

"Oh, you'll rest, my lord," said the doctor, offering a brimming spoon. "Open!"

"What is that?" Nicholas demanded.

"Laudanum," Breeden pronounced. "I cannot help a cadaver, and I'd hate to have come all this way for naught. Open, and swallow."

Eleven

"It first occurred when I was twelve," Nicholas said, giving account to Dr. Breeden. He was propped up with pillows in his bed, while the doctor sat in the Chippendale chair alongside, close enough so that they could converse low-voiced. Even though Mills kept watch outside the master bedchamber, they decided to guard their speech, and continue to endow the manifestation with the name of *Nero*, in case they were overheard. "I believe it was the emotional impact of Mother's death that set off the transformations. Before that, I hadn't a care in the world in my prepubescent bliss."

"You say your father was bitten by a wolf."

"In India, yes."

"Did he suffer from similar manifestations?"

"I don't know, Dr. Breeden. I was in my cradle when he passed. That's why I'm concerned about Mr. Mallory. I have no idea how that bite is going to affect him. Will he be as I am . . . or something worse, like the wolf that bit my father?"

"Has Nero ever bitten anyone before?"

"No, and that's another thing that worries me. Is the manifestation evolving into something . . . more?"

"It was my papers on lycanthropy that prompted your invitation, was it not?"

"Yes. I read them with much interest, just as I have devoured every bit of material ever penned on the subject."

"You are not a lycanthrope, my lord. That is not to say that the wolf that bit your father wasn't a werewolf, however. I wish we knew more about that."

"But . . . Nero attacked Alex. He meant to kill him, Dr. Breeden. Believe me, I *know*."

"Nero was protecting his mate, my lord. If lycanthropy were involved, he would have torn *her* throat out as well. There have been many documented accounts of werewolves worldwide. Some in which the victims only imagine themselves transformed—that is to say, the transformation only takes place in their mind—and others where an actual physical transformation occurs. There are more cases of the former, of course, but either way one common thread binds all cases ever recorded: rampant, indiscriminate violence and blood lust. Nero is not a killer. If he were, he would have turned on the baroness the minute your steward left and deprived him of his kill, not gone to her for stroking and reward. From all accounts, never once was she fearful of her life in Nero's presence. That, my lord, is not in any way characteristic of a lycanthrope."

Nicholas thought on it. "What *is* it then?"

"We will get to the bottom of this, my lord," said the doctor, "but first, I need to know what triggers these manifestations. Are they connected perchance to the phases of the moon?"

"No, they have occurred in moon dark as well as when the moon is full, and all the phases between—even in broad daylight. They come upon me when I am angry, emotional . . . and aroused. The hellish thing is that I cannot control them. They control me."

"Has the transformation ever occurred during sexual congress? Forgive me, but I do need to ask some rather personal questions, my lord."

"No, not thus far," said Nicholas, "but there has been precious little sexual congress of late—not since the incidents have become more frequent. I've lived a rather celibate life these past few years."

"Then, why on earth did you marry, my lord? I'm given to understand that your nuptials are quite recent."

Nicholas heaved a ragged sigh that brought his posture down and sent ripples of pain through his shoulder. It had only been two days since the bullet was removed. He would not let the doctor know about the pain and risk being dosed with the opiate again. The subject at hand had to be broached now, before he got out of that bed again, no matter the cost.

"I am hounded by the *ton* to enter the marriage mart," he began. "Scads of invitations arrive on a daily basis, which I must decline. No wife, no mistress—people were beginning to talk. I've had to have my servants turn away at the door, some well-meaning callers determined to draw me into the social whirl. I cannot leave Ravencliff, for fear of this madness coming upon me at some inopportune moment in some ballroom, opera house, or open market. I've been abroad, Dr. Breeden, trying to live a normal life, and I was very nearly found out in just such a situation. That's why I've become somewhat of a hermit here. I needed to marry to put paid to the hounding that I become an active part of society, and I couldn't even do that other than by proxy."

"But to send your steward, my lord?" said the doctor. "What sort of woman—"

"No, no, Sara is quite well to pass," Nicholas interrupted. "She's the daughter of a knight, Sir Jacob Ponsonby, a Colonel in the army, before he died and left her scorched. There was no male heir, and none to designate. The Crown took back the land, and her personal assets were not great enough to keep her out of the Fleet. Colonel Ponsonby served with my father in India at the beginning of the occupation, as I told you. What I didn't tell you, or her, is that he was with my father when the wolf bit him, and it was he who killed the animal and saved my father's life. They were close friends—military chums. Father mentions him repeatedly in his journals, including the incident of the wolf. You are welcome to peruse them if you wish, though I have done again and again and found no clue to this nightmare that plagues me now.

"When I heard of Sara's misfortune, I offered for her at once. She was hardly in a position to refuse. I took advantage of that, hoping that putting her in my debt might be enough to keep her here once I made my intentions plain and she realized the benefits of the arrangement. The Fleet is an odious place. It would have pleased my father that I do such a thing for the daughter of his friend, but my motives were more selfish than philanthropic, Dr. Breeden. I am . . . so lonely."

"What were the terms of the arrangement, my lord, if I may be so bold as to inquire?" the doctor queried.

"It was an honorable proposal. I explained that I wanted to marry for the reasons I've already told you—that I required a hostess to preside over gatherings at Ravencliff, such as your visit here now, and that since I did not want an heir, sharing my bed was not part of the arrangement. Furthermore, she would be treated like a queen, want for nothing, and gain title and lands. I own properties abroad that are not attached to the estate. It was a very attractive offer, Dr. Breeden. I am a man of means, and a generous one."

"Forgive me, but you hardly needed to marry. Except for the title as part of the package, you could have taken a mistress, my lord. London is swarming with all sorts of prospects these

111

days—gentlemen's daughters, society mavens, respectable widows—all quite well to pass, who would jump at the chance to broker such an arrangement."

"No," Nicholas returned. "A mistress would have expected bed sport, and I couldn't risk it. Besides, the way mistresses are flaunted in Town these days, taking one wouldn't have exempted me from the marriage mart. It would have made me even more desirable.

"I foolishly imagined that sharing my bed might be a concern. I was counting upon Sara's relief that she hadn't been brought out here to be ravished by a total stranger to get me past that hurdle. I was hoping that once we'd gotten beyond that awkward bit, we might settle into some sort of amiable platonic relationship beneficial to us both. It isn't quite working out that way."

"You expected her to live a life of celibacy as well, my lord?" said the doctor, clearly nonplussed.

"Of course not," Nicholas replied. "I told her I would not object to her taking a lover, as long as she was discreet and it wasn't Alex Mallory. He resides here much of the time, and that would have been awkward. I was soundly upbraided for making such a suggestion."

"I shouldn't wonder."

"What else was I to do? I thought I was offering her a practical solution to a problem I hadn't anticipated. Added to it, she couldn't imagine why I wouldn't want an heir. She even questioned my sexual preference. You can certainly see why I cannot have children. I cannot risk passing this . . . whatever it is on to another generation. The madness must end with me. I couldn't tell her that, of course. I did say that there was a defect in the blood that I did not wish to pass on. It was half-truth, and I doubt she believed it. God knows what she believes."

"Yet she has remained," the doctor mused.

"Unfortunately, there is a mutual attraction," said Nicholas.

"Why is that unfortunate?"

"Surely you can see the impossibility of such as that? I am aware of her attraction to me, and I've done everything in my power to keep her from realizing that it's mutual—even to the point of boorish behavior that disgusts me."

"You are falling in love with her."

"That is something else I didn't anticipate."

"Love conquers many things, my lord."

"Not this."

"Do not sell love short, Baron Walraven."

"There is . . . something else," Nicholas said. He couldn't meet the doctor's eyes. The man saw more with that silver gaze than any man had a right to see. "She has become . . . attached to Nero," he murmured.

There was a long silence. It tasted of death. Not even the sun shone on that moment. Clouds scudding before the risen wind had obliterated it, and though it was midday, the room was clad in bleak semidarkness.

"How did that happen?" said the doctor at last.

"I am at fault," Nicholas confessed. "It was the only way I could be near her . . . close to her . . . bear her touch . . . touch her myself. It is torture. I live with her scent. It is with me always. It is *in* me. *She* is in me. Nero gives me what little I will ever have of her—the innocent, unconditional love of a mistress for her pet."

"This must cease."

"I have tried."

"A man was nearly killed, my lord. We do not yet know how badly he was mauled till we find him, and that is the least of the danger in such an association. The hopelessness alone! How do you bear it? The baroness believes that Nero is dead. I implore you, let him stay so."

"He very nearly was, wasn't he, Dr. Breeden?" Nicholas murmured.

"Do you always remember what has occurred during the transformations once they are over, my lord?"

113

"For the most part, yes—in bits and pieces according to their importance, the way you remember parts of a dream."

"What does happen usually?"

"Nothing memorable," said Nicholas. "Nero runs off whatever emotion it was that summoned him. He and I both have an affinity for the sea, and he haunts it—runs the strand in a way that I long to do, but never could in my two-legged incarnation, through the surf, over the rocks. He bathes in the tide pools, and races the wind, free, as I can never be free as long as we are joined.

"Sometimes, he prowls the house, observing the servants, and Alex. You would be amazed at what those occasions yield. He roams at will, virtually ignored, privy to all sorts of shocking tidbits. Through Nero's eyes, I know who's diddling whom, and who would like to be. Who can be trusted, and who cannot. What the servants really think, and how they gain and cull and hone the bits of information they gather for their deuced *on-dits*. Every estate in the kingdom should have a Nero wandering about, Dr. Breeden. There'd be far less skullduggery afoot, I guarantee you."

"How long has Nero lived in this house, my lord?"

"Nero has had many incarnations over the years . . . and many names, but he is still the same creature, my alter ego. We are one. What am I, Dr. Breeden . . . man, or animal?"

"I shall have to see this manifestation with my own eyes in order to make a positive assessment of your . . . malady, my lord," said the doctor, "but from what you tell me, it appears that something of the wolf has been transferred to you from your father through the blood upon conception. You yourself were not bitten, so the taint is diluted in you. The mold has been broken, as it were, and you are, in my estimation, what is known as a nonviolent *shapeshifter*. Werewolves are technically shapeshifters as well—anyone who changes form would fall in that category—but not all shapeshifters are werewolves. The term covers a broad spectrum of entities, the werewolf being the darkest, most violent creature, as different from you in your affliction as night from day."

"Can you help me, Dr. Breeden?"

"It is too early to tell, my lord," said the physician. "There is no cure, if that is what you're asking, but there are other ways of . . . dealing with the problem. You will have to be patient, and you will have to trust me."

"Just tell me there is hope."

"There is always hope, my lord, but for now you must rest and mend. You haven't fooled me, you know. You're in pain. I shall dose you with laudanum, repair to my suite, and read those journals you spoke of, if you will allow. Will you give me leave to tell the baroness that Nero is dead?"

"No, Dr. Breeden," Nicholas murmured, looking him in the eyes. "That, I cannot do."

The doctor processed his reply without speaking. This time Nicholas met his mercurial stare, meaning to punctuate and underscore his words that there be no mistaking his resolve. It was the doctor who broke eye contact.

"Very well, my lord," he said. "Though I implore you, think on it . . . objectively. We shall take the matter up again, when you've had time to consider the consequences."

The doctor dosed him and left him then, his bushy brows knit in a contemplative frown. Mills stepped in as he quit the chamber, and Nicholas beckoned his valet closer. The laudanum was beginning to work, and he needed to have his say before it rendered him inert.

"What is it, my lord?" said Mills.

"Is there any sign of Alex?" he asked.

"No, my lord, he seems to have disappeared without a trace."

"That is impossible. Did you go round to the stables and inquire of Watts, as I told you to?"

"I did, my lord. All the horses and carriages are accounted for, and Watts wasn't even aware that Mr. Mallory had returned, much less disappeared. He arrived by post chaise."

"This is impossible. He has to be somewhere. He cannot just have vanished into thin air." He shook his head in a vain attempt to forestall the effects of the opiate. "Breeden's given me a proper dose, by God," he grumbled. "I'll be out before I have this said."

"You need to rest, my lord. Everything is being done that can be done. You need to mend, so you can take command again."

"You've searched the house?"

"We have, my lord, a thorough search from top to bottom."

"Search it again! He knows where most of the hidden chambers are. He's hiding in one of them—he has to be. He must have left a trail of blood. He was badly bitten. Did you follow it? I should think that would have been your first course of action, Mills."

"Begging your pardon, my lord, but Nero left a trail of blood as well. One trail ended here, the other at the landing. He must have bound the wound somehow."

"Look again. He may have bled somewhere else. Mills, he has to be found. We do not know how Nero's bite will affect him. He may be as I am, or he may be something far worse. There is no way of telling. Do you understand what I'm saying to you?"

"Merciful God, my lord!" the valet breathed. "Suppose—"

"Is her ladyship guarded?" Nicholas interrupted.

"The hall boys, Peters, Clarke, and Gibbons are taking turns outside her door, my lord, whether she is in her suite or not. She is watched day and night. They have orders to alert us at once if Mr. Mallory should approach the tapestry suite. What should we do with him if he does surface, my lord? You cannot see him as you are."

"Get those . . . damned pistols, for one thing," said Nicholas, his speech thick and slurred as the laudanum took him deeper. "Then turn him out—*no*, you cannot . . . I am not

116

thinking clearly. He must remain until we *know*. You will have to . . . confine him somewhere until . . . until I can confront him. Just *do* it, Mills . . . however you must. Everything depends upon it."

Twelve

Something was wrong, very wrong. It had been three days, and still Nicholas hadn't returned—neither had Alexander Mallory or Nero. Sara was beside herself. None of the servants would tell her anything. She was kept confined in her suite at Mills's instruction, acting in Nicholas's stead. The reason given her was that Alexander Mallory was doubtless deranged and dangerous, and until he was apprehended and disarmed, she was safer in her suite.

She should be in the dining hall extending hospitality to their guest in Nicholas's absence. She wanted to prove herself to this strange husband, who evidently thought of her with no more regard than he did a piece of his furniture. What had taken him away from Ravencliff? What "urgent business" was it that was more important than taking a coach to London to marry his bride? She couldn't imagine it. How could she have been so wrong about what she'd felt in that one delicious unguarded moment in his strong arms?

Dr. Breeden had been to see her several times during her confinement. He'd been pleasant and reassuring on those occasions, and he'd told her that he was quite content to sup alone and repair to his rooms early to peruse some of the tomes from Nicholas's impressive library. She mustn't reproach herself. All would be well. Nicholas would soon return. Hopefully Mr. Mallory would be found by then, and things would go back to normal—whatever that was. Sara hadn't had one normal experience since she'd entered Ravencliff Manor.

It was Nero's absence, however, that troubled her most of all. No one had seen him since the shooting. He'd been seriously wounded, and he hadn't returned to her suite. Fear that he had crawled off somewhere to die gave her no peace. Dr. Breeden hadn't been very encouraging. Though he said that dogs often crawled off to lick their wounds when injured and sometimes survived, he also said the longer his absence the less likely that would be. It didn't bode well, and by the end of the fourth day of her confinement, Sara had memorized every tapestry in her suite, as if she willed Nero to materialize from among the hunting hounds that lined her walls. She had to do something. She had to get out of those rooms before she went mad.

It was late. Nell had long since retired. Outside a wicked wind had kicked up, and the sound of angry breakers beating on the rockbound strand and rolling up the cliff was music to her ears. The racket would cover any noise she might make exiting her suite. There would be a hall boy posted outside. She was counting on the hour to find him nodding, or if it were Peters on watch, that he would have stolen away for one of his customary nocturnal assignations with Nell. The latter was evidently the case. When she eased her door open, the bench the sentries occupied in their turn was vacant. *Bless the boy!* She stepped into the corridor, and pulled the door to, leaving it slightly ajar for Nero. Just in case.

She had no plan. Just getting out of that suite had emboldened her to the point of recklessness, and why not? She was

Baroness Walraven, wasn't she? Who was to stop her? Certainly not her enigmatic, absent, unfeeling husband. Puffed up with that, she strolled over the second-floor hallway, gaining confidence in her liberation with each forbidden step.

She was still dressed. She had cried off when Nell came to prepare her for bed. The seed of this escape had been germinating for days, waiting for the perfect moment to sprout. She should have put her pelerine on over the thin white muslin frock, however. The halls were drafty, the dampness penetrating. Would it be this way all summer as well? She shuddered to wonder.

Having reached the grand staircase, she hesitated on the landing, glancing upward toward the restricted third floor. It suddenly struck her that now, during Nicholas's absence, would be the perfect time to have a look inside the master suite in hopes of unearthing some clue, some nugget of understanding of the man she'd married. Curiosity egged her on, and moved her up the third flight of the carpeted staircase on feet that made no sound.

That she had no idea which suite was Nicholas's didn't matter. She would find it, if she had to throw every door open until she did. Other than that it was a turret room in the north wing, which would put it on the west side of the corridor facing the sea, she had no idea where to begin. Never having been out on the cliff to view Ravencliff from the sea side, she could only speculate as to where the turret suites were located. Since the bifurcated staircase divided the house into north and south wings, she turned right, and began her search.

She'd just poked her head into the second chamber on the left side of the corridor, another suite where the furnishings were draped with Holland covers, when a door halfway down the hall came open, throwing a puddle of candlelight onto the crimson carpet. She ducked inside the chamber she'd just checked, leaving the door open just enough to see who passed by on the way to the stairs.

Sara's heart pounded in her breast, thudded against her ribs. Pressed up against the crack in the door, she held her breath in anticipation of the author of the heavy footfalls coming closer. Not the footfalls of one of the servants, certainly, who were well skilled at moving about without making a sound. No, these footfalls had no care for discretion, their owner was weary and borne down. When he passed, she gasped in spite of herself. It was Dr. Breeden!

What was this? The doctor's rooms were on the second floor, not the third. She had chosen them herself, and Mrs. Bromley had made them ready. Sara waited until he disappeared in the shadows of the landing below, before stepping into the corridor again. No candlelight flooded the hallway from the chamber he had vacated now, only a thin sliver of light seeped out from under the door. She crept toward it.

Had Nicholas returned, and not sent word to her? Had she been patiently awaiting his return to be released from her chambers for naught? Hot blood surged to her temples. The heat of it narrowed her eyes. She would not knock. Grasping the knob, she threw the door open . . . and stopped dead in her tracks, teetering on the threshold of a well-appointed sitting room. Nicholas stood beside the hearth, naked to the waist, a brandy snifter in his hand. His left shoulder was wrapped with heavy bandages. When he spun to face her, the look in his eyes—half horror, half pain-laced rage— would have backed her down if she weren't rooted to the spot.

"Step inside and close the door," he said, setting the snifter on the mantel.

"W-what's happened to you?" Sara breathed, taking a step nearer, her gaze fixed on his bandaged shoulder.

"Stand where you are!" he thundered. "Come no closer."

"When did you return?" she said, halted by his words,

breath-suspended, as he took up the snifter again, swirling the liquor in it as if he expected to extract his answer from the glass.

"I've never been away," he said at last, and flushed some of the liquor down.

"I . . . I don't understand," Sara murmured.

"You shouldn't be here," he said, gazing in her direction again. Looking into those hypnotic obsidian eyes was torture, but she couldn't tear her gaze away. His sensuous mouth had formed a hard, lipless line, and the muscles were ticking along his jaw. It was a mercy when he began studying his snifter again.

"What do you mean you've never left the house?" she said.

"Exactly that."

"How have you hurt yourself?"

He hesitated. "Alex shot me," he said, meeting her eyes again.

Sara gasped, and her hand flew to her lips.

"I didn't want to worry you," said Nicholas. He finished the brandy, and set the snifter aside. "Dr. Breeden has been treating me, and as you can see, I'm recovering well under his care."

"Was that fair? I have been waiting for you to return, so that I may be released from the prison you've imposed upon me, Nicholas."

"Which is where you should be right now," he snapped. "What are you doing up here at this hour? You were told not to come up here *at all*. Alex is still at large, Sara. You are at risk abroad in this house now, and I am still not fit enough to protect you. You were safe in your rooms under guard until we sort all this out. I must insist that you return there at once, and stay there until I personally come and give you leave to quit your chambers."

"You say that Mr. Mallory shot you? Mr. Mallory shot *Nero*, my lord."

"There were . . . two shots fired," he returned.

"No one has seen Nero since," she said. "His was a shoulder wound, too, I think. He was bleeding profusely, barely able to run—yet he led Mr. Mallory out of my suite. If it has taken this long for you to stand on your feet again, despite Dr. Breeden's expert doctoring, what of him, alone, with no one to look after him? Is he dead, Nicholas? Is that something else you're all keeping from me?"

Again Nicholas hesitated. "Nero can take care of himself, Sara," he said.

"So said Mills, but I don't see how. That bullet would have had to come out, just as yours did, for him to survive."

"If he were dead, he would have been found," said Nicholas. "That we have not is a good sign. Put Nero from your mind. You've become too attached to him. I warned you that such an attachment was unwise."

"Yes, you did, but nevertheless I shan't rest until I see him again," she replied. "May I sit? I do not easily become overset, but all this has quite unsettled me."

"No," he replied. "You cannot stay here. I've said all there is to say. I will fetch my dressing gown and see you back to your rooms. You are to *stay* in them, Sara, until I say otherwise. I shall visit you there, now that I'm able, and once I see fit, I shall come and escort you down to meals personally. I am sorry that I deceived you, but I knew you would never stay in your suite if you knew I'd been . . . shot. Only Mills and the doctor are aware. They were needed to see to my wound. The rest were told, as you were, that I am away, and that's how it must remain. The others all have their duties to perform and none could be spared to keep you from falling through any more walls."

Sara held her peace. She watched him walk barefooted through an adjoining door that led to his bedchamber, catching a glimpse of a massive raised bed made with sumptuous quilts and creamy linens. He snatched his dressing gown from the lounge beside a hearth lit there as well, and walked back into the sitting room attempting to shrug the uncooperative satin garment on over his bandaged shoulder.

"Here, let me help you with that," she said, instinctively reaching to untangle the robe he'd twisted by trying to slip it on one-handed.

"Don't!" he gritted, but it was too late.

As if they had a will of their own, her hands slid from the tangled dressing gown to his broad chest, her fingers buried in the silky mat of black hair. The heart beneath hammered wildly, shuddering against her open palms, and his ragged breathing became rapid as he stared down into her eyes, his own glazed and dilated in the hearthlight.

"My God, Sara, *don't* . . ." he murmured.

Sara scarcely heard over the thunder of her own heartbeat. It had gone too far for her to stop. His scent overwhelmed her, drifting from his hair and moist skin, salty-warm, clean, and feral, laced with brandy. How could she ever forget?

Her arms slipped around him. What was she thinking? That was just the trouble; she *wasn't* thinking. His closeness was like a drug, drawing her under, blurring the edges of right and wrong, dissolving reason.

Every sinew in the long, lean length of him responded to her touch, though his firm grip on her upper arm made a valiant attempt at resistance. It was like petting a snarling dog with a wagging tail. Which should she believe? The physical evidence of his arousal stretching his faun-colored pantaloons, the bruising pressure of it swelling against her belly through the thin, white muslin, put paid to that decision. All at once, he groaned. The wounded arm slipped around her waist. Crushing her closer still, he cupped her head in his other hand at the base of her neck, swooped down like his namesake the raven, and parted her lips with his own skilled mouth in a kiss that drained her senses.

His silken tongue entered her mouth, drawing hers to it. She tasted the brandy he'd just drunk, warm, earthy, and mysterious on her tongue, but more mysterious was the man himself. His very essence was in her now, but she wanted more, she wanted all of him—all of the promise in that dynamic body—and she wanted it not just for the moment, but for all time.

He buried his hand in her hair and deepened the kiss—primitive, feral; all things wild under Heaven lived in it. Like a starving beggar let loose at a feast, he devoured her with those bruising lips, and yet there was a facet of tenderness in him, a practiced restraint lying under the surface of his passion like a sleeping animal that defied the rest. What would it take to rouse that sleeping beast? She was on the verge of finding out.

He freed his fingers from her hair, which had fallen over her shoulders, and reached for her breast and the stiffened nipple budding into tight awareness, straining against the embroidered muslin bodice. Sara groaned, and he slid the puffed sleeve down, spread the décolleté, and exposed the shuddering breast beneath to those lips that had left her weak and trembling in his arms. A deep, guttural groan escaped her throat as he leaned down. His tongue encircled the hardened nipple, drawing it into his mouth, teasing it taller—sucking relentlessly until her loins were on fire with icy hot waves of forbidden sensation that weakened her knees. But was it forbidden? They were married after all. Then he straightened and possessed her lips again, and she leaned into his arousal until it responded to the pressure of her undulating motion, growing harder still. It was as if Nicholas had burst into flame and ignited her, setting loose white-hot tongues of fire along the sexual stream flowing between them. It was magical . . . until he broke the spell.

Throwing his head back, he loosed the closest thing to the howl of a dog she'd ever heard, and let her go. It reminded her of Nero's plaintive howl. The sound spread gooseflesh the length of her body, and left her trembling in the chill that had come between them in the absence of his warm arms around her.

"Nooo," he moaned at the end of it. "No, Sara . . . *no!*"

Sara scarcely drew breath, watching him struggle toward composure. His chest was heaving, and he raked the ebony hair back from his sweaty brow with a trembling hand as he fought to control his breathing.

"Why, Nicholas?" she murmured. Covering her breast, still wet from his lips, she took a step closer.

"*No,* I said," he repeated, backing away as she advanced. "Stay back. Come . . . no closer."

"But, why, Nicholas," she pleaded. "You want me. I *know* you want me. I felt how you want me just now. How can you stand there and deny it?"

"I want you, yes," he gritted out, filling his empty snifter. He downed the brandy in one rough gulp. "You are a very desirable woman, Sara, and I'm hardly made of stone, but I cannot have you—not now . . . maybe not ever. It isn't fair to either of us to live with false hope. It's best that we stick to the original agreement."

"I don't understand."

The breath left his lungs on a long, empty sigh. "I know you don't," he said, "and I'm sorry for that. This here just now . . . never should have happened. It shan't again, I assure you."

"But I want it to," she murmured through a tremor. "If you do not want children—"

"Sara, it's not that simple," he interrupted. His misted eyes were dark pools of red fire catching glints from the hearth, and his moist skin glistened with sweat. "This whole arrangement was a mistake," he said. "I see that now. If you find that you cannot abide by it, I shall take steps to release you. It would be best if we do that now, before things become . . . more involved . . . Before we go too far."

"It's already too late for that," said Sara. "If you would

only explain yourself. All this time, I thought it was something in me that repulsed you—"

His mad, humorless laugh interrupted her.

"I did . . . until tonight, Nicholas. You'll never convince me of that now. What in God's name can it be?"

"God has nothing to do with it, Sara," he snarled. He began to prowl the edge of the Aubusson carpet before the hearth in the same manner that he had done several times before in her presence, only now, he was shaken, and it showed. Was it the injury that had drained him so, or what had just occurred between them? She didn't speak, watching him travel the textured rug for what seemed an eternity before he stopped in his tracks and faced her. "All right," he said, "since you will not make it easy for me to end it, I shall have to take the initiative. I owe you an explanation, it's true, but that cannot be just yet. Before I could even think of carrying you through that door to my bed, we would need to talk, and I would have to be assured that you would keep what I tell you in the strictest confidence, that what I confide be held no less than sacrosanct—inviolable."

"Done," she said.

"No, it isn't that easy, Sara. I have to be certain of it. At the moment, I am not, or I would have put it to you long ago."

"What can I do to convince you?"

"Nothing! That's the hellish part, and such a conversation between us cannot even be considered until all this business with Alex is settled. You must be patient. If you cannot be, I shall have Watts bring the brougham 'round, and have you away at once to one of my other properties until permanent arrangements can be made for you elsewhere."

Sara gave it thought. Something dark and dreadful lurked between the lines, but she could not read it. Perhaps it was better that she could not. All she knew then was that, no matter the consequences, she could not let him send her away.

She could not bear never to see him again, never feel those strong arms, those hungry lips—the anxious pressure of his manhood leaning heavily against her. Even with the broad span of rug between them, the ghost of his arousal haunted her, sending white-hot ripples of achy heat through her most private regions. A fresh surge of hot blood rushed to her temples at the realization of the power this man had over her even from a distance. They no longer needed to touch; he was in her soul.

"Very well, Nicholas," she said, her voice steady, for all that she was a shambles then. "I shall be patient, but not for long. That would be cruel."

"I will never harm you, Sara," he said. "That is the reason we are having this little talk. I am not a cruel man. I want this situation dealt with just as much as you do. Do we have an understanding?"

"Yes, Nicholas."

"Good," he said, bending to retrieve his dressing gown, which lay forgotten until that moment in a heap on the floor. The minute he picked it up, she took a step closer, of a mind to help him into it, but he held up his hand, and flung the robe down again. "Ohhh no!" he said. "Enough! I shall see you to your rooms just as I am. Come."

Exiting the suite, he took up a pistol from the gateleg table beside the door, and cocked it. Sara hadn't noticed it lying there until that moment, and a shattering chill raced the length of her spine. She gasped in spite of herself.

"Just in case," he said, ushering her into the corridor without touching her. "Stay close to me. There are no hall boys stationed on this floor, which reminds me, how did you get past Peters? It was he stationed outside your suite at this hour, was it not? Was he nodding again? It wouldn't be the first time—lazy gudgeon."

"I saw no one outside my suite, Nicholas," she said. She would not betray Peters. To do so would bring retribution down upon Nell also. Nicholas would keep his secrets, so would she keep hers. Hoping that Peters was still closeted with the abigail when they reached the tapestry suite, she stayed close to her husband's side, wishing she hadn't promised to keep her distance. The corridor was very dark, and her heart had begun to pound again, but not with arousal this time.

They had nearly reached the landing, when something moved toward them from the dimly lit south wing, stopping them both in their tracks. For a moment, Sara's heart hung suspended in her breast, until the familiar four-footed padding on the carpet that she had so longed to hear these past few days echoed toward them.

"*Nero!*" she cried, as the animal materialized out of the shadows. At sight of them, it stopped in its tracks, slowly exposing its fangs.

To her surprise, Nicholas shoved her behind him, and raised the pistol. "Stay back!" he commanded, squeezing the trigger.

"*Noooooo!* Are you mad?" she cried, spoiling his aim. With both her hands clamped around his wrist, she deflected the bullet toward the ceiling as it discharged. The reverberation was deafening. The acrid odor of gunpowder rose in her nostrils, and a spurt of flames burst from the pistol barrel, all but scorching her skin, as plaster and fragments of a shattered candle sconce rained down over them. Loosing a guttural snarl, the animal bolted and skittered back the way it had come, disappearing in the darkened south wing hallway.

"You little fool!" Nicholas thundered at Sara, sprinting after it. "Get back to your rooms at once, and bolt the door! *That isn't Nero!*"

Thirteen

The pistol shot brought Mills on the run in his nightshirt, his own pistol drawn, which he handed to Nicholas in exchange for the empty gun. Dr. Breeden, wearing his dressing gown and slippers, and carrying a candle branch, joined them minutes later, and all three set out on a search of the south wing chambers.

"Well, we needn't speculate any longer over the effects of Nero's bite, Dr. Breeden," said Nicholas. "I just saw with my own eyes what might well have been Nero himself, and we both know the impossibility of that. There are no other wolves at Ravencliff."

"You were aiming to *kill*, my lord?"

"No, certainly not. When it bared its fangs, I meant only to wound it, to bring it down and end this madness, and I would have done if the baroness hadn't spoiled my aim."

Smythe and the footmen came running, tugging on their livery coats, their wigs askew, and their hose and breeches twisted. Mills shuffled back and met them at the landing, as more servants came pouring through the green baize door below.

"All is well, all is well," he called down to Smythe and the others. Nicholas and the doctor ducked inside the nearest chamber—it wouldn't do to be caught out pistol-shot, when one wasn't supposed to be in residence. "I was cleaning his lordship's pistol, and it discharged accidentally," the valet explained. "I was just now coming to reassure you."

A rumble of out-of-rhythm murmurings replied to that, as the servants began filing back to their quarters. After a moment, Nicholas stepped out into the corridor again.

"See what you can do with this mess, Mills," he said, gesturing toward the bits of broken plaster littering the carpet, "and replace the sconce. Those lazy buffleheads will never notice the ceiling, bent over with their ears pressed up against the doors in this house spying on their betters. Just take away the obvious."

"Yes, my lord."

"Once that's done, I want you to find Peters, and remand him to Smythe. I want the boy sacked, Mills. This is outside of enough. I told you what would be if he misstepped again in this house, regardless. See to it. He left his post tonight, and her ladyship was with me when . . . this occurred. Smythe knows the consequences of disobedience. See that someone else is posted outside the tapestry suite at once. Make certain whoever replaces Peters understands that the same fate shall befall him if her ladyship is left unguarded again. *Ever!* Then join me in my rooms."

"Yes, my lord," said the valet, set in motion.

One by one, Nicholas and the doctor threw open the doors in the south wing, and searched each suite, but there was no sign of the animal. He seemed to have vanished into thin air.

"Where could he have gone?" said Breeden, as they exited the last chamber.

"This house is veined with escape routes," said Nicholas. "Smugglers occupied it for centuries before the Walravens came to Cornwall. He could have ducked into any one of them, or melted into the shadows and passed us by when we entered one of these suites. He could be anywhere in the house by now. He has been obsessed with its intricacies since a child."

"What are you going to do?"

"Alex keeps rooms here, which he occupies when he isn't off on business for me. They've been checked a dozen times, but not by me. I want to walk through those rooms now. I'll know if he's been in them."

"Let us go and do it then, my lord."

"Oh, no, I cannot impose further upon you tonight, Dr. Breeden," Nicholas said. "There has been nothing but chaos in this house since you arrived."

"I shan't sleep in any case now," said the doctor. "Besides, you've overreached yourself by the look of you, and will doubtless have need of me before the night is out. You're a reckless young fellow, aren't you, my lord? You're hardly fit enough for heroics just yet. Let me go with you, and then we shall talk. I need to know what occurred here just now."

"Then I shall fetch my dressing gown," said Nicholas. "The wound must be concealed. Baron Walraven has just returned, whether he's 'fit enough' or not."

Sara threw herself across her bed, muffling her sobs in the counterpane. What did Nicholas mean, it wasn't Nero? Of course it was Nero, and he'd almost shot him. He'd meant to *kill* Nero, and would have done if she hadn't spoiled his aim. Minutes before, he was holding her in his arms, those incredible arms, driving her to the brink of ecstasy. Why did he stop? What secret was he keeping, and why didn't he trust her with it?

There was still no sign of Peters, and no one had come to replace him. Sara climbed down from the bed and opened the door a crack. There was no question that Nero needed refuge, what with Nicholas prowling about armed, and she prayed he'd come to her. There was no sign of Nell, either, and she undressed on her own, slipped on her ecru night-dress, and climbed into bed. She was exhausted, and her head hardly touched the pillow, when she dropped off to sleep to the wail of the moaning wind.

At first she didn't recognize the sound that woke her. Not until the familiar padding of the animal's feet bled into her strange, disquieting dreams. They dissolved in the presence of that beloved sound, and she vaulted erect in her bed. He was marking his territory again, raising his leg and sprinkling the carpet in the same semicircular arch around the bed that he'd marked before. Having done, he shook himself, his whole body rippling, from the thick, shaggy ruff of silver-tipped black fur about his neck, to the tip of his bushy tail.

"*Nero!*" she cried, reaching toward him, but he passed her by, and stretched out on the rug before the mellow fire in the hearth, licking ooze and crusted blood off his left foreleg.

"I could have sworn your wound was higher . . . in your shoulder," Sara mused. She shrugged. "It all happened so fast, I must have been mistaken." She slid her feet to the floor. "Poor thing . . . That looks infected. Will you let me have a look?" she murmured, starting toward him.

The animal stopped licking his wound. He didn't growl, but his lips curled back, exposing vicious-looking fangs. He had never bared his teeth to her before, and it stopped her in her tracks.

"I know, boy," she soothed. "My dogs never wanted to be disturbed when they were injured, either. One nearly bit me once when I tried to give aid, but you wouldn't do that, would you, Nero? Not to worry, I shan't interfere, and I shan't tell Nicholas that you are found, either. We dare not risk it, not after what he nearly did tonight."

The animal didn't move. He was poised to spring, though she couldn't imagine it. Nevertheless, the hairs on the back of her neck had risen, flagging danger. His nails were curled under, seeking traction from the thick, sculptured rug, the sinews in his forelegs standing out in bold relief. For the first time since she'd met her canine friend, she feared him— enough to inch toward the bed. The minute she sat on the edge of it again, the animal's attention returned to his wounded leg. There was no sound save the rhythmic lapping of his long, pink tongue.

Sara said no more. She climbed back into bed, taking care not to make any sudden motions. He was in pain, and obviously out of sorts. He was following her every move with his dark, firelit eyes. Pulling the counterpane up to her chin, she closed her own, but she didn't fall back to sleep again until the animal got up and padded out of her chamber shortly before dawn.

Nicholas and Dr. Breeden made their way back to the master suite after searching Alexander Mallory's apartments. The steward's bed hadn't been slept in, and there was no sign that he had been there in recent days. In the absence of Mills to keep watch against eavesdroppers, they repaired to Nicholas's dressing room, where the doctor examined his wound, and dressed it with fresh bandage linen.

"Bind it tightly," Nicholas gritted out. Though it was mending, the wound was still sore, and he'd taxed it. "The bandages mustn't show through my clothes."

"You shouldn't be up and about yet, my lord," said the doctor. "This here is hardly healed enough for what you've put it through tonight. If you won't pace yourself, I shall have to dose you."

"No, no laudanum," said Nicholas. "I need my wits about me now. There is no doubt that it was Alex I nearly shot tonight. I saw the dried blood on his leg where I . . . where Nero bit him. This doesn't bode well for me, does it, Dr. Breeden?"

"It eliminates the possibility that your condition is all in your mind, my lord," said the doctor, "but then, we knew that already, didn't we."

Nicholas nodded. "What troubles me, is that we haven't seen Alex himself since the incident. Is it possible that he cannot transform back into human form?"

"Anything is possible, my lord. It's hard to say what you've passed on to him, or what he was susceptible to. In these cases, one thing seems to be the rule. Unlike the werewolf, the nonviolent shapeshifter tends to take on the personality of its human host. That is to say, what you are in human form, so will you be in your animal incarnation—with the strengths, weaknesses, and extraordinary abilities of that incarnation, of course. What sort of man is Alexander Mallory?"

"Alex is a bit of an elbow bender, Dr. Breeden. He's amiable enough when he isn't drinking, but when he's foxed, there's no telling what he'll do. He doesn't imbibe on a regular basis. At least, he never has in the past while attending to my business, or I would have sacked him long ago, childhood friend or no. Liquor brings out the worst in him. He's a bit of a womanizer as well. I don't know what set him off this time, but both vices were working against him that night."

"Jealousy," said the doctor.

"I beg your pardon?"

"Your wife is a very beautiful young woman. Unless I miss my guess, he is smitten, wishing he were the bridegroom in earnest. No doubt he feels that since there is no longstanding relationship between you and the baroness, considering that you are virtual strangers, he has just as much of a chance to win her affections."

"She did imply that there was something amiss, but she assured me she had it in hand."

"Evidently not, my lord," said the doctor through a humorless chuckle.

"You say that the animal takes on the character of its human host. Nero was in a blind rage when he attacked Alex. Mightn't that color what Alex has become? Mightn't it make him more . . . violent?"

"No," said the doctor. "Any animal that bites is angry, my lord. The man bitten would not become violent from the bite, unless, of course, he were violent to begin with. Whatever inherent traits are at his core are what he will carry into animal form. It's like heredity. If the man is gentle and kind, so will his wolf be. If he is brutal and vicious, his wolf will be also. The personality of the man will be the personality of the wolf, unless we are discussing werewolves. In that case, the wolf becomes what his attacker is, a bloodthirsty predator. We have already established that you are no lycanthrope, my lord."

"I wish I knew more about Father," said Nicholas.

"Researching these . . . phenomenon is speculative at best," said the doctor. "Most scholars agree that one has to be bitten by a werewolf to become one. There are exceptions to every rule, of course, but you are not one of them, my lord. Neither is Mr. Mallory. Whatever your father passed on to you at conception was a weakened form of what he was—an altered strain, if you will. You will always be what you are. You will never be what he was, whatever he was; nor will you pass what he was on to anyone else. The condition is not progressive. There are no lycanthropes here. I knew that the moment your letter arrived in the post. Your case is quite unique among my studies. Though all manner of similar tales abound in India, I have never personally come upon anything quite like it before. That is why I was so eager to take you up on your kind invitation to come out here. If nothing else, you may rest assured that neither you, nor Mr. Mallory are now, or ever will be, werewolves."

"Then, Alex will always be . . . as I am?"

"He will be what he has become, yes, my lord. What will you do if he does surface? Will you sack him?"

"What—and have him do to another what Nero has done to him? How could I?"

"What, then?"

"Perhaps . . . whatever you can do for me might help him as well, assuming you can do anything for me." His tone was pleading, but the doctor didn't respond to it.

"You're certain Nero has never bitten anyone else, my lord? Think carefully."

"No—never."

The doctor sighed. "You need to confide in the baroness," he said, "and you need to do it at once."

"I cannot do that," Nicholas snapped. "I will lose her! She might even disclose my situation."

"You do not know that."

"I cannot risk it."

"She thought that wolf tonight was Nero. What if he were to bite *her*, my lord? You've said she leaves her door ajar. She needs to know."

Nicholas shook his head. "Not yet," he said. "She will be watched—*I* will watch her. I will scarcely leave her side until Alex is dealt with."

"Forgive me, but is that altogether wise, my lord?"

"What do you mean?"

"What happened between you two before that wolf appeared tonight?"

Was he so transparent, or was this man clairvoyant as well?

"Come, come, my lord, I cannot help you unless you let me," said the doctor.

"I very nearly lost my head," said Nicholas. "I let my heart rule, and I nearly transformed right there in front of her. I cannot stop it, but I always know when it's going to happen—when I need to shed my clothes and let it happen, just as I know when I'm about to change back. But for that, I would have been caught out long since."

"And, you also know what triggers the attacks?"

"Yes. Tonight, I was aroused."

"How did you prevent the transformation?"

"I . . . I broke contact, came to my senses and put her from me before the transformation began. I . . . I couldn't let her see what happens."

"That was control, my lord. You *can* do it; you need help perfecting how."

"My God, help me then—whatever the cost—whatever you can do."

"There are several things, my lord, and we shall try them all. To begin with, Mills tells me he prepares an herbal cordial of skullcap, linden, and hops for you each evening."

"Mrs. Bromley prepares it. Mills sees that I take it. It's supposed to relax me, and keep me calm."

"That may continue, but I shall make it from now on," said the doctor. "Do you have a kitchen garden?"

"Yes. Mrs. Bromley prides herself upon it."

"I shall need henbane and angelica to begin with," said the doctor. "You needn't trouble her. I will know them on sight, as well as any others I require. We shall dispense with the hops in the cordial. While it has long since been hailed as a cure for uncontrolled sexual desires, it obviously isn't working for you. It has excellent properties for inducing sleep, however, which would be beneficial. I would suggest an external application. An herbal pillow, perhaps, filled with hops mixed with lavender tucked inside your bed pillow—very effective. I will have Mrs. Bromley prepare one. Meanwhile, we shall try angelica as a replacement to adjust your libido instead—a good deal of it—and see how we fare; but not in the cordial; separately, taken in wine. Don't look so stricken, my lord. All this is temporary. Have you roses—the briar rose in particular?"

"Y-yes, quite a number of varieties," said Nicholas, still dwelling on the angelica. "I cannot name them all, but we have an excellent groundskeeper, Henry Gibbs. I shall introduce you. He's tended the estate since Father was alive. He takes particular pride in the roses. There's a walled garden off the courtyard, somewhat sheltered from the gales, though the wind spreads the perfume through the whole house when they're in bloom."

"Good," said the doctor. "The ancient Celts used the root of the briar rose to doctor infected wolf bites on themselves, and on their animals, and it was once touted as a cure for rabies, widely used in the Orient . . . and in India. Its properties will be beneficial—just how beneficial, remains to be seen. The baroness must have this also. I would suggest a tea made of rose hips—a minimum of eight 'fruits,' as they are called, a day, steeped well and sweetened with honey. I shall instruct Mrs. Bromley. The taste is quite pleasant—"

"If I can get her to take it without telling her why," Nicholas interrupted.

"I shall see that she takes it," said the doctor. "I shall prescribe it as a tonic to set her to rights after her ordeal in the priest hole. Your dose will be more potent, combined in the cordial. There will be other herbs as time goes on, but we shall not try too many at once. We shall see how each one affects you until we reach a satisfactory combination. I tell you all this, because I want you to be aware of my methods. I want you to know what I am using, and why."

"Do you really think any of this will help?"

"Not if you don't believe," said the doctor. "We have established that your condition is not all in your mind, my lord, but your mind is not exempt from it. You've just proved that in the way you forestalled the transformation. Next, we must teach that mind how to think, but not tonight, or should I say 'this morning'? Dawn is soon upon us, and we have much to do, but first you need to rest, and I need a walk in the garden, if you will direct me. Herbs are best collected when the dew is still upon them."

Nicholas nodded, and got to his feet, leading the doctor out. "We must find Alex, Dr. Breeden," he said, as they left the chamber. "Before more harm is done."

"Of course, my lord."

"There is a gun room below stairs. I will have Mills fetch

you a pistol. If you are going to roam about on your own here now, I'm afraid you shall have to do so armed. From what I've read, I understand that silver bullets are required. Unfortunately, we haven't any. I'm afraid you'll have to make do with lead."

"We shan't need silver bullets to defend against the wolves in this house, my lord; those are only necessary in the case of werewolves. Unfortunately—for you, that is—an ordinary pistol ball is all that is required to kill a shapeshifter."

Fourteen

Sara woke at the crack of dawn to the soft mewling sobs coming from her dressing room, where Nell was laying out her toilette. Shrugging on her wrapper, she followed the sound to find the abigail red-faced and teary-eyed, ordering the sprigged muslin frock Sara would be wearing to breakfast. One look in her direction, and the stricken girl burst into a fit of wailing.

"Whatever is it, Nell?" Sara said, sitting her down on the lounge. "What's happened?"

"He's been sacked," the girl moaned. "The master come home and sent him off before sunup, and it's all my fault."

"Who's been sacked?"

"My Jeremy . . . you'd know him as Peters, my lady. He was ta stand guard outside your door last night, but you was retired, and he sneaked off ta be with me. Now I'll never see him again!"

"Evidently his lordship isn't aware of your part in this, or he would have sacked you as well," said Sara.

"I wish he did!" the girl moaned. "Oh . . . oh, my lady, I

141

didn't mean . . . it ain't that I don't want ta be your lady's maid . . . and I really need the wages, it's just . . . I *love* him, my lady!"

"I know that, Nell," said Sara. She could relate to the girl's misery. The physical aside, she was falling in love with her strange, brooding husband as well. There, she'd *admitted* it. She'd realized it the moment she entered his sanctum sanctorum and found him wounded—realized he could have been killed, that she might never have seen him again. How could she have borne it?

They too were separated, but their separation was crueler. They were close enough to touch, close enough to kiss, to embrace, to make love, but there was a barrier between them, an invisible shield of Nicholas's making, and she didn't know why he'd walled himself in, or how to penetrate the barricade he'd built between them. She hadn't the skill. She was too inexperienced, and he was a man of the world—far too sophisticated to succumb to the transparent wiles of such a pitifully inept goose as herself, when it came to affairs of the heart. The worst of it was knowing, since that night, that he felt something for her, too—something he obviously didn't want to feel, something he wouldn't allow. But why? She hadn't imagined it. It was in his kiss, in the strong arms holding her close, in the bruising pressure of his arousal leaning against her, in his very breathing, hot and steamy against her flesh.

"Ya won't tell him, will ya, my lady?" the girl sobbed, jolting her back to the present. Sara's hands were trembling, her palms moist, and her innermost regions—those secret places Nicholas had awakened at her very core—were palpitating from the mere memory of that brief embrace.

"No, I shan't tell him," she said, "and there's something that you shan't tell him either."

"W-what would that be, my lady?"

"It concerns Nero."

"That scruffy old dog? Fie, my lady! Nobody's seen him or Mr. Mallory either, since they had that set-to. For all we know, he's crawled off and died o' that wound, and good riddance, I say!"

"He hasn't," said Sara. "I saw him just last evening."

"Well, the master better no' set eyes on him. Smythe says, more'n likely, he'll be after gettin' shot o' that dog for good and all after what happened with Mr. Mallory."

"Yes, well, not while I draw breath," said Sara. "If Nero chooses to visit, he will be welcome here in my rooms. I intend to leave my foyer door ajar in case he does, and I do not want his lordship to know. That animal is treated shamefully in this house. Why, he's thin as a shadow. He looks like a half-starved wolf, instead of the house pet of a baron."

"The master'll skin me if he finds out," the girl protested.

"He won't find out, Nell, unless you tell him."

"But the hall boys," the abigail said. "They're ta be keepin' watch out there night and day, my lady. They'll see that old dog comin' in here, and I'll be sacked for fair!"

"You leave the hall boys to me," said Sara. "I shall see that they are dismissed from their duties. This shall be our little secret, Nell. You will keep mine . . . and I will keep yours. Do we have an understanding?"

Sara abhorred the necessity of such a tactic, but she jumped at the chance to employ it nevertheless. These were extraordinary circumstances. Baron Nicholas Walraven wasn't going to take any more shots at her beloved Nero if she had anything to say about it.

"Nell?" she prompted during the girl's silence. "I've kept the bargain already, you know. I was questioned about Peters. I knew where he was, and with whom. I've known all along that you two sneak off to meet, but I held my peace. You owe me as much in kind. Now, I shall ask you again . . . do we have an understanding?"

"Y-yes, my lady," the abigail mewed.

"Good! Now, you had best dry those eyes, and help me into that frock before his lordship arrives to escort me down to breakfast."

The abigail had just finished tucking the last green grosgrain ribbon into Sara's upswept coiffure, when Nicholas's knock sent the girl scurrying to the foyer door. Had Sara left it ajar last night after the animal left? Her heart sank. Nicholas pushed it open with his finger before the maid reached it, answering that question. Nonetheless, Sara squared her posture and met him with her most fetching smile in place, despite his tight-lipped scowl. They passed the new hall boy stationed outside her suite as if he didn't exist, though she was bursting to get her teeth into that issue, and neither spoke on their way to the breakfast room, except for the barest amenities.

Sara breezed through breakfast playing the perfect hostess; Nicholas's raised eyebrow on more than one occasion during the meal was proof positive that she couldn't be faulted in that regard. It was a shallow victory, but a victory nonetheless, and she claimed it like a polished trophy. It wasn't until afterward that it began to tarnish.

Dr. Breeden excused himself early. Mrs. Bromley had given him space in her herbarium for preparing his herbals, and he was anxious to attend to his just-picked specimens before the effects of the morning dew upon them were lost. Sara was delighted. The study was Nicholas's domain. Her victories had been won in the cheery breakfast room, with its urns filled with flowers, creamy table linens, and breathtaking view of the gardens through the diamond-fretted windowpanes. She accepted a second cup of coffee, and adjusted her position in the chair as though she were battening down for the onslaught of a Cornish flaw.

"There is something I should like to discuss with you, Nicholas," she said, taking a swallow from her cup. "You did say that if I had any questions . . . or issues, I should bring them directly to you . . . first." That last got his eyebrow up, and his own cup suspended. Why did he always look like an animal ready to spring whenever they conversed on serious topics?

"Yes?" he said, his voice edged for battle.

"It concerns the hall boys outside my room. I want them removed."

"That is impossible, Sara," Nicholas said.

"Why?" she persisted. "It is my suite, is it not? I do not wish an armed guard posted there day and night. I feel like a prisoner. I had more freedom in the Fleet!"

Nicholas vaulted out of the carver's chair, scudding it out behind him, and tossed his serviette into his empty plate.

"Please leave us," he charged the footmen collectively. "Close the door after you, and if I find you with your ears pressed up against it again, you can all collect your wages. Is that clear?"

A monotone rumble replied, as the footmen tripped over one another retreating, and Nicholas resumed his place at the table looking daggers.

"That wasn't necessary, Nicholas," said Sara. "They all know I'm under guard."

"Yes, but they don't know why, and I'd rather they not be privy to . . . certain matters. They've enough ammunition for manufacturing *on-dits* as it is. The breakfast room is not the place for such a conversation, Sara."

"Oh, I know," she served, "but it seems to be the only place in this house where we can converse on equal footing. If that is due to the footmen eavesdropping, then I say—God bless them for it!"

"You will have hall boys stationed outside your door until Alex is found and dealt with," said Nicholas. "That is not negotiable now, nor will it ever be in future. Have you so soon forgotten what occurred in your suite?"

"You do not trust me, and that is insulting."

"I do not trust *him*, and you are evidently no match for his prowess. So much for keeping him in his place."

"That's not fair. I was sound asleep when he . . . when—"

"When he tried to molest you?"

"He was foxed, Nicholas."

"And you would have been raped just the same but for . . . Nero. How did Alex gain entrance, Sara? I'll tell you how, you left the door ajar—just as I found it up there when I came to fetch you down to breakfast. I should think you'd have learned your lesson . . . unless—"

"Don't you dare finish that sentence, Nicholas Walraven, *don't you dare!*"

Nicholas heaved a mammoth sigh. "Sara," he said, in that sensuous baritone voice that melted her to the marrow. She could deal with his anger, but not that deep, resonant silkiness that had the power to arouse her from across the room. "This is hardly a permanent situation," he went on. "Once Alex is found—"

"*Find* him, then!" she cried, vaulting to her feet. She had to call the anger back. It was her only defense against this paradox of a man who had tied her heart in knots. "Because, I tell you here and now, I did not come to Ravencliff to be held prisoner. I could have stayed where I was for that!" Did he flinch? The muscles in his broad jaw were ticking, and he was on his feet again, but he made no move toward her, and she went on speaking while she still had the upper hand. "I will not stay where I am held captive again—never again!" she seethed, hurling her serviette down. "And, do not forget, I *saw* that last night, Nicholas. You nearly killed that poor animal. The servants in this house are just as hard-hearted in that regard. I've heard them talking. Why Nell alone is harping on getting rid of him each time she opens her mouth. I don't know what is going on here, but I warn you—you can mark my words, nothing had better happen to Nero in this house. Ever! Not while I'm residing in it."

Spinning on her heel, she marched out of the breakfast room. This time, there wasn't a footman in sight.

* * *

"Sara!" Nicholas called after her, tossing his serviette down. There was no reply, and he skirted the table and strode out into the corridor. She had already reached the second-floor landing. Through the gloom that presided over the halls, fair weather or foul, he caught a glimpse of her sprigged muslin frock melting into the shadows as she turned toward her suite. He bolted after her, but the thunderous crack of the front door knocker echoing along the hallway stopped him in his tracks. *Who the devil can that be?* he wondered. The knock came again. It sounded urgent. The racket brought Smythe shuffling along the corridor tugging at his frock coat and muttering complaints.

The butler scarcely acknowledged him as he passed, and Nicholas raked his hair back, his eyes oscillating between Sara disappearing and the sound of raised voices funneling along the great hall at his back. He was ready to spring, but in which direction? Like a pendulum, swinging this way and that, he swayed there, trying to decide.

"The Devil take it!" he mumbled at last. Spinning around on the heels of his turned-down boots, he sprinted down the corridor toward the front door.

Smythe was standing in the open doorway arguing with three men in drab stuff breeches, short coats, and low-crown wide-brim hats. *Guards from the Watch?*

"What the deuce is going on here, Smythe?" Nicholas demanded, ranging himself alongside. "I could hear you clear back to the breakfast room."

"Captain Renkins, m'lord," the leader spoke up before the butler could answer. He doffed his hat. "Your man here don't seem to understand. We have to come in. There's been a complaint."

"What sort of complaint?" said Nicholas, struggling with a sinking feeling in the pit of his stomach. What was this now?

"We've come about a vicious dog," said the Captain.

"That *animal* again?" the butler grumbled low-voiced.

"That will be *all*, Smythe. I'll handle this," said Nicholas through clenched teeth. Dismissing him with a look that booked no argument, he turned to the guards. "Gentlemen, if you will follow me . . . ?"

He led them to the study. No use to have the whole house privy to this new press, though he had no doubt the rafters would be ringing with it once Smythe reached the servants' quarters. Ushering the guards inside, he closed the door behind them, and took his seat behind the desk

"Now then, gentlemen," he said, "what is all this about a dog?"

The three men stood ramrod-rigid before him, the captain in the center seeming the only one possessed of a tongue. The others stood like bookends at his side. Nicholas did not invite them to sit.

"The young chap says it might be rabid," said the captain. "He's got the village in an uproar over it, m'lord. Folks won't rest easy now until we know. We'll have to see the animal to be certain."

"What 'young chap'?" Nicholas asked, as the blood drained away from his scalp. His nostrils flared, and the short hairs on the back of his neck stood up as gooseflesh riddled his spine.

"Fella by the name of Jeremy Peters—says he was one of your staff here till you sacked him. Says he was of a mind to give his notice anyway because the animal attacked him. Folks ain't safe with a creature like that roaming about."

"Ah! That explains it," Nicholas responded, with as much authority as he could muster. "Peters was sacked for diddling one of the maids when he was supposed to be at his post—not that that's any business of the Watch. Your 'complaint' is nothing more than the vindictive ramblings of a disgruntled servant, plain and simple." He surged to his feet. "Now, if that is all, you really must excuse me. I have urgent business to attend to this morning." He started toward the door, but the captain's gruff voice turned him back.

"That may be, m'lord," Renkins said, "but we still have to have a look at the animal."

"There is no dog!" Nicholas said in a raised voice. Anger sent hot blood rushing to his temples, and he worked white-knuckled fists at his sides, wishing he could get his hands upon the traitorous hall boy. He took deep measured breaths in a vain attempt to quell the rage building inside. He dared not succumb to anger now and risk transformation before their very eyes.

"That's not what your butler said," the captain returned. "I heard him plain as day just now."

"My butler, sir, has gone addled with age. I keep him here out of pity. I am master of this house, and if I say there is no dog, there is no dog! And even if there were and it were rabid, would I be standing here denying it—putting my household at risk? Would that not have been the first thing out of my butler's mouth when he opened that door out there? I assure you, gentlemen, if there were a rabid dog on Ravencliff, I would have sent for you myself."

"It's not just your butler, m'lord. The whole village is in an uproar over the tales your hirelings have spread about the animal you keep out here."

"Then Peters must have put them up to it. The little tart he's diddling is still in my employ. She is the baroness's abigail until I can find a suitable maid to replace her. Then, you shall have more *on-dits*, I have no doubt, because the girl will be sacked as well. Now, gentlemen, I don't mean to be rude, but I really must be about my business."

"Young Peters says that dog you ain't got out here bit your steward, and that he ain't been seen since. What have you got to say to that, m'lord?"

"I dismissed my steward a sennight ago," said Nicholas seamlessly. "He was bitten all right—*jug*-bitten, not dog bitten, I assure you. When he sobers up and hauls his arse back out here for the rest of his belongings, I shall send him 'round to tell you so himself."

The three men stood their ground, studying him. Did they believe him? The captain's knit brows and pursed lips didn't bode well.

Transformation was imminent. Between his argument with Sara and this new press, it was only a matter of time before Nero made a liar of him. The soul-shattering palpitations had begun inside—the dizzying nausea and narrowed vision that always warned him it was time to shed his clothes in preparation, for the phenomenon had begun. That couldn't happen here, in front of three guards from the Watch, and he sketched a dramatic bow and swept his arm wide in one last attempt to be rid of them before it was too late.

"Very well, gentlemen," he said, "since I see we shall have no peace until I submit to this ridiculous affront, be my guest. Search the house from top to bottom if needs must—anything so that I can get on with my affairs. I have a house-guest in residence—a prominent London physician. I am behindhand for a tour of the estate I promised him this morning. He's going to think we are barbarians here on the coast: servants spreading scandalous lies, guards banging our door down at the crack of dawn. . . . If you would rather take the word of a lying little weasel of a put-off malcontent than that of a baron, have at it! I shan't stand in your way, just stay out of mine. And if you find a dog on this estate, I shall have Cook roast it with an apple in its mouth and I will eat it for my supper. You gentlemen may join me. Well? What are you waiting for? Get on with it, then." He reached the door in three strides, and flung it wide with a clammy hand.

Standing motionless until then, the captain broke his trancelike stance, and meandered toward the door. The others followed. Were they going to take him up on the offer? Nicholas held his breath as the captain on the threshold turned to face him.

"That won't be necessary, m'lord . . . for now," he said. "But if I hear of any more complaints, you can bet your blunt that we'll be back, and if there is a predator lurking about, we'll run it to ground, sure as check—four-legged or two."

"Just what is that supposed to mean?" said Nicholas.

"It means, m'lord, that I ain't so green as I'm cabbage-looking. Something just don't set right with me about this, and if I have to come back out here over it, I won't be put off till I've found out just what that something is."

"Just so," said Nicholas, frosty-voiced. "If something un-toward were afoot, I would insist upon it. Now then, if Peters encountered a dog it must have been a stray—none of mine. And if I set eyes upon it, I shan't need you to run it to ground, I assure you. I can hold my own at Manton's Gallery with the best of them. Rabid dog indeed! Now, good morning, gentlemen."

Nicholas slammed the door to the master suite with force enough to set it off its hinges, bringing Mills from his adjoining rooms, clothes brush and Nicholas's best dinner jacket in hand.

"Has something untoward happened, my lord?"

"Untoward? You might say that, Mills," said Nicholas. "We've just had the guards in from the Watch."

"The *guards*, my lord?" Mills asked. "Whatever for?"

"It seems that Peters has spread the tale that Nero attacked him, and bit Alex."

"Oh, my lord! What are we going to do?"

"Nothing, Mills," Nicholas pronounced. "They've gone . . . for now. But they will be back, I have no doubt. The whole staff has been spreading rumors in the village that we have a rabid animal out here."

"Did you convince them otherwise, my lord?" said Mills.

"I wouldn't count upon it. I told them to go ahead and search the place, and they cried off."

"Was that wise, my lord, considering? Suppose they had

taken you up on it? I wouldn't try that strategy again as things are here now, if you take my meaning."

Nicholas scarcely heard. "By God," he said, pacing like a caged animal. "The staff is going to be called to account for this. Before I'm through, they'll wish they'd kept their traitorous jaws from flapping. No one leaves this house again until I've addressed this with every servant below stairs. Pass the word."

"Y-yes, my lord," said Mills."

"And that's not the whole of what's come down upon me this bedeviled morning!"

"There's more, my lord?"

Nicholas nodded. "My lady wants the hall boys dismissed. You know I cannot do that. She's still leaving that damned door ajar, and don't you dare say 'whose fault is that,' or so help me God . . ."

"I haven't said a word, my lord," the valet defended.

"No, but you don't have to. You were thinking it. You read like a book, old boy."

"What are you going to do, my lord?"

"She thinks I mean Nero harm," said Nicholas, pacing the oriental carpet. "I cannot explain it to her, Mills. She wouldn't believe me if I did. Hah! *I* don't even know what we're dealing with. How the Devil could I presume to explain it to her? She's certain it was Nero that I nearly shot, and she means to protect him. She loves that animal."

"She loves you, too, my lord," said the valet in a small voice.

"That doesn't help me, Mills," Nicholas growled, "it only makes matters worse, if that were possible. Besides, I think you're wrong—I *pray* you are. I think you'd be of a different opinion if you heard her down there just now."

"Begging your pardon, my lord, but mightn't you curtail Nero's visits to her suite for a time?"

"You know the limits of my control over Nero. It's too late for that in any case. She'd only go off in search of him. That would be catastrophic now, what with Alex prowling about, and her penchant for finding Ravencliff's pitfalls. She's right. He has to be found, and quickly." He reached inside his waistcoat and produced a small pocket pistol, ignoring the valet's gasp. "I had to see that Dr. Breeden was armed," he went on, exhibiting the gun. "I can hardly have the man blundering about without protection. While I was at it, I chose this for myself. I couldn't very well go around toting a dueling pistol at the ready. This is compact enough to conceal on my person."

"Is . . . is it loaded, my lord?"

"It wouldn't be much use if it wasn't, would it, old boy?"

"I expect not. I'm just afraid . . ."

"The only thing you have to be afraid of, Mills, is that I should come face to face with Alex without it. Now, fetch my greatcoat—the one with the pockets."

"You're going out, my lord?"

"I'm in need of a walk on the strand," Nicholas replied. Stripping off his indigo superfine jacket and oyster-white brocade waistcoat, he handed them to the valet, and unbuttoned his shirt halfway down the front. "Believe me, you'd best hurry."

"Y-yes, my lord," said the valet, skittering off. He returned moments later with the caped greatcoat, and helped Nicholas into it.

"See that her ladyship is escorted to the breakfast room when the time comes," Nicholas said, jamming the pistol into his coat pocket. "I doubt I shall be back in time for nuncheon."

Sara should have been working on the rest of the menus for Dr. Breeden's stay, but she was far too overset to take that on. Traveling back and forth before the window in her sitting room, she tried to order her thoughts. The storm had blown over, but the wind still had its bluster. Though the sun remained hidden behind dense cloud cover, the drafts seeping in around the mullioned panes seemed milder, if such a thing could be.

The hall boy was still stationed outside. How she hated imprisonment, for that was how she saw her situation. Nothing had been settled. She should have stayed until she'd won her freedom. Now she would have to confront Nicholas again over the issue. Her posture collapsed. He would never give in, but then, neither would she. Nero had to have access to her. The poor starved creature needed food, and friendship—someone he could trust. But she couldn't betray Nell; the abigail was right that she would be blamed if they were caught out. So the hall boys had to go.

Passing by the window, Sara glanced below in time to see Nicholas descending the stone steps hewn in the cliff, his greatcoat spread wide on the wind. She rang for Nell. It was only minutes before the maid scurried in, sketching a curtsy, but it seemed an eternity to Sara, her eyes fixed on the place where she'd last seen Nicholas on the cliff.

"Fetch my pelerine," she charged the girl.

"Ya can't go out, my lady!" the girl breathed. "The hall boy'll see ya."

"The hall boy will see us both, Nell," she replied. "We are going to take a little stroll. I am allowed, so long as I'm escorted. I shall make a comment regarding the drafts in this mausoleum to excuse my wrapper for the benefit of my jailer out in that hall. Now *hurry*. You are going to show me how to get out on that cliff."

Fifteen

Under protest, Nell led Sara to a side door, recessed in much the same manner as the priest hole door was, behind the back stairs. Obscured by tapestries, the exit was well disguised, something left over from the house's smuggler days, Sara surmised. She never would have found it on her own. A narrow passageway connected it to a rear entrance to the servants' quarters that she didn't even know existed. It was a true service entrance, which didn't make any sense unless one were a smuggler, because the cliff was not accessible from the main drive. Only through the narrow gate in a high stone wall was it possible to reach the cliff from the front of Ravencliff Manor. That portal, hewn of thick, seasoned timbers and crisscrossed with iron bars, like something that belonged on a medieval fortress, was always locked; as a safety precaution, so said Nell.

Sara dismissed the abigail, and stepped out onto a narrow skirtlike shelf only a few yards wide, tufted here and there with sprouting weeds. It was carved in the flat table of granite rock, and from it the house rose into the dismal sky. A low, stacked stone fence similar to the one barring the cliff from the road on the approach to Ravencliff was all that protected the edge. It, too, was in disrepair, riddled with holes carved over time by the sea. A narrow opening revealed the deep steps hewn in the face of the cliff that led to the strand below. It was a daunting drop, softened only by gradual sloping halfway down that was slightly less perpendicular. A jutting crag on the left offered some shelter from the wind, and convenient niches were carved out, where, depending upon the weather, one descending could get a grip if not a firm hold upon the wet rock, slimed with algae and debris flung there by the sea. The rocky wall was damp from the morning mist now, and Sara wondered if it ever did dry out.

She paused a moment on the brink, her pelerine spread by the wind just as Nicholas's caped greatcoat had been earlier, and scanned the shoreline below in both directions, but there was no sign of Nicholas. He had to be down there somewhere, and it was the perfect place to finish their discussion, with no prying eyes or listening ears. Surveying the distance down again, she could see why she had been warned against doing what she was now about to do, but there was nothing for it. She had to go down. She might not get such an opportunity again. Taking a deep breath of the salt sea air, she lifted the hem of her sprigged muslin frock and began her descent.

Clouds of waterfowl soared overhead, cormorant, tern, and gull among them. There were some species she couldn't name, but all shared the same tertiary plumage in varying shades of white and brown and gray—the color of the brooding sky bleeding toward her. They were one brotherhood flocking inland: a flapping mass of squawking frenzy collecting on the stone apron above. Gracefully, they sailed over the gated wall to litter the drive and huddle in the courtyard just as she'd seen them do on other occasions when dirty weather was brewing. Another storm was on the way.

Ducking low-flying birds, Sara reached the strand without incident, and stopped to catch her breath. The rocky shoreline, edged in sand, looped around in a semicircular arc toward the north, to disappear beyond the sheer face of another ancient crag. The strand was straighter to the south, though the beach was foreshortened there by outcroppings—fallen boulders, tide pools formed by coves and natural jetties, and what debris the cliffs gave back to the sea. It was a rugged stretch of land, lonely and desolate, yet possessed of an ethereal beauty that drew her like a magnet.

It was still neap tide. The full moon that would bring the rush of spring tide was still a few days off. It should be safe enough for a brief walk on the strand. Nicholas certainly wouldn't stay down on the beach if there were any danger. With that to bolster her courage, she began her stroll high along the hard-packed berm to the south, as far away as she could manage from the surf lapping at the shore and creaming over the broken shingle. The surf crawled higher as she progressed, but she scarcely noticed. Something black lying in a heap half-hidden among the rocks in a little cove several yards down the beach caught her attention, and she decided to investigate.

The wind had picked up, rippling the object, and lifting into the air something white lying beside it then tumbling it along the sand until it snagged on another rock. Sara hurried toward it, scrambling over rocks that formed one of the natural jetties, passing what she now recognized as a man's coat—Nicholas's coat—wedged between two boulders. She snatched up the white object. It was a shirt. Holding it to her nose, she inhaled Nicholas. There was no mistaking his evocative scent. Still there was no sign of him, and she carried the shirt back to his greatcoat to discover his pantaloons, hose, and drawers strewn about, as well. His Hessians were lying amongst the seaweed, east of the spot, and she climbed over the rocks and collected them, uniting them with the rest. This took some time, as the rocks were slippery, half-hidden in the weed, and she lost her footing more than once retrieving them.

By the time she reached the pile she was making, the wind had whipped the waves into fearsome breakers, their issue inching ever closer and leaving dark lace-edged rings on the sand. She paid them no mind. She had lost all track of time. Where could he be without his clothes? Had he gone for a swim in one of the tide pools? It was warmer, being May, but not *that* warm, and the wind had a definite bite. Hardly weather for swimming. Why, hearths were still lit in the house, and probably would be for some time. Were all Cornishmen so rugged, she wondered? The man must be mad.

She returned to her chore. The clothes would surely blow away again if they weren't well anchored between the rocks, and she set about the task of layering them in such a manner that might help prevent them from disappearing.

All at once she realized what she was doing. The man was wandering about out there somewhere *naked*. What if he should return and find her there? She glanced up and down the strand. Still no sign of him, and her hands moved a little faster ordering his clothes.

She arranged everything in a neat pile and lifted the coat, intending to lay it over the lighter garments, then anchor the lot with the Hessians. It was heavy. Trying to fold it, she came upon one of the reasons—a pistol in the pocket. She almost dropped it, realizing what it was for. He still meant to kill Nero! Should she take it? He had a well-stocked gun room. He would only get another, but that would take time. Should she, or shouldn't she? While she was debating that with her back to the sea, she paid no attention to the wail of the wind, or the roar of the breakers rolling up the coast. It wasn't until a blast of salt water knocked her off her feet that she realized she'd been cut off. She was trapped—walled in by the jetties—her access to the north beach obliterated by crashing waves that left her floundering in waist-high water.

Icy cold, it snatched her breath away. The pelerine was weighting her down, and she began to flounder, until she tried to regulate herself to the ebb and flow of the rushing water. She would not panic. Once she caught the rhythm of the ocean, she tried to scramble higher when the water receded, but the sand beneath the sucking waves undermined her footing, pulling her back toward the sea—toward the undertow. She dared not slip out far enough to be caught in it, or she would surely drown.

She was losing her grip on the rocks. Just when her strength began to fail, something pulled her back toward the natural jetty—something that felt like a set of jaws sunken deep in her soggy pelerine. Shaking the soaked hair out of her eyes, she squinted, for they smarted from the salt. She blinked, clearing her vision, expecting to find Nicholas towering over her, but it wasn't Nicholas. There, with his claws dug into seaweed and rock, and his sharp teeth sunken in the saturated wool of her wrapper, stood Nero on the jetty pulling her toward it, away from the rising tide.

He seemed to have adopted the same strategy, tugging her closer as the waves receded until she got a grip on the rocks and let him pull her out of the cove to the strand alongside. Conditions there were no less treacherous. It had happened just as Nicholas said it would. The beach had flooded in seconds, cutting her off, and she wasn't out of danger yet. The stone stairs seemed so far away. How could she have come all that distance? How would she ever get back? The waves were coming faster now, driving her higher, pinning her against the sheer-faced wall of Ravencliff.

Nero still had a hold on her wrapper. He'd torn it, and it was dragging, but he wouldn't let go. He was in front of her, backing up, dragging her toward higher ground, and the steps.

"My God, Nero, don't let go!" she cried, as he shifted his jaws for a firmer grip. The shaggy ruff of silver-tipped hair about his face was plastered wet to his head; and his eyes, those dark, penetrating eyes, never left her face as he inched her along toward safety. He whined as if in reply, seeming to take great care to catch nothing in those clamped tight jaws but fabric. "Sometimes, I do believe you are more human than any of the two-legged creatures in this godforsaken place," she observed, indulging in a giddy laugh now that safety was almost within reach.

Still whining, the animal continued to back toward the steps, his breath puffing from flared nostrils, his broad chest expanding and contracting visibly. His ribcage seemed about to burst for the labor, but he didn't let her go until they reached the stone staircase. He barked then. It was the second time she'd heard his bark, and it rooted her to the spot. The first time she'd heard it, he was menacing Mallory. There was triumph in it now. Deep and rich, guttural and mellow, it sounded more like the bark of a wolf than a dog's high-pitched cry. He shook himself then, and when she flung her arms around his neck, thanking him for his labor, he washed the salt from her face with his long, pink tongue.

"I love you, you brave boy," she murmured. "I see you're in a better humor this morning." She tried to see his wound, but his chest and forelegs were plastered with seaweed, mud, and ooze.

He nudged her toward the steps then, and she started to climb thinking he would follow, but he didn't. He barked again, then turned and raced back the way they'd come through the creaming surf and flying spindrift, and disappeared toward higher ground above the cove, his plaintive howl living after him. It was only then that Sara realized the sea had claimed her Morocco leather slippers.

She began to climb. Her clothes were clinging wet to her body, and her hair had come loose from its confines, the grosgrain ribbons hanging limp about her shoulders. She was so cold, her teeth were chattering, but it was gooseflesh unrelated to the chill that froze her halfway up the cliff. What of Nicholas? Had he been cut off by the storm, as well?

No, he was too clever for that. He must know another way to reach the house, too. Still, his absence didn't settle well on her, and she continued to climb, anxious to reach Ravencliff before he did, and order herself before she had to face him again.

Nell was waiting beside the service entrance door, wringing her pinafore into a hopeless twist, as Sara picked her way barefoot over the rocky apron.

"Oh, la, my lady!" the girl cried, tears streaming down her face. "I'd given ya up for dead."

"Has the . . . master returned?" Sara panted, crossing the threshold just before the rain came.

"I dunno, my lady," said the maid. "I ain't seen him."

"Thank you, Nell. How long have you been standing here?"

"Since I made your excuses ta Dr. Breeden for nuncheon, my lady. I done that as soon as ya left."

"Then, there must be another way up here from the strand. No one could survive down there in that. If it weren't for Nero, I'd have drowned. The strand disappeared in seconds, Nell."

"That scruffy old dog, my lady?"

Sara nodded. "It was, indeed."

"How are ya ever goin' ta get past the hall boy like that?" the abigail whined.

Sara thought for a moment. "I'm not going to have to," she said. "Go up and fetch my hooded cloak. Pretend you're taking it below to press it off with the flat iron or something, if anyone questions you. Then go back up and occupy that hall boy—get him away from that door however you have to, so I can get back into my suite."

"But how, my lady?"

"I'm sure you'll be enterprising, Nell. How did you manage it with Peters? Try not to get caught out this time. You weren't very clever then. If you had been, Peters would still be here with you. I knew it all the while, and I haven't said a word to his lordship about your assignations with that boy. I've kept my part of the bargain, just as I said I would. I needn't remind you that you owe me for that—not just about Nero's visits, either. If you fail me now and it all comes out, because it surely will, I shall have no choice but to tell the truth. He cannot dismiss me, but he will sack you in a heartbeat."

Sara regretted her words the minute they slipped out; the girl's stricken look was more than she could bear. It wasn't like her to be mean-spirited, but if Peters hadn't sneaked off to meet the little abigail, none of this would be happening. It was beyond the beyond.

"I'm sorry, Nell," she said. "I'm overset. I'm soaked to the skin, and I need to get into a hot tub, else I come down with pneumonia. Here's what let's do . . . tell the boy—whatever his name is—"

"It's Wallace, my lady, beggin' your pardon."

"Very well, tell Wallace to go and fetch water for my tub. Tell him you'll stand guard until he returns. The minute he's out of sight, collect my cloak and bring it down—not here. I cannot be seen in the halls looking like this. Someone will surely tell the master. I shall wait in the alcove by the stairs. Hurry now. His lordship could return at any moment."

The girl scampered off then, and Sara crept along the hall and waited in the shadows. Minutes later, Wallace hurried along the hallway on his mission, and Nell came shortly after with her cloak. Once safely back in the tapestry suite, Sara closed herself inside her sitting room out of the servants' sight, while each in their turn carried up the water to fill her tub.

Outside, the storm had worsened. Horizontal rain slid down the windowpanes in sheets, and wind gusts rattled the glass. Sara could scarcely see below, though she strained her eyes, and wiped the fogged window hoping for a glimpse of Nicholas's black greatcoat sailing over the edge, but the apron below and the stone fence that housed the steps were vacant.

Nell came to fetch her once the tub was filled, and she walked through the suite, hesitating in the foyer. No. She would *not* lock the door. She would leave it just as she always did, just free of the latch, but not noticeably open. The sentries weren't guarding her against four-legged intruders, only the two-legged kind, Alexander Mallory in particular. Nero had saved her life twice. If he wanted to take refuge in her rooms, he was welcome. With that decided, she moved on toward her dressing room, and the waiting tub.

"*Bloody hell!*" Nicholas trumpeted, bursting in on Mills, who was preparing his toilette for the evening meal in his dressing room.

"Oh, my lord!" the valet breathed, staggering back from him. "Where is your shirt—your good pantaloons, and hose? And where has your bandage gone? Oh, now! Look at your coat! I shall never be able to beat the sand out of it."

Nicholas glanced down at what was left of his clothes, and hurled his Hessians to the floor. He stood barefoot, wearing only his drawers underneath the caped greatcoat hanging off his shoulder. It dragged on the carpet, filthy with beach debris.

"I would have returned before the storm hit, but for the baroness," he said. "Perhaps I should tell her to *do* the things I do not wish her to do. Perhaps then we might have order instead of chaos in this damnable house." He reached into one soggy greatcoat pocket and produced the pistol, then drew Sara's Morocco leather slippers from the other and tossed them on the lounge.

"My lady went down on the strand?" said Mills. He was incredulous.

"She did, and but for Nero, she would have drowned down there."

"*Nero*, my lord?"

"I couldn't very well confront her naked, old boy, now, could I? That delayed me, and I'm fortunate to have escaped with my life, let alone my drawers." He peeled off his great-coat. "Where is Dr. Breeden?" he queried, tossing it down after the Hessians.

"In the herbarium preparing your cordial," said Mills, stooping to gather the coat and boots.

"He will be happy to know that the deuced 'cordial' seems to be working, else it would all have been over down there just now."

"Oh, my lord! You were able to control the transformation?"

"After a fashion," said Nicholas, "until her damnable shoes came crashing down on my head riding a wave." He gestured toward the waterlogged Morocco leather slippers.

"Oh, but that is such good news, my lord!"

"It's too sporadic to be good news yet, old boy. Let us just say that it's progress, and leave it for now, shall we?"

"You will want your bath, my lord," said Mills, shuffling off to dispose of his wet burden. "I shall see that it is prepared at once."

"No bath," Nicholas said, halting the valet in his tracks. "I should think I've had enough cold water for the moment. Fetch me a towel, and my dressing gown," he said, stripping off his drawers. "I'll have a word with her ladyship. I cannot let this go by unaddressed, Mills. It's far too serious."

Mills handed him the towel. "Shouldn't you dress first, my lord?" he asked.

"There isn't time," Nicholas said, snatching Sara's shoes from the lounge. "Let us just say that I've used up my ration of progress for the day, and let it go at that. Now, fetch me that damned dressing gown, and for God's sake, *hurry!*"

Sixteen

Sara was chilled to the marrow. Despite the gauzy voile wrapper she wore into the bath, she was shivering, the hot, perfumed water notwithstanding.

"It's no use, Nell," she said. "I shall get out now. I doubt I shall ever be warm again."

She surged to her feet in the hip bath just as Nicholas burst through the dressing room door. A startled gasp escaped her throat as he reached her in two strides, tossed down her shoes, and clamped both hands around her upper arms.

"This is twice now that I have returned your shoes to you, madam," he seethed. "If I come by them again, I shall keep them." He glanced toward the abigail. "Leave us!" he charged, and Nell scampered off, a cry on her lips glancing back as he lifted Sara out of the tub.

Sara swatted his hands away from her arms, and tried without success to cover all her charms at once. The thin, wet voile was transparent, clinging to the contours of her body like a second skin as the water flowed the length of her, outlining every curve. Nothing was denied his eyes, which feasted upon her like a half-starved animal.

She glanced down at what had him so enthralled. Her breasts had stretched the wet fabric taut, and her nipples were clearly visible, dark and tall, showing through the cloth. The wrapper gapped in front, and his hooded gaze followed the sliver of exposed flesh to the mound of golden hair between her thighs that she didn't have enough hands to hide. Her breath caught in sputters, and she tugged the wrapper closed, but it was no use. She could as well have been naked.

Why she was covering up, she couldn't imagine. This was her perfect opportunity, was it not? Judging from the look of those sensuous obsidian eyes devouring her, it wouldn't take much to seduce him. It had nearly happened on their last encounter, when they were both reasonably clothed. Now, they were both nearly naked. He had nothing on underneath that dressing gown. It was carelessly tied, showing her a glimpse of dark hair below his waist, and the hint of an arousal challenged the burgundy satin.

Her breath caught again, and she tugged her wet wrapper closer around her. It was no use. She couldn't play herself false. She was no seductress. She wouldn't know where to begin—but he did. It was in his eyes, in the rapid rise and fall of his broad chest, in the hot breath puffing against her face, as he stooped over her. His scent wafted toward her, threading through her nostrils, surrounding her, entering her. She drank him in, as foxed by his closeness as a lord in his cups. Oh, how she wished she were more experienced! How she wished she could spread his dressing gown wide, and slide her hands beneath it, burying her fingers in the soft, silky hair she'd dreamed of fondling again since the night she braved his chamber. All she could do was stand and gaze with longing anticipation of that magnificent body impacting with hers.

All at once, his demeanor changed. It was as though he'd just awoken from a trance. He seized her arms again and shook her. She cried out, unprepared for rough handling, but he made no move to let her go.

"You were told not to go down to the strand," he snapped.

"How would you know where I've been?" she challenged. "You're never about when you're wanted. Are you having me followed whenever I leave my room now?"

"I saw you . . . climbing back up," he said. "And if I had not done, one of the servants would have told me. They are well aware of the dangers, even if you are not. You could have drowned."

"But I didn't, thanks to the poor dog you're trying to kill," she sallied. "What were you doing down there, Nicholas? Do you often bathe in the ocean in such weather?"

"I have lived here all my life," he returned. "I am accustomed to . . . bathing in all sorts of weather, but my habits are not the issue here. Your obedience is."

"My *'obedience'*?" she cried. "How dare you presume to treat me with no more regard than you do that dog!"

"Sara, your safety is important to me, and I explained to you that trust was paramount in this relationship. Blind obedience is trust. You agreed to that when you accepted my proposal."

"And you evidently look down upon me for doing so. I was afraid you might. Alexander Mallory certainly did. Why should I expect more from you?"

"Do not include me in that company," he growled.

"I was wrong to come here . . . to hope for your respect."

"Balderdash! You know better." He loosened his grip, but he didn't let her go.

"I know nothing of the sort! You treat me like one of the servants—someone you can order about . . . someone beneath you. While that may be true, I am hardly a scullion. I am the daughter of a colonel in His Majesty's Royal Army—a knight, and a hero recognized by the Crown, who fell prey to the lure of the gambling hells, and died in dun territory.

Do not tar me with the same brush. The only gamble I've ever taken was coming here. As you can see, I have no talent for it."

"Why did you agree to this?" he murmured.

"I was dying in that place," she said, "eating maggoty food, fending off two-legged predators, when I wasn't fending off the four-legged variety. I wouldn't have lasted, having to fight and claw my way through each day—each *hour*—with nothing save more of the same to look forward to. Oh, I could have borne it in the physical sense, I suppose, but it would have made me like the others . . . someone I couldn't bear to become—someone I would have *had* to become in order to survive. Your . . . invitation came at a most fortuitous moment. They were coming to select girls for the brothels from among the younger prisoners. I would most certainly have been taken. Virgins bring a higher price. The jailers would have been only too happy to turn me over for a handsome reward. Your missive was like an answer to my prayers, as if all my dreams had come true. But those dreams have turned into a nightmare."

Something terrible lived in his eyes—rage and terror beyond bearing, and she looked away. She was close to tears, but she wouldn't give him the satisfaction.

"Why did you climb down to the strand?"

"I was following you."

"Why?"

"To finish our conversation earlier. I did take advantage of the footmen's presence in the breakfast room to make my point, but there are some things even I choose not to discuss in front of the servants. I wanted to speak with you alone. It seemed the perfect place to do that."

"What did you want to say to me, Sara?"

"That doesn't matter anymore."

"Why?"

"Because it isn't important. I want you to let me go, Nicholas. I shall seek employment as a governess, or a companion—whatever respectable position I can find—and pay back every halfpenny you've spent upon me if it takes me the rest of my life. I beg only that you do not return me to that place. I would rather be dead than sold to a brothel."

"You are my wife, Sara, I cannot let you go," he said.

"So I *am* a prisoner here, after all!"

"No," he groaned.

"What then? What am I, Nicholas? I don't know what you want. *You* don't know what you want. One thing I do know, you do not want me. I'm a bride who isn't a wife, a companion who isn't even a friend. I want to be both, but you won't let me, and you won't tell me why. How dare you speak to me of trust? *How do you dare!*"

His eyes were boring into her—those terrible eyes that had the power to melt her resolve. She couldn't meet them. All at once she was in his arms. Crushing her close, he took her lips with a hungry mouth, and parted them with a skilled tongue and one swift thrust. It took her breath away. Cupping her head in his hand, he tasted her deeply, feeding on the moan in her throat, matching it with his own feral growl that seemed to come from the very depths of him, resonating through her body in a way that weakened her knees.

He slid his hand along her arched throat, and spread the wrapper wide, then tore the sash from his dressing gown and wrenched her against his naked hardness. Sara held her breath. Seizing her hand, he drove it down to his sex. She uttered a muffled cry through lips trapped beneath his bruising mouth as it responded to her touch, throbbing like a pulse beat. He drew his head back, gulping air, his hooded eyes dilated with desire.

"Does this feel as though I do not want you, Sara?" he panted, wrapping her fingers around his engorged member. "It is all I can do to resist you . . . to keep from ravishing you, but I can, and I will, because I *must*. I cannot have the luxury of you in that way."

"But why?"

"I cannot tell you why . . . not yet . . . perhaps, not ever. That remains to be seen." He released his grip on her wrist. Her flesh was on fire. It was as though molten lava were flowing through her belly and thighs, moistening the mound between her legs that pulsed like a heartbeat matching the rhythm of his manhood—his very life shuddering against her fingers. She let her hand slip away, and he leaned back, closing her wrapper with painstaking control. "I am asking you to trust me," he went on, "to do as I say, and give me time. I told you once that, please God, this is only temporary."

"I shall not embarrass you in front of your guest," she murmured, trying to sound as though she had command of her runaway emotions. It fell flat. How could he believe it, when she could not? She was a shambles, mortified and cold, standing there in the clinging wet negligee. Her whole body ached for the passion in his, which he denied her. *Why?* It was time to force the issue. "I shall advertise at once," she said.

"You cannot do that," he barked. "Baroness Walraven cannot go into service. You know better than to suggest such a thing."

"Well, be that as it may, you have until Dr. Breeden leaves to explain yourself, my lord," she said, "because, unless you do, when his coach arrives I shall leave in it with him."

"And go where?" he returned.

"I've no idea, only that I must. If you cannot answer me by then, I will have to conclude that I am right, or that you are mad. Either way, I will go mad if I stay. I've said my piece. It's your coil to unravel now, Nicholas."

He snatched a towel from the chiffonier. "Cover up. You shall catch your death," he said, as though he'd just realized she was standing barefoot in a puddle of scented water, in a wrapper still dripping on the parquetry. "I shall make your excuses. You cannot come downstairs in such a state. I shall

170

have Mrs. Bromley fetch up a dinner tray, and an herbal tea to warm you. Dr. Breeden has prescribed a rose hips tonic . . . to build you back up after your ordeal in the priest hole."

"I don't need 'building up,'" she snapped.

"You will do as he says," said Nicholas unequivocally. "I shan't have consumption on my conscience. It's burdened enough over you as it is."

"To borrow your favorite phrase, 'do we have an understanding,' Nicholas?" she said, clutching the towel against her.

"Sara—"

"And I want the hall boys dismissed from my suite at once," she put in. "I will not live under guard."

"That has already been done," he said on a sigh. "I . . . I concede on that one point, but only so long as you keep your doors latched. Alex has not turned up yet. While he is at large, you are in danger. I know you do not understand this, but you must obe—humor me in this." He tugged his dressing gown closed in front. He was still aroused, and he raked back the damp hair from his brow. She took a step toward him. "*No!*" he growled, backing away. "Do not touch me! Do not tempt me . . . again—*never again!*"

"Very well, Nicholas," she said, "but there is one more condition. Do not think to harm that dog. You are not to lift one finger against him again, or I shall have the guards in. I shall leave in the clothes I came in. You may keep everything you've given me, but when I go, Nero goes with me."

He turned on his heel and stormed from the dressing room then. She flinched when the door slammed, though she watched him fling it shut. Frozen to the spot, she stared after him for a long moment. When she took a step toward the bell pull to summon Nell, her foot caught in something and she tripped. It was Nicholas's dressing gown sash. Snatching it up, she ran through her suite, through the bedchamber to the foyer only to pull up short on the threshold.

The door was wide open, and there, in a crumpled heap at her feet, lay his dressing gown spilling into the hall. Nicholas was nowhere in sight.

Nero ran in circles before the hearth in the master suite dressing room, his plaintive howl echoing over the voice of the storm. Faster and faster he pranced, his sharp nails clacking on the hearthstone and his footpads thudding on the Aubusson carpet, as his path grew ever wider, skirting Mills, who was standing with a quilted throw at the ready.

He howled again, a mournful supplication trailing off on the wind, and sprang into the air, no more than a blur of shaggy fur and sinew expanding to Nicholas's full height, surging into a sweaty mass of naked flesh and muscle, whose cords were strung like bowstrings. Panting and heaving like the animal he had left behind, Nicholas dropped to his knees before the hearth, his tousled head bowed.

It had happened again. Twice in one day. Dry sobs and a moan left his throat, and he pounded the parquetry at the edge of the rug with both his clenched fists.

"Take ease, my lord," said Mills, covering him with the throw. "It's over now." A mad, misshapen laugh was Nicholas's reply, and the valet took hold of his arm. "Here, let me help you up."

"I left my dressing gown behind in her rooms," Nicholas groaned, struggled to his feet.

"You have other dressing gowns, my lord," said the valet, settling him in the wing chair. "I shall fetch you another at once."

"That isn't the point," Nicholas returned. "How shall I explain it?"

"I'm sure I don't know, my lord. Calm yourself. There's nothing to be done about it now. I shall be but a moment."

Nicholas leaned his head back against the tufted chairback, and indulged in a long, lingering moan. No region of his body was exempt from the pain of the stressful transformation, no tendon spared the torturous effects of strain. Making matters worse, his libido was charged, as it always seemed to be when he was exhausted. He was beyond exhausted now, and there had been no release. His sex still throbbed for need of her—still grew for want of her, and he shifted uneasily in the chair.

Mills shuffled back across the threshold carrying a blue brocade and satin dressing gown, and helped him into it. His cordial waited on the chiffonier, and the valet brought it to him.

"Drink it, my lord—all of it," he said, offering the strong-smelling concoction.

"It's too late for the damnable nostrum now," Nicholas snapped, refusing the glass.

"For this time, perhaps," the valet persisted. "Please, my lord, you were doing so well."

Another mad laugh was his response, and after a moment, Nicholas took the glass and tossed back the cordial with a grimace.

"You mustn't be discouraged, my lord."

"Mustn't I?" Nicholas growled. "I've dismissed the hall boys from her suite, and made a fool of myself doing it after swearing not to."

"Was that wise, my lord?"

"It was *necessary*," Nicholas returned, "else one of them see what happened to me just now. I knew I was at risk for the transformation when I went down there. That's why I couldn't chance it fully dressed. It was a wise decision. I almost didn't make it out of her rooms, Mills. I know she won't lock that door, and now she's unprotected. I shall have to keep watch myself, whenever I can, which shan't be easy, while Dr. Breeden is in residence. I've neglected him shamefully what with all this."

"Believe me, he understands, my lord. Why, he's closeted in that herbarium below stairs day and night. He isn't here to socialize. He knows that."

"I want you to make up the bed in the green suite across the hall from my lady's apartments, and take some of my things down there. I'm too far removed up here to be any use in an emergency should one arise, which is almost a foregone conclusion considering her past record in this house. Do it yourself. I do not want the staff privy to this. It will only arouse suspicion, and give the servants more fodder for stories we can ill afford here now."

"Yes, my lord."

"You shall attend me here as usual during the day. I will have to fend for myself in the green suite, so see that I have everything I need. You cannot be seen coming and going."

"Yes, my lord. I shall attend to it while you are at dinner."

"My lady will not be joining us in the dining hall. She is having a tray in her rooms. Take care that she doesn't see you, and look sharp. I needn't remind you that Alex is still missing. I shall be closeted with Dr. Breeden in the master suite after dinner until quite late. Perhaps you ought to stay in the green suite until I relieve you. She has given me an ultimatum. I have until the doctor leaves to explain myself, or she will leave also. I cannot let her do that, Mills. She has nowhere to go, and she'll end up right back in that bridewell carted off to the brothels."

"Very well, my lord," said the valet. "Begging your pardon, but don't you think you should tell her? With Dr. Breeden here to address both your concerns—"

"Tell her what, Mills?"

"About her real role in this madness. It is, after all, the reason you chose her—because you felt of all the females in the realm, this one might be persuaded to understand . . . to end your loneliness. My heart goes out to you, my lord, but you have to take the initiative and trust someone. You cannot expect it of her and not return it in kind."

"If I tell her the whole truth, about her father's involvement in all this, I shall have to tell her the rest."

"Not necessarily, my lord. Mightn't you just tell her

enough to appease, just . . . something? You cannot let her go, my lord. You love her . . . and she loves you."

"Well, it isn't quite that simple, old boy, because she loves someone else, as well."

"My lord?"

His lips gave a wry smile. "She has just informed me that when she leaves, she's taking Nero with her."

Seventeen

"The technique I wish to try is not my own, my lord," said Breeden. "I learned it under the tutelage of Anton Mesmer over forty years ago. I was not yet twenty, as green as grass, and awestruck by the great theosophist, unable to believe my good fortune in being able to study at his home and hospital on the Landstrasse in Vienna. Early on, he practiced healing with the use of magnetized objects with much success, but shortly after I joined him, his methods changed. You see, he began employing what he called 'animal magnetism' in his practice, and that was the beginning of his downfall, I'm afraid."

"Animal magnetism, sir? Wasn't there some sort of brouhaha about Mesmer, and his practices?"

The doctor nodded, taking a sip of sherry from his glass. They were seated in the sitting room of Nicholas's suite, where the doctor had assembled an eclectic assortment of objects on the drum table.

"Yes, there was," said Breeden, "and still is. According to Mesmer, 'animal magnetism' is a substance, an invisible liquid, if you will, which can neither be seen, felt, smelled, touched, or tasted, that every man does possess, in different degrees of strength. This substance can be employed to heal . . . and to adjust the consciousness, so that suggestions might be given the recipient of the therapy that will evoke behavioral change."

"But we have already dismissed the theory that my condition exists only in my mind."

"Yes, we have," said Breeden. "However, the mind can be trained to overcome all sorts of physical behavior."

"And you are hoping—"

"I am hoping that some of Anton Mesmer's theories might benefit you, my lord. To what degree, I cannot say. You are quite correct about the brouhaha. It's only fair to warn you that he was denounced as a charlatan in Austria for his animal-magnetism therapy. He went to Paris, where he wrote a report hoping to redeem himself, in which he stated that animal magnetism was not some sort of mysterious secret cure-all as the Austrians feared, but rather a scientific phenomenon that wanted study in order to reap its benefits for mankind.

"His cures were phenomenal. The clergy, of course, attributed all that to the Devil, but the French aristocracy revered him as a saint. He had much success, and the favor of the Queen of France, but the King ordered an investigation. While the appointed committee could not fault Mesmer's results, they would not sanction something too illusive to be perceived by the five senses, and he was denounced again. Then came the Revolution. With neither fame nor fortune, and having lost what friends those attributes attract, he left Paris and settled somewhere near Zurich. Then two years ago, he went to Meersburg, where he died this past March, working amongst the poor. I tell you all this because I shan't use methods of which you do not approve. My personal belief is that the man was ahead of his time, and that one day his methods will be appreciated—even revered. There is no question that they work; how well in your case, remains to be seen."

"You have used these methods on others?" said Nicholas.

"Yes, but none with your particular affliction."

"What must I do?"

"Relatively little, my lord," said the doctor. "Little more than you've already done."

"I don't understand. . . ."

"When you were shot, and in pain, while we waited for Mills to bring Mrs. Bromley's nostrum, I used my 'powers,' if you will, of animal magnetism, which Dr. Mesmer helped me develop in my training, to ease your suffering. Do you remember?"

"I remember you telling me to concentrate upon your words . . . upon the candle."

"And what happened, my lord, when you did as I bade you?"

"The pain was lessened. We had an almost normal conversation."

The doctor nodded. "I was trying to see if you would be receptive to my methods."

"And . . . was I?"

"To a degree," said the doctor. "You have a very strong will, my lord; stronger than most. You fought the passionflower tea to a fare-thee-well in order to stay in control, and suffered needlessly for it. I believe the only reason my method succeeded somewhat was because you were unaware of what I was doing, and you were in great pain. It remains to be seen if I can treat you with full knowledge of the process. You need to learn to trust, my lord."

"So says Mills as well," Nicholas responded on the tail of a weary sigh. "I have too long trusted no one but myself completely enough to relinquish control to another—not even to him, and he has seen me through this nightmare from the beginning."

"Mills was your father's valet as well, I believe you said?"

"Yes."

"And he can give no insight into your father's condition after being bitten in India?"

"Only that Father suffered from dreadful headaches, and often became irritable. The wound never healed, and toward the end, he spent more time away from Ravencliff than he did on the estate. Whatever his condition, he confided in no one, which was probably why Mills insinuated himself into my dilemma early on. He sensed that something was terribly wrong. Father shut him out, and Mills was devastated when he died. I don't believe he has ever recovered from the guilt of not being able to help Father while he lived. He was determined not to let that be the case with me.

"I'm sure you've noticed that our relationship is something more than simply that of valet and master, and that I oftentimes allow him to speak out of turn, as it were. Aside from the obvious, Mills has been surrogate father, father-confessor, mentor, guardian, and friend to me since I could stand without my knees buckling, and the conventional rules are often bent where he is concerned. The staff is accustomed to it, but it can be jarring to an outsider used to more formal interaction between the upper classes and their servants, which is why I mention it. Also, do not be afraid to employ him in your methods, and feel free to question him however you will. I am too close to the situation to be objective, and his opinions might be of help to you. He has witnessed almost all of my transformations, the latest just this afternoon."

"I shall avail myself, of course, my lord," said the doctor. "Meanwhile, there are several things I wish to try." He gestured toward the drum table. "I have set out several objects here that I would like to use in conjunction with animal magnetism. You will see there a simple magnet, and several other metal objects that have been magnetized as well. I shall lay them so"—he illustrated by laying his fingers on

Nicholas's brow and temples—"while employing much the same method that I did when you were shot. It is most relaxing, which is what is needed if we are to achieve any measure of success."

"And those glasses there?" Nicholas asked, pointing to several brandy snifters containing varying levels of water.

"A glass *armonica*," said the doctor. "A primitive one, I will allow, but effective nonetheless. Dr. Mesmer had astounding results with the armonica. It is nothing more than a musical instrument, and Anton Mesmer loved music above all things. He was quite an accomplished pianist and cellist, you know. It is hardly unusual that he would find a way to utilize such an instrument as the armonica in his practice. When one moistens one's fingers and runs them around the rim of the glass, a tone is produced, depending upon the amount of water it holds. Therefore, glasses set out containing different measures of water produce different sounds. The result is music of a sort. I shall employ all these methods to induce a temporary trancelike state in you, my lord, during which I shall introduce a suggestion to your subconscious mind that will hopefully carry over into your conscious state once you awaken."

"That is all?"

"That is much, my lord. If we succeed—I say 'we' because I cannot do this alone—I will have ordered your mind to reject the transformation. What you must do is relax your guard, and trust me to do so. Nothing can be done lest you believe we will succeed."

Nicholas heaved a speculative sigh, and considered it.

"What I am saying, my lord, is that you must put yourself in my hands completely."

"I know what you're saying," said Nicholas. "And I shall, of course, do everything in my power to aid your success, but—"

"*Our* success," the doctor interrupted. "And there can be

no 'buts,' my lord. You will either comply, or I will proceed without your knowledge to affect such a state in you that can be reached by autosuggestion. It is that, or I shall thank you for your most gracious hospitality and leave you as I found you. The choice is yours, which is why I have explained it so thoroughly. There is no risk. We shall either succeed, or we shall fail. The worst that can happen is that you will remain as you are . . . unchanged."

"There is no choice, Dr. Breeden," said Nicholas. "Proceed with your experiments, and let us see how we fare, eh?"

"As you wish, my lord."

"If we do succeed, is there a chance I could be cured?" Nicholas inquired.

"There is no cure, my lord," the doctor returned. "We do not even know what it is that we are trying to cure. The most we can hope for is to stop the transformations; the least, that we be able to control them satisfactorily enough for you to enjoy a somewhat normal life."

"Does that include cohabiting with my bride? Forgive my bluntness, but it is at issue, and I need to know."

The doctor hesitated. "Without animal magnetism treatments, you haven't a prayer, my lord," he said flatly. "That is, if your performance today—despite my new cordial designed to ease you in that regard—is any example. And above all, no matter what, to bring a child forth from your union could pass the condition on in either the same, or a lesser form. It's impossible to say for certain."

"But it . . . might be possible to consummate this marriage?"

"I say again, at the risk of repetition, you need to tell my lady. She ought to be prepared, no matter which way the pendulum swings. If she were willing to risk it, that might ease the tension in you that makes transformation under those circumstances likely. If on the other hand she is content to remain your wife without conjugal fulfillment, knowing your predicament, that gives you another option. If she is not, or if the situation is too repugnant to her, she needs to know it now, before things go too far between you."

Nicholas sighed deeply. "She has given me an ultimatum. I am to explain myself before you leave, or she plans to leave for London with you. I cannot tell her the truth and risk her carrying tales if she chooses to leave Ravencliff, and if I don't tell her, I shall lose her. There is more. You know, of course, that she is convinced it was Nero that I fired upon. She believes I mean to be rid of him one way or another, and she intends to take him with her when she leaves."

"That isn't possible, my lord!"

"But she doesn't know that."

"All the more reason why you must tell her."

"Mills thinks that I should tell her something short of the whole truth, something to appease her while we sort out this coil."

"A half-truth?"

"Exactly."

"Or you could let her go, concede that you've made a ghastly mistake, and put the whole unfortunate business behind you."

"It's already too late for me to do that. I didn't expect to fall in love with her. That was not part of the bargain, and I have done everything within my power to discourage her. I've allowed her to perceive me as an ill-mannered tyrant, and a boor. I've insulted her intelligence . . . hurt her feelings. She has no idea who or what I am as a man . . . as a gentleman, and still . . ."

"Love, my lord, will go where it's sent. Cupid's arrow has never been known to give quarter to obstacles it its path. If it is true love, it will withstand the truth. If it is illusion, it will fall by the wayside."

"But at what cost?"

"Whatever the cost, it is not too dear for the purchase of truth. No union can be built on a foundation of lies."

"Every instinct in me warns to hold my peace."

"Then you must follow those instincts, but at the very least examine them thoroughly."

"There is something else that we need to discuss before we commence," said Nicholas. "I had to dismiss the hall boy outside my lady's suite. If I hadn't, he would have seen me transform this afternoon. I shall take his place."

"*You*, my lord?"

"I shall be sleeping in the green rooms across from the tapestry suite until all this business with Alex has been resolved. He must be found, and no one but you, Mills, and myself can search for him now. It's been too long, Dr. Breeden. He would have transformed back by now if he could. Unless I miss my guess, he remains in wolf form. We needn't expect that the baroness will not lock her door. She means to protect Nero from *me*, and that leaves her vulnerable to *him*. I doubt I shall do much sleeping, but I shall be better able to help her from there than from this distance, and she must be monitored."

"A wise decision, my lord."

"No one but Mills and yourself must know this, Dr. Breeden. I cannot have the servants bandying it about, making their own conclusions. The guards came 'round this morning because of *on-dits* they've been spreading in the village about Nero, and Mills tells me that a plot is hatching below stairs to kill him outright. They must not be involved in any of our activities here now."

"I quite understand."

"Keep your pistol loaded and at the ready. I shall see that Mills is armed as well. Just take care which wolf you shoot."

Nicholas was too agitated for the magnet treatment to work. It wasn't like he hadn't warned the doctor; there were just too many thoughts tumbling around in his mind to allow Breeden's soft voice to come to the fore. The magnets didn't present enough outside stimulus to attract and capture his attention. All he could think of was Sara, and how close he'd come to consummating their marriage. His loins ached to finish what he'd started, his heart was standing in the way of common sense, and his head was reeling with dilemmas—one greater than the next.

It was not so with the armonica, however. The doctor had prepared the glasses to give off pleasant tones not unlike the soft strains of a lullaby. Aside from a dwindling fire in the hearth, only one candle branch was lit on the drum table. Nicholas's eyelids began to slide shut in the soft semidarkness, as he reclined on the lounge listening to Dr. Breeden's skilled fingers extract music from such simple elements as glass and water.

"That's it, my lord," Breeden murmured, his soothing voice seeming to flow on the strange melody. "Listen to the music. Let it carry you away. See where it takes you. Imagine yourself floating in the quiet waters of a tide pool. Let the water buoy you . . . let it bear you up. You are drifting now, free of all cares. They are draining away, flowing out to sea. They are almost out of sight. You can no longer recognize them. They cannot return. The music bars their way. You feel lighter as you float in the water. You are protected, like a child in its mother's womb. Drift, my lord . . . just . . . drift—"

"Would one of you please tell me what is going on here?" said a soft voice from behind.

It was Sara, standing on the threshold, Nicholas's burgundy dressing gown and sash looped over her arm.

Eighteen

Nicholas vaulted off the lounge at sight of Sara, and Dr. Breeden's fingers struck a discordant, high-pitched squeak as he gripped the edge of the snifter he was circling. The glass shattered, piercing his thumb.

"This belongs to you, my lord," Sara said to Nicholas, dropping the dressing gown on an antique Glastonbury chair beside the door. "You left it behind on my doorstep."

Nicholas swallowed. He was caught out, and he cast a sidelong glance in the doctor's direction, but there was no help for him there. Breeden was binding his wounded thumb with his handkerchief.

"What the Devil are you doing up here at this hour, madam?" Nicholas snapped. Anger had always been his best defense with her. He was hoping he hadn't lost his touch, but he was still groggy from the doctor's experiment, and at a distinct disadvantage. "You could have rung for one of the servants to return it. Did you hear nothing I said earlier? There are dangers here of which you know nothing."

"Well, I think it's time that I did know something," she said, tapping her foot, "beginning with *that*." She gestured to the dressing gown. "You seem to have a propensity for going about in the nude, sir. This is thrice now that I have come upon your clothes without you in them. Would you care to explain this quirk?"

"I would not," he snapped. *Thrice?* He could only recall two occasions, both that very day. When was the third? "I dismissed the hall boys from outside your rooms in good faith," he said. "I can just as easily reinstate them. The house rules are simple. Why can you not abide by them? You have come to harm twice now for defying my authority and ignoring my directives. I should think by now you'd be ready to yield to the dictates of common sense, madam! There are dangers—"

"Yes, yes, dangers of which I am unaware. So you've said. I can give no credence to any such 'dangers' without an explanation of them. If they are not serious enough to warrant being clarified, they are of no consequence to me, sir, and I cannot—no, *will not*—take them seriously. Well? I am waiting, Nicholas. Tell me what dangers lurk in wait for me in your house, sir."

Just then Mills skittered to a halt on the threshold, his arrival raising Nicholas's eyebrow.

"Well done, old boy," Nicholas said, his voice edged with sarcasm.

The valet winced, then glanced about and settled his attention on the doctor, who was still fumbling with his injured thumb.

"You're bleeding, sir," he said, "let me help you."

"It's nothing, Mills," said Breeden. "Just a scratch."

"How have you cut yourself?" said Sara, craning her neck toward the drum table. "Is that some sort of parlor game you two were playing when I came in just now? Somewhat hazardous I should think, if it results in bleeding."

"Perhaps I should leave," said the doctor. "It's late, and I need to tend to this. We shall resume tomorrow, my lord."

"I would appreciate that you stay, Dr. Breeden," said

Nicholas. "Mills, help him with that in my dressing room."
He flashed narrowed eyes at Sara. "This shan't take long."

"Yes, my lord," Mills responded, leading the doctor away.

Nicholas spun toward his wife. "Have you gone addled?"
he seethed. "As soon as Mills comes out of that dressing
room, I shall have him escort you back to your rooms, and
you are to *stay* in them, madam."

"Not without some explanations," she returned, taking a
seat on the lounge with a flourish. Why did she lean forward
like that? The neck on her oyster-white muslin frock was
problematic. The last thing he needed was to be reminded of
what lay barely concealed beneath that fetching décolleté.

"You gave me an ultimatum, and I agreed to adhere to it in
the time allotted—not here in my rooms, with . . . with an
audience, for God's sake! Have you lost all sense of propriety?"

"I prefer to call it a 'challenge,' my lord, our little bargain.
But you put paid to that when you shed your dressing gown
on my doorstep. I want some answers, and I am not leaving
these rooms until I have them."

Nicholas began to pace the carpet. Mills was right. He had
to tell her something, but what? The woman was intelligent
to a fault. She would not be easily duped. There was one consolation, however, and he almost laughed aloud when it
came to him. The answer she so eagerly sought was so
bizarre that the very intelligence that led her to this moment
would never accept what he laid at her feet. Literally. He
hardly believed it himself, and that the doctor did was only
due to his theosophical persuasions. Had he been a conventional medical practitioner, Mark Breeden would have certified Nicholas a bedlamite; he was certain of it.

"I am waiting, my lord," his wife said.

"I am . . . unwell, Sara," he began, stopping in front of her
as inspiration struck.

"You look perfectly sound to me," she said, her gaze sliding the length of him. It settled uncomfortably on the bulge

in his faun-colored pantaloons. "All essential parts in working order," she concluded.

"What ails me cannot be seen by the naked eye. It is an internal problem, and Dr. Breeden's visit is not entirely a social one, which I am sure you have gathered. He is here to attempt to correct it, and he may need to extend his stay if these interruptions continue." It was half-truth, but truth nonetheless.

"You're serious," she murmured, clouding. "It isn't something . . . grave?"

"It could be, which is why I need my privacy right now."

"What sort of illness is it, Nicholas?"

"Oh, it isn't contagious," he responded. "I suffer from . . . lapses, and often cannot remember what has transpired during them afterward." The muse he'd courted for inspiration was still with him. The yield was sheer genius if he did say so himself. He had managed to put paid to both issues at once . . . or had he? Why was she looking at him like that? *Pop!* went his euphoria.

"And you couldn't tell me all this before?" she said. "I don't believe you, Nicholas. There's more to it, there has to be. There is no reason why you couldn't have confided that from the first. I am hardly bird-witted. I want you to tell me the truth."

Nicholas threw his arms into the air. "I have done!" he thundered. "But you wouldn't recognize truth if it sneaked up and bit you on your beautiful behind."

"I beg your pardon?" she breathed.

"I shall say it again: I suffer from lapses. The condition is . . . hereditary. They often come upon me when I am angry . . . or aroused, and I am neither saint nor eunuch, which is why I cannot let what happened between us earlier continue. There was never to be anything . . . physical between us. You were told that at the outset. I made it quite clear to you. That is the truth. Since you do not believe me, would you have it from Dr. Breeden?"

"Yes," she said flatly, folding her arms.

"It is all quite true," said the doctor, entering with Mills through Nicholas's adjoining bedchamber, his thumb bound in linen. "His lordship did not wish to worry you, my lady, nor did he wish to raise your hopes." He exhibited his thumb, and crooked it toward the broken glass Mills was attempting to clear away. "That contraption is part of my method," he explained, "a glass armonica, after the fashion of Dr. Anton Mesmer."

"The charlatan?"

The doctor smiled. "The very same," he said, raising her eyebrow. "He was denounced twice, it's true, and accused of black magic as well—a victim of little minds, which is often the way with genius. His methods are revolutionary, my lady, but they have proven most successful. *I* have succeeded with them, and one day his practices will astound the world. Of that I have no doubt."

"What does that armon . . . that thing do?" she queried.

"It relaxes the subject, so that the practitioner may address his subconscious in hopes of alleviating problems which exist in his conscious state."

"It does sound like black magic," she mused.

"To the untrained, I expect it would," said the doctor. "Put your mind at ease, my lady. Whatever your differences with his lordship, set them aside for now. They will impede the process. His mind must be clear and free of stress if I am to succeed. You may rest assured that what we undertake here is for the good, and let us be about this business privately."

"This is all very well," said Sara, rising, "but I have yet to hear what 'dangers' keep me prisoner in my rooms. What insight can you offer in that regard, Dr. Breeden?"

"None, my lady," he replied. "I am not qualified. My expertise does not extend to house matters."

"I can answer that," said Nicholas, "but I doubt my lady would wish me to do so in company."

"To the contrary," said Sara, "go right ahead. I have nothing to hide."

"Very well, but you were warned," Nicholas responded. "Alex Mallory has designs upon you, Sara. The circumstances of our marriage encouraged him to act upon them. He knew we were strangers, and evidently thought that since ours was not an affair of the heart, he might have a chance to win your affections. No doubt he hoped to engage you as his mistress. You told me yourself that he was flirtatious on your journey. You also told me that you had the matter in hand, and I believed you. That was an error on my part."

"Nicholas—"

"Oh, no, my lady, you wished to hear this, and so you shall," he interrupted. "He, whom you had 'in hand,' stole into your rooms foxed and took advantage of you while you were sleeping. He climbed into your bed, put his hands on you—despite your struggling—and very nearly violated you. He has not been seen since, and he has not left Ravencliff. He is hiding somewhere in this house, no doubt biding his time until he can continue his pursuance of you, or revenge himself upon you for your rejection of him. He was badly bitten in that process as I recall. If what I say were not the case, madam, he would have surfaced by now and humbly begged our forgiveness for behaving like a jackanapes in his altitudes, and that would have been the end of it.

"I have known Alex much longer than you, Sara. He is an elbow-bender of some repute, though he has never let his drinking interfere with his situation here before. He knows I will not tolerate it, because I know how ugly he becomes under the influence of liquor. When I say that there is danger, you can take me at my word. That I have not gone into the matter in detail with you before is simply because I did not want to frighten you, but perhaps it is best if I have. This is an enormous house. There are many places where he might hide. We are doing everything in our power to find, and to deal with him, but until we do, I must insist that you abide by my rules. They are for your own protection. If you continue to leave your door open, you are inviting him to return and do worse. That is why he entered your suite in the first place. Finding the door ajar, he assumed it was an invitation for him to do so. He told you that *himself!*

"Now then, it is very late. Mills will see you back to your suite, and make certain you are locked in for the night. I will come and collect you myself at the breakfast hour. This will be the way of it until Alex is dealt with." He nodded a silent command to Mills, who went at once to her side. "Now, good night, Sara."

She made no reply as the valet led her away. Her face was blotched scarlet, and her beautiful blue eyes were downcast. Nicholas's heart sank. He hated himself for embarrassing her. Every instinct nudged him toward sprinting after her, taking her in his arms, and begging her forgiveness. Instead he stood his ground, ramrod-rigid, his hands clenched in white-knuckled fists at his sides.

"Damn and blast!" he gritted.

"Well done, my lord," the doctor said.

"Do you think she believed me?"

"*I* believed you. Do not reproach yourself, my lord. You told her the truth, just not the truth entire."

"I wish I shared your confidence," said Nicholas, "but something in her eyes just now chilled me to the marrow. She isn't convinced. I'm certain of it."

"You shall have to put all this from your mind now, and get back to the business at hand," the doctor said. "I am most encouraged, my lord. Before the interruption, you were very close to allowing me access to your subconscious. We shall try again tomorrow."

"How serious is that?" Nicholas asked, nodding toward the doctor's bandaged thumb.

"It is nothing. Mills is quite capable. We doctors make the

worst patients, I'm afraid. He provided the extra hand that was needed to bind it properly."

"Forgive me for imposing upon you to remain. I haven't lost all semblance of chivalry—although I cannot imagine why, what with this damnable role-playing-the-ogre charade I'm forced to take on to keep Sara at her distance. I knew she would never accept an explanation on the strength of my word alone."

"I quite understand. Mills and I heard much of that conversation from the other room. I simply made my entrance on cue. Get some rest, my lord. We shall get an early start in the morning, and see how well we fare."

"I doubt I'll get much rest, Dr. Breeden," said Nicholas. "Once I've had a word with Mills, and given my lady time to settle down, I shall keep an eye on her apartments from the green suite . . . Just to be sure."

Sara's door seemed open a little wider than she recalled having left it, when she and Mills reached the tapestry suite. She was too overset to tax her brain over inches, however. Besides, everything seemed in order when Mills poked his head in and glanced about.

"Where is Nell, my lady?" he asked.

"I excused her for the evening," she replied. "His lordship has dismissed Peters. He was her sweetheart, and she has fallen into the dismals. It was the least I could do."

"His lordship will not be pleased," said the valet.

"I do not particularly care if his lordship is pleased, or not, but I'm sure you'll go running off to give account."

"We are only concerned for your welfare, my lady."

"Then go tell him what you will, and leave me to my rest. Believe me, I have had enough adventures for one day."

"Yes, my lady," said the valet. Sketching a bow, he turned to go, and had nearly closed the door behind him, when she called him back.

"Wait, Mills," she said. "If I were to ask you a question, would you tell me the truth?"

"I make it a practice always to tell the truth, my lady," he replied.

"Is his lordship's illness serious . . . I mean *really* serious?"

"We are hoping not, my lady," said the valet. "Dr. Breeden is a celebrated healer. We must put our faith and trust in that, and let him do his work unhindered."

He had replied without answering. The man was a study in diplomacy. Was there no one in the house to speak the truth in a firm and direct manner?

"What I want to know, Mills, is whether or not his condition is cause for alarm. I am no milk-and-water miss. I do not come to pieces in a crisis, and I could be of help if needs must."

"His lordship's condition has been with him since a child," said the valet. "It is hardly a cause for alarm. It is . . . unpleasant, and he is in hopes that the doctor's treatments will make it easier to bear. There's really nothing you can do. I will, however, pass on your concern, and your kind offer of assistance."

"Thank you, Mills," she said, as he bowed again and shut the door between them, ending the conversation.

Sara turned away. Despite Nicholas's eloquent oration, she would still have to unravel the coil herself. It wasn't that she didn't believe him. She couldn't shake the feeling that he was holding something back—that they *all* were.

She yawned and stretched. It was fast approaching midnight. It had been a long day. She was just about to enter the bedchamber, when she remembered the door, and crept back to leave it ajar for Nero. That done, she snuffed the candles, and passed through the bedchamber door only to pull up short before a pile of her clothing strewn about the carpet, and a visitor on her bed.

"*Nero!*" she scolded. "Did you make this mess? What a

naughty dog. Come down from there. That is my bed, not yours." It was a playful scolding, and the animal didn't move. Reclining on her pillow, he continued to watch her cross the room. "I see the armoire door is open. Nell must have left it so. Did you pull all this down from inside? You must have done. Shame on you, Nero! This isn't like you at all."

Sara ventured nearer, standing arms akimbo. His leg looked better. Maybe that accounted for his arrogance, or maybe he was just exhausted and out of sorts from his labors on the beach. There was no evidence that he had been down on the strand now. His shaggy coat had dried, and it didn't smell as clean as it might have if he'd just come in from the salty air.

"I wonder if you understand me," she mused. "Sometimes, you seem as though you do, and then on other occasions, like now, it is as though you've come from the wild. I don't know why that should surprise me, considering the way you are ill-used in this house."

The animal blinked, then continued to stare.

"Well, I shan't desert you," Sara said. "You can count upon my protection even more now. He means to kill you, Nero. He's carrying a pistol—I saw it. He intends to shoot you. You must take care in coming here." She dropped her hands to her sides. "Oh, what am I saying, you're only a dog. You don't have the slightest idea of what I'm talking about, do you, boy? No, of course you don't. Well, you cannot spend the night in my bed. You shouldn't be prowling about, either. It isn't safe. You shall have to go wherever it is that you do go, before you are caught out. I would feel dreadful if it were my fault. I shall probably be leaving Ravencliff soon, and when I do I shall take you with me, but not tonight. Get down, boy."

She took a step nearer, but when she reached to nudge him off the counterpane, he stood and hunched his back. Hackles raised, he curled his lips exposing fearsome fangs, and loosed a guttural snarl that stopped her where she stood. Glaring eyes bore down upon her, glowing red. Sara's breath caught in her throat. He looked ready to spring.

Fear spread gooseflesh over her skin, and her hands began to tremble. This was the second time he'd turned on her. He hadn't been the same since Alexander Mallory shot him. She could hardly blame the poor animal, but there could only be one alpha, when it came to a dog and its master. She had enough experience with dogs to know she had to keep the upper hand. There was a porcelain basin and pitcher of water on the dry sink beside the bed, and she snatched the pitcher just as the animal lunged at her, and emptied its contents full in his face as he sprang. The snarl died to a whimper, and he bounded off the bed and streaked out through the foyer door, shaking himself as he went.

Sara's hands were trembling. The echo of his sharp teeth clacking against the porcelain pitcher just inches from her fingers still rang in her ears. She set the pitcher down, and stripped the wet counterpane from the bed. It would dry beside the fire with no one the wiser. Had she taken command? She wasn't sure. For the moment perhaps, but there needed to be another gesture of her disapproval so that there be no question, and she locked the foyer door. Just for tonight. Then, when Nero was calm, and she had beaten back her fear enough to face him without him smelling it, she would unlock the door again.

The room was a shambles, but she dared not wake Nell and explain what had happened. She set about ordering it herself. The last articles of clothing she picked up were the peach silk nightdress and wrapper she had worn the night Alexander Mallory tried to molest her. They had been laundered, the bloodstains removed, and Nell had set them out for her before she retired. By the look of things, Nero had dragged them about the room and marked them just as he had the carpet, and she tossed them into the fire. Seeing them again brought it all back, and she shuddered, took another gown from the chiffonier, and readied herself for bed.

Snuffing out the candle, she climbed into the four-poster. Across the way the dying embers in the hearth had sprung to life again, fed by the cloud of peach silk she'd consigned to the flames. She sighed, trying to forget the images of that other night, of the terror she'd felt beneath Alexander Mallory's demanding body, of the fetid odor of strong liquor on his breath, and the words he'd whispered in her ear: *"You left the door ajar for me, just as I knew you would, didn't you, my lady. You won't be sorry . . ."*

Her eyelids began to droop, but those words wouldn't fade away. Again and again they echoed across her memory, giving her no peace until all at once she vaulted upright in the mahogany four-poster, her heart pounding in her ears.

"How could Nicholas possibly know Alexander Mallory told me that . . . *himself?*" she murmured.

Nineteen

The weather turned fair at the end of the week, and dispositions improved somewhat. Sara kept to herself, dividing her time between her apartments and the vast Ravencliff library during the day, perusing what tomes she found there that might offer insight into Nicholas's mysterious condition. Dr. Breeden resumed his treatments, and Nero made no more visits to Sara's apartments, though she'd left her door ajar since the morning after the incident. She was beginning to worry that her punishment had been too severe. No one had seen Nero in days. It was as if he had vanished in thin air.

Sara finished her menus for the duration of the doctor's stay, which was more than half over. Her ultimatum, as far as she was concerned, had not been met. Nicholas was holding something back; she was certain of it. If he didn't give her credible explanations in the next few days, she would be forced to keep her word and leave Ravencliff, something that would break her heart to do. It would also break her heart to stay as things were between them—loving him, and wanting him with no hope of fulfillment. She had gambled with drastic measures, and failed, unless he chose to yield to her demands and tell her what was really wrong with him, and why he wouldn't make love to her, when it was obvious that he longed to take her in his arms and consummate their marriage.

Also in question was why he wanted to harm Nero. It was one thing to want to be rid of a dog by finding a home for it elsewhere, but Nicholas meant to kill the animal, which she would not let him do. She would take Nero with her if it came down to it, but she couldn't take him if she couldn't find him, and time was running out.

When Smythe came that afternoon to tell her Nicholas wished to see her in the study, Sara collected her menus and followed him below, assuming it was those he wanted to see. She found him pacing before the unlit hearth. For the first time since she'd entered the house, the weather was warm enough that fires could be dispensed with during the day, though she'd been warned that at night, and in dirty weather, she might expect hearth fires all through the summer to chase the dampness in the old house.

"Please be seated, Sara," he said, gesturing toward the lounge.

"I've brought the menus," she said, laying them on his desk before taking her seat.

"That's what I wanted to speak with you about," he said. "We shall need several more . . . more than several, come to that. The doctor will be staying on awhile."

"How long a while?" She had been expecting something like this, and it proved her theory. There was something he was keeping from her. If his condition couldn't be addressed in a fortnight, it was serious indeed.

"He has consented to stay on until he is satisfied that he has done all he can do for me, and until this business with Alex is resolved."

"What is this 'business' with Mr. Mallory, Nicholas, and what has it to do with Dr. Breeden?"

Nicholas hesitated. He wouldn't meet her eyes, though

she inclined her head until he had no choice but to face her, or turn away, which is what he did. It was a simple enough question. Why was he struggling so with it?

"Dr. Breeden has kindly consented to remain until Alex is found," he said. "Nero bit him, if you recall. He will need tending once he surfaces."

"The bite was hardly serious enough to detain the doctor, Nicholas. I saw it happen. It wasn't all that deep."

"Any dog bite is serious," he returned.

Sara's heart leapt. Was he afraid that Nero might be rabid? Her mind reeled back to the animal's behavior of late. That might explain his strangeness, and Nicholas's as well. Could that be why he tried to kill Nero, why he was going about armed? She couldn't bring herself to believe it, much less address it.

"And you expect me to put my life on hold indefinitely for all this?" she said.

"You made a bargain, Sara."

"So did you."

"And I have kept it," he sallied, spinning to face her. "I told you what you wanted to know, and I asked you to trust me."

"What is really wrong here, Nicholas?" she murmured. "And how is it that you haven't found Mr. Mallory in all this time? In a house full of servants with precious little to do, how is it that someone hasn't turned up something? Are you even looking?"

"Of course we're looking," he snapped, "and the servants in this house have much to do. A house this size hardly runs itself."

The look in his eyes was devastating. There was something under the surface of that hooded gaze that grabbed her heart like a fist. He wore no waistcoat or jacket, though his neck cloth was tied to perfection beneath modest shirt points that framed the shadowy cleft in his chin. His breathing was rapid and audible, the rise and fall of his well-muscled chest stretching his Egyptian cotton shirt to its limit. Her eyes drank in the rest of him—the hands fisted at his sides, the skintight black pantaloons that left nothing to the imagination, tucked into polished Hessians. He looked like an animal about to spring, just as he always did during their encounters. She wanted to rush into his arms, to feel them, strong and warm around her again, clasping her fast to that magnificent body denied her, making an end to her longing for more of him. If only he'd never touched her, if only he hadn't let her taste what she could never have, but he had, and she would never forgive him for it. She rose to her feet, and fought against the burning ache in her heart and loins with her tongue, edged like a knife blade.

"Well, the staff evidently isn't looking very hard," she said. "Perhaps they need help. I would be only too glad to assist—anything to have this unfortunate business over with. Let me see," she said, tapping her chin with her forefinger, "you paint Mr. Mallory as an elbow-bender. Do you have a wine cellar?"

"Of course we do," said Nicholas.

"Has it been searched?"

"I'm sure it would have been first on the list."

"But you don't know for certain," she said, answering her own question. "Very well, we shall leave that for the moment. It seems to me that I heard Mr. Mallory tell of the many passageways and secret hiding places in the house. He seemed to have knowledge of them—even to a dungeon below stairs. He went on and on about it on our way here from Scotland. I suppose they would have been 'first on the list,' as well?"

"Sara—"

"Come, come, my lord, these are not difficult questions. It is only the answers that seem difficult for you, which I find quite telling. Why is that? Could it be that you don't really want to find Mr. Mallory, or could that be a moot point? For all I know, shut up in my rooms with no more freedom than

200

I had in the Fleet, he could have been found and dealt with long since, sir. Can it be that you are using him as an excuse to keep me here? That's it, isn't it? You don't have to answer. I can see it in your eyes. Well, it won't work. None of this was part of the bargain I made with you when I arrived here, but you are *not* going to kill that poor animal! I *am* taking him with me, Nicholas. You want to be rid of Nero? Consider it done." She turned to leave, but his raised voice arrested her.

"Where will you go, Baroness Walraven?" he said. "A baroness cannot go into service, and you cannot return to the Fleet. I paid a staggering sum to free you from that odious place. Have you no care for that, madam?"

"You are an enterprising fellow. I'm certain you have friends in high places, connections that might recommend your petition to the Archbishop of Canterbury or the Court of Arches, or some such to affect an annulment. Perhaps you could approach Parliament to grant a divorce since our 'marriage' is a sham, so that I might take a position as governess, or companion, or perhaps marry a proper husband and eventually pay back your 'staggering sum.'"

"Such things take time Sara—years. I don't even know if—"

"And as to where I shall go while all this is accomplished," she cut in, not giving him a chance to answer, "I am not entirely bereft, sir. I have a distant cousin in Shropshire, the widow of a vicar, a poor relation on in years, whom I haven't seen since a child it's true, but I am quite certain she would take me in gladly, and welcome the company."

He reached her in two strides. "Don't leave me, Sara," he murmured, crushing her close in his arms. His hot, moist hands were trembling, and the misted eyes riveting her were pleading and sad. "I'm asking only for time—just that, a little time."

"You've had time, Nicholas," she said, struggling against the very arms she ached to hold her. "Let me go, you're only making matters worse."

"I will never let you go. You are my wife, Sara. There is no other 'proper husband' for you—*ever!*"

"Don't you see the hopelessness of this?" she said, pushing against his hard chest, with both her hands. His heartbeat thumped against her fingers, and her hands slipped against the soft cushion of hair beneath his shirt, the shadow of its blackness visible through the fine cotton. She remembered the silky feel of it against her flesh. His scent was all over her, his salty, feral essence laced with whatever spirits he'd fortified himself with for this encounter, but she was the one who was foxed. He possessed the power to inebriate with a look alone. His touch was exquisite agony.

"Just a little longer is all I ask," he murmured close in her ear. His hot breath on her hair and skin sent shivers of icy fire through her blood. Her heart and mind were racing, pulling in opposite directions. He was all she ever wanted in a man, except for this secrecy, this barrier that kept them apart. He was otherwise above reproach. The man exuded honor, strength, and kindness—all the qualities that fostered love, but what drew her to him more than all the rest was a glimmer of tragic vulnerability about him, a mystique like that of the warrior-poets of old. It melted her heart. But this she dared not let him see . . . at least not yet.

"Sara, please . . . ?" he whispered.

"Odds fish! Now, I've done it!" said a remorseful voice from the threshold.

It was Dr. Breeden. Sara hadn't even heard him knock.

Raking his hair with a shaky hand, Nicholas let her go. Uttering a groan that echoed every battling emotion raging through her body, Sara spun on her heel, and fled.

"I am sorry, my lord," said the doctor. "I did knock, and I could have sworn I heard you invite me to enter." They had repaired to the library, where Nicholas was showing him some of the volumes he'd collected over time that might prove relevant to his malady. They had already gone through two-thirds of the collection, exhausting the most informative first. What remained didn't hold much promise, but Nicholas was determined, and the doctor was willing to peruse anything remotely associated with his chosen field.

"It's all right, Dr. Breeden," Nicholas said. "You may have done more good than harm. She wants to leave, and I can't say as I blame her, but I cannot let her go—and no, I cannot tell her," he added, answering the doctor's look. "Don't even ask it. She thinks I'm using Alex's absence as an excuse to keep her here. She doesn't think we're even looking for him. How can I tell her that we aren't looking for *him*, but for the wolf he has become?"

"That's all we're apt to find, my lord. It's been too long."

"I shall have to pass the word soon that I've dismissed him, and call off the search, except for you and Mills, and myself, of course. I have already told that tale to the guards. I've been holding off here because of Sara, but I can't forestall much longer. She also thinks I mean to shoot Nero, and I cannot refute that, either."

"Nero has not visited her lately?" said the doctor.

"No . . . if I could only be sure, but it's still too soon. We are making progress—at least, we were until just now. It very nearly happened in that study. If you hadn't come in on us when you did, she would have come face to face with her beloved Nero forthwith."

"I'm sorry to hear that," said the doctor, his posture deflated. "I was so encouraged. Perhaps a stronger cordial is what's wanted; I shall see to it at once."

"She is everything that I have denied myself all these years," said Nicholas, "everything I've always wanted. What I admire most is her indomitable spirit. I think I fell in love with that before her body tempted me, because we are so alike in that regard. We fight for what we want, for what should have been ours, but for circumstances beyond our control, and through no fault of our own. I reached for that kindred spirit long before I reached for the sweet flesh that houses it. Despite the shocking indignities she endured in that place, she has not lost her poise and grace. She has not come from it hardened, or sour for the experience, only grateful to be shot of it."

"She is a lady, my lord."

"In every sense of the word; I knew that from the first. A lightskirt would have jumped at my proposal, taken me for all I possess and been only too glad to take a lover for what remained, settling in quite content to be indifferent to me. Despite her fears, for she did have them—Sara was like a frightened rabbit at our first meeting. She accepted me to save herself from being sold into the brothels. I represented the lesser of two evils, and while she took the challenge eagerly, she was anything but resigned when she arrived here. The hellish thing is, I never expected her to fall in love with me, or that I might fall in love with her. That wasn't part of the plan. Ours was to be a platonic, congenial, mutually beneficial relationship, which would put paid to the *ton* hounding me. It was to address my loneliness for the basic elements of human companionship in this accursed exile, and in return she would have my eternal gratitude and all her heart could ever desire. I was a fool to imagine that the physical aspect would not enter into it with the right woman. Hah! I never expected to *find* the right woman shut up in this tomb, and I am not prepared for it. Needless to say, my experience with the opposite sex has been mostly abroad, and with a different sort of woman—one who made no demands of a personal nature, only a monetary one. There was never a risk of falling in love."

"What did you do to avoid conception on those occasions?"

"It wasn't a concern. You're a physician. You must know that Birds of Paradise are well skilled in the art of contraception. They handle that themselves, their livelihood depends upon it."

"And there were no transformations during those intimacies, my lord?" the doctor queried.

"No."

"Then, why do you fear it so now?"

"There is never any pressure or angst when heart and loins are disjoined," said Nicholas. "The sex act was nothing more than a clinical bodily function—a form of release that in a way helped the situation as I see it, like drawing off water from a spigot. This is different. This is an all-consuming fire that ignites the madness, and if it can cause the change to come upon me without consummation, I shudder to think what the results might be, were I to take that magnificent creature of a wife to my bed."

"Could part of that fire not be in the anticipation?" said the doctor. "Mightn't the risk of it—the fear of the change occurring and frightening her out of her wits—be the catalyst—the tinder, if you will—that ignites it?"

"And . . . if it were?"

"You need to *tell* her, my lord. All roads come back in that direction."

Nicholas shook his head. "It isn't just that," he said. "I've said it before, and I mean it. I cannot pass this nightmare on to any offspring. I would rather cut off my cods than risk that."

"Right now, we must set that issue aside; there are other ways of dealing with it," said the doctor. "We need to concentrate upon my cordials and treatments to train your mind to reject the transformations, and worry over passing the condition on once we've conquered that."

"What 'other ways'?" Nicholas cut in. For the first time since the treatments began, there was true hope in his heart, and in his voice.

"Patience, my lord," said the doctor. "No stone shall be left unturned, I assure you. We shall talk on this topic again, but first we need to take care of the business at hand before we move off in another direction."

"Anything," said Nicholas. "I cannot lose her, Dr. Breeden. She is no jinglebrain. She's hardly ignorant of the law. She wants me to petition the Archbishop of Canterbury for an annulment, or Parliament for a bill of divorcement."

"Can you do that? Do you have the connections?"

"I do," said Nicholas, "but either would be a lengthy process, and difficult. It could take years. She means to go to a distant cousin in Shropshire meanwhile, and take a situation as governess or companion, or even marry again after all is said and done in order to pay back what I've spent on her. I cannot let her go. If I do, I'll never see her again. I would not be able to go after her. What am I going to do, Dr. Breeden?"

"We'd best be about our work," said the doctor. "There's only one thing to do in order to put paid to that plan, my lord; you've got to turn my lady's head around so that she doesn't want to leave you. You've got to consummate your marriage, and *quickly*."

Twenty

"If you will not go with me, I shall go alone," said Sara to Nell, who had dug in her heels refusing to show her any more architectural oddities in the Norman manor. "There is no danger of being caught out, Nell. His lordship and Dr. Breeden repaired to the library right after dinner. They will be closeted there half the night, and it's impossible to do it during the day. There are too many servants about."

"The master'll sack me for fair if he finds out, my lady. I'm supposed ta be keepin' an eye on ya so ya don't come ta harm."

"Which is just what you will be doing, because I'm going off exploring—with or without you, so, if you want to do as he bade, you'd best come with me right now. No one else in this house seems interested in finding Mr. Mallory, and since my future here depends upon it, I must take the responsibility upon myself."

"Depends upon it, my lady?" said the maid, nonplussed.

"Never you mind. Just do as I say."

"What if you do find Mr. Mallory?"

"You let me worry about that. Now, take that candle branch and light our way."

Sara had no idea of the mission she'd undertaken until an hour had passed and they hadn't gotten below the first level of Ravencliff's meandering corridors, and rooms within rooms. They avoided the third floor altogether, as well as the wing that housed the library. It wouldn't do to tempt fate.

Most of the secret rooms were on the seaside, and all were reached through actual suites by surreptitious means: false walls, dummy fireplaces—one even had a wardrobe, whose rear panel gave access. Obscured by the buttressed seawall, a narrow passageway on the far side of these hidden rooms ran parallel to and slightly below the main corridor, joining them like links in a chain that led to the cliff through yet another rear entrance to the house. This she assumed was one of the smuggler's tunnels Nicholas had spoken of. The house was a literal maze of hiding places. How many more could there be? Would she ever find them all?

She unearthed several more priest holes as they progressed. These, however, were level with the entrance, not sunken lower as the one she'd fallen into. Nevertheless, she approached them with caution, and did not venture past their thresholds. The last one, however, impressed her as the most perfect hiding place of all, since it was nearly invisible hewn in the arch of a recessed alcove. It marked the yawning entrance to a tunnel—black as coal tar pitch—that sloped farther downward. Nell stopped in her tracks when they reached it.

"No, my lady," she said. "I won't go another step. The dungeon's down there, and there's ghosts and devils in it." She leaned close, whispering, "We hear them in the servants' quarters sometimes—whistlin' like the wind and howlin' like wolves. You'll not get me down there. I'll give my notice first!"

"That is ridiculous, Nell," Sara scoffed. "There are no such things. If you're hearing sounds from down below, they're no doubt coming from drafts seeping in from the outside. Don't you feel them? My ankles are freezing."

"You ain't gettin' me down there, and if ya set foot in that tunnel, I'll go straight ta the master, I swear it, I *will*."

Sara breathed an exasperated sigh. She had no doubt that the frightened little maid meant what she said. She couldn't risk it. Now that she knew the way, she could come on her own. Vowing to do just that, she conceded mock defeat, and turned back along the corridor.

They hadn't gotten past the priest hole when a rumble of discordant sound exited the tunnel, a bloodcurdling, heart-stopping howl.

"*Nero!*" Sara cried. "So this is where he goes."

Nell ran back along the corridor the way they'd come, taking the candle branch with her, a troop of screams exiting her throat. Sara raised the hem of her skirt and dashed after her, while she could still see. There were too many twists and turns in the passageway to risk becoming separated from the abigail in the deep dark. Her heart was hammering in her breast. When she reached the girl, she spun her around and clamped her hand over the abigail's mouth.

"Be still!" she said, shaking her. "You will bring the whole house down here. It's only Nero. There's nothing to fear." The howl came again, more distant. "See? You've scared him more then he scared you. You've driven him deeper in now. I can hardly hear him anymore."

"That nasty old dog!" Nell snapped. "I wish the master would hurry up and get shot of him. He came after me, ya know, a few days back. He come tearin' outta your rooms just as I was comin' up from the servants' hall—soakin' wet he was. I told him ta shoo, and he come at me—showed me his teeth, and growled at me, he did. He was droolin' all over the carpet, too. I thought sure he was goin' ta bite me, but he run off growlin', when I stamped my foot at him."

Cold chills raced the length of Sara's spine. That must have been the night she'd doused Nero with water—so much for teaching him a lesson.

"Have you seen him since?' Sara asked.

"No, my lady, but I'm goin' ta tell the master first chance I get. That dog useta be a nuisance, poppin' up outta nowhere and scarin' us half outta our wits, but he never harmed nobody. Now he's gone bad, and he could be dangerous."

"Don't tell the master," Sara said. "Nero hasn't been himself since Mr. Mallory shot him. I'm sure that's all it is. You'd be out of sorts if you were shot, too. I haven't been able to get close enough to see if the bullet is still lodged in him. He is probably in much pain."

"That may be, but I still think the master ought ta know."

"You just leave Nero to me," said Sara. "Whatever the master needs to know, I will tell him. Now, we'd best hurry. Do not dare run away and leave me again! The candles are nearly burned to the sockets; hasty motion will snuff them out altogether, and I do not relish the thought of groping through these passageways blind in the dark."

Whimpering, Nell scurried along the dank corridor, despite Sara's warning. Did the girl not hear a word she'd said? The candles began to flicker, their feeble flames drowning in the melted wax with the abigail's haste. It splashed on Sara's frock, and on the bare skin of her hand and forearm, as she tugged on Nell's sleeve, slowing her pace. It was too late, one candle expired, and then another, spreading the acrid odor of smoke and burnt tallow. Only one candle remained lit, and Sara jerked the girl to a standstill.

"Now look what you've done," she snapped, trying to steady the candle branch in Nell's trembling hand. "*No!* Don't tilt it! The tallow will extinguish the flame."

"Oh, my lady, it's goin' out!" the abigail shrilled.

"Be still!" Sara seethed. "Give it here!" Snatching it from her, she held it upright, a close eye on the fading wick. The candle was disappearing into a pool of wax in the socket.

There was precious little time left, and the passageway was unlit. "Why couldn't you have chosen a branch with fresher candles?" she scolded.

"They was fresh when we set out, my lady," the abigail defended.

"Never mind," said Sara. "Where are we? Which of these panels did we come through? They all look the same to me."

"This one, I think," said Nell. "No . . . that one there on the left. Oh, I dunno, my lady. I'm all mixed up!"

"Well, you'd best un-mix yourself posthaste, my girl. Dawn will shed no ray of light here, and this last candle is spent in seconds!"

Nothing would quiet the abigail. She was clearly struck with terror, whining and trembling—rooted to the spot. Another sound bled into the noise, stopping Sara's free hand in midair as she felt the damp wall for an exit from the passageway. A low, guttural growl behind them spun her around to face two shiny eyes glowing red-gold with reflected light from the candle before her motion snuffed it out. Nell screamed, and started to run. The last thing Sara saw was the flashing gleam of sharp fangs. The last thing she heard was the patter of the animal's feet, its long nails clacking on the flat stones underfoot, before she darted after the hysterical abigail, seized her arm and drove her through the panel she'd been searching for. It opened to the safety of one of the inner chambers, and swung shut behind them. Above Nell's shrieks, Sara could still hear the whines and growls on the other side, and the frantic scratching as if the animal were trying to dig its way through stone a foot thick.

She sagged against the wall. The candlestick lay somewhere on the other side, where she'd dropped it. It didn't matter. It couldn't help them now, with the candles all snuffed out.

"Will you stop that infernal caterwauling!" she snapped, giving Nell's arm a shake. "This is serious here. I have no idea how to get through to the other side. You brought me into this secret chamber. You have to collect your wits and get us out of this!"

"I . . . I can't see!" the girl wailed. " 'Tis black as sin in here. I'm afeared o' the dark, my lady."

"That is unfortunate," said Sara. "There is nothing in the dark to harm you, Nell. We've left the danger behind. And that's another thing. *Never* run from a threatening animal. Never show your fear. That poor dog is in pain. This is evidently his domain, and we have intruded upon it. Dogs can be very territorial, but Nero would never harm me. You, however, do not seem to share that distinction, since you say he snapped at you once already. He probably tastes your fear. He knows I do not fear him, and I mean him no ill."

"Then, why is he scratchin' and growlin' like that, my lady?" said Nell.

"I shan't presume to get inside the mind of a pain-crazed dog," Sara responded. "He is probably trying to get to me. I'm the only friend that poor animal has in this house. There isn't time to puzzle it out. Stop that sniveling! We have to get out of this maze of smugglers hideaways, and back to the house proper before we're missed."

Sara took off her shoe and set it on the floor against the panel they'd just come through. "Start feeling your way along the wall," she said. "Once we reach my slipper, we'll know we've come full circle. That way at least we will know where one exit is."

"That won't matter a whit ta me, my lady," snapped the abigail. "I ain't never goin' back inta that dog's domain again!"

"Then help me find the way back into the outer chamber," said Sara, nudging her along.

The room was sparsely furnished, though each time they bumped into a table, or settle, Nell's whimpers became outcries. Sara had long since given over trying to silence the girl. It wasn't until they reached the back of the armoire they'd come through earlier, and pushed through it into one of the legitimate chambers, that the abigail quieted. Light from the full moon flooded the room, and while Nell held the armoire panel open, Sara ran back for her shoe.

"Hurry, my lady!" Nell cried. "Just, please hurry."

Sara needed no prompting. It had grown late. All she could think of was getting back to her suite before one of the servants, or Nicholas himself, caught her out. Once safely inside, Sara's hand hesitated, hovering over the doorknob.

"You ain't thinkin' o' leaven that open, are ya, my lady?" Nell breathed. "Not after all o' this just now!"

"I am," said Sara, "and it's nothing to you, Nell." She glanced down at her frock. It was splotched and streaked with mildew and dust. Her hands and arms were likewise decorated, and she could only imagine the state of her face, and her hair, which was hanging on one side where it had come loose from its combs. "I know it's late, but I shall want a good soaking," she said. "Have the hip bath filled, and then you may retire. I shan't need you again tonight. I shall manage on my own. This frock will have to go straight into the dustbin. It's beyond saving."

"Beggin' your pardon, my lady," said Nell, pulling herself up to her full height, "but I won't be goin' back inta them passages again, no matter what ya say I owe ya. I'll give my notice first, or ya can sack me as ya like."

"I shan't need you to, now that I know my way," Sara returned.

The girl gasped. "Ya can't mean you're goin' back down there?" she cried.

"If needs must, but not tonight. The only place I intend to go now is into a nice hot bath, and then to bed."

Rose oil never smelled so sweet, and silkened water, fragrant with the woodsy aroma of rosemary, never felt as delightful as it did that night. Sara nearly dozed in the bath. She hated to leave it, and she didn't until the water began to grow cold around her. Nell had left a stack of towels on the chiffonier, and she dried herself, and towel-dried her hair, but when she turned to collect her nightdress and wrapper, it was to find that she had an audience. Nero was sitting in the doorway, his head cocked to the side, his long, pink tongue hanging down in a manner that almost made it seem as though he was smiling at her.

"Nero!" she gushed. Though she'd left the door ajar, this was the last thing she'd expected. He seemed docile now, but dared she trust that deceptive image? She took a cautious step closer. "Have you quieted down?" she crooned. "Yes, I see that you have." She braved another step nearer and he rose, wagging his long, bushy tail as he pranced in place.

Sara discarded the towel wrapped around her, and wriggled into her nightdress—a gauzy shift of butter-colored lawn, so fine it was almost transparent—and squatted down, stroking Nero's damp, shaggy coat.

"You've been outside, haven't you?" she said. "The sea air seems to have calmed you. You took another route back into the house proper, too. You know them all, don't you, boy?"

The animal whined and shook himself, nuzzling her hand, licking it with that soft, warm tongue.

She braved a look at his wound. Inching her fingers along his foreleg, she spread the fur and found it higher up.

"It *is* in your shoulder," she marveled. "Why, it's nearly healed. This doesn't hurt you, does it? Then, what on earth was wrong with you before? Was it Nell? You don't like her, do you, Nero? I wonder why? Maybe you sense that she isn't all that fond of you." She surged to her feet. "Well, that's no excuse for being rude. You frightened her half out of her wits. You won't do that again, will you, boy?"

If a dog could look nonplussed, this one did. His expression extracted the closest thing to a giggle that had passed her lips in days, and she ruffled the thick fur about his neck.

"All right, play dumb," she said, "but I'd better not have a pitcher of water handy if you do it again. You need to learn some manners, boy—though I'm not surprised, considering the fine example your master sets for you."

She nudged him aside, and walked into her bedchamber. Nero padded after her, gazing at her in the oddest way before loosing the most mournful howl she had ever heard. It sent the fingers of a crawling chill along her spine and puckered her scalp with gooseflesh. All at once, he bolted and streaked into the sitting room, and out through the open foyer door.

Sara had had quite enough roaming about for one day, but she poked her head out into the corridor just the same to follow his direction with her eyes. To her amazement, he didn't head straight for the landing as he had in the past. Instead, he disappeared in the shadowy recesses of the green suite across the way.

Sara stared after him. What on earth was he doing in there? Should she investigate? It was only across the hall. She shifted from one bare foot to another, deliberating for several moments before throwing caution to the winds and venturing out into the deserted hallway. It was only a few short steps, and she entered the darkened chamber. She found herself in a well-appointed sitting room. Soft, diffuse light coming from the bedchamber beyond showed her that the room was empty, and she followed the shaft of moonglow, taking slow, measured steps.

"Nero?" she called. Her voice was no more than a hoarse whisper. Suppose Mallory were hiding there? She almost turned back at the thought, but it was too late for that. Instead, she crossed the bedchamber threshold only to pull up short at sight of Nicholas standing in the middle of the Oriental carpet. He was naked and aroused.

Twenty-one

Sara gasped aloud. Nicholas stood rooted to the spot, his hypnotic obsidian stare riveted on her.

"N-Nero?" she stammered. "Where—"

"Gone," said Nicholas. "I chased him off."

"W-what are you doing here like . . . like *that?*" she said, stumbling over every word.

"Preparing for bed," he snapped, grabbing his shirt off the floor in a vain attempt to cover his nakedness.

"Here?" she said. "Why here? Why aren't you preparing for bed in your own suite?"

"Because I cannot keep an eye on you from my own suite," he pronounced.

"*Oh!*" Sara seethed in exasperation, slapping at her nightdress with a balled-up fist. She spun, making a dash for the door, but he threw down the shirt, reached her in two strides, and spun her toward him.

"You don't think you need watching?" he asked, close in her face. "Look at yourself! Wandering the halls half-naked in that nightdress. It's as transparent as a cobweb. You may as well be naked. What if you'd come upon Mallory?"

"You're a fine one to speak of going about naked, my lord!" she retorted, struggling in his arms. "You seem to be separated from your clothes again, yourself. And I wasn't wandering the halls. I merely stepped across the corridor because I saw Nero enter here. He had just left me, if you must know, and I wondered what he was up to. He hasn't been himself of late, and I'm concerned about him. It's a good thing, too, because no one else seems to be. Everyone wants to be rid of him—*you* want to shoot him. Don't dare deny it! I saw you, remember. Perhaps you've already disposed of the poor animal. Oh, my God, if you've harmed that dog—"

"What do you mean, he hasn't been himself?" Nicholas interrupted.

Sara's mouth dropped open. There he was, in the altogether, gripping her upper arms like a madman as though he hadn't the slightest notion that he was stark naked, and what had gotten his attention? Nero's peculiar behavior.

"Answer me, Sara!" he said, shaking her gently.

"Nicholas, please . . . ," she murmured.

Steering her to a wing chair beside the unlit hearth, he sat her in it. "Don't move," he cautioned. Snatching his dressing gown from the bed, he shrugged it on with rough hands. It was too late. She'd already seen what lay beneath—the broad shoulders, the lightly furred chest, the narrow waist, and well-muscled thighs, the magnificence of his sex. His body was burned into her memory, just as his scent was. Every instinct urged her to vault out of that chair and run, but she could not—*would not*. Her body was on fire for him.

"How is Nero . . . different?" he persisted, standing over her, arms akimbo, his broad chest heaving.

"For the most part he's been playful and loving," she said. "There's no question that he's protective of me. It's just since he was shot that there seems to be a change."

"What kind of change?"

"Oh, it isn't that he's changed completely. It's just that sometimes he frightens me now. He never did before."

Dawn Thompson

"Frightens you how? Come, come, Sara, I need to know."

"Why?" she snapped. "Do you want me to give you more ammunition? Do you want me to load the gun that kills him? I think not, my lord."

"Bloody hell!" Nicholas thundered. "Nero is *mine*. If he is out of sorts, Mrs. Bromley can concoct a remedy. Why do you insist that I mean to kill that animal?"

"Because I saw you try to!" Sara snapped. "Or was that during one of your 'lapses'?"

Nicholas didn't speak. His posture collapsed, and his hands fell limp at his sides. He looked so lost in that moment she was tempted to melt. After careful deliberation, she decided that she would tell him, but not because of that—because there might be help to be had for Nero if she did.

"It started with little things," she said. "The way he tried to take over my suite, the way he'd curl his lips back in a silent snarl. He wouldn't let me examine his wound, and then just now, he let me spread the fur—even let me touch it."

He seemed to turn as pale as the moonlight filtering in through the leaded panes. Several times he opened his mouth as if to speak, but didn't, and she couldn't read his thoughts. His body tensed again. The veins in his neck were standing out in bold relief, and the muscles in his jaw began to pulsate in a steady rhythm.

"Once, I found him in my bed," Sara went on. "He had pulled down some of my things from the armoire and dragged them about. When I scolded him and tried to nudge him off the bed, he sprang at me—"

"He didn't *bite* you?" Nicholas cut in, taking a step toward her. For a moment she feared he was about to spring as Nero had.

"N-no," she murmured, catching her breath. His sudden motion had disarmed her. "I . . . I doused him with water from the pitcher by my bed. His teeth banged against *it*, not me. And then, the next time I saw him he was just as he was tonight, like the old Nero, the one I would never fear. The one I love. I thought perhaps he might be in pain and that it had him out of sorts, but he didn't seem so earlier at all."

"When was the last time he seemed . . . out of sorts?" Nicholas murmured.

Sara fell silent. If she were to answer that, she would have to tell him of her exploration of the secret chambers. That would implicate Nell, and that she would not do.

"I . . . I can't recall," she hedged, "but nothing of that nature ever occurred before Mr. Mallory shot him."

He lifted her out of the chair and took her in his arms. She couldn't see his face, but when he spoke, there were tears in his voice.

"Sara, I must ask you to trust me," he said. "Please believe me when I say that I mean no ill to that animal. He is as much a part of me as these hands that hold you."

"But you said I shouldn't become attached to Nero, that he might be leaving, and then you . . . you—"

"I know what I said," he interrupted. "And, yes, he may have to leave us, but not in the way that you accuse. You must keep the door to your suite locked whether you are in it or not, until Alex is found and Nero is . . . seen to. You should have told me all this long ago. You are in danger . . . more danger than I knew," he added absently.

"How can I be in danger when you are standing guard over me so relentlessly?" she snapped.

"Sara, Nero is part *wolf*," he said. "Wolves are . . . unpredictable. You must obey me. I will lock you in before I see you come to harm."

"I thought from the beginning that he might be!" she cried. "I've never seen a wolf, of course, but I have seen pictures of them in books in my father's library. Now I can really see Nero's beauty. He cuts a poor figure as a dog, I will allow, but as a *wolf* he is splendid."

"And he could be . . . dangerous. Promise me you will do as I ask."

"Nicholas . . ."

Pulling her into his arms, he cupped her face in his massive hand, and gazed into her eyes. He seemed to be memorizing every inch of her face, every pore in her skin, which was on fire under his scrutiny. The throbbing had begun inside, pounding like a heartbeat, moistening her sex. Why was he looking at her like that, with those misty eyes dilated in the moonlight? When he spoke, it didn't break the spell; it heightened it to a more intimate plane, stoking the fire that had ignited a passion she didn't even know existed. *There* was the real danger—in getting too close to that fire, in letting it mark her, burn her, spoil her, forever shackled to a hopeless love. Nevertheless, she let the flames engulf her, let them gobble her up.

"Sara, my God, if anything were to happen to you, I believe I would run mad," he murmured against her lips before he took them. He tasted of salt, and of sweet wine lingering on his skilled tongue as it entered her, parting her lips, plunging deeper, extracting the moan waiting in her throat to be released by his ardor. It mingled with one rumbling in his own throat, and he devoured it, just as he devoured her resolve and her inhibitions, stripping her bare of them.

His hand left her face and roamed lower, his fingers lightly caressing her arched throat, and the notch at its base. They crept along as he felt for the pulse, for the thrumming blood pumping there, and slid his mouth over the spot, his silken tongue feeling for the pulsating flow until she shivered. The ghost of rough stubble on his face against her tender skin sent shock waves through her sex. What had he awakened? Every fiber of her being longed for him, ached for him. Her blood was racing through her veins, through the pulse point he caressed. Surely, he could feel her passion. It was coursing through her in rhythm with the shuddering heart in his tight chest pressed against her.

He untied the silk ribbon that drew the neck of her shift closed with trembling fingers, and spread it wide, fondling her shoulder and then her breast, the fullness of which he crushed against his open palm. He worked the hard nipple between his thumb and forefinger, then took it in his mouth—sucking, nipping, extracting another moan from the very depths of her. The sound he made shot her through with searing heat and cold chills all at once. It was something she might have expected to come from Nero's throat, rather than his.

He slid her nightdress down until it puddled at her feet. Then, shedding his dressing gown, he scooped her up in arms of muscle become so rock hard, the cords in them seemed about to snap. Laying her on the bed, he gathered her against him.

No man had ever seen Sara's naked body before, much less touched it. The fingers of a blush stole over her skin from head to toe, a steamy rush of hot blood riding the thrill of the experience, especially when his skilled hand lingered over the mound of soft, moist hair between her thighs. They were properly wed, and yet there was a glimmer of something forbidden in his embrace. Had he lodged that in her head with his constant insistence that there be no physical aspect of their arrangement? Could it be her inexperience—her maidenly modesty—or was it because the marriage was by proxy that it didn't seem real? She wouldn't delve deeper into the cause. Whatever it was, it heightened the effect beyond imagining. That facet of the forbidden flamed, and caught her in a firestorm that would not be quenched.

Capturing her hand, he drew it to his lips and kissed her moist palm, then crimped her fingers around his sex; Sara's breath caught as it responded to her touch. She gasped again as his mouth opened hers, and as his deep, feral moan resonated inside her. Her heart leapt at the sound of it—more animal than human—flowing through her body.

She buried her hand in his hair. How soft it was, like silk between her fingers. The fine hairs on the back of his neck were standing on end. His hackles were raised, every sinew in him tensed against her. His heart seemed as if it were about to leap from his chest the way it pounded against her breast.

"God help me," he murmured.

Spreading her legs, he reached between and began stroking her there. Those fingers, so gentle, so nimble for their size, petting her swollen sex wrenched a dry sob from her that she hadn't even realized escaped until it rang in her ears. It seemed to be coming from an echo chamber far off in the distance, as was his heart-stopping howl. There was no other word to describe the sound he made. It belonged in the wild, not in that bed. His eyes were black coals burning into her, dark with arousal, almost aglow in the moonlight. Something in that look excited and terrified her all at once. Raw passion had overtaken him, and yet he was holding back. What ecstasy, if he were to let it out. Sara would settle for nothing less, and she arched herself against him.

There would be pain. She was prepared for it. What she wasn't prepared for was the slow, tantalizing movements of this masterful lover, who seemed determined to spare her even the slightest hurt. Each stroke of his fingers was bringing her closer to the rapture she reached for, and she did reach for it, her hands splayed across his lightly furred chest, following the straight line of diminishing hair striping his flat belly, pointing like an arrow to the thick, veined shaft of his sex. He moved with the stealthy grace of a sleek jungle cat, responding to her caresses, and when he spread her legs wider and eased himself between them, she held her breath in anticipation of his very life moving inside her, filling her, making her whole.

All at once, a bloodcurdling scream echoed along the corridor outside, mingled with the guttural snarl of a savage animal. The scream came again, then another—a troop of them, piercing and shrill, growing more distant, as were the growling snarls. Then a howl, mournful and deep, rang through the hallway. Then silence.

Sara's heart skipped its rhythm. "Nell!" she cried. "That was *Nell!*"

For a split second, Nicholas froze in place before he leaped from the bed and snatched his dressing gown from the floor where he'd dropped it.

"Stay where you are," he charged. "Do not move from that bed!"

Nicholas didn't give his wife a chance to reply. Snatching his pocket pistol from the gateleg table, he burst from the chamber, despite her cries, and ran along the corridor in the direction of Nell's screams. He found her lying in a pool of blood beside her chamber door, and sank down beside her with a groan. The servants were coming; their milling voices echoing from below brought him to his feet again. He dared not linger. There was nothing he could do. He couldn't go back to the green suite either, without being seen. That was the worst of it. Sara was vulnerable and unprotected. Mallory was roaming the halls of Ravencliff in wolf form, and she thought he was Nero. The intensity of the passion that had nearly consummated their marriage, and the shock of finding the abigail savaged, was enough to trigger a transformation without the terror of being helpless to protect Sara. He couldn't shapeshift before the servants, or Sara, either. It wasn't safe to transform *at all*. He couldn't appear as Nero when everyone in residence would surely be gunning for him now, and he bounded up the back stairs on the verge of madness over the whole circumstance, and just in time burst into his master suite sitting room, where Dr. Breeden was interviewing Mills.

Running through the suite, a howl preceding the transformation, he plunged through the dressing room door—no more than a blur—and Nero landed on all fours, still tangled in the burgundy brocade dressing gown.

Sara sprang from the bed and wriggled into her nightdress. She would not obey Nicholas's command. *He's going to kill*

Nero! was the only thought in her mind, as she ran from the bedchamber. Outside, the patter of many footsteps out of rhythm, and the racket of shouting voices wrinkled her scalp with gooseflesh. She cracked the door and peered into the dimly lit corridor, watching the servants—some in their dressing gowns and wrappers—streak by. Mrs. Bromley, Smythe, Robbins and Searl, and a stream of hall boys and scullions, all running north, past her suite. Mills and Dr. Breeden were not among them, conspicuous in their absence.

"Where's the master?" someone shouted. "Somebody fetch the master!"

"We'll have to send for the guards!" Mrs. Bromley wailed.

"Not until we've told the master," Smythe returned. "I'll go up and fetch him down."

"We're all goin' ta be killed in our beds if that filthy animal's not caught. I won't sleep a wink till he is! I'll give me notice!"

"Be still!" the butler snapped. "Collect your wits, Mrs. Bromley. There's no time for hysteria here now."

"*She's dead*, Smythe," the housekeeper moaned, bursting into tears.

Sara did step into the hall at that. Nobody noticed her. They were all gathered at the north end of the hallway in front of Nell's chamber, which adjoined her own. Her heart was pounding in her ears. It was all she could do to put one foot in front of the other. Where was Nicholas? Why hadn't he come back? Didn't he know she'd be worried?

"*Her ladyship!*" Mrs. Bromley shrilled. "Has anyone checked on her ladyship?"

"I . . . I'm here," Sara said, venturing nearer. "What's happened?" She was almost afraid of the answer—afraid she'd heard correctly. The very air tasted of calamity, of death.

The teary-eyed housekeeper gasped and rushed to her side. "You'll catch your death out here in that thin gown!" she cried. Turning her around, she led her back toward the tapestry suite. "Go on back inside, put your wrapper on before you take a chill, and lock your door, my lady. This here is not for your eyes."

"What has happened?" Sara demanded, digging in her heels. They had reached her suite, but she wasn't crossing the threshold until she knew. "I'm not going anywhere until you tell me!"

Mrs. Bromley broke into tears. " 'Tis Nell, my lady . . ." she wailed.

"What's the matter with Nell?" Sara cried, still praying she'd heard wrong.

"She's dead, my lady," the housekeeper moaned. "Nero's tore her throat out, and he's on the loose in here somewhere. He must've gone mad. The men are huntin' him now. They're goin' ta shoot him on sight. Now, you go back inside, and lock yourself in till one of us comes and tells ya it's all right to come out again."

Twenty-two

The sound of shrill cries and raised voices from below had begun to funnel up the grand staircase from the second floor, and Mills shoved the doctor into the dressing room after Nero, and shut the door.

"Hold him!" he cried. "Don't let him go until I see what's happening."

Mills skittered through the suite, closing the doors as he went in a frantic attempt to stifle the howling, snarling, whining din he'd left behind in the dressing room. He didn't wait for the knock he feared imminent. He burst out into the corridor just as Smythe came running.

"What the Devil's going on down there?" he barked at the breathless butler. "We can hear the racket all the way up here with the doors closed. I was just coming to see."

"Where's . . . his lordship?" Smythe panted.

"He isn't here," said Mills. "What's happened, man?"

"It's Nell," said the butler. "She's dead, and Nero's killed her."

"*Nero?*" Mills breathed. "Have you attics to let? You know that animal hasn't a vicious bone in his body."

"She's dead just the same," snapped Smythe. "Her throat's torn out, and she's got two fists full of dog hair, Mills. We'll have to have the guards in, and it's his lordship that has to send for them. Where's he gone at this hour, then?"

Gooseflesh receded the valet's scalp. His mind was racing. It couldn't have been Nero. He would stake his life upon that, but Nero would take the blame, since no one else except Dr. Breeden and himself knew there was another animal loose in the house. But why had Nicholas come bursting in like that just now? In all his years attending him, not once had he ever seen his master transform *clothed*.

"He asked that we not wait up for him," he said, closing the door to the master suite, and leading the butler back toward the staircase. He dared not risk Nero bursting out as Nicholas had just burst in; his demeanor alone would damn him. "I believe he said something about a walk on the strand. He often does when the weather permits. The moon is full, and it's warmer at last. You know how he does. He could be gone for hours."

"What are we to do?" asked the butler. "We can't just leave her there like that!"

"She will have to stay as she lies until his lordship returns," said Mills.

"What about the guards?"

"That is up to his lordship, Smythe, we cannot presume to have them in without his authority. I'll come down. We shall cover her, and send the others back to bed. They shouldn't be abroad here now until we know what's what." Another terror struck. "W-where is her ladyship?" he asked, swallowing his rapid heartbeat.

"Mrs. Bromley's with her in her suite," said the butler. "She's dreadfully overset. You can imagine—"

"Yes, yes, I can," Mills cut in. "Go on back down. I was just in the midst of something. I'll finish up, and join you directly. Where . . . did it occur?"

"Right in front of her rooms adjoining my lady's. Nell was evidently trying to reach her chamber, when the animal . . . attacked her. We heard her screams clear to the servants' hall, but then we're closer down there than you are up here in the turrets."

"I didn't hear a thing until you lot started making enough of a din to raise the roof," said Mills.

"Shouldn't we fetch the doctor?" the butler queried.

Smythe wasn't aware that Dr. Breeden was closeted in the master suite. So be it. He was needed right where he was. Nero could not be left alone now. It only took seconds for the valet to respond.

"The doctor has retired," he said. "If the girl is dead, we needn't wake him. There's nothing he can do, after all. The master is concerned that he isn't getting enough rest on his holiday, what with all the urgencies that have occurred in this house since his arrival. Tomorrow will be soon enough to bring him into this, unless his lordship decides otherwise when he returns."

"I expect so," said the butler. "It just seems . . . there should be someone in authority to deal with this."

"We shall just have to wait for his lordship," Mills replied. "Now, go back down and keep order. He shan't appreciate coming back to chaos. I shall join you directly."

Mills ran back into the master suite and bolted the door. Streaking though the bedchamber, he burst into the dressing room and shut that door as well. Having shed the dressing gown, Nero was running in crazed circles, his broad chest heaving, drool dripping from his tongue and spotting the rug. His high-pitched whine ran the valet through like a javelin.

The doctor stood, slack-jawed, watching Nero's every move. The minute Mills moved away from the door, Nero lunged and attacked it. Mills gasped. The lower door panel was rutted with scars from Nero's fangs and claws. Splinters littered the parquetry. He'd nearly chewed through it.

"Extraordinary," said the doctor. "I've never seen the like."

"Well, I have," snapped Mills. "Not quite to this degree, I will allow, but he has good cause."

"Why? What's happened?"

"My lady's abigail, Nell Critchton, is dead. Her throat has been torn out. The consensus is that Nero killed her, but we both know not. There isn't a drop of blood on him that I can see. 'Twas Alex Mallory in wolf form, I'd stake my life upon it, but Nero is sure to catch the blame."

"Good God!"

"There's no time to tell the whole of it here now. I shall fill you in later. I must go below. Will you be all right . . . you aren't afraid?"

"I'm a scientist, Mills. I've come in close contact with far worse than this. My whole experience here is invaluable to my research. No, I'm not afraid. Nero poses no threat to me, but I daresay I wouldn't know how to hold him if he breaks through that door."

"Nero, *stay!*" Mills thundered, and the wolf ceased his relentless assault on the door, looking up with eyes so full of desperation, the valet's own eyes teared. "She is safe," he soothed. "You have my word." He turned to the doctor. "See if you can calm him," he said. "He will stay as he is as long as he is excited. They need him below, and he cannot roam these halls like this now. He will be shot on sight. Just see if you can hold him till I get out. I shall be back as soon as I can. Bolt this door when I leave. Whatever you do, do not let him out of these apartments!"

The minute Mills closed the dressing room door, the doctor threw the bolt, and Nero resumed his attack on the panels. The sound raised gooseflesh along the valet's spine and he spun on his heel, ran back through the suite, and into the corridor. There was no time to lose.

Sara paced the carpet in her bedchamber. Mrs. Bromley was the last to leave; she'd stayed to comfort her. The others had

long since trickled back down to the servants' quarters behind the green baize door. Where was Nicholas? No one had
seen him, and everyone was looking for him. She'd had a
cursory visit from Mills, who'd said that Nicholas had gone
for a walk on the strand. That couldn't be. He was with her
until it happened, and then he disappeared. What were they
keeping from her? And where was Nero? No one had seen
him attack Nell, but he'd been convicted of the crime
nonetheless. They would find him, and they would kill him,
but not if she found him first.

Pulling her wrapper closer about her, she unlatched her
door and poked her head out in the hall. There was no one
about. She shuddered at sight of the quilt mound covering
Nell's body farther along the corridor, half hidden in the
shadows, and fresh tears welled in her eyes. She blinked
them back, and glanced in the other direction. There was no
sign of Nicholas, or of Nero.

She was just about to close and latch the door again, when
she recalled seeing Nero enter the green suite earlier. Could
he have gone there to hide? Without a second thought, she
crossed the threshold and tiptoed across the hall. It wasn't
far, and if she didn't find him there, she would concede defeat for the moment and return to her suite until morning.

Once inside the bedchamber, she lit the candle branch and
glanced around the room. Her gaze fell on the rumpled
bed—very nearly her conjugal bed—and more tears threatened, reliving the intimacies she and Nicholas has shared in
it. She felt again the phantom of his arousal leaning against
her thigh, the warmth of his short breaths puffing on her
naked skin, his deft fingers and hungry mouth quickening
her heartbeat, awakening her to pleasures she scarcely dared
imagine. Why hadn't he come back to her? Where was he
now? It was beyond bearing.

"Nicholas?" she called. Her voice was no more than a
hoarse whisper. He didn't answer. She knew he would not.

But maybe Nero would. Again and again, she whispered, walking from room to room, but he didn't respond either.

Walking back through the bedchamber, she spied Nicholas's dressing gown sash lying on the carpet. He'd left in such haste that he hadn't bothered with it, and she picked it up and raised it to her nose. It held his scent. She inhaled him, taking deep, slow breaths, then looped it over her arm and was about to exit the chamber when Nero came bounding out of the south wing shadows and streaked past her into the room.

Sara closed the door, set the candle branch down, and knelt beside him. Whining, Nero stood, hackles raised, feet apart, his proud head bowed. His chest was heaving, and he panted as though he'd run his heart out. His eyes, gazing into hers, were wild feral things glowing in the halo of candleshine, and she threw her arms around his neck and sobbed into his shaggy fur ruff.

"You didn't do it, did you, Nero?" she moaned. "There's not a drop of blood on you *anywhere*. Oh, I knew you didn't! I knew you couldn't have, and they're going to kill you!" He licked her face with his long pink tongue, and pranced in place. "You couldn't have cleaned yourself, either," she said. "You haven't been outside, have you? Your fur isn't damp. You don't smell of the sea"—she breathed him in—"you smell . . . of *him* . . . of your master."

All at once, voices bled into the silence. Someone was running along the corridor outside. Sara held her breath. It was Mills, and Dr. Breeden.

"Are you sure he came this way?" Mills panted.

"No more sure than you are," said the doctor, likewise out of breath. "He's led us a merry chase, but I could have sworn he turned down here."

"Her ladyship's door's ajar. My God, you don't suppose . . . ?" Mills said.

"There's only one way to find out," said Breeden.

"Keep that pistol at the ready, but do not shoot unless you're certain. I don't like the look of this."

Sara gasped. "They're entering my suite!" she panicked. "When they don't find me . . . !" She jumped to her feet. "We cannot stay here. Come, Nero!" But the wolf stood his ground. "You have to come *now!*" she whispered. "While they're occupied. It's all right, I know a place." Still the wolf wouldn't budge, and she tied Nicholas's dressing gown sash around his neck, snatched up the candle branch, and dragged him out into the corridor.

It was a struggle, but she finally persuaded him to follow. Together, they ran toward the landing, down the staircase, and into the main floor north wing unseen. It was a moment before she recognized the chamber she and Nell had entered to access the secret room and the smuggler's passageway. Her heart was hammering against her ribs, and though Nero was keeping pace with her, he was hardly resigned, balking at every turn.

"I'm trying to save your *life*," she scolded, prodding him through the false back in the armoire. "They are both armed. Oh, God! If you could only understand me!" she moaned.

The candle branch that was left behind on her first exploration was still lying where she'd dropped it, and she set it upright on the floor beside the panel to mark her way back, and pulled Nero along. The passageway was steeped in shadow. The walls, bleeding with moisture, glistened in the candlelight as they made their way toward the tunnel.

"We're almost there," she panted. Her lungs were burning from gulping the stale, dank air, and she could scarcely hear the clacking of Nero's long nails on the rough stone surface underfoot. It seemed a longer distance this time somehow, but the yawning black mouth of the tunnel finally loomed up before her, and she turned into the little alcove that sheltered the hidey-hole she'd noted when she'd explored the passageway with Nell. The door was a narrow wooden panel that swiveled in much the same manner as the one she had fallen through.

Positioned among other similar timbers along that recessed wall, it didn't look like a door at all. It took all her strength to move it. Inside, the room was level with the entrance, but Nero hung back, straining against the tether. It was all she could do to hold him.

"No, Nero!" she snapped. "You have to go in. You'll be safe here until I can think this through. The guards will come. They'll never find you here."

Still he held back, whining, pulling against her grip until she stepped inside and called him over the threshold.

"See?" she said, as he followed after her. "You can see in the dark—I know you can. I'll bring you food and water in the morning. You must stay here until the guards are gone. I won't let them harm you. I *won't!*"

He seemed confused, and she took advantage of the moment to run out and slide the panel shut. Tears welled in her eyes at the sound of his muffled howl from the other side. It reminded her of the howl that had so frightened Nell. Poor Nell. She dared not think of that then, and she ran back along the passageway with that mournful howl ringing in her ears.

She reentered the house proper with ease, but she moved with caution. It was almost first light. Soon the servants would be about their morning chores—sooner than usual no doubt, considering the circumstances. It wouldn't do to be caught wandering the halls in her nightclothes.

There was no sign of life until she reached the staircase. Then, tall shadows bleeding across the second-floor walls above soon took on human form. The footmen were fitting the sconces with fresh candles. The gloomy halls were lit day and night, the candles replenished accordingly. She couldn't go up until the footmen moved on to the third floor, and she ducked behind the staircase and melted into the shadows to wait. It seemed an eternity before she heard their footfalls on the carpeted stairs above. Still she waited, giving them ample time to set about their tasks before tiptoeing up the staircase, and skittering to her suite.

Her foyer door was ajar just as she'd left it. Mills and Dr. Breeden must have left it as they'd found it so she wouldn't know they'd gone inside. She glanced across the hall. The door to the green suite was open a crack also. She hadn't thought to close it in her haste to flee with Nero earlier. She hesitated. Could Nicholas be inside? If he was, he had some explaining to do, and without hesitation she stepped over the threshold.

The first gray streamers of a feeble dawn were showing at the windows, breaking the magic spell of the night before, when for a brief moment—a blink of time's eye—heaven had opened to her, only to shut its gates too soon. Would they ever open to her again? Not unless Baron Nicholas Walraven became willing to trust her with his heart, and all its secrets.

The suite was empty, and she stepped out into the hall again, and went to her own across the way. The rooms were in semidarkness, the fires having gone out, and she'd left no candles lit. The light of dawn wasn't as generous on the west side of the house at that hour, and she could barely see, but the sound of motion close by stood the hairs on the back of her neck on end, and drew her scalp taut with gooseflesh.

"W-who's th-there?" she stammered, straining the darkness with darting glances for someone to materialize.

A heavy snort that bordered on a growl replied, and she followed the sound to the glimmer of two shining eyes, and a flash of long white fangs beneath curled back lips.

"Nero!" she gushed. "How did you get back here?"

Twenty-three

Mills hadn't closed his eyes all night, nor had he left Nicholas's sitting room in the master suite. Dr. Breeden had begun to doze, reclining on the lounge across the way. The valet didn't have the heart to disturb him, though he should; the stiff horsehair antique wasn't large enough to accommodate the doctor properly.

Should he go down again and look for the baroness? He'd been debating it. He was weary of body and spirit from trekking up and down the grand staircase through the night to no avail. Now dawn had broken, and there was still no sign of the baron, the baroness, or Nero, either. No one had seen any of them since the incident, and fear of another calamity had parched his throat and kept him from his slumber. He wouldn't rest until he knew. He'd failed the father; he would not fail the son. Nicholas was like his own. Hadn't he practically raised him since a child, when the strangeness began? Where would it end? Or had it ended already? He shuddered to wonder.

One of them should have returned by now. If not Nicholas, surely Nero would have come . . . if he could. That worried him most of all, with everyone in residence gunning for the animal, and he shuffled back into the dressing room for another look at the staved-in door. In all his years, he had never seen the like. He had never witnessed Nero in such a taking. He had gnawed and clawed the lower panel of that door until he'd weakened it enough to crash through. It happened so quickly there had been no time to react, and they couldn't have stopped him in any case. Nero had streaked through the suite—all but knocking them down—and then disappeared, no more than a blur, in the shadows of the staircase landing by the time they'd reached it. He had one thing and one thing only in his mind: his mate. And woe betide the soul who got between him and his purpose. They had both been wise enough not to attempt it.

Mills squatted down and fingered the broken door panel. Splinters were scattered on both sides of the door, but larger pieces littered the bedroom side where Nero had burst through. Mills glanced upward. The door was more than twice his height. It would be a mammoth undertaking to repair, let alone replace. The wood was centuries old. That mattered not to the deranged wolf that had done the damage. How was he ever going to explain this to the rest of the staff? He'd had his challenges with his master's transformations over the years, but nothing ever to equal this. The others in the house suspected something, he was certain. How could they not. But never in a million years would they possibly imagine Baron Walraven's secret . . . unless they came face-to-face with it, which was what the valet now feared most of all.

"I'm sorry, Mills," said the doctor, who had crept up behind him. "Don't reproach yourself. There was nothing either one of us could do. I couldn't calm him, much less hold him."

"I'd barely gotten back inside when he came crashing through this panel," said Mills. "I could have sworn I'd closed the sitting room door behind me."

"You did," said the doctor. "He bit down upon that door handle until he opened it. He tried that in the dressing room, too, but I'd thrown the bolt above, and he couldn't reach it."

Mills gave a harsh chuckle. There was no humor in it. "Well, to comfort us at least we have the knowledge that he tried to keep the damage to a minimum," he said, getting up stiffly. "He didn't . . . you haven't been bitten?" he asked.

"No," said the doctor. "He wasn't interested in me, though I will admit I didn't give him a chance to be. I have never seen anything like that in all my years of researching such phenomena. What could have happened to set him off like that? His lady was in no danger—at least, not then. Have you found her?"

"No, and his lordship should have returned by now, in one incarnation or another. I'm worried, Dr. Breeden. I've been up and down those stairs all night. I cannot imagine why one of them hasn't surfaced by now. I daren't alert the others to help in the search. They aren't aware, and we cannot wait any longer. We cannot leave the girl lying dead in the second-floor hallway indefinitely. It's unthinkable that she's been left there disrespected like that this long, and we mustn't move her until we've had the guards in. I haven't the authority to send for them—none of us does. In his lordship's absence, the next in line for dealing with house emergencies would be her ladyship, and she's gone missing as well. We've got to find her."

"Does the abigail have family?" said Breeden.

"No, and that's one blessing, at least, but it doesn't negate the seriousness of the situation. All below stairs are that girl's family, Doctor, and have been since she joined the staff ten years ago. They will want justice for what's happened, and we all know what that means. While we both know he's innocent, Nero's life is forfeit here now. Why hasn't he made the transformation back? I cannot understand it."

"How long does it normally take for him to transform when he's this overset?" Breeden queried.

"That's just it—I have never seen him this overset. If anger or upsetment causes the change, he runs off that energy until he's calmed, and then becomes himself again. When aroused, it often takes longer. We don't know exactly what set him off this time, but whatever it was, judging by the way he came tearing in here, it's nearly driven him mad. As long as he stays so, he will remain as he is. The hellish thing is, whatever that might be, he needs to be himself to solve it. He cannot do it as the wolf."

"Then we've got our work cut out for us, Mills," said the doctor. "I thought as much, when animal magnetism had no effect upon him in wolf form. We need to have him back, so I can work on him in his human incarnation. Where shall we begin? I suppose I ought to examine the girl. I shall be able to help with that when the guards come, without damning wolf or master. You can count upon it."

"No, not yet," said Mills. His tired mind was racing. Nothing seemed real anymore, except the premonition of impending doom that had gripped his heart like a vise. "One of us should remain here until his lordship returns," he decided. "I'd best go below and see if her ladyship has gone back to her rooms first. We must send for the guards. Then, I shall keep watch here while you examine the . . . body." He looked the doctor in the eyes. "I am so sorry that all of this has been put upon you, Dr. Breeden," he said, gesturing to encompass the entire circumstance.

"Nonsense," said the doctor. "This is just the sort of thing that normally fuels my passion. Though, I wish it weren't happening to those I have grown fond of. It's rather difficult in these circumstances to look at all this with a clinical eye."

"I shan't be long," said Mills, walking back through the bedroom.

"Have you got your pistol?" the doctor called after him.

"I'd be loath to use it," said Mills. "But yes."

* * *

Sara backed steadily away from the snarling animal in her foyer. Was he out of sorts because she'd locked him in the alcove chamber? How did he get out? He'd lost the dressing gown sash she'd used for a leash, and it didn't seem likely that he would follow her without one in his present humor. He couldn't escape. She'd closed the foyer door this time.

"Let me pass," she scolded. "I shall have to fetch something to tether you with. You cannot stay here. The day has begun. Some of the servants are already at their chores. You're going back to that room, whether you like it or not. Don't you know I'm trying to help you, Nero? You aren't safe here now."

Inching along, she eased her way into the bedchamber. Shaking moisture from his shaggy coat, the beast followed her as far as the threshold then sat, his penetrating eyes watching her every move as she backed toward the wardrobe.

"How did you get so wet?" she asked. "You've been out on the strand again, haven't you?"

The animal made no response, but when she reached inside the wardrobe, he got to his feet, his hackles raised, and his lips began to curl. It was a silent snarl this time, but there was no mistaking its warning.

"It's no use," she snapped. "You may as well behave. I'm not going to let them kill you."

The words were scarcely out, when a knock at the foyer door wrenched a loud, guttural snarl from those curled-back lips, and when the door came open, the wolf sprang and leaped through it, driving Mills down as it fled.

Sara's scream, Mills's outcry as he hit the floor, and the thunderous crack of his pistol shot rang out in rapid succession. Sara reached him before he could stand scanning the hallway for some sign of the animal, but it was vacant.

"You've killed him!" she shrilled at the valet sprawled below.

"No, my lady, I missed," he gritted, soothing his bony elbow, which had taken the brunt of the impact. "The fall spoiled my aim, more's the pity."

Dr. Breeden came running at the pace of a man half his age, and knelt beside the fallen valet.

"Are you all right, Mills?" he panted. "H-he didn't bite you?"

"No, he did not," the valet said, allowing the doctor to help him to his feet. "Just knocked the wind out of me making his escape."

"Come. Let me have a look at your arm."

"No, not just yet," said the valet. "The others are going to be up here any moment. "If you would help, go down and tell them to stay below stairs until further notice—all of them. I would have a word with her ladyship before I join you again." He turned to Sara, sweeping his good arm toward her sitting room. "My lady," he said. "We must talk."

Sara took her seat on the lounge, and bade the valet be seated also.

"Are you really all right, Mills?" she said. "You don't look it."

"I will be fine, my lady," he said. "Where have you been? We have been beside ourselves searching for you after what occurred here last night."

"I have been looking for his lordship," she snapped, "who doesn't seem to have a care that someone has been killed here!"

"My lady, you cannot wander about here now unattended. It simply isn't safe until these matters are resolved."

"Aren't you presuming too much authority here, Mills?" she said. He was only a valet, after all. He had forgotten his place.

"No, my lady, I am not," he responded, getting to his feet. "The master would have my head if you were to come to harm in his absence. He has left you in my charge."

"And where is he off to this time, your master?" she insisted.

"He stepped out for a walk on the strand last night," said the valet, "before the tragedy . . . as I told you."

"And, he's been gone all night?" she queried.

"He sometimes spends the night on the strand in fine weather, my lady. We are so often deprived here, what with the prevailing winds that never cease, and the currents on this coast that make short work of fine weather more often than not at this time of the year."

"You're lying," she said flatly, surging to her feet.

"I beg your pardon, madam?" the valet breathed.

"I said, you are lying, Mills," she repeated. "He went for no walk on the strand last night. He was with me in the green suite until Nell's scream parted us. He ran out to see what had occurred, and he never returned. Now will you tell me what has become of your master?"

"With *you*, my lady?" the valet murmured.

"With me."

"Praise God!" he murmured in an undertone.

"I'm waiting, Mills. Where is my husband?"

The valet's posture collapsed. "I do not know, my lady, and I did not want to overset you."

"Well, I am overset, Mills," Sara said. "Nero did not harm Nell. I will never believe it. You tried to *shoot* him just now."

"My lady, you must leave such matters to us," he said, "but if you would be of service to this house, there is an urgent matter that needs your immediate attention."

"And, what might that be?" She was verging upon being rude, but there was nothing for it. If he could not give her an honest answer, he hardly deserved civility. What did they all know that she did not, and why wouldn't they tell her? If she were in such danger, as they all professed, why would no one tell her from whom, or from what?

"Nell has not died . . . of natural causes, my lady," he said.

"The guards must be called in. In the absence of his lordship, the authority for that falls to yourself. The body cannot be removed and prepared for burial until they've come and gone."

Sara sank back down on the lounge. Finally, something for her to command as mistress of Ravencliff, and she would have given anything to designate it to someone else. Tears welled in her eyes. Of course the guards must be called in. The poor girl had lain all night where she'd fallen. Of course Sara must be the one to give the order, and in so doing, she would seal Nero's fate. Where was Nicholas? Her heart was breaking.

"I'm sorry, my lady," said Mills. "There is no other way."

"Of course," said Sara. "Send someone to fetch the guards at once."

"It would be best that you keep to your apartments until they've come and gone, my lady," said the valet. "I do not know if you are aware, but they have already been out here once over tales that were told in the village. This will be difficult now because of that. You had best leave the guards to me. It would stand to reason that you would be in a taking after such an event. If they insist upon questioning you, it would be best that you actually *be* in a taking, if you follow my meaning, and offer as little by way of explanation as possible. If you will permit me, you were asleep when the scream woke you, and by time you exited your suite, the servants had gathered 'round the . . . body, and you were so overset Mrs. Bromley saw you back to your rooms, and stayed to quiet you."

"You have it all sorted out, don't you?" Sara said.

"Yes, my lady."

"What of his lordship? Where was he when all this was taking place?"

"His lordship has been called away on urgent estate business. He left Ravencliff before the tragedy. I helped him pack, and saw him off."

"Yes, of course," Sara replied. "Why doesn't that surprise me? The last time his lordship was 'called away' on urgent business, I found him in his rooms recuperating from a pistol shot. You were trying not to overset me on that occasion, too, as I recall. What would I find if I stormed the bastion up there now, Mills?"

"N-nothing, my lady," said the valet. "He is not there, I assure you."

"Then you shan't object if I see for myself."

"I would rather you not, my lady," said the valet. Why did he look as though he was about to expire? He'd suddenly gone as white as the morning mist drifting past the window. Indeed, the mist had more color. "I shall send Mrs. Bromley up with an herbal draught to calm you, and she will remain closeted with you in your suite until the guards have come and gone."

"After I've visited the master suite," Sara returned, storming out through the foyer door.

Mills's spindly legs were no match for her long, agile ones. She reached the third floor before he negotiated the landing, and burst into the empty master suite sitting room.

"Nicholas?" she cried, moving on to the bedchamber, but that was empty as well, except for Dr. Breeden, whom she found on his knees brushing up wood splinters with the hearth broom.

Sara skittered to a halt and gasped. "What on earth has happened here?" she murmured, staring at the gaping hole in the dressing room door.

"Nothing to cause you concern, my lady," said Mills from behind, clutching his elbow. His breath was coming short, and his color had not been restored, for all the blood-pumping experience of chasing her down two corridors and up a wicked flight of stairs. "'Tis just a little . . . architectural mishap."

"It looks rather like something more," she replied, arms akimbo.

"Well, I assure you, it's being addressed," said the valet. "And now, my lady, as you can see, his lordship is not here, and I really must insist that you return to your suite and lock yourself in. I shall see you there, and have Mrs. Bromley attend you straightaway. I shall need you to draft a missive to summon the guards?"

"Yes, of course," said Sara, her eyes still following the doctor's movements. He had pried some of the splintered wood away from the lower door as if it were something he did as a daily occurrence, and was stacking it neatly against the dressing room wall.

"Very good," said Mills. "Once I have it in hand, I shall have the stableman fetch them at once."

"I will do that," said the doctor, "and I will accompany her ladyship to her rooms, and remain with her until Mrs. Bromley arrives. Meanwhile, you will sit and calm yourself, Mills, or by the look of you, the guards will have two corpses to deal with when they arrive."

Twenty-four

Sara moved through the hours that followed like an automaton, with no more life than the little mechanical poppets sold at the fairs. Watts, the head stableman, brought the guards. They arrived at the noon hour, on the heels of a blustery squall that chased the morning mist with howling winds and torrents of horizontal rain. It couldn't have been more ill timed. They were too few in number to do a thorough search of Ravencliff, only a brief walk-through of the most-used chambers, and Nero's favorite haunts, pointed out by the staff.

A complete search of the house couldn't be conducted without more men, and a search of the grounds could not be managed in such a gale even if they were more in number. Despite Mills's account that he had fired on the animal that had killed Nell, and driven it from the house, the matter could not be laid to rest until every corner of the house and grounds had been searched and the animal responsible caught and killed before it attacked again. What this meant to Sara was that as soon as the gale subsided, they would be coming back. She had to find Nero, and hide him away in the alcove room again. It was the one place in the house where he would be safe from the guards. With any luck, they wouldn't even find the secret passageway, but if they did, the entrance to that hidey-hole was virtually invisible. She would be more careful in locking the panel this time. That was the plan, and it saw her through those hours, with only one thing left unsettled. Where was Nicholas?

The guards found no fault with Mills's explanation of Nicholas's absence. They did question Sara, as she knew they would, but she followed the valet's direction to the letter—even to feigning a swoon when the interrogation became awkward—and they contented themselves with the accounts of Mills and Smythe and Dr. Breeden, whose medical report and corroboration of the servants' accounts went a long way toward satisfying the investigators.

Permission was given to remove the body for burial. The nearest undertaker was brought from Padstow, and with Mrs. Bromley's help, he prepared Nell and placed her body on a bier in the morning room, where she would remain until the storm passed over. The coffin, illuminated head and foot with candle branches, was closed, which was a mercy. The little abigail had been brutally savaged.

Sara refused to believe that Nero had done such a thing, but if he had not, who could have committed such a heinous assault? All signs pointed to Nero—the manner in which Nell was killed left little room for argument. Nell didn't like the animal, and lately, when he was out of sorts, she'd feared him. Dogs were known to attack humans in whom they sensed fear, and Nicholas said Nero was part *wolf*. Who knew what that combination bred? Had the feral instinct in him surfaced? Had Nell become a victim of it? Sara thought of the times she'd felt fear in Nero's presence, and, yes, it had emboldened him on all occasions. No! Not her Nero. She would never believe it. There must be another explanation.

She decided to take her meals in her rooms. She was perfectly fit to go down to the dining hall, but it would be harder for her to collect food for Nero from there, and get it back to her suite without the footmen or Dr. Breeden noticing. It was a much better plan to play the overset mistress in earnest. She did, however, spend her time in between by keeping vigil in the morning room. It was the least she could do for the little maid who had been such a faithful servant.

One by one, the staff members filed in as their time allowed. All the while, Sara's eyes were trained on the morning room door in anticipation of Nicholas striding through, but he never appeared. The candles were nearly burned to their sockets, when Mrs. Bromley came to replace them.

"Fie, my lady, are ya still down here, then?" she scolded. "It's half-eleven. Do ya mean ta tell me nobody came ta see ya upstairs?"

"I put them off," said Sara, rising. Her limbs were stiff. She couldn't imagine from what. Sheer tension, she supposed, and she soothed the back of her neck, and stretched.

"Nobody can be spared to replace her," said the housekeeper, laying a hand on the coffin. "You'll have to be content with me, comin' as my duties allow, till the master returns and we can bring another maid from the village ta attend ya. This has always been a man's house, my lady. Menservants is what we've got mostly, but for a few chambermaids and scullions, none o' which is fit ta offer ya."

"Don't worry about me, Mrs. Bromley," said Sara. "I'm well accustomed to managing on my own. I'll be fine." This was good news. She needed no witnesses to what she was planning. "Has the master returned?" she asked.

"No, my lady, neither Mills nor Smythe knows when he's expected, neither. Why, Smythe didn't even know he'd gone off—none o' us did, only Mills. It must've been somethin' what come up suddenlike."

"I expect so," said Sara.

"Look here, I can do this later," Mrs. Bromley said, laying the candles aside. "Let me see ya to your suite. You're goin' ta need your rest. The rain's slackin' some. If the storm blows over by mornin', so's the groundskeeper can dig the grave, we've got the burial ta deal with."

"Where will it be?" Sara wondered.

"We've got our own graveyard, my lady," Mrs. Bromley informed her. "It dates back ta the days when Ravencliff was a priory, or some such. It's all consecrated proper. Watts'll fetch the vicar down from Padstow when 'tis time. 'Tis what the master would want. He's offered it ta us all for our final restin' place, so long as we stay in his service, and those o' us who have no other scrap o' ground ta go inta when the time comes are grateful for it."

"The master is a very generous man."

"That he is, my lady. Nell had no folks livin'. We was her only family, so ta speak. 'Tis a fine cemetery, my lady—'tis where she'd want ta be, where her friends can visit her now and again, and not cast off on some strange parish. Why, his lordship's father and mother are buried out there, and them that went before and all. She'll be keepin' good company, she will."

"I think I will go up," said Sara, letting the housekeeper lead her. "I'm quite exhausted."

"I can ready ya for bed, but I can't stay with ya, my lady. There's just too much to be done here now."

"That's quite all right, Mrs. Bromley," Nell replied. "If the master should return, I want to be told at once—no matter what the hour."

"O' course, my lady, and ya lock yourself in up there, ya hear? We don't want no more untoward happenin's in this house. My poor ol' heart won't stand it."

"Yes," said Sara. "I'll be sure and do that."

Dr. Breeden repaired to the master suite to keep the vigil with Mills after dinner. They were closeted in the sitting room sipping sherry, which Mills poured one-handed, his left arm being confined to a sling.

"How is that elbow?" the doctor inquired.

"Mending," said the valet, as convincingly as he could manage. It was swollen and throbbing; a nasty sprain.

"Hmmm," growled the doctor. "Old bones mend slowly. You'd best favor that for awhile."

"I never expected to make 'old bones,'" the valet observed. "I'll be careful. Thank God it wasn't my pistol hand. I never doubted Nero—not for a second—but I'd never seen him in such a taking before, and that worried me. It was as if he had gone mad. Now we have proof positive that my faith in him was well-founded. The master was with her ladyship when Nell was killed. He left her to find out what happened, and never returned. He wasn't there when the rest of the staff arrived, and he never returned to my lady. Where could he be all this while, Dr. Breeden? I've wracked my brain over and over, and I cannot puzzle it out."

"It was Mallory's wolf incarnation that killed the girl, that's obvious, but we cannot tell that to the guards. They'll have us carted off to the madhouse." The physician gestured toward the dressing room. "Did you see the look on their faces when they saw that door?"

"I think they accepted my story, that we were trying to confine the animal until they arrived, and that he chewed through the wood, knocked me down, and escaped the house when I tried to stop him with my pistol. It was the only thing I could think of."

"They believed you, of course, but it made them all the more anxious to continue the search until the animal is found and destroyed."

"What we must do is have the master back, and make certain that never happens," Mills replied.

"I doubt they believed the animal was a stray—not after the tales your hall boy told in the village. Especially not that Captain Renkins, strutting and preening and gloating that he'd known something untoward was afoot out here. I don't envy his lordship, he's going to have the Devil's own time convincing him of that once he returns. What bothers me is that his lordship hasn't changed back in all this time. He should have done by now, unless, as you say, he is still in the same state of distress. The other alternative is too terrible to consider."

Mills entreated the doctor to elaborate with a silent stare. He couldn't bring himself to voice what was gnawing at his reason, either.

"That he has met with a similar fate as poor Nell," said Breeden. "We have to face the possibility, Mills. You yourself have said that Nero is a docile wolf. We both know Mallory's incarnation is not. I wonder are they equally matched."

"Considering how we last saw Nero, I would have to say yes, Doctor." Mills defended. "After all these years, I can almost read Nero's mind. Some, if not all, of his distress was over my lady. I thought so then. I'd stake my life upon it now. His lordship had been with her just prior to finding Nell savaged. He came here right after, and transformed before our very eyes. He loves her very much, Dr. Breeden. He won't be calmed until the stress of that is alleviated."

"Then, we must find him and calm him, Mills, as quickly as we can."

"Why? You think he might never change back if we don't?" Gooseflesh riddled the valet's spine until the bones snapped.

"I cannot say for certain," said the doctor. "Studies such as these are all speculative at best. We're plowing untilled soil, as it were. There is scant material on shapeshifters to draw from, and there doesn't seem to be a defined pattern of behavior that threads through all the known cases. I'm groping in the dark here, and I certainly hope I'm wrong, but Mallory was in a blind rage when he transformed, wasn't he, and he hasn't changed back, either . . . has he?"

Sara locked the door to her suite while Mrs. Bromley waited outside. Once the housekeeper's heavy footfalls receded along the corridor, she unlocked it again, and left it ajar for

Nero, just as she always did. Everything was in readiness. The food she'd collected was bundled away with the sash from her blue voile gown, which would suffice for a leash, and she'd climbed into bed to wait wearing her nightdress and wrapper. All that remained was for Nero to make his appearance.

Outside, the wind had died to a sighing murmur and the rain had ceased tapping on the window glass. The soft moaning echo of the sea crashing on the shore below began to lull her to sleep in spite of her resolve to stay awake. She dared not give in to it. If Nero didn't come to her, she would have to go to him, wherever that might be. The burial would certainly take place in the morning, now that the storm was passing. Then the guards would return, and they would find him, and they would kill him.

If only Nicholas weren't so set against her in this. If only he were as fond of Nero as she was, and she could have appealed to him—but he wasn't, and she was almost glad of his absence. If he were in residence, he would be first in line with a loaded pistol against the poor animal. These thoughts fed her dark, disturbing dreams as she dozed, all tangled into recollections of his deep, sensuous kiss, the power of his strong arms around her, the pressure of his hardness—the taste and feel and scent of him. She awoke with a start to a different scent, the musty odor of unwashed animal fur. Her eyes came open with a start.

"There you are!" she murmured. "I knew you'd come. I have a present for you." She lifted the food parcel from the dry sink next to the four-poster, and waved it in front of his nose. "Ah-ah-ah, not yet," she said, sliding her feet to the floor. "You have to be a good boy and come with me first."

Slipping the loop she'd made in the sash over his head, Sara pulled it tight enough that he couldn't slip out of it, took up the food parcel and candlestick, and led the animal out into the deserted hallway. It wouldn't be deserted long. It was nearly first light, and she hurried below, thankful that he was more interested in the food than proving his alpha-wolf status. He was in one of his moods again, nipping at the parcel, and blowing snorts through his nose that were too close to growls for her liking.

"No, you have to wait," she scolded, holding the parcel out of his reach. He did curl his lips back then, but they were nearly at the alcove room and, with the end of her mission in sight, resolution overcame fear.

He was used to traveling the passageway; that was obvious in the way he almost led her at the end, but he seemed to want to go into the tunnel, and she had to pull him back into the alcove. He'd nearly ripped open the food parcel, and she had to set the candlestick down to keep it out of his reach while she groped for the panel.

"All this could have been avoided, you know, if only you'd stayed in here," she said, feeling for the spring mechanism. "I don't know how you did get out, unless you tripped a spring on the other side. You mustn't do it again. The guards will be here in the morning. They will *shoot* you on sight if they find you roaming these halls."

It was becoming harder and harder to hold him. When her hands released the spring, she cried out in relief and nudged the narrow timber aside, expecting to find an empty chamber. Instead, two shiny dark eyes glowing red-gold in the candlelight glared back at her, and a tousled mass of silver-tipped black fur trailing a burgundy brocade dressing gown sash heaved through the opening, trampling a mound of splintered wood.

Sara dropped the food parcel and leash, as a rumble of bloodcurdling snarls echoed along the corridor. Before her wide-flung eyes, two streaks—no more than a blur—of shaggy, hackle-raised fur leaped into midair and collided, their bodies locked chest to chest in a tangle of muscle, sinew, and bared fangs, flinging drool and foam.

"My God!" she shrilled. *"There are two of you!"*

Nero had a death grip on the other wolf's shoulder, but

when Sara's screams distracted him, the beast broke Nero's hold and lunged for her with deadly aim at her throat. Again Nero sailed through the air, impacting the other, spoiling its aim and clamping sharp fangs into the shoulder of his barrel-chested adversary, until the wolf yelped its discomfort.

Still concentrating on Sara, the animal lunged again, and again Nero clamped down with deadly jaws, this time on the back of the wolf's neck. It screamed, spun, and plunged yowling into the tunnel, dragging Sara's blue silk sash behind it.

Nero threw back his head and loosed a triumphant howl that reverberated along the passageway once, twice—three earsplitting times, before he began to run in circles, backing Sara against the wall as his path widened in the narrow confines of the corridor. Then there was no more room to run. On the cutting edge of yet another mournful howl, he sprang through the air, and Nicholas emerged from the silvery blur of fur and fang and muscle, surging to his full height, before dropping spent and breathless to his knees, naked, at Sara's feet.

Staggering upright, Nicholas tore the dressing gown sash from his neck and spun toward her, shaking his damp hair out of his eyes, his broad chest heaving, glistening with sweat. For a split second, their gazes locked in the flickering semidarkness as the candles faded, then failed altogether just as Sara did, collapsing unconscious in his arms.

Twenty-five

Grinding out a string of blue expletives, Nicholas scooped Sara up, and carried her along the passageway to a different panel than the one she had come through. He needed no light to find his way. Possessed of night vision in both incarnations, he traveled the convoluted passageway with ease to a hidden door obscured by a tapestry. It led to the back stairs, and he took them two at a stride to the third floor, and stepped out into the shadowy corridor.

No one was about. It was still at least an hour before dawn. Hoping that Mills and the doctor had retired to their respective rooms, he made his stealthy way to the master suite unseen, and laid Sara on the bed. She looked so pale and still lying there. If he hadn't felt her sweet breath puffing against his skin as he carried her, he would have sworn she was dead.

The catastrophe had happened. There was nothing to be done about it now, and he raked his wet hair back from a pleated brow, and yanked his burgundy dressing gown from the wardrobe in the corner. Untangling the sash Sara had tied around Nero's neck, he cinched it about his waist ruthlessly. He didn't even remember bringing it with him from the lower regions.

Sitting beside her on the bed, he began a frantic search of her person, praying he would find no wounds. He had not bitten her, of that he was certain, but Mallory's wolf had come close on several occasions—too close. His hands were trembling, his heart hammering against his ribs as he examined her slender throat, her arms, hands, and legs. Nothing. No blood, no break in that translucent skin anywhere.

"Thank God," he murmured, heaving a mammoth sigh. Should he wake her? God, no! Let her stay so, at least until he'd formed some sort of defense. What that would be, he had no idea, and he began to pace the carpet, his hands clasped in white-knuckled fists behind him in a vain attempt to give birth to a plausible explanation. All at once, a shuffling sound at his back spun him around to find Mills, in his nightshirt, one arm in a linen sling, the other aiming a flintlock at his middle.

"Oh, my lord!" the misty-eyed valet gushed, lowering the pistol to his side, as though it weighed ten stone. "Praise God in His heaven! We'd all but given you up."

"Shhh," Nicholas hissed, nodding toward Sara.

"What's happened?" the valet murmured.

"The worst," said Nicholas, drawing him into the sitting room, for fear of waking Sara. "It happened right in front of her."

"Is she . . . ?"

"No. She's just fainted," said Nicholas. "What have you done to yourself?"

"The other animal knocked me down, and spoiled my aim. Dr. Breeden's seen to it. It's nothing. Where have you been, my lord? We have been half out of our minds with worry."

"I was with Sara in the green suite when Nell screamed.

Another moment, and there would have been no more talk of petitioning the Archbishop of Canterbury. I went to see what had occurred, and found Nell . . . what was left of her. I knew at once it was Alex, and I knew something else, too. He has been visiting Sara as well. She thought *Nero* was suffering from changes of mood, and she was concerned because he frightened her at times.

"To make short of it, I felt the transformation coming on. I couldn't go back to Sara, and I couldn't stay with the body, either. It would have happened before the staff, they were nearly upon me. I ran up the back stairs, and got here just in time."

"So that's what put you in such a taking. My lord, in all these years—"

"I was aroused. Then the shock of Nell, and the fear of Sara welcoming that bastard into her suite, thinking it was me . . . I believe I did go mad, Mills. Then it got worse."

"But, where have you been all this while, my lord? The guards have come and gone, and they are coming back to seek out the animal and kill it."

"Good!" Nicholas flashed. "Let them kill it, because if they don't, I will."

"But what if it's *you* they kill? If you transform again here now, it will be your last."

"I shall make every effort not to," said Nicholas. "But as things are, I can promise nothing."

"We searched everywhere for you, my lord—*everywhere!*"

"Not quite everywhere, old boy," Nicholas returned. "After Nero broke out of here, he ran to the green suite. The brouhaha was over, and fearing I would be shot on sight, her ladyship made a tether of this sash"—he slapped at it—"and shut me in the alcove chamber below. The timber there that forms the door is more than a foot thick. Nero had chewed halfway through it, when she came below just now with the other wolf in tow. We fought, and at the end of it, Alex's wolf ran off, and I changed right before her eyes. There was no way to prevent it, Mills, and when it happened, she dropped like a stone."

Mills heaved a ragged sigh. "What will you ever tell her, my lord?" he breathed.

"That is exactly what I would like to know," said a voice from the bedroom doorway that spun them both around.

It was Sara.

"Leave us, Mills," said Nicholas, not taking his eyes from hers. Why couldn't he read that look?

"Very good, my lord," said the valet, bowing as he left.

"Sit down, Sara," Nicholas said, sweeping his arm toward the horsehair lounge.

"I think that I shall," she replied, making her way to it—on unsteady legs, he noted, and why not? She'd just witnessed her beloved pet change into her naked husband.

"We need to talk," he said.

"A mild understatement, I daresay," she said with a humorless chuckle. "Where is Nero? And where did that other dog come from? Tell me I didn't see what I think I saw down there just now."

"Not a dog," said Nicholas. "It was a wolf . . . the wolf that killed Nell. He just tried to kill you, as well." She drained of all color before his eyes. *God, don't let her swoon again!* He needed to have this said now, while he had the courage. "Let me pour you a glass of sherry," he offered, reaching for the decanter on the drum table.

"I do not want sherry," she snapped. "I want answers, Nicholas. What in God's name is going on here? Where has Nero gone? What have you done with him?"

Nicholas bypassed the sherry, and poured himself a brandy. Would she understand something that he didn't really understand himself? Would he be able to convince her to stay once he'd told her? Would she ever be able to love him—accept him as the bizarre phenomenon he really was? By the look of her then, it didn't bode well.

"I have done nothing to Nero, Sara," he said. "Nero and I

257

are one entity . . . or rather, two forms of the same entity. We are one and the same. I've always told you I meant him no harm."

"How can you be? That's insane! You said yourself that I shouldn't become attached to that dog, because you were planning to get rid of him. What? Were you contemplating suicide . . . meaning to get rid of *yourself?* Why did you bring me here, then? That's ridiculous!"

"No, the servants told you I was planning to get rid of him. That was the story I told them. They know none of what I'm about to tell you, Sara, and it must remain so. I told you that you shouldn't become attached to Nero because he might be leaving us. That is why Dr. Breeden has come . . . to help Nero leave us."

"I don't understand any of this," she said, shaking her head.

"I'm going to try to help you understand, Sara," he said, "but you have to bear with me, and promise to hear me out. Much of this is new to me as well, and it's difficult to speak about. I have never done with anyone but Mills, and the doctor."

"All right, go on, then—explain," she said, folding her arms beneath her bosom, "but I may as well tell you, I think you're quite addled."

"Before I was born, my father served in India, where he was bitten by a wolf," Nicholas began. Her eyes were riveted to him, and he started to pace, taking sips from the snifter. "Your father was stationed with him out there, and it was he who killed the wolf that attacked, and he who saved my father's life. When I heard that the daughter of Father's comrade-in-arms, as it were, had been imprisoned for debt, I pressed my suit immediately. Had I known of your distress beforehand, you never would have gone to Fleet Prison."

"So it was a philanthropic venture, our union?"

"Partly that, and partly what I've already told you, that I wanted to marry to put paid to the hounding of the *ton.*

Then, too, I was so terribly lonely, Sara. I had hoped that our arrangement would ease that somewhat, and dared not even begin to hope that Dr. Breeden might be able to help me find a way to live a normal life. But all that was before I met you. Now, it's quite something else."

"What 'else' is it, Nicholas, exactly?" she murmured.

"My God, don't you know I'm in love with you?" he said. "You've stolen both our hearts . . . mine and Nero's, don't you know that? Couldn't you feel it in my arms in that bed?"

"I thought I did," she said. "I hoped I did, but we are not discussing that here now. You need to trust me with the rest of this—whatever it is—before we address that issue."

"Of course," he responded. "Forgive me. Father's wound would not heal, and he was mustered out. I never knew him, Sara. He died, of complications related to the wolf bite, while I was still in my cradle. Mills was his valet as well, and he nursed Father, but Father distanced himself from Ravencliff at the end. He died alone abroad, and my mother never recovered from the loss. She passed when I was twelve. It was then that my . . . condition came to light."

There was nothing in her face, and he went on praying she would keep her word and hear him out. "Whenever I am angry, overly excited . . . or aroused," he went on, "I change into the form of a wolf—the wolf you know as 'Nero.' I cannot help it, or prevent it happening, but I always have fair warning—enough time to shed my clothes before the change occurs. The trouble is, while I can feel it coming on, I cannot control it. Dr. Breeden has been trying to help me do that, since there is no cure. That is what was going on when you came in on us with this deuced dressing gown. He was attempting to speak to my subconscious mind, just as Mesmer did with his patients."

"A . . . *werewolf*?" Sara breathed. "Is that what you're telling me you are? I thought werewolves were nothing more than fiction—made-up tales to frighten children!"

"No, Sara, not a werewolf, though that's what I thought,

too, until Dr. Breeden diagnosed it properly. It seems I am what is known as a *shapeshifter*. Werewolves are shapeshifters of a sort, as well. Anyone with the ability to transform would fall into that category, according to Dr. Breeden. But the werewolf is a different entity entirely—in a class all its own. An evil, predatory entity at the other end of the spectrum of creatures with the ability to take on other forms. And like yourself, I'd always believed such beings were creatures of myth.

"As near as we can tell, my father passed the condition on to me when I was conceived. We don't know what the wolf that bit him was, or what he passed on to my father. He's taken that to his grave, so all we can do is try to deal with what exists in me."

"I . . . I thought that what I saw down in that passageway was some clever sleight of hand," Sara murmured, "some trick of the mind, but you're *serious!* You actually believe that you and Nero . . . !"

"We are," he said at her hesitation. "Now do you understand why it had to be a proxy wedding, why I cannot leave Ravencliff—even to marry? Can you imagine what you just saw happening on the dance floor at Almack's, or in the middle of Hyde Park one Sunday afternoon? Now do you see why I want no heirs to pass this nightmare on to, why I dared not risk consummating our marriage? That almost happened anyway, and I changed right after I left you. I barely made it to the master suite before it happened, and they locked me in the dressing room, until Nero chewed through the door panel and came back to be sure you were safe. Then you shut me, or rather Nero—it's so difficult for me to separate us—up in the alcove chamber, where he stayed until just now. The minute I saw that you were safe I changed back. Unfortunately, you were there when it happened. I never meant for you to find out in that way."

"Are you saying that you changed because of what nearly happened between us?"

"That, and finding Nell, but what nearly drove me mad

was learning that the wolf that killed her had been visiting you, and that you thought it was *Nero*. I knew you were in danger, and I couldn't change back to protect you. I was too overset to calm myself and let the change occur."

"Where did that other wolf come from, Nicholas?" she murmured.

He hesitated. Did she believe anything he'd told her thus far? There was no way to tell. That face would be perfect in the gambling hells; no one would ever guess her hand. He heaved a ragged sigh, stopped pacing, and set the empty snifter down. He hadn't even realized he'd drained it until he tried to take another swallow. If she didn't believe what had gone before, she would never believe what he was about to tell her now.

"Do you remember the night that Alex came into your room and nearly raped you?"

"That's not something I'm likely to forget," she said.

"Nero bit him, didn't he? And then Alex got his pistols and shot him in the shoulder. What did you find when you entered my suite several days later? That's right," he said to her gasp. "You found me recuperating from a *shoulder wound*."

"But there were two shots fired!"

"The other missed," he said succinctly. "I ought to know, I was there, and I was fortunate. Alex held the record at Manton's Gallery several seasons ago. He's an excellent shot, when he's sober."

Sara gasped again. "That's how you knew he told me himself that he assumed I'd left the door ajar for him! You . . . or rather Nero, *heard* him say it."

Nicholas nodded. Was he gaining ground? He hoped so, because the next words out of his mouth were either going to prove his position, or damn him as a bedlamite in her beautiful eyes.

"Nero bit Alex, Sara," he said, "and Alex hasn't been seen since . . . but the other wolf has, hasn't he? Nero was the only animal in this house until that night."

"Are you trying to tell me that Mr. Mallory has become . . . as you are, because you . . . *Nero* bit him?"

"The condition can be passed on in that way, just as a werewolf passes its affliction on to its victims. Let's not lose sight of the fact that my father passed this madness on to me after he was bitten—a weaker strain of what he must have been. This is not an exact science, Sara. You have only to ask Dr. Breeden. No two cases are alike. That is why he was so anxious to come out here and study mine. When did you first notice a change in Nero's behavior?"

Sara was silent apace. "It was after the shooting," she said. "I thought that was what caused him to be out of sorts."

"Dr. Breeden says that the personality of the man will mirror that of his animal incarnation. Alex and I are polar opposites. While we look the same in wolf form, our animal incarnations are different enough for you to have noticed a behavioral change. What else did the wolf do that made you fear him?"

"His general demeanor was different. He didn't greet me in the usual way, wagging his tail, nuzzling to be petted . . . almost seeming to smile. He seemed indifferent—"

"Thank God!" Nicholas interjected, in genuine relief.

"By that, I mean, instead of jumping up on my bed, he would lounge on the hearthstone, curling his lips back in a silent snarl when I tried to approach him and a genuine snarl when I attempted to examine his wound that time."

"Where was that wound, Sara?" Nicholas asked, hoping this would sway her.

"In . . . his *foreleg!*" she breathed. "It happened so fast, I was confused. I thought what I first had taken for a shoulder wound was actually . . . lower. *I wasn't wrong.* Oh, Nicholas!"

He nodded. "Alex carried the wound Nero gave him into his animal incarnation, just as Nero carried the gunshot wound into my human incarnation."

"If all this is possible, why hasn't Mr. Mallory changed back?" said Sara.

"We do not know," Nicholas replied. "He was foxed, and in a blind rage when Nero bit him, and I was nearly running mad the last time I transformed. You know how long it took me to change back. That was the longest it has ever taken. Perhaps he's confused, and not knowing what's happened to him, he cannot change back. Perhaps his intellect isn't developed enough, or he remains in a state of distress that won't allow him to change. Or perhaps the untreated wound has poisoned his blood. There's no way to be certain."

"This is . . . impossible!" Sara murmured.

"Impossible, but true."

"What happens to you when you . . . transform? How do you know when to change back?"

"Nero runs off the energy that caused the change until he calms, and then it just . . . occurs."

"So, this is why I've so often found you in a state of undress?"

"Yes. You said once that such had occurred thrice. I can only recall two occasions, plus this last, of course."

"Do you remember the night that we met on the stairs? You were wearing your dressing gown, and I'd been following Nero . . . oh, my God! You *knew* I had been!"

"Yes, because Nero was with you just prior to that," he said.

"I sought you in the study earlier, and saw your clothes and muddy boots on the floor, but you weren't there. I couldn't imagine why you had discarded them there, of all places."

"Ahhhhh, so that was it," he realized. "I discarded them there, because that is where the transformation took place. I'd been out on the strand, trying to walk off the effects you were having upon me all the way 'round, and I barely made it to the study before it happened. It often happens out there, but not on that occasion. As I've said, I cannot control it."

"Then . . . that day when I climbed down to the strand and found your clothes . . . ?"

"The day Nero saved you from drowning, yes. He nearly got cut off that day. There are several other ways to access Ravencliff from below, but not in a squall—they flood too quickly—and not in wolf form. I barely changed and made it back before that stretch of beach disappeared. As it was, half the clothes you saved for me are lost at sea, and those I did manage to salvage went straight into the dustbin."

Sara shook her head and lowered her eyes. Were those tears glistening on her lashes?

"But this . . . I don't know, Nicholas," she murmured. "I . . . just don't know."

"What other changes did you notice in 'Nero'?" he asked. "It's important, Sara. I need to know."

"Nothing specific that I haven't already told you . . . except the time he dragged my clothes out of the wardrobe, I had to burn a nightdress and wrapper. He'd urinated upon them."

"Nero marked his territory in your suite as well, that is why Alex's wolf did that. He was canceling that out, claiming it—claiming *you*—for himself. Bloody hell!"

"He did it more than once."

"Go on," Nicholas growled, raking his fingers through his damp hair. "Anything else that you can recall."

"When I found him in my bed that time . . . the night I doused him with water from the pitcher on my nightstand, I later learned that when he left me, he menaced Nell, but she shooed him off. I told her not to run from him . . . not to show her fear. Oh, Nicholas!"

"You're sure he didn't *bite* you?" Nicholas interrupted. "Not even the slightest scratch?"

"No, he didn't," she replied. "The cold water chased him, and I did lock the door afterward that time. I wanted to teach him some manners. That . . . wasn't Nero?"

Nicholas's heart was pounding. He wanted to take her in his arms and hold her and kiss her and shake her all at once.

He did none of it. He took deep, tremulous breaths, and swallowed his rapid heartbeat.

"No, Sara, it wasn't," he said. "How long ago was that?"

"Just before . . . Nell. She told me he had snapped at her, too."

"Did he come back afterward?"

"No," she said. "That was the last, until just now, when I brought him below . . . and found you."

"How did you find that room down there?" he snapped.

"Nell showed me the way. We heard a howl in the tunnel, and then *one of you* appeared, and we ran back into the house proper."

"That wasn't Nero, either, Sara."

"You're frightening me now!"

"Good! Somebody has to. Do you finally understand why you must keep your door locked? Nero will not be returning to your suite, but that other wolf surely will, and it will kill you, Sara, just as it killed Nell."

"Why couldn't you have told me all this from the start?" she moaned.

"Would you have believed me, if I had?"

She hesitated. "No," she said low-voiced. "Probably not then. I don't even know what to believe now. This is preposterous!"

"Well, there it is," he said, the words slumping his body. "I didn't tell you, because I didn't want to lose you."

"That is unfortunate. You should have trusted me enough to take the chance," she said, rising from the lounge. Dawn was breaking. The first bleak ribbons of a cottony fog were pressed up against the windowpanes, throwing a distorted shaft of light on the floor between them. "The storm is over," she observed. "The vicar is coming this morning for the burial, and then the guards will doubtless return to finish searching the house and grounds for . . . *Nero*, the mad dog they think has killed her!"

265

"Sara . . ."

"Not now, Nicholas," she murmured. "I need time to sort all this out. We must see to Nell first. We owe her that much. . . . *I* owe her that much."

"Will you promise me that you'll lock your door until the other wolf is found . . . and dealt with?"

Sara nodded.

"Nero gave him a few more wounds just now. That will only serve to rile him more than he is already. I will be in the green suite each night until this is resolved, and I will be armed."

When she started to move past him, he took her in his arms, but she held him at bay with both her tiny hands pressed against his breast, and would not look him in the eyes.

"Not now, Nicholas," she said. "Please . . . don't! I need time to think."

Nicholas hung his head. "Of course," he said. The words tasted of bile. The worst of it was, she was right: He should have trusted her. He should have taken the chance. Even Mills had said as much.

"I love you, Sara," he said. "I don't want you to leave me, but you are not a prisoner here. I told you that at the start. If you cannot accept this situation—accept me, and our arrangement under these circumstances—I shall use my connections to petition the proper authority to release you from your vows. Either way, it will be a lengthy process. I shan't lie to you; it could take years. I'm not trying to persuade you, only to make you aware, but you needn't be cast upon poor relations if it comes to that. I have other estates, where you could be housed in comfort pending resolution. In return, I ask only that you not betray my secret. I shouldn't want this bruited about, or I will likely be hunted down like the animal . . . that I am."

Sara made no reply. She burst into deep, wracking sobs, broke free of his embrace, and fled.

Twenty-six

Nicholas moved through the motions of the burial with a close eye upon Sara, who gave him no opportunity to continue their conversation. He would not press her. He watched in rapt amazement as she stood at the graveside, consoling the servants, taking matters in hand in a way that he himself never could have done, as though nothing had happened between them, though she would not meet his eyes. It was just as well. She had been crying. Despite a liberal application of talc, her fair skin was painted with blotches, and her eyes were nearly swollen shut. It seemed natural enough, considering the solemnity of the funeral rites amongst a collection of grieving servants beneath a dreary watercolor sky all shades of gray. But if she had dosed him with her teary-eyed gaze, he would have been hard-pressed to meet it, knowing that he had put the tears on those soft rose-petal cheeks.

Anticipation of the guards descending upon Ravencliff had everyone on edge. As the day wore on and they didn't come, Nicholas took matters into his own hands. Wearing a caped greatcoat, and armed with a pair of Harcourt flintlock dueling pistols in his pockets, he set out to comb the manor from top to bottom, and every inch of the grounds. Stopping first at the tapestry suite, he knocked and waited, encouraged that the door was closed, and reassured when Sara threw the bolt, barely cracking it open.

"I told you I needed time, Nicholas," she said, opening the door a little wider, but not wide enough to admit him.

"I haven't come for your answer," he said. "I've come to give you this." He exhibited the pocket pistol he'd been carrying all along. "And to show you how to use it."

"I don't want that, Nicholas."

"It's no longer a matter of what we want, Sara. You need to be protected. Just be certain before you shoot. Nero will never menace you." He shoved it through the door. "Here, take it. Be careful. It's loaded."

Sara hesitated. "I . . . I don't like guns," she said.

"Take it!" he insisted, "and this." He handed her a small case lined in burgundy baize. "The implements and ammunition you need to reload are inside. Do you see this key? It fits into the tool that allows you to remove the barrel for loading and cleaning. Here, let me show you."

"I know how to load a pocket pistol, Nicholas," she snapped. "My father was a military man, remember? I even carried a muff pistol once, on a journey from Nottingham to London. Father insisted, because of the highwaymen who frequented that quarter."

"I'd like to hear the whys and wherefores of that, by God, but it will have to wait for another time. Keep that pistol by you, and keep this door locked. I shall collect you at the dinner hour, and return you here afterward. Then, after my session with Dr. Breeden, I shall retire across the way in case you have need of me."

"You don't have to do that, Nicholas. I'm hardly a child," she snapped.

"It's that, or I post the hall boys outside your suite again. You decide."

Sara heaved a ragged sigh. "Do as you please," she said with a shrug.

"You realize, of course, that you cannot discuss the situation at table. You know how the servants eavesdrop in this house. The last thing we need here now is to have more tales circulating in the village."

"You needn't worry," she said. "I'll behave." She took his measure. "Where are you going now, with those?" she said, nodding toward the dueling pistols protruding from his pocket.

"Hunting. Now lock this door," he pronounced, and waited while she closed it and slid the bolt.

Nicholas searched until twilight deepened the shadows and he had to light a candlestick, but there was no sign of Mallory. Convinced that the wolf was hiding somewhere along the passageway in one of the secret chambers, he haunted the lower regions, and followed the tunnel to its end, to the dungeon, and the revolving panel that gave access to the granite apron that edged the cliff. Nero had used it many times to exit the house.

Nagging at the back of his mind was the recollection that Alex Mallory had always been fascinated by the intricacies of Ravencliff; its many hiding places, branched corridors, access doors, and false walls. The steward knew them all—but so did Nicholas, or at least he thought he did. Some he hadn't visited since a child, and others Nero frequented on a regular basis.

There was a way to lock the tunnel exit, though it hadn't been employed in years, a tongue-and-groove mechanism hewn into the top of the panel that, once activated, prevented the panel from swiveling. A man could work it, but a wolf could not. If he were to engage it, and the slabs meshed inside the wall, he would be locking the wolf either in, or out. He would also be depriving himself . . . or Nero of an exit route if the need should arise. He tried to put himself in the mind of the wolf, and gave it only passing thought, before he tripped the mechanism. The grating rumble of stone against stone echoed along the corridor. It was a gamble, but unless he missed his guess, the wolf was somewhere in the house and would surface soon enough with his exit route removed. Counting upon his instincts not to play him false, he retraced his steps, but the lower regions were vacant.

A search of the grounds on the courtyard side yielded nothing either, and he dragged himself back to the house at the end of it, drenched with the evening mist, and chilled to the bone, as was often the way of it long into summer in soft weather on the Cornish coast.

There was no way to repair the damage before the evening meal, though he did opt for a change of clothes, and ordered the hearths lit again in the dining hall, and in the master, tapestry, and green suites. The house was dank and musty, the old walls bleeding with mildew and rising damp. That had never bothered him before. Somehow, everything bothered him now.

Sara accompanied him to the dining hall in silence. Her eyes were still puffy and red, but the blotches had either faded, or been doctored more expertly with talc. He suspected the latter. The conversation was congenial, though forced during the meal. Dr. Breeden watched Sara's every move just as he did, but she was the perfect hostess, above reproach, and Nicholas began to relax—as much as was possible under the enchantment of her closeness.

The low-cut décolleté of her sprigged muslin gown drew his eyes. He'd already tasted with his lips what lay beneath. How sweet it was to suckle at those perfect breasts. How magical to feel the silky softness of her skin beneath his fingers, rough by contrast; to feel the tall rosebud nipples harden against his tongue. How well they fitted together, as if she were the missing part of him, without which he had never been whole. What ecstasy it would be to feel himself live inside the soft, moist warmth of her, filling her, moving to her rhythm. He'd imagined it a thousand times, but it could never be. His indigo breeches began to pinch, and he changed position in the chair. It didn't help. He was tight against the seam, and thankful that he was seated and would be for some time.

Her scent was all around him—in him—threading through his nostrils, the subtle sweetness of gillyflower and roses chasing the stink of damp and decay. He inhaled it in deep breaths disguised as stifled sighs. Soon, the roses would bloom in the gardens, and flood the house with their perfume as they always did in summer, but their scent would pale before hers now, and torment him forever if she were to leave.

After the meal, he returned her to her suite, and waited while she threw the bolt. No words passed between them, except for a strained "good night." Afterward, he dragged himself back up to the master suite sitting room, where Dr. Breeden had set up the armonica, and was waiting with his nightly cordial, while Mills and the footmen readied his bath.

"It's no use," Nicholas said, after half an hour of the doctor's treatments. "There's too much on my conscious mind for it to give way to my subconscious, I'm afraid. I'm sorry."

"Not to worry, my lord. We've plenty of time."

"That's just it, we don't," Nicholas said. "The baroness saw me transform last night. How she hasn't fled the place by now is a mystery, and a miracle. It may still happen. She hasn't given me her answer yet, but I'm afraid I know what it will be."

They hadn't had time to converse since it occurred, what with the funeral, and Dr. Breeden had been shut up in the herbarium half the day. Before long, Nicholas had told him everything that had transpired since he'd carried Sara up from the lower regions. When he finished, he raised his bowed head, his misty eyes pleading.

"What am I going to do, Dr. Breeden?" he asked.

"You need to consummate your marriage, my lord, if you mean to keep her."

"It nearly happened before all this. But now . . . I can't very well force her, and I haven't the right to stand in her way if she wants her freedom. She is young and vital . . . she deserves so much more than I have to give . . . than I *can* give under the circumstances."

"But you love her, my lord," said the doctor, "and she loves you, or she would be gone by now, I'll be bound. I saw her at table tonight. She's been crying. At first, I thought it was because of the abigail's death, but now I see it was quite something else."

"Marrying her . . . bringing her here was a mistake," said Nicholas. "I was a fool to think I could live some semblance of a normal life." He surged to his feet and began to pace the carpet. "The least I can do, is try to rectify it before . . ."

"Before what, my lord?" the doctor prompted. "If you were about to say 'before it's too late,' don't waste your breath."

"I shall wait for her decision, and act accordingly. There aren't grounds for a Parliamentary divorce. There's been no adultery, and I am not a fiend threatening her life. Besides, even if there were a way, it could take as long as a year. Parliament has to be sitting, for one thing, and its regular business concluded, before such an appeal could be addressed. The cutoff date for petitioning has already passed for this year. I would have to wait until the end of November to petition. An annulment might be arranged, and I have the connections to do it. I shall have to look into it. I must have been mad to let it go as far as it has between us. There's always the outside chance that I could transform right in the conjugal bed!"

"Not . . . necessarily now," said the doctor.

"Why, not now?"

"She knows," the doctor said flatly. "The fear that it might happen no longer exists. That alone may well keep you calm enough to make love to your bride."

"And you think I ought take that chance?" He stopped pacing, loosed a guttural chuckle, and shook his head. "I may be half mad with all of this, but I'm not addled."

"I think, my lord, that you might test the theory. She already knows. The worst that could happen is transformation, and you will have enough forewarning to spare her and yourself any embarrassment if it does happen."

"All well and good, but there is still the matter of passing the condition on, as my father passed it on to me, to be considered. I will not take that chance."

The doctor heaved a sigh. "Who told you the condition could be passed on through the blood, my lord?"

"Why, no one. I just assumed, because Father passed this on to me in that way—"

"There are no statistics on that, my lord," the doctor interrupted. "We do not even know if your particular condition can be passed on in that way, considering that it is a weaker strain, and something entirely different from that transmitted by the wolf that bit your father. Again we've got the cart before the horse, my lord. Those are gray areas."

"All the more reason to be wary," said Nicholas.

"Wary yes, but closed minded? Never! I am first and foremost a scientist, my lord. For the sake of argument, let's just suppose that—despite all possible precautions—conception occurred. We know that the shapeshifter's animal incarnation takes on the personality of its host—case in point, Nero: fiercely loyal, good natured, well mannered, nonviolent unless provoked. In short, a gentleman wolf, if you will allow, just as you are a gentleman, my lord. If the condition is transferable, the worst that could happen would be that your offspring would be as you are."

Nicholas shook his head in adamant disagreement. "With the same fears, the same restrictions?" he said. "Condemn it to a life of forced exile from the world, and all its joys and

Dawn Thompson

pleasures, when I have the right to spare it such a sentence? No—*never!*"

"But, do you really have that right?"

"Yes, I do," Nicholas snapped. "I would not wish this madness upon my worst enemy, let alone my own flesh and blood. I am not my father's son in that regard. I am not so blinded whoring after an heir that I cannot foresee the pitfalls of my actions."

"All right, then, that is your prerogative. There are other ways that cohabitation can be managed to your mutual satisfaction—age-old ways of addressing the problem with herbs that go back to Biblical times. That cordial there"—he nodded toward it—"already contains ingredients that will help, and her ladyship can be instructed in certain internal and external methods also."

"What sort of 'methods'?"

"For example, French prostitutes have used a sponge affair for years, my lord. The same method is used here now by prostitutes and courtesans, and those whose health is too fragile to survive childbirth. You mentioned once that lightskirts and courtesans usually take care of such matters. Trust them to know how. They've been at it since time out of mind. Treated with certain herbs, the sponge I mentioned can be quite effective. A salve made of the herbs themselves is another alternative. Believe me, my lord, the situation is far from hopeless. I can have what's needed sent from London. She will, however, not be able to use either the first time."

"Nothing can be done until the baroness decides," said Nicholas.

"Would it help if I were to speak to her about your condition?" said Breeden. "Perhaps coming from me . . ."

"No," Nicholas responded. "It must be her decision and hers alone. I won't have her swayed. There's no need of convincing. She *saw.* Now it's a matter of her being able to live with what she saw."

"As you wish, my lord, but if you should change your

mind, I would be only too glad to rise to the occasion. Meanwhile, with your kind permission, I shall have one of your staff send word on to London for some supplies I have need of, and the article I described to you for my lady, in anticipation of a happy outcome to all this, eh?"

"In anticipation," Nicholas mused. The poor man was doing his best, after all. The least he could do was humor him. "Well, then," he said, gesturing toward the armonica. "Shall we try again?"

Though they did try, again and again, nothing significant was gained that Nicholas could see, and nothing would be, as far as he was concerned, until Alexander Mallory was found in one incarnation or another, and justice was meted out accordingly.

For the next three days, foul weather prevented the guards from returning, and Nicholas haunted the convoluted corridors and passageways of the old house armed with loaded pistols. By night he kept his vigil over Sara, wide-eyed from the green suite across from her own until dawn, catching only brief snatches of sleep when it overpowered him. Still, she had not given him her decision. She hadn't spoken alone with him, for that matter. Why hadn't she decided? Was her hesitation a good sign, or a bad one? Could she be waiting for the situation with Alex Mallory to be resolved before she committed to belief in what he'd told her? Was it proof she wanted? There was no way to tell, and his brain hurt from trying to make sense of it.

Calm, he had to stay calm. That was becoming harder and harder to do as the tensions mounted from all directions. He dared not transform with the whole house gunning for Nero, but now Sara *knew*. With that obstacle removed, while Nero was still being hunted, he could at least cancel the search for Alex Mallory in his human form. Dr. Breeden was in accord that it wasn't likely Mallory would transform if he hadn't by now, and Nicholas decided to spread the tale that the steward had reappeared and been sacked. If he did change back and surface afterward, it could always be said that he'd sneaked back in via one of the smugglers' entrances he was so fond of. It was a gamble, but there was no other alternative. He would just have to deal with that if it occurred.

On the morning of the fourth day after the funeral, Smythe presented himself on the study threshold. From the look on the butler's grim face, Nicholas was loath to bid him enter.

"What is it, Smythe?" he said.

"Begging your pardon, my lord," the butler said. "I've come to voice some concerns from below stairs."

Nicholas set his quill down with painstaking control, and folded his hands atop the ledger he was working in.

"Concerns?" he parroted.

"Yes, my lord," said the butler. "The truth of it is we're all afraid below stairs . . . of the dog . . . of Nero . . . after what's happened to Nell."

Nicholas wanted to blurt out: *Nero wouldn't harm a hair on any of your heads, you nodcock! Though he should, judging from some of the tidbits he's discovered spying on you lot below stairs.* He took a less inflammatory tack.

"Have you seen the animal since, Smythe?" he said. The servants' quarters were the only area in the house he hadn't searched.

"That's just it, my lord, we haven't, but the food keeps disappearing."

"Food? What food? Don't tell me you've been setting food out for that animal?" He surged to his feet. He was well aware that Sara had been feeding it, but all that ceased after he told her the truth, and he'd been hoping hunger would drive it into the open. His blood was boiling.

"Y-yes, my lord," said the butler, taking a step back from him. "We always left food out for him in the past, you know that. Then, after what happened to Nell, we stopped, but food went missing from the larder—meat, and fowl mostly, a good deal of it, so we started leaving food out for him again, for fear we'd be next if we didn't. He made a fine mess below, my lord."

"And you're just coming to me with it *now?*" Nicholas thundered.

"Mrs. Bromley thought—"

"The Devil take Mrs. Bromley! You are head of staff below stairs, Smythe. Since when does Mrs. Bromley dictate your actions?"

"I-I'm sorry, my lord," the butler stammered. "I . . . we didn't want to trouble you with it, what with the funeral and all."

"There'll likely be more than one of those in this house if you don't 'trouble me' in future," Nicholas snapped. He sank into the chair again, raking his hair back with stiff fingers. How much should he confide in the butler? Certainly not all, but enough to clear Nero's name, since he would still be a very visible part of the household when all was said and done; it was that or replace the entire staff. Right now, he was angry enough to do just that. "Sit down, Smythe," he said.

"My lord?"

"*Sit!*" Nicholas barked, while the butler dropped like a stone into the nearest chair. "There's no use my telling you to keep what I'm about to tell you to yourself," he went on, "because the walls have ears in this house, tongues wag, and the only purpose doors serve is to give the servants something to lean against while they eavesdrop!"

"Y-yes, my lord."

"Nonetheless, I must insist that you refrain from carrying tales in future, because there shan't be a staff member left below stairs when the sun sets upon the day that you do. I'll sack the lot of you! Considering what's been going on in the village, you can count yourself fortunate that you all still have positions here. If one more word ever travels beyond that gate down there, you will collect your final wages without references. I would have done it the day the guards came out here, but with all the press come upon this house I really haven't time to seek replacements at the moment—though I am so at my wits end with the lot of you at this point, I'm ready to brook the inconvenience. Do we have an understanding?"

"Y-yes, my lord."

"Good! Just in case you aren't convinced that I am aware of the goings on above *and* below stairs in this house, be apprised that I know my idiosyncrasies are bruited about on a regular basis amongst you. I know you eavesdrop to fuel your *on-dits*. I know when you do it, and how you do it, and whom you tell your tales to. I know that Millie, the scullery maid, nicks small game birds from the game room on the eves of her days off. I do not choose to address this, because we have plenty of game on Ravencliff, and I am aware that she's done this to help feed her infirm mother, and siblings, since her good father, whom I knew and admired, passed on.

"It has just come to my attention that the footmen lay abed half the morning, while the hall boys do their tasks for them. I know the boys do this out of fear of a hiding, and anticipation of a reward at the end of it. I also know there's precious little reward, and hidings aplenty, whether the tasks are done or they aren't. This commenced when her ladyship joined our household. What? Did you imagine that I would be so preoccupied with my lady bride that I wouldn't notice? Never think it! I am aware of everything that goes on in this house.

"I know that a plot was afoot below stairs to poison Nero with some of the arsenic the grooms use to get rid of the rats in the stables. Well, Peters has been sacked, hasn't he? Oh, yes, I know he was at the bottom of it, and you shan't find so much as a grain of arsenic on the estate now, either. Let the rats overrun the place! You lot are next! If you—any of you— ever lift one finger toward that animal, I will see you jailed. Do not think to put me to the test.

"I know that you and Mrs. Bromley have acquired a taste for the French wines in my wine cellar—that when one is brought up for the table, two walk out of the cellar on a regular basis, and I know that you and Mrs. Bromley imbibe also on a regular basis closeted together, when your duties permit, of course. Is that sufficient, or shall I go on? The list is quite lengthy. We could be here half the morning."

"Yes, my lord . . . I mean, no, my lord."

"Mmmm," Nicholas grunted. "These matters are on your head, Smythe, no one else's. As butler here, it is your duty to me, and to this house, to see not only that everything runs smoothly, but that honesty and decency abound in it. Overlook the birds. Let the girl take them, and I do not mind that you're nicking a little wine now and again, so long as you don't get foxed on your watch, but the business between the footmen and the hall boys must stop, and you are the one to stop it. If you do not, I shall hire a butler who will, and if it does not stop forthwith, the footmen will find themselves booted out bag and baggage without recommendations. Am I plain?"

"Y-yes, my lord."

"Now then, the very next time something untoward, like what you just told me about the food occurs, and you do not come to me with it straightaway, you will collect your wages. *That*, you may repeat. You may shout it from the rafters, because you all have good cause to fear, but not to fear Nero. He did not kill Nell. I know because he was with me when she was killed. There is another . . . animal loose in the house."

The butler gasped. "*Two* dogs, my lord?" he said, giving a start.

Nicholas nodded. "Do not ask me how it got in, or where it came from. That is not the issue. There are too many ins and outs to this old mausoleum to be counted. One of you may even have inadvertently let it in thinking it was Nero.

They look very similar—similar enough to have come from the same litter. I was shocked myself, when I saw them together."

"My lord, I never dreamed . . . !"

"Tell me something, Smythe . . . has Nero ever threatened you?"

"Why, no, my lord . . . that is to say, other than popping up at odd moments and giving us all a fright, he's always been a congenial sort. That is, until Mr. Mallory shot him. Since then, he's been downright vicious at times."

"Have you seen Mr. Mallory since that occurred, Smythe?"

"Why, no, my lord," the butler breathed. "That was a while ago. When we couldn't find him after, we assumed he'd finally . . . come to his senses, and that you'd sent him abroad on an errand again. He's gone off more than he's in residence."

"Mmmm," Nicholas mused. They hadn't been searching very hard, the lazy lot! Maybe that was just as well. "Mr. Mallory has been sacked," he said, "but some of his belongings are still here. In case he returns for them, I'll want to know of it at once. We didn't exactly part on good terms. I didn't take kindly to him drinking himself into his altitudes, attempting to molest my bride, and shooting my dog."

"Yes, my lord."

"Now then, is there anything else, Smythe?"

"Just that we need a new maid for her ladyship, my lord," said the butler. "Mrs. Bromley is worn to a raveling, trying to keep up with her regular duties and assist the mistress as well, though her ladyship has been most gracious in excusing her. It just isn't right that she be left to fend for herself so much of the time . . . especially now."

Nicholas frowned. "I agree, Smythe, and you can tell Mrs. Bromley that a new abigail will be had just as soon as the animal that killed Nell has been caught and dealt with. I shan't bring another servant into this house until it is safe to do so. That might just be the incentive to enlist the staff's help in the search. Alert everyone below stairs that there is another animal roaming Ravencliff, that it is dangerous and that they are not to approach it, but to come to me at once if they sight it. I do not want any of you to do anything that will put you in harm's way, but if you see that animal, I want to know of it at once. Is that clear?"

"Y-yes, my lord."

"You may arm yourselves—with the exception of the hall boys, and scullions, of course—but take care not to shoot Nero. He will never menace you. The poor animal has already been shot once. Go off half cocked, and you will answer to me."

"Very good, my lord," said the butler. "But, what shall I do about the food?"

Nicholas rolled his eyes, and heaved a ragged sigh. "As long as you feed the animal, it will be content to stay hidden. Stop feeding it! Lock up the larder, and the game room! Leave no leftovers in the kitchen! For God's sake, man, use your head! I'm trying to starve it to flush it out, and you're filling its belly. We are at cross-purposes here. You're no slap-skull, Smythe. Use the brains God gave you."

"Y-yes, my lord," the butler murmured.

"Very well, then, if there's nothing else, you are dismissed, but you'd best be prepared. The foul weather is finally at an end. Tomorrow should be a fair day, and we can expect the guards swarming over the place to complete their search. After this fine news, I shall have them begin with the servants' quarters. I needn't tell you to see that everything is as it should be below stairs."

"N-no, my lord. I mean, yes, my lord," the butler stammered.

"Very well then, carry on," Nicholas concluded, going back to his ledger.

He penned three characters and set the quill aside again, taking his aching head in his hands. It was beyond bearing. He was half mad anticipating Sara's decision, losing faith in

Dr. Breeden's experiments, and now this. There was no use trying to attend to anything until the animal was found. Reaching into the drawer in his desk, he yanked out the loaded pistol he kept there, rose to his feet, and stormed from the study.

Twenty-seven

Nicholas was absent from the breakfast room at nuncheon. He prowled the passageways until twilight robbed the light, with no results, then dragged himself to the master suite draped in cobwebs, slimed with mildew and dust, and precious little time to put himself to rights in time for the evening meal.

"I abhor the lies," he growled, submerged to the neck in his tub of herb-scented water.

"You cannot tell them the truth, my lord," said the valet.

"Having your rooms adjoin mine has its drawbacks, old boy," Nicholas regretted. "If you'd been housed below stairs with the rest of the staff this never would have happened. You'd have seen them feeding that damned animal. All this time wasted. Bloody hell!"

"Would you like me to take a room below, my lord . . . at least until all this is over?"

"What, and give them something else to talk about? No, Mills. I need you where you are. Besides, it's too late. The damage has been done. I think I've put the fear of God in them enough to keep anything similar from happening again."

"Yes, my lord."

Nicholas struck the water a vicious blow with his fist, showering Mills in the process. "Why won't she decide?" he said. That was what was really bothering him. He could think of nothing else.

"Might I point out that she has not run screaming from the house as you predicted, my lord? I would take that as a good sign."

"The guards would hardly let anyone leave until the investigation is completed to their satisfaction. We can count ourselves fortunate if they don't call Bow Street in. There's been murder done!"

"By an *animal*, my lord. Why, Dr. Breeden's testimony alone—"

"Yes, yes, I know, Mills, but you can trust me when I say they'd be on us like hounds on a rabbit if one of us tried to leave Ravencliff now."

"All right, my lord," the valet said, "cast aspersions where ye may, the fact still remains that she has not left, nor does she seem about to leave, the house. Why, just look at the way she conducted the funeral affairs. She had it in control in a manner that rocked me back on my heels."

"I do not want to pressure her. I told her I would give her time, but it's been four days, Mills. How much more time does she need?"

"Evidently more than four days, my lord."

Nicholas's eyebrow shot up, and his lips formed an exasperated crimp. Mills met the expression by dumping a bucket of tepid water over his head, and Nicholas shook like a dog, showering more water over the valet still glistening from the last.

"There's no need to drown me!" Nicholas snapped.

"Fine talk of drowning, my lord, when I am wetter than you," Mills countered, setting the bucket down. "Have a care. You need to calm yourself. Now is not the time for Nero to roam freely through the house, with half the inmates bearing arms and ill-equipped to use them. We shall be hard-pressed to come off all of a piece as it is, without presenting them any valid targets, my lord."

Nicholas sighed. "No one has seen Alex since the shooting," he said. "Below stairs, they thought I'd sent him on an errand. It isn't likely that he's able to change back if he hasn't by now, so says Dr. Breeden. I've spread the word that he's been sacked for his conduct, but that some of his belongings are still here, and that I want to know at once if he returns to collect them."

"Wise decision, my lord," said the valet. "How are the sessions going?"

Nicholas shrugged. "Nero hasn't visited since he left me in the alcove chamber."

"That's a good sign," said the valet, holding the towel, as he climbed out of the tub.

"If this keeps up, Breeden tells me I'll be ready to try and transform at will soon."

"But that's excellent news, my lord!" cried the valet.

"I wonder," Nicholas replied. "Suppose I cannot? Or, worse yet, suppose I can, and I cannot change back . . . like Alex? I'm almost hesitant to try."

"I wouldn't advise conducting an experiment until after the guards have come and gone, my lord," the valet opined. "They still think it was Nero that killed the girl."

"I'm not ready in any case, Mills. I've too much on my mind. Besides, who knows if anything the doctor is about will do one bit of good?"

"You have not corrected your problem with trust, my lord," observed Mills, "and until you come to grips with that, I fear that nothing will work in your favor—not the good doctor's efforts, or resolution with her ladyship. Forgive me for speaking my mind, but this is your most grievous fault. I've told you many a time you cannot expect blind trust from others when you are not willing to give it yourself. Now perhaps, you finally begin to see the folly of that tack."

"I told her the truth, didn't I?" Nicholas snapped.

"After a fashion, and after the fact. I pray not too late. I told you from the start that you might consider telling her. Trust must exist for love to survive, my lord. Love will wither and die on the vine without it, sure as check."

"And you are an expert in this area, eh?" Nicholas chided.

"Let us just say . . . that I have learned from my mistakes, my lord, and would spare you such a costly lesson."

It was impossible for Nicholas to imagine Mills in love. When had that happened, he wondered? Yet, judging from the faraway look in the valet's misty eyes, he didn't doubt that it had at some point in history. Mills rarely showed emotion, and never in recollection had he betrayed such thoughts, or let anyone glimpse his private side.

"I appreciate that," said Nicholas on a sigh, "but you know my situation isn't something I could 'trust' to just anyone. I believe that Sara is probably the only woman in the kingdom I could safely trust with it. She has honor and integrity—and at such a young age. I've never met a woman like her."

"And you never will again," said Mills. "You are learning, my lord. Just remember, no lesson comes without a price. Trust does not come too dear for what you're seeking—from either her ladyship or the doctor."

It was late, and Mills helped Nicholas into his evening toilette, consisting of black pantaloons, superfine tailcoat, and burgundy brocade waistcoat. Once his neck cloth was engineered in the intricate Oriental wrap fashionable that Season, he hurried below to escort Sara to the dining hall, hoping for some sign that would end the torment and put his mind at ease. There was none. Except for the barest amenities, no words passed between them.

During the meal, while she was bright and engaging with Dr. Breeden, Sara did not address him directly, or make eye contact. When he tried to instigate a response, her replies were polite and succinct, but that was as far as it went.

She was the picture of loveliness in buttercup-yellow muslin scattered with tiny green satin bows, her upswept hair haloed in the nimbus of candleshine. There were no more telltale signs of weeping painting her cheeks, and her eyes were no longer swollen and red as they had been more often than not over the past few days. They were a clear aqua blue, like the transparent curl of an ocean swell, and only a delicate blush tinted the apples of her cheeks. Whether that meant she'd gotten over her sorrows, or they no longer mattered, was unclear, and his heart sank fearing the latter.

After the meal, when he returned her to her suite, it was in silence. He didn't try to draw her out. Resisting every instinct in him crying that he seize her in his arms, bury his fingers in the shimmering gold of her hair, and taste again those petal-soft lips, he stood on the threshold, bowed while the door was closed in his face, and retreated to the master suite, where Dr. Breeden waited.

Since time was of the essence, they had foregone the custom of brandy in the drawing room after the meal for some days, and had it instead in the master suite sitting room. Despite his hermit's existence, Nicholas had until then managed to maintain the rituals of the times. That could no longer be, in these circumstances. The doctor didn't seem to mind. He had been most accommodating—as anxious to resolve Nicholas's problem as Nicholas was. Would he one day be part of another of the good doctor's treatises—anonymously, of course? Nicholas had no doubt that such a motive moved the man through his paces with the persistence of a juggernaut. Still, he'd decided to give way to Mills's advice, and as he and the doctor sipped their brandy before the session, he commenced to do so.

"I must confess to something," he began, swirling the brandy in his snifter. "I haven't been fair to you, Dr. Breeden. Mills pointed that out to me earlier. I'm not going to make excuses for myself. There is no excuse for wasting another man's time, but I've lived so long with hopelessness, I haven't put myself completely in your hands."

"Oh, I know that, my lord," said the doctor. "It's quite to be expected."

"Then, too, I have a gnawing fear that if I raise my hopes only to have them dashed here now, when so much depends upon it . . ." Nicholas shook his head. He couldn't finish the thought.

"Rather like taking a dreadful, foul-tasting tonic, only to find that all was for naught when it doesn't work, eh?" said the doctor.

"Mildly put," Nicholas replied, through a humorless laugh.

"But accurate," the doctor said. "You mustn't reproach yourself, my lord. We are dealing with an ailment that medical science does not even want to admit exists, and you are under greater strains than any man should have to endure. I frankly do not know how you stand it, but you do. I should like to study *that*. It defies reason."

"There is a certain discipline that is by-product of this . . . condition," said Nicholas, "but I cannot take credit for it. It's part of the process, and you either stand up to its demands, or succumb. I learned early on that if I were to survive, I had to steel myself against it—form a shell around myself, where some part of me could exist normally, if such a thing could be. I thought it served me well enough . . . until her ladyship. Now, I see how empty that shell was, and I shall never be able to crawl back into it after tasting what I've missed of life."

"I am here to do all in my power to see that you never have to, my lord," said the doctor.

"Then I must do more to aid you in your efforts," Nicholas said. "Mills says I lack trust, while I demand it of others. He's right, of course. He always is. I've made a clean breast of it with the baroness, though he faults me for not doing so at the outset. Now, I should like to try and be more open to your treatments. If I can show her that I can at least control the transformations, it might make a difference. Oh, I don't know, Doctor, but I shall try harder."

"Do not try too hard, my lord," said the physician. "There is no quick solution to controlling your malady. What's wanted is openness, and a relaxed state."

Nicholas's lighthearted laugh replied.

"I know, my lord, it is much to ask under the circumstances, but necessary. Remember, we are charting new waters here, and we have only just begun to plumb the depths, as it were. When you enter here for these sessions with me, leave the world without for this brief time."

"I shall make every endeavor to do so," said Nicholas. "But while I am closeted here with you, the baroness is vulnerable, unprotected, and quite frankly, judging from past experience, I cannot trust her not to take matters into her own hands. With such as that weighing on my mind, and the threat of a shapeshifter wolf on the prowl, leaving the world on the doorstep is rather impossible."

"Does it help to talk about these things? Sometimes voicing them aloud brings relief, and I am a good listener."

"There are just too many 'things' banging about in my brain, Dr. Breeden," said Nicholas, draining his snifter. "For example, to take just one: As you know, if she should decide to leave me, I offered to use my connections to see our marriage dissolved. I've been consulting several legal volumes in the study. That shan't be as easy a thing to manage as I first thought—if it can be managed at all. An annulment could actually take longer than a divorce, and nonconsummation is not a valid reason to petition for one. Impotence is, but I am *not* impotent—far from it. None of the other 'valid' reasons apply. We are not closely related, or secretly married to others, nor did we use the wrong names on a special license, and there were no parents or guardians to dupe. While I'd thought a year's wait for a Parliamentary decree was a lengthy period, I'm now beginning to think that it may be the only alternative, since my most useful connections are with Canterbury through my father. I have no impressive Parliamentary favors to call in, and a church divorce is useless. It could be had more quickly, but it amounts to nothing more than a legal separation and neither of us would be able to marry again. That matters not to me, but what of her ladyship? She's young, and vital. I could not damn her to that, or make a whore of her, because that's what would be. She would have no choice but to take a lover. My God, what have I done?"

"Let's not borrow trouble, my lord," said the doctor. "I should think it's deposited enough in our account as it is. If worst comes to worst, a way will present itself, and we shall avail ourselves of it . . . even if we have to bend the truth a bit. You are no longer alone in this. Now, loosen your grip on that empty glass, and set it aside before you cut yourself as I did. Close your eyes, my lord. Listen to the armonica. We have much work to do."

Despite the warm, scented bath Mrs. Bromley had drawn for her, Sara couldn't sleep. Dressed in her ecru nightdress and wrapper, she paced from room to room, from tapestry to tapestry, like a caged animal, studying the artistry, etching every stitch in her memory, wondering what had become of the new ones Alexander Mallory was supposed to have brought back from London—anything to take her mind off the real issue at hand. It was no use. The subject matter of the beautiful wall hangings brought Nero to mind, and thoughts of Alexander Mallory brought the image of another wolf, and the cold reality that her husband was a shapeshifter. The ramifications of that were beyond imagining, and yet it was a reality.

Had he suffered enough? No, not yet. Had she? Oh, yes, there was no question. Could she bear to continue the punishment? Would it do any good? Probably not, but she wanted Baron Nicholas Walraven to think twice before denying her his trust again . . . if she were going to stay, of course. That still remained to be seen.

Anger had dried her tears: anger that he had let her discover his secret in such a shocking manner, anger at herself for falling so desperately in love with the man. How hard it had been to ignore his pleading glances, to disregard the sadness in those hypnotic obsidian eyes that devoured her, that spoke to her soul and melted her heart. The only way was to avoid his gaze altogether. She did it for his betterment, and for her own, for she would not stay where there was deception, and she could not leave. It was a hard lesson, but her lesson to teach. He had to earn her love with trust, and she needed to be certain he would never deceive her again.

As far as Sara was concerned, their agreement, such as it was, was nullified in the shadowy passageway outside the alcove chamber in the bowels of Ravencliff Manor. It could be all or nothing now, and to her thinking, she'd earned the right to set the ground rules. This had been the longest four days of her life. Was it enough? Had he learned the lesson?

She went to the window. Outside, stars winked down from the indigo vault. There was no moon, at least not one she could see from her vantage, though silver spangles of moonlight danced eerily on the ink-black water, becalmed for the first time since she'd arrived on the coast. Was it an omen—if so, of what? That the crisis was past . . . or was it just another calm before another storm? Either way, looking at that sky, it was a fair assumption that the guards would come in the morning. A ragged sigh brought her shoulders down, and after a moment, she turned away.

Padding through the foyer to the sitting room, she spied the handgun Nicholas had given her on the table beside the door. What if she were to shoot the wrong wolf with it? No. She would take no chances. Picking it up gingerly, she deposited it in the table drawer, out of the way of temptation.

She started on her way again, but a noise in the corridor stopped her in her tracks—footfalls, heavy-sounding and weary, making no attempt at stealth. Tiptoeing to the door, she leaned her ear against the panel listening. They had stopped outside. Sara held her breath, but he did not hold his. On the other side of that door, Nicholas emptied his lungs just as she had done.

Tears welled in her eyes at the sound. She blinked them back. After a moment, the footfalls receded along the corridor. Then there came a soft, metallic click, as the door to the green suite closed across the way, sending shivers down her spine. There was something final in the sound. Something palpable, which struck her with terror. It tied knots in the invisible cord stretched between her and the man she loved more than life itself, despite and because of the nightmare and how he bore it. Something that, if not grasped then with both hands and held tight, would be lost forever.

Bursting from her suite, Sara crossed the span of carpeted hallway between with quick, light steps, and followed him inside.

Twenty-eight

The unseen moon wove its magic in the green suite as well, throwing shafts of silver light through the mullioned panes, where dust motes danced. Sara moved on bare feet that made no sound through the foyer, and entered the bedchamber. Nicholas didn't see her at first. His back was turned. He'd stripped off his jacket, neck cloth, waistcoat, and shirt, and stood bare to the waist before the window in his stocking feet, gazing out over the garden.

How broad his shoulders were, how narrow his waist. He seemed like a statue standing there, with the moonlight playing on his bare skin, casting shadows along the indented length of his arrow-straight spine, laying a silvery sheen over the black satin pantaloons that left nothing to the imagination in the area of his taut buttocks and well-turned thighs. No padding girded those limbs. Sara remembered her father availing himself of such devices, as was the way of it amongst men not so endowed trying to adapt their less-than-perfect figures to the fashions of the day. No corset held Nicholas's well-muscled, washboard-stomached middle in check either. She had lain naked against that hard, lean body. She had known the silkiness of his lightly furred chest against her breasts. She had felt the strength in him, the thickness of his sex pressed against her, and the discipline of restraint keeping it in control, that made every sinew in him tighten like steel bands, and every muscle contract and flex against her as though it were about to burst.

Just the sight of him standing there thrilled her to arousal, readied her for the consummation of a passion she didn't even understand. All she knew was that he filled her with strange, forbidden warmth; forbidden, because feelings this shocking had to be. This searing, moist heat that invaded her loins in his presence was a scandalous thing that made her hands go clammy and her whole body shiver, with delectable cold chills despite the fire inside. Only being wrapped in those strong arms would stop her quaking. Only the feral scent of him, sweetened with herbs, and fresh with the salt of the sea could give her a reason to breathe. Only the pressure of his mouth opening her lips beneath could slake her insatiable need to taste him deeply, and completely.

What other pleasures that body held in store, she couldn't imagine. Still, despite that she wanted those pleasures until her very bones ached for them, another saner voice inside nearly convinced her to creep out as she had crept in. That was, until he bowed his head and raked both hands through his hair, then dropped them at his sides. It was a gesture of defeat, and all of her defenses plummeted to earth right along with his posture.

"Nicholas . . . ," she murmured, her hoarse voice scarcely more than a whisper, though it boomed through the quiet like a thunder roll.

Her husband spun so fast to face her that she saw only a blur, like the blur she'd seen in the passageway, when Nero leaped into the air, and Nicholas emerged naked before her. Like a spurt of déjà vu, it riveted her to the spot, but oh what it did to her equilibrium, and to her quivering sex. Her breath caught in a dry throat. She was on fire for him.

For a moment he didn't move. His obsidian gaze devoured her, glistening with reflected light from the shadows. He didn't seem real, backlit by the split shaft of illusive moonglow spilling in around him, bouncing off him, like a fractured aura. It almost seemed to shine through him, as if he were a wraith standing there, staring at her, ready to disappear in a puff of ethereal mist should she breathe and break the spell.

The moment seemed to go on forever. Then he sprang again, reaching her in two graceful strides, more animal-like than human. Now she recognized the feral energy in his makeup that had always been there, in the way he moved and prowled and surged and paced. Was it a carryover from his Nero incarnation, or were man and animal one creature, separated only by a hairsbreadth of unearthly distance, or the beat of a palpitating heart?

For a moment, he didn't speak. His eyes moved over her with the skeptical anticipation of one dying of thirst, fearing that the oasis before him was no more than another mirage, a trick of the eye come to torment him. She could barely stand to look into them. He inhaled her—nostrils flared, almost like a dog . . . like a *wolf*, his straight Celtic nose raised in the air, those mad, staring eyes finally hooded. As if in a trance, he moaned, and his eyes came open, drinking her in.

Trembling hands reached for her—enveloped her—folded her in his strong arms. He groaned again, and she slipped her arms around his waist, drawing him closer still.

"You are real," he whispered. "I wasn't sure. I've conjured you in my mind so often, I was afraid you were nothing more than another apparition come to haunt me."

"I'm real enough," she said, "but for a moment just now, I viewed you the same, like a ghost in the darkness."

"Does this mean that you've decided?" he asked, his voice quavering.

"It means . . . that I love you," she replied, looking him in the eyes. "That has caved in my common sense, undermined my scruples, and defeated my resolve." He drew her closer still, holding her face against the soft hair on his chest. His skin was afire beneath her cheek, his heart thump, thump, thumping its rapid rhythm in her ear. "It means that my need of you is so great, I have no shame," she murmured through a dry sob.

He tilted her face up until their gazes met. Were those tears in his eyes, glistening in the darkness? Her own eyes misted, looking into them.

"You won't be afraid?" he said.

"Afraid?"

"If anything . . . untoward should happen. Like what occurred in the passageway," he whispered, brushing her brow with his lips. They were hot, and dry. "I'll know in time to distance myself, but still . . ."

"Why would I be afraid?" she said. "I love you both, and I would be loath to think that either of you would harm me."

The breath left his lungs in a rush of hot, moist whispers against her face, her hair—her arched throat. She couldn't understand his words, only the meaning behind them, the utter relief in the sound of primeval love binding them to the moment, and to each other.

Seizing her head, he cupped it in his massive hand and took her lips, opening her mouth, deepening the kiss with a teasing tongue that drew hers after it. The swift motion thrilled her, just as it had in the past, and she buried her hand in the soft silkiness of his hair, holding him fast until their trembling lips parted moist, and breathless.

"You're cold," he murmured against her mouth. "You're trembling."

"Not cold," she whispered back, their lips still touching, "I've never felt like this before. It's as if my bones are melting."

Nicholas stripped off the rest of his elegant toilette, tossed the clothes on the lounge with the rest of his things, and stood naked before her. He untied the ribbons that closed her wrapper, and slid it down over her shoulders, then the gown, until they fell in a cloud at her feet.

The shaft of moonlight, brighter now, spilled over them through the windowpanes. He was aroused, his sex touching her, as he slid his hands over her shoulders, down her arms, and reached for her breasts. As he caressed them his thumbs grazed her nipples, extracting a soft moan from her throat that drew her closer. Circling the puckered outline of each nub with one finger, he teased the hardened buds until they grew tall, coming closer and closer to the tips, leading her to the brink of ecstasy in rapturous torture, as his lips descended upon first one, and then the other. Sucking, tugging, nipping lightly. She shuddered in delight, every nerve ending in her body tingling in anticipation of what those skilled fingers, that merciless tongue were about to do to her next.

"You are . . . exquisite," he panted, his hot breath puffing against her moist skin. "You taste . . . of sweet cream . . . and of roses. I cannot drink my fill . . ."

Her sex was on fire, moist, swollen—palpitating with arousal. He took her hand, and guided it along the shaft of his engorged member, hot and hard yet silky to the touch. Her breath faltered as it responded to her caress, just as it had in the past; only now, it was as if it were a separate entity. He was no longer holding back. He was hers.

All at once, he lifted her into his arms, kicked her night-dress and wrapper out of the way, and carried her to the bed. Throwing back the counterpane, he set her down between the sheets, climbed in beside her with a sinuous motion that took her breath away, and took her in his arms. His moves were seamless. He never broke stride. His lips never left hers. His hands never ceased caressing, exploring, bringing her to the brink of rapture she feared would melt her very soul.

This was no amateur; here was a skilled lover. Sara's heart began to beat a little faster. She wasn't even sure what was

Dawn Thompson

expected of her. How would she ever please him? Suddenly, there was no impending threat of doom, no murderous wolf stalking the halls of Ravencliff, no guards about to descend upon the place, pistols at the ready. They were the only two people on earth, and his pleasure was all that mattered to her. If only she were wise enough. If only she were confident enough. If only she were skilled enough to pleasure him, the way he was pleasuring her.

His shaking hand slid along the curve of her thigh, and then crossed over, his fingers probing the private place between, which throbbed, and ached, and reached for his caress. Leaning back, he looked her in the eyes.

"Are you sure?" he asked.

"I'm sure," she said, meeting his black gaze, those dark, dark eyes dilated now with desire and searching her face.

"Wolves mate for life, Sara," he said, his voice like gravel.

"I know, Nicholas. . . ."

He pulled her closer then, the breath leaving his body on a long, ragged sigh.

"Will I ever see Nero again?" she whispered in his ear. She hadn't seen him since the incident. She had to know.

His handsome mouth became a lopsided smile, and dawn broke over Sara's heart. How like a mischievous lad he looked in one respect, while, in juxtaposition, lurked the master of seduction—hot breath puffing from flared nostrils, hooded eyes glazed with arousal. The intrigue of that set off earthquakes in her soul.

"Sometimes," he said, kissing her cheeks, her brow, her arched throat between words, "I think . . . you love . . . that animal . . . more . . . than you . . . love me."

"And whose fault is that, then?" she asked, delivering a playful swat to his arm. "Creeping into my chamber, letting me hand-feed you, nuzzling my hand, washing my face—letting me make a pet of Nero to replace the hounds I loved so and lost."

"It was the only way that I could touch you . . . be near you, feel the cool softness of your fingers on my brow, taste the sweetness of your skin, inhale the scent of you. If you think that I was not in torment, think again."

"You cannot be jealous of yourself, Nicholas, so do not be. Have you no idea how I longed to touch you from that very first day, when I reached out my hand, and you backed away from me—told me you didn't want to be touched?"

"If I had let you touch me then you would have seen what you saw four days ago right there in that study, my Sara. I knew the minute I set eyes on you the folly of my fine 'arrangement.' "

"And so, I turned to Nero," Sara continued. "He filled the gap that losing my dogs had rent in my heart. I had a pet again, and it was he who received the affection I so longed to bestow upon you—and would have done, if you had only let me, Nicholas. I've been so lonely. I saw the torment in you, and I longed to soothe it away. The odd thing is, I saw it in Nero also, and you haven't answered my question. Will I ever see him again? To me, you are and always will be separate entities."

He gathered her closer still. "Sooner than you care to, if we aren't careful," he murmured, taking her lips with a hungry mouth.

After a moment that mouth inched lower, following the curve of her throat, pausing over the pulse beating there, his tongue seeking the life force pumping through her. Sara shut her eyes and groaned as he spread her legs and began stroking her between them again. His touch was light and rapid, delving deeper with each stroke. She arched her body against the pressure, reaching for she knew not what until it came—a surging, searing firebrand of palpitations coursing through her body. Waves of icy fire moved through her, like ripples on calm water once a stone breaks the surface.

All at once, he withdrew his hand, and filled her with his

sex. The groan that left her throat as he glided inside her on the dew of her first awakening seemed dredged up from her very core. She had no control over it. It came unbidden, of its own volition, mating with the moan in his own dry throat, as his mouth closed over her trembling lips. The mingled sounds resonated through her body. Was that her heart, racing so savagely? Or was it his? Or was it both their hearts, pounding, shuddering one against the other.

The hard buds of her breasts were buried in the silk of his chest hair. They seemed to catch fire, and new pleasure-pains shot through her loins like molten lava, as she moved to the rhythm of his thrusts. How he filled her. How perfectly they fitted together. Lost in a firestorm of excruciating ecstasy, she yielded to every nuance of his love. Her body became malleable in his hands, responding to the fever in his blood.

There should have been pain, but there wasn't. She'd expected it—steeled herself against it, but it never came. She felt only the pressure of his sex, the gentle strength as it moved inside her at the height of the icy-hot surges that canceled out pain and thought and reason—canceled out all but awareness of him. But it wasn't just *him*. They were no longer two separate people. They were one. That is what transported her—lifted her out of herself—riveted every cell in her body to his with pumping spurts of liquid fire.

Like sand beneath an ebbing wave, all restraints were washed away in that brief blink of time's eye. They had mated for life. All the world seemed to hold its breath. In that magical consummate moment, there was no more threat, no more danger, only love.

It was, alas, too fleeting. All at once he tensed against her. The discipline returned, and he withdrew himself before his bursting life could fill her with the warm rush of his seed. Instead, he crushed her hand around his sex and called her name as it pumped him dry.

All at once his breathing changed from quick and shallow to deep, shuddering gasps. His brow was running with sweat, and he dropped it down on her shoulder, and gathered her close, burying his hand in her hair.

"Why did you do that?" Sara murmured.

"I meant . . . what I said," he panted. Snaking a handkerchief from beneath his pillow, he put it in her hands. "I cannot risk passing this nightmare on. It must end with me. It needn't be this way always. Dr. Breeden has solutions. You need to talk to him. Nothing could be done this first time in any case. I'm sorry, Sara . . ."

"Sometimes what we fear the most turns out to be the least of our fears, when all is said and done," she murmured.

"Sometimes yes, but not *this* time. You must trust me, Sara, to know what is best for both of us. I love you. I will not see you tortured in that way—mother to such a creature as I am—and I will not inflict such a legacy upon an unsuspecting innocent: condemn it to the life that I have been forced to live because my father had to have his deuced heir."

"Until now," she whispered. "Is it so dreadful . . . now? Nicholas, you're making strides. Dr. Breeden is committed to the task of teaching you to control your transformations. Once you have done, you could teach your son to do the same if needs must . . . couldn't you?"

"Shhh," he said. Wrapping the counterpane around her, he gathered her close, and grazed her temple with his lips. Those *were* tears glistening in his eyes. She longed to kiss them away. "Go to sleep, my Sara," he murmured, his voice husky and strained.

She said no more. Now was not the time. He was choked with emotion, and from the look of it, trying to prevent himself from shapeshifting then and there. All at once, it was so clear, as though a candle had suddenly blazed in her fogged brain. It wasn't that he didn't want a child. It was that he didn't *dare* want a child. He'd built a wall around his heart and soul that longed to be complete, because he thought he never could be. That was obvious, and it hurt her far more than any of the rest. That was the torment she'd seen in the eyes of man and wolf from the very start. She didn't recognize it until now, and she bit her lip until it bled to keep from crying.

Snuggling close, she clung to Nicholas, running her fingers through the soft hair on his chest. The heart beneath had calmed now—slow, steady beats rode shuddering breaths. The moist skin beneath her face was still flushed; the long, lean length of him pressed against her still blazed with the heat of their joining.

"Don't ever leave me, Sara," he murmured against her brow.

Sara didn't answer, except to draw him closer into her arms. There was no need of words. Her body spoke volumes with more eloquence than her lips could have done.

He sighed then, and she began drifting off to sleep to the music of his deep breathing. To the rise and fall of his chest, as though her head were a boat riding the gentle swells of a sea becalmed. Outside, the actual sea breathed deeply as well. Lace-edged combers lapped at the strand, foaming over the rocks and boulders, whispering in the tide pools, murmuring among the cairns and caves and hidden places. The voice of the wind had stilled. It would be a fine day tomorrow. Sara wouldn't think about that. She lived in the here and now, curled in her husband's strong arms, listening to the symphony of man and nature, letting it spiral her down, down, down into what would have been the perfect sleep, except for one nagging question still tugging at her heartstrings. How could she make that life live inside her? How could she make him complete? It was her only desire.

She awoke in the morning with a start to the crack and boom of thunder rumbling along the strand, and bright sunlight flooding the bedchamber. How could that be? Vaulting upright in the rumpled bed, she rubbed the sleep from her eyes.

Nicholas was not beside her. Her heart leapt. The indentation his body had made in the feather bed and down pillow was still there. It was cold to the touch. Where had he gone? When had he left her? What time could it be?

The thunderclap came again. It seemed louder now, but that was because of the echo. Changes in the weather at sea amplified sound along the strand. Men were shouting now, and more thunder rumbled. Sara stared at the shiny bright morning showing through the windows, gleaming through the mullioned panes, and listened to another crack and boom. No! Not thunder—*gunfire!*

She sat bolt upright, clutching the counterpane to her naked body, riddled with chills despite the warm sun streaming through the window. It was as though an icy fist had gripped her spine and paralyzed her where she sat. Her nightdress and wrapper lay nearby on the floor where Nicholas had discarded them. She was just about to reach for them, when a rapid knock at the door froze her again. Before she could reply, it came open, and Mills burst inside.

"Begging your pardon, my lady," he cried. "his lordship . . . ?"

"N-not here," she stammered. The valet's face was the color of ashes, and his faded gray eyes were glaring. She had never heard him raise his voice before. "My God, Mills, what is it?"

"Do you know where he's gone, my lady?" the valet persisted.

"No . . . I just woke, and he wasn't here. What's happening?" she shrilled.

The valet's eyes oscillated between the pile of clothes on the lounge, and Nicholas's boots carelessly strewn on the floor. "Those are the togs his lordship wore down to dinner last evening," he murmured, as though he were thinking out loud. "I dressed him myself." Rummaging through the armoire, he seized Nicholas's dressing gown, then flung it away with a groan.

"What is it, Mills? Will you *please* tell me what's going on?"

"The guards have come, my lady," Mills said. "They've cornered a wolf on the beach."

Twenty-nine

Sara took no time to dress. Clutching her nightclothes about her, she ran to the tapestry suite, wriggled into her striped muslin morning frock—the first dress her hand fell upon when she reached into the armoire—and tugged on her pelisse. The halls were empty, but it wouldn't have mattered if they were teeming with staff; she raced down the stairs, along the first-floor corridor to the servants' entrance, and burst out onto the apron.

Below, the sound of gunfire—of pistol balls glancing off granite rock—of something heavier than a handgun resounding over the rest—wrenched a cry from her lips. It turned Mills around, as he shuffled toward the stone steps with Nicholas's greatcoat looped over his arm.

"My lady, *no* . . . go back!" he called over the sound of the wind, which had risen suddenly, heavy with the taste of salt. "It isn't safe. Let me handle it, I beg of you!"

"Let you throw that over his dead body after they *kill him*, you mean?" she cried, gesturing toward the coat as she ran by him. "I'd rather you throw it over mine!" Just for a split second, she glimpsed a flash of steel beneath the greatcoat, and stopped in her tracks. *Mills was armed.* "What do you mean to do with that?" she shrilled, pointing toward the pistol.

"My lady, please! Go back to the house and let me handle this."

"You're going to *shoot* him?" Her shrill voice sounded back in her ears, amplified by the wind.

"There is no time for this, my lady. I implore you, go back to the house!"

"You *are*! My God, you *are*!" Sara cried, making a lunge for the pistol.

Mills held her at bay with a firm hand. "If needs must," he said. "It is something we have prearranged in case of just such a situation, my lady. I must bring him down . . . wound him, nothing more, before *they* do. He will not transform right away . . . the shock will prevent it, and I can see him safely back inside before it subsides and spare him what they will do with him if he is captured alive . . . or what they will see if they . . . kill him. *No*, my lady! Let go of the pistol. I do not want to hurt you. That could be Mr. Mallory down there, and if it is, I shall need it! You mustn't interfere!"

"My God!" Sara screamed. "How will you tell the difference? Why, you might . . . you might . . . !" The thought was too terrible to give substance with words.

"Trust me, I will know," said Mills, "That, too, is prearranged. Let . . . *go*, my lady!"

It was no use. The valet's grip upon the weapon was unequivocal. The look in his eyes gave her feet wings, and loosing a groan she bolted toward the brink, flew over the edge of the seawall, and began climbing down to the strand below.

The beach was swarming with guards running helterskelter over the sand, guns blazing. The acrid odor of gun smoke rode the wind, invading her nostrils until her eyes teared. Her vantage, halfway down the stone stairs, gave her a clear view. They were converging upon the little cove where she'd found Nicholas's clothes, and a blur of silver-black fur trying to reach it. It was too great a distance, and they were gaining on him.

"*Noooooo!*" she shrilled, slip-sliding the rest of the way down.

Mills and Dr. Breeden weren't behind her now. Where had they gone? It didn't matter. Lifting her skirt, she kicked off her Morocco leather slippers, threw off her pelisse, for it weighted her down, and raced along the hard-packed sand at the water's edge. She was lighter on her feet than those ahead of her, and passed them by with ease, ignoring their shouts that she halt. Nero was still within pistol range. *Why did he stop?* She swallowed her rapid heartbeat. Her lungs were burning from the salt. *He's coming back! He's running right into them!*

Shots rang out. Nero raised his head and howled into the wind, then ran straight toward her and toward the guards attempting to fire around her. Glancing back, Sara saw two of the officers drop down on one knee, taking dead aim at Nero advancing.

"No, Nero, go back!" she screamed, putting herself in the line of fire.

More shots resounded, and the jolt as one of the pistol balls impacted her lifted her off the ground. It happened so fast there was no pain at first as it spun her around. The strand appeared sideways—sand and sky tilted before her blurred vision as she crashed to earth in a crumpled heap of striped muslin, and white batiste petticoats.

A whistle, piercing and shrill, rose above the pandemonium. Where was Nero? Why couldn't she see Nero? He had been so close. Heavy footfalls pounding the hard-packed sand reverberated through her body, as a sea of faces converged upon her—strange except for Dr. Breeden's, as he pushed through the others gathered there, and knelt beside her. All at once, excruciating pain ripped through her back and shoulder, and she groaned.

"N-Nero . . . ?" she begged, but she didn't hear his reply. Something blotted out the sun and the faces and the rumble of discordant voices. The pain was beyond bearing now. Waves of nausea threatened. White pinpoints of fractured light starred her vision. Then they were gone. The sky turned black, and the last thing she heard was the deep, mournful howl of a wolf trailing off on the wind.

Nicholas sat in his stocking feet on the lounge in the tapestry suite sitting room, his head in his hands. He was wearing the rumpled black satin pantaloons and Egyptian cotton shirt he'd thrown on the lounge in the green suite the night before. Beyond the closed door to the bedchamber across the way, Dr. Breeden and Mrs. Bromley worked over Sara. Time meant everything and nothing then, only that it was passing with no word of her condition, and he'd been barred from her bedside—locked out in his own house, when she could be dying.

Nicholas had no idea how much time had passed when Mills burst in through the foyer. He didn't even look up; his eyes were so brimming with tears he couldn't have made out the valet's clear image in any case.

"The guards have gone, my lord," said Mills, "All except for Captain Renkins, that is. He's waiting in the drawing room for news of her ladyship."

"Bastards!" Nicholas seethed, pummeling his knees with clenched fists.

"'Tis a wonder they didn't cart you off as well," Mills scolded. "You nearly planted the captain a leveler, not to mention me!"

"Do you think they'll return?"

"*They* won't, my lord. There'll be no more dog hunts on the strand after what occurred today, but the captain will no doubt be haunting you until this coil has been unwound. You can bet your blunt upon that. This day comes dear, and he hasn't forgotten that you told him there was no animal on the estate. How you weren't carted off, charged with assault, I will never know. You must take yourself in hand! I cannot do this any longer. I'm a bit too old to get between and hold you back, like I did when you were a lad. I am ill-equipped to be a referee, especially with this deuced lame wing. I'll be stiff as a coat rack tomorrow. Then who'll tend you?"

"They shot my wife, Mills!" Nicholas reminded him.

"Aiming at *Nero*," the valet served. "What ever possessed you to turn back? You were nearly at the cove. You could have lost them in the cave in the rocks, and come back to the house by the old way, through any one of the smugglers' tunnels, with plenty of time to spare. Just as you did the last time you got caught short out on the strand evading my lady. But no! You ran right into the line of fire. I never saw the like, and for a moment I thought they might have cornered the other wolf, after all; your actions were that foolhardy!"

"I was trying to protect her. She'd put herself deliberately in harm's way trying to protect *me*. And I couldn't have made the cave. I barely made it when they abandoned pursuit. They would have found it, and followed it straight to the Manor otherwise, no doubt stumbling upon me in the altogether. My God, she didn't think they'd fire, and they *shot her down!*"

"The wolf trying to do the man's job, was he?" Mills said. "Well, now you see the folly of that, my lord. God forgive me, what sort of 'treatments' is that man in there giving you? Your common sense has always been infallible, until he started tampering with your head."

"It's not my head, and it's not the doctor's fault." Nicholas groaned. "I have never been in love before." He gestured toward the bedchamber. "But that in there is not entirely my fault, either, Mills," he said. "Why the Devil did you let her go down there? Why didn't you stop her?"

"*Stop her*, my lord?" the valet ground out through a mirthless laugh. "Wild elephants could not have stopped her. She saw my pistol and tried to wrest it out of my hands. I had to tell her what we prearranged, but that only made matters worse. She fought me like a tigress until the doctor came running, and then she ran off and climbed down to the strand."

Nicholas dropped his head back into his hands, and raked them both through his hair. The valet shuffled away and, after a moment, shuffled back.

"Here," he said, offering a half-filled brandy snifter. "Have this, my lord. You look like death itself."

Nicholas took a swallow from the glass, but the click of the bedchamber door latch opening turned his head, and he surged to his feet, thrusting the snifter back at Mills, sloshing its contents down the front of the valet's heretofore impeccable white waistcoat.

Mrs. Bromley waddled into the sitting room, grim-faced and teary-eyed, a bundle of blood-soaked linens caught up in her apron. A groan escaped the bedroom when she opened the door, and Nicholas lunged, dancing with the woman in the doorway, trying to get past her.

Mills slapped the snifter down on the drum table, and took a firm hold upon Nicholas's arm. Nicholas paid him no mind, trying to circumvent the housekeeper's girth and gain entrance to the bedroom.

"Out of my way, Mrs. Bromley!" he charged.

"Beggin' your pardon, my lord," the housekeeper said, "the doctor says you're not ta go in till he sends for ya."

"I have to know!" Nicholas insisted. "I have to see her. She's in pain, goddamn it, woman. Is he giving her nothing to ease it? Stand aside, I say!"

"Don't, my lord!" the valet pleaded. "The last thing any of us needs right now, is you on the verge of madness here. You must calm yourself, to prevent more . . . harm done."

Nicholas read between the lines, but it didn't matter; Sara's groans were more than he could bear. He was the

:ause of them, and he would run mad if he couldn't see her
'or himself—hold her, touch her, tell her her sacrifice had not
)een in vain.

"Bring his cordial, Mrs. Bromley," Mills said in an aside to
:he housekeeper, while trying without success to pry
Nicholas's fingers away from her arms. "Let go, my lord!
'ou impede progress."

"Why has she not been dosed?" Nicholas raved. He didn't
want to hurt the woman, but by Heaven if she didn't make
way. . . .

"She can't have no more laudanum," said the housekeeper. "She's had more than what's safe as it is. I'm goin' ta
fetch one o' me cordials. Please let me pass, my lord, we're
doin' all that can be done."

"Is she . . . will she . . . ?"

"We dunno yet, my lord. Please let me by!"

"Let him come!" boomed the doctor's voice from the bed-
:hamber. "I've only hands enough to tend one patient here
now."

Mills let him go, and Nicholas reeled through the bed-
:hamber door, ran to the bed, and dropped down on one
knee beside Sara.

She seemed so small lying there tossing beneath the
quilts, her hair like spun gold fanned out on the pillow. He
:aptured her hand, and kissed it.

"Sara, can you hear me?" he murmured, searching the
glassy, vacant eyes that seemed to see right through him.
'She doesn't know me, Dr. Breeden!" he despaired.

"She wouldn't know her own mother after the dose I've
given her," said the doctor. "You cannot stay here, my lord.
You do more harm than good. If you would have me finish
my job and see her through the worst of this, you must away,
and let me."

"How bad is it?" Nicholas asked, his eyes riveted to the
blood-soaked bandages the doctor was applying to the
wound, exerting pressure.

"The pistol ball didn't quite go through," Breeden replied. "It lodged close to the artery. I've got it out, but she's lost much blood, and I now must clean and cauterize the wound. You cannot be here for that, my lord, or we will have Nero all over again."

Nicholas glanced toward the poker propped in the blazing hearth, and his scalp drew back taut.

"Mrs. Bromley kindled the fire," the doctor said. "I'm waiting only for that there to heat enough to do the job."

"And then . . . ?" Nicholas murmured.

"We wait, my lord," said the doctor. "Fever is our enemy now. You must trust us to do what has to be done. She lives! After what she's just come through, believe me that is a good sign. Now please, I beg you, leave us."

"You do not understand," Nicholas murmured against her cold fingers pressed to his lips, "This is all my fault. I took her to my bed, and I got through it without . . . changing, but afterward, I couldn't hold it back. She was sound asleep when it happened. Nero should have stayed there with her. He should have curled up on the hearth and let her find him there when she woke, but no . . . I tried to run it off out on the strand . . . and then the guards came. If only she hadn't come down there . . . if only—"

"If she hadn't, you would be dead, my lord. You could not have outrun them; there were too many. They would have shot you dead, and learned your secret, because in death you would have shifted back as you are now. Think of the repercussions of *that*, my lord, and thank the stars above that she did what she did. Where did you go? I didn't see. I was ministering to her ladyship."

"Everyone converged upon the baroness," said Nicholas. "Mills whistled, and Nero obeyed. It is a signal prearranged between us . . . in case of an emergency. I barely made it into the tunnel before I changed back. I dressed and came as fast as I could."

"And nearly got yourself hauled off by the guards. What-ever possessed you to go at them like that?"

"What would you have done if it had been your wife lying there in a pool of blood on the beach? How would you have dealt with the bastard that fired the pistol standing slack-jawed and indignant—spouting all that horse shit that he was only 'doing his duty'?"

The doctor heaved a nasal sigh. "Probably the same, my lord," he said, "but I am not a shapeshifter. You're thinking with your heart and not your head. Men who do that in such a crisis usually are killed. You must focus on the larger picture here, and keep control, or you will undo all that we have accomplished. Whether you realize it or not, you have managed to control the transformation to a de-gree, and under the worst possible conditions. I call that progress."

"I wasn't even thinking of that," said Nicholas. All he could think of was Sara, so still and pale and out of reach, though his hand tethered hers like an umbilical cord, in a desperate attempt to feed her life through the power of his will alone.

"How is it that you changed back so quickly in that tunnel, my lord?"

"I had to!" he cried. "I had to know. I feared she was *dead!*"

The doctor nodded. "So you fought your way back," he said. "Could you have done that when I first arrived here? You needn't answer. I remember what occurred when we locked you in your dressing room, and when my lady shut you up in the alcove chamber. Could you have changed back on either of those occasions? I think not, my lord. Don't fly in the face of fortune. Now I want you to take yourself off and rest, and let me get on with this here."

"You know I won't do that, Dr. Breeden. I shan't leave this suite until I know that she will live."

"Have it your way, but you *will* leave this room," said the doctor, as Mrs. Bromley entered bearing a tray heaped with fresh bandage linen, antiseptic, and several of her remedies. "Wait where you will, however you will, but you shan't cross that threshold again until I summon you. Now leave, and let me try to have this done while she is still too drugged to feel the worst of it."

Nicholas staggered to his feet, cast one last look at his semiconscious bride, and stumbled out of the room like a man in his altitudes. Mills awaited him in the sitting room, and presented him with the prescribed cordial. Nicholas tossed it down in one savage gulp, and began to pace the length of the Aubusson carpet.

"You defeat the purpose of that which you've just drunk, my lord," the valet pointed out. "You need to calm yourself, and rest. You court the inevitable as you are, and you can ill afford to have it come about here now, with the captain of the Watch wandering about."

Nicholas stopped in his tracks. "She could die, Mills," he said. "If she does, you can rest assured that Nero will tear his throat out, your captain of the Watch!"

He said no more. Pacing and prowling throughout the day, he kept a close eye upon the bedchamber door, but it remained locked. There were no more sounds from inside, and Mrs. Bromley didn't emerge again. Was that a good sign? There was no way to tell. If only one of them would come out and tell him *something*.

Smythe went to the drawing room several times at Nicholas's insistence, trying to persuade Captain Jenkins to leave, but the man refused to go, which only served to infuriate Nicholas more and more with each attempt as the day wore on. The butler returned with word that the captain wasn't about to leave until he knew how Baroness Walraven fared, since it was his bullet that brought her down, but that was the least of Nicholas's worries. On the other side of that towering door his bride lay suffering on what could well be her deathbed, and it was his fault. That challenged his sanity, and Nero waited just under the surface of his departure from progress.

When twilight robbed the light, and Mills lit the candles, Nicholas could stand no more. He strode to the bedchamber door, and called out: *"Breeden!* In God's name!"

After a moment, the doctor stepped into the sitting room, and closed the door behind him. Haggard and pale, he took a ragged breath, his sharp eyes lusterless in the nimbus of candle shine.

"Is she . . . ?" Nicholas pleaded.

"She is holding her own," the doctor replied. "There's fever, but Mrs. Bromley's remedies are addressing that. We should know more by morning."

"Is she conscious?" said Nicholas.

The doctor shook his head. "No, my lord, and that's a mercy. We have the laudanum, and Mrs. Bromley's herbal remedies to thank for it, and that she's healthy, young, and strong."

"I want to see her," Nicholas said. "I must!"

"You cannot disturb her, my lord. She needs to rest."

"I shan't wake her, Dr. Breeden. I beg of you . . . just for a moment—only that . . ."

The doctor hesitated. "I expect we'll have no peace unless I allow it," he said. "Two minutes. No more."

"Granted," said Nicholas, pushing past him into the bedchamber, as the housekeeper left it carrying more linens and an empty tray.

How pale Sara looked, like a ghost in the soft semidarkness. Nicholas swallowed his rapid heartbeat, and knelt on one knee beside her, taking her hand in his just as he had before, and as before, it was lifeless and cold. She drew shallow, rapid breaths, and he turned to the doctor at his side.

"The fever," Breeden explained.

Nicholas leaned close, whispering in her ear. "I'm here, Sara, and I . . . we have come to no harm. Come back to me, Sara. My God, don't leave me . . . !"

The doctor gripped his shoulder. "Come away, my lord," he said. "She doesn't hear you."

"I've heard it said that those in coma do hear what goes on around them," Nicholas said. "I pray it's true, because if she dies thinking it was all for naught . . ."

"Believe me, the moment she is coherent, I will personally tell her that you were not harmed. You have my word. Now come away."

Nicholas got to his feet, staring down through misty eyes.

"Mrs. Bromley has gone off for a lie-down," the doctor said. "We shall spell each other through the night. If there is a change, you will be summoned at once."

"You shan't have far to go to find me," Nicholas snapped, storming out of the room and into the sitting room, where Mills waited.

"How does my lady fare?" asked the valet.

"She is alive," Nicholas told him. "She isn't conscious. There's fever. We won't know more until morning."

"She is in good hands, my lord," said the valet. "Please come away and rest. You need to keep control. It's too dangerous here now to take risks."

"Control, Mills?" snapped Nicholas. "If I do not occupy myself with some task here, I will run stark staring mad. Fetch me my turned-down boots, and my pistols."

"What are you going to do, my lord?" the valet breathed.

"First, I shall evict that bastard waiting in the drawing room—for his own damned good, I assure you. Then, I'm going hunting."

Thirty

Was it the wind whispering in her ear? It sounded so desperate. But then, the Cornish wind had moaned like a creature possessed since first she'd experienced it in the buffeted post chaise, the day she arrived at the brooding manor. All that seemed a lifetime ago. This wind had no motion, only sound. A pity. She would have welcomed it to cool the fever raging in her. Was it calling her name, or was she dreaming?

The sound came again, and she stirred. Why couldn't she open her eyes? Her eyelids were so heavy, and her head was swimming. There was pain, too, a dull nagging pain in her back and shoulder. Why was she propped on her side?

Someone groaned. It was a moment before she realized that the sound had come from her own dry throat. The whispering grew louder . . . no, not the wind . . . someone *was* calling her name.

Her eyes fluttered open a crack, but she couldn't see. Everything in her line of vision resembled moiré silk: all wavy, shifting and fluid. Was it day or night? Whose hand was that on her forehead, so gentle, and cool? She leaned into it, and groaned again.

"Nicholas . . . ?" she murmured.

All at once the featherbed sagged with his weight, and strong arms slipped around her without changing her tilted position. Cool lips brushed her brow, so soothing against her hot, moist skin. What a delicious dream.

"Have a care, my lord!"

Was that Dr. Breeden's voice? Someone else cried out. Could it be Mrs. Bromley? What were they doing in her dream? Another voice bled into the rest that she didn't recognize. At first, she couldn't make out what it was saying. It sounded far off in the distance. Then, as it gained volume, the strong arms holding her fell away, and the body weight bringing the featherbed down was lifted sharply.

"That was a damned fool thing to do," said the strange voice. It was gruff, and common. She didn't like it. It hurt her ears. "Running straight into the line of fire like that," the voice was saying, "interferin' with Guard business. She could've been killed, and that's a fact."

"Well, you can thank Divine Providence that she wasn't," Nicholas's voice growled. "As it is, your superior will have my report of what occurred down on that strand, sure as check. You can bet your blunt upon it!"

"You wasn't even there, m'lord!"

"I saw nonetheless, from the Manor. I was on my way down to tell you, you were firing on the wrong animal. You haven't heard the last of this, Renkins."

"Oh, so now you admit there *was* a dog out here all along, do you, Walraven?" the stranger barked. "I thought as much. If you had owned up to it when I came out here the first time, we wouldn't be having this here now, would we? It's your fault the baroness is lying in that bed. You may as well have shot her down yourself!"

There was a scuffling sound, loud shouts, and . . . was that Mrs. Bromley screaming?

"Let go of me, Mills!"

Nicholas?

"*Enough,* my lord!"

"Hold him, you lot!" the gruff voice boomed. "If he lays a hand on me he'll go before the magistrate—baron or no!"

Sara flinched, and moaned, wishing the bizarre dream would end.

"There are *two* animals on this estate, you nodcock!" said the voice that sounded like Nicholas. "One is my own, the other a stray that we have been trying to get shot of. I chose not to divulge that when you first came 'round, because I didn't want to chance harm coming to the wrong one. That is neither here nor there. If you'd bothered to consult me before going off half-cocked out there, all this could have been avoided. Her ladyship knew you had cornered the wrong animal. She knows the difference, and since you and your men obviously do not, *I* shall find and destroy the animal that killed my servant. You, sir, are a menace! I want you off my land."

"You knew we was comin'," said the captain. "You should've chained that dog up, then."

"I must insist that you take this elsewhere," the doctor said, his voice raised and edged. "You are disturbing my patient. My lord, *please.*"

Heavy footfalls receded then, carrying the voices away, though Sara heard them still, arguing and shouting, even after the door closed upon them. Then she slept.

It took three days and a gradual reduction of the laudanum dose before Sara fully regained consciousness. The captain of the guards had gone, and Nicholas hovered despite the insistence of Mills and the doctor that the crisis had passed. The fever had broken. There was no sign of infection, and no reason to believe she wouldn't make a complete recovery.

Mrs. Bromley's herbal salves, poultices, and tinctures were given much of the credit for her recovery. The salves and poultices of flaxseed, foxglove leaves, and milk thistle healed the wound and dulled the pain, and her borage and balm tinctures, and fresh-squeezed black currant juice addressed the fever. The latter, sweetened with honey, was the most palatable, but Sara endured it all with a cheerful heart, despite her worries over Nicholas who, during his absences from the tapestry suite, prowled Ravencliff like a man possessed, loaded flintlocks at the ready. Thus far, to no avail. It was during one of those absences that she decided to speak to the doctor about the one nagging matter that only he could help her resolve.

She was never left unguarded. When Dr. Breeden took himself off for a lie-down or one of Nicholas's treatments, Mrs. Bromley attended her, Nicholas relieving her in his turn. That evening, she was alone with the doctor, who had just finished changing the dressing on her wound.

"If you continue to improve at this rate, I shall allow you out of bed for short intervals commencing tomorrow," the doctor said, dosing her with one of his rare smiles.

"Dr. Breeden," she said, "there is something I wish to discuss with you . . . some questions I need to ask you regarding Nicholas's condition."

"Whatever I can impart without betraying professional confidence, my lady."

"This shouldn't encroach upon confidentiality," she said. "Much of it concerns the condition, rather than Nicholas himself."

"I see," said the doctor, taking a seat in the Chippendale chair beside the bed. "How may I assist you, then?"

Asking intimate questions would not be easy. It went against her sensibilities, but this was far too important to let refinement stand in the way, and he was a doctor after all. Nevertheless, the hot fingers of a blush crawled up her cheeks, hotter than the fever she'd just overcome.

"Is th-the . . . condition always passed on through the blood?" she got out, despite the lump in her throat. "That is to say . . . if we were to have children . . . ?"

The doctor hesitated. "His lordship doesn't want to take that chance, my lady."

"I know, Dr. Breeden. What I'm asking is . . . would there be a chance that a child might not be . . . infected, if that's the right word? I am ignorant of such things. All this is so new to me."

"We simply do not know," said the doctor. "There's precious little precedent to go by in these cases, and what documentation there is, isn't conclusive, I'm afraid. That is why his lordship does not want to risk it."

"It isn't that he doesn't want an heir, Dr. Breeden," said Sara, "it's that he's *afraid* to want children. I'm certain of it. He would rather deny himself the right of fatherhood, than inflict such a thing upon his offspring."

"Has he said that, then?

"No," said Sara. "He didn't have to. I see it in his eyes—in the sadness I see there whenever we discuss it."

"I see," said the doctor. "You have discussed it, then . . . at length, my lady?"

Sara was silent. How was she to tell him that the husband she worshipped withdrew himself from her body to prevent conception? Nicholas did say, however, that she ought to have this conversation with the doctor. She decided to begin with that.

"His lordship did suggest that I speak with you . . . about alternatives," she murmured.

"Ah!" said the doctor, "of course. There are several methods that you might employ, herbal salves for one. The right combination of herbs can be quite effective. And then there are devices that courtesans have used since time out of mind. A sponge affair, infused with the herbs of which I speak, has proven quite reliable for some time now. French courtesans have used it for ages. It's only just gained popularity here over the last decade, but it is easily obtained, my lady."

"How . . . unnatural," Sara mused. She couldn't imagine

how such a device should be used, and she wasn't brave enough to inquire. "Is there nothing . . . else?"

"Do your courses come regularly, my lady?"

"Yes . . ."

"That being the case, halfway between would be a dangerous time, during which you could abstain, but the calculations would need to be precise, and there's no way they can be. Each individual is different. There is no set pattern. Your physical makeup is peculiar to yourself, and what might be the case one month could be entirely different the next. Many outside influences affect the female cycle. That would without a doubt curtail the instances of safe cohabitation drastically, and you might well conceive once or twice before you'd gotten it right. It is the most natural method, but the least effective, and if you are thinking of suggesting such to his lordship . . ." He shook his head. "I wouldn't. There's just too much risk involved."

This was not going well. Her embarrassment was profound, and had gained her nothing. Hot tears stung behind her eyes. She blinked them back. She would not outfit herself like a whore, and he was right, Nicholas would never agree to anything as risky as second-guessing nature. She would not trick him, either, but neither would she have his solution to the problem continue. It was her coil to unwind, but maybe . . . just maybe the good doctor might be able to point her in the right direction. It would mean being frank with the man, but she'd come this far. . . .

"Dr. Breeden, perhaps I should rephrase my original question," she said. "Is it a certainty, in your opinion, that his lordship would pass on his condition to his offspring?"

"Of course not," he responded. "Nothing is known for certain. That's the insidious element in this."

"That being the case, is there a direction you might suggest I take that might persuade his lordship to leave such matters to Divine Providence?"

The doctor smiled. "You do not need my suggestions for

that," he said. "Women's wiles have always had the ability to conquer we unsuspecting males. If such a thing can be done, you are the only one to do it—of that I'm as certain as I am that the sun will rise tomorrow."

"I wish I shared your confidence," said Sara.

"This is very important to you," said the doctor, epiphany in his voice.

"It is vital, not only to me, but to him, and he doesn't even know it."

"Explain."

How was she to tell him that she'd felt the pent-up power of emotion in him longing for release in her arms; felt his ache to embrace that release, and how he beat back the temptation to yield to the surrender that would make him whole?

"I am not just speaking of pleasuring a husband. There are many ways of doing that. What I want goes much deeper. It involves the spirit, and his God-given right to reproduce. He will never be whole no matter how we love, unless we love . . . completely."

"And what of you, my lady," said the doctor. "Are you not complete?"

"I am not the issue, Dr. Breeden," she said. "It is not my fulfillment in question, it is his. I want to give him this. I simply do not know how, but I do know that I shan't rest until I have accomplished it."

"Accomplished what?" said a deep sensuous voice from the doorway that shot her through with heart-stopping waves of liquid fire. Nicholas strolled closer. His lopsided smile broke sunshine over her soul despite the dreary gray mist pressed up against the window, and the awkward conversation.

"Getting out of this bed," she said, without missing a beat.

"Is that something in the offing?" Nicholas asked the doctor.

Breeden nodded. "If she behaves, I might allow several brief periods out of bed tomorrow," he said.

"But that's wonderful news!" Nicholas said, sinking down on the bed beside her.

"If I may trust you to see that she does behave, I shall go and consult Mrs. Bromley about the dosage."

"Don't worry, she's in good hands," said Nicholas.

"Hmmm," the doctor growled. "I shall return directly."

The minute he crossed the threshold, Nicholas took Sara in his arms. Burying his hand in her hair, he took her lips in a burning kiss that left her weak and trembling.

"Nicholas . . . I've been wanting to speak with you alone," she said.

"Well, we're quite alone now, my love," he murmured while showering her face with soft kisses.

"Don't," she said, resisting. "I'm serious, Nicholas, we need to talk."

Now was the perfect time to broach the subject of children. There wouldn't be a better moment. He would never agree for himself. Would he agree for her? If it were true that he wouldn't want to live without her, maybe . . . just maybe . . .

"I spoke with Dr, Breeden as you suggested," she began, "and I'm afraid that I do not find his . . . unnatural alternative methods of preventing conception acceptable. May I speak my mind?"

His hands slipped away. "Of course," he said his voice like fingernails drawn across slate. He was steeled against what she was about to say; that was evident. His posture clenched. The muscles in his jaw were pulsating in a stiff, steady rhythm. The sinews in his rock-hard biceps, stretched to their limit of strain, were visible bulging through his cotton shirt, but she had begun, and there was no turning back now.

"I love you, Nicholas," she said, her voice quavering. "And I will never deny you pleasures of the flesh. *Ever.* But I want to give you children . . . or at least to try, and I do not believe you have the right to deny me this."

"I have every right, Sara," he responded, surging to his

feet. "We've been all 'round this. I cannot conscience bringing another creature such as myself into this world. It wouldn't be fair to it, *or* to you."

"I have already seen the worst that it could be in that passageway below," she countered. "Now, I will admit that it was somewhat of a shock that first time, but were it to occur before me here this minute, I wouldn't even blink, because I love you—all of you—*both* of you. What makes you think that our offspring wouldn't find such a mate as you have found in me? What makes you so certain that our child would even be afflicted, when Dr. Breeden is not certain himself? Do you presume to know more than he?"

"I cannot presume to take that chance," said Nicholas. "If he is not sure our child would be affected, he is not sure it wouldn't, either."

"From what I understand, your condition is a lesser form of your father's affliction. It would stand to reason that your child, if it were afflicted at all, would have a lesser strain than you. No matter what, it shan't be the other way 'round."

"We do not know that."

"We do not know *anything*," she snapped. "That is my point. How can you deny me fulfillment on mere speculation? I call *that* not fair." She hesitated. What she had in mind to say next could well drive a wedge between them that would separate them for life, or it could turn the tide. There was no way to be sure. He had moved away and begun to pace the carpet. "Don't you want children, Nicholas? My children?" she murmured. He stopped dead and fixed her with his gaze. She couldn't read the message in those eyes, or didn't want to, though she met them bravely. If he were to say no and mean it, it was over. The issue would be put to rest with a word. But if he could not, there was hope, and she held her breath waiting—clinging to that hope—for what seemed an eternity.

"That isn't fair," he said around a tremor.

"How not?" she returned. "You haven't been fair with me

325

from the beginning, and I love you in spite of it. You have lied to me—*blatant* lies, and lies of omission. You have put my life in jeopardy for the sake of pride, and your stubborn lack of trust. I want to know. I believe I have a right to know. I nearly *died* out on that strand, Nicholas. When one comes that close to one's mortality, one sees all things from a new perspective. One cannot help but be honest with oneself in such a situation. I am asking that you be as honest with me, as I have been with myself. Can you—*honestly* now—stand there, before me and before God, and tell me that you do not want children . . . have no liking, or need, or patience or . . . whatever, for children—mine or anyone's? That is all I'm asking. It is not a difficult question."

He reached her in two strides, sat back down beside her, and took her in his arms. Tears gleamed in his eyes, glistening on his long, dark lashes, catching glints of reflected light from the dreary day showing at the window. Sara couldn't meet those eyes. Though he blinked back the tears swimming there, they triggered her own.

"I cannot want children, Sara," he murmured, his hot breath grazing her ear, setting it afire. "I cannot afford the luxury of wanting what I cannot have. That is why I closed the door on that prospect early on, and why it was never part of the arrangement."

"There is no more 'arrangement,'" Sara reminded him. "You put paid to that when you consummated our marriage. Everything is changed now, Nicholas. We are one. You are no longer responsible for yourself alone. You have me to consider. You needn't answer now. I realize that you need time to think. What I'm asking is simply this . . . for the sake of my fulfillment as your wife, would you leave the consequences of our cohabitation in the hands of God, and love me as any woman has the right to expect to be loved by her husband?"

"Sara . . ."

"You are becoming more and more adept at controlling

your transformations with Dr. Breeden's help," she went on, laying her finger across his lips. "Is it that you fear to take the responsibility of teaching your son to overcome his affliction if needs must, just as you have done—because you *will* conquer this, you know. I feel it and I know it! Can you trust enough . . . are you *brave* enough to put our future in the hands of Divine Providence . . . not for yourself, but for *me?* That is what I need to know before we go forward. Search your heart, Nicholas . . . search it deeply, and well. When you can answer that question . . . come to me."

Thirty-one

Nicholas dragged himself up to the master suite to dress for dinner. Mrs. Bromley's entrance at that critical moment with Sara's dinner tray spared him answering her question, but nothing would spare him Mills's inquiry. Was the man a clairvoyant? Nicholas was beginning to think so.

"Oh, my lord!" the valet breathed. "Has her ladyship taken a turn for the worst?"

"No, Mills, *I* have," Nicholas snapped. "She wants me to leave this madness in the hands of Divine Providence, and chance having children."

"Yes, my lord."

"*'Yes, my lord?'* Is that all you can say, Mills?"

"Yes, my lord," said the valet. "A wonder she hasn't broached the subject with you sooner."

Nicholas stared. "You agree?" he asked, slack-jawed.

"She does have a point, my lord," said the valet, "and it is her prerogative to want children. She is a fine, healthy young woman, who, I strongly suspect, would make a fine mother—just as you would make a capital father, my lord, but for this 'madness.' Do you never long for such a life?"

"Of course I do, or I did . . . before I put it out of my mind. It isn't possible, Mills. I couldn't bear to pass this on to a child . . . to have it realize one day—just as I did on the brink of awakening to life and its pleasures—what I have done, and hate me for it—"

"The way you've always hated your father for what he's done to you, my lord?" the valet interrupted. "Forgive me, but you have, with the help of Dr. Breeden, made phenomenal progress, and will I have no doubt one day be able to control the transformations completely. At least, that is the doctor's prognosis. What you have done, so could your offspring do, my lord, and with less difficulty, since you have already set the example. And it may not even happen. There are no guarantees that your offspring would be as you are. To deny yourself on speculation"—he shook his head—"that is . . . unfair, to the both of you. You've managed well enough, when all is said and done, my lord. You've found your mate, without ever leaving this prison you've made for yourself. I would hate to see you lose her."

"*Lose her?* I cannot lose her, Mills. How could I ever live without her now?"

"I think it's time I tell you something that you ought to know, my lord," said the valet. "It concerns the father you hate so for bringing you into this world. Your father, God rest him, never knew what was happening to him—not when you were conceived. Then, he thought only that he had a festering wound left behind by the wolf bite that would not heal. He wasn't driven to get an heir despite his affliction, as you have always accused. He and your mother were very much in love. It surprised me, that, because so many of his peers indulged in social marriages for the purpose of breeding, and had mistresses for their pleasure. He never even knew what malady he had, let alone how it might affect you. If you must hate, hate the wolf that caused all this, not your father. He was its victim, just as you are."

"But I *do* know, Mills," Nicholas flashed, "and it's within my power to prevent more harm being done."

"The question is, my lord, do you have the right to exercise that power? And if you do exercise it, how will that affect your relationship with my lady?"

How did this subject become open for debate? It had always been a closed issue—the one part of the arrangement that was nonnegotiable. Now it was staring him in the face, and those he loved were against him two to one.

"Things are different now, my lord," Mills went on. "You do not just have yourself to consider any longer. Give your head a rest, and search your heart. Rational thought has thus far gained you naught in this that I can see, save error. If my lady has no qualms—"

"Stubble it, old boy—just stubble it. There are other coils to unwind before we start on that one." The conversation needed changing, and Nicholas was too worn down from his discourse with Sara to stand up to the valet, who was *always* right—except in this . . . he was certain. "We have to find Alex. Has everyone forgotten that?"

"I certainly haven't, my lord, and I cannot see how you have, considering that you've haunted the halls of Ravencliff—pistols drawn—for nigh on a sennight now."

"Well, good! Now help me change, so I can eat and continue the haunting."

Sara set her dinner tray aside for Mrs. Bromley. Had she done the right thing, giving Nicholas an ultimatum? There was no way to tell. If only she'd had a few minutes more to plead her case. If only Mrs. Bromley hadn't made her entrance at that precise moment. It had ruined her appetite, and half the food was still under the lids of the silver servers. She hoped the woman wouldn't peek beneath until she left the tapestry suite; she was in no humor for a lecture.

It was odd not having someone hovering. She hadn't been alone since she regained consciousness. She wasn't afraid. The door was closed, after all. It hadn't been left ajar since she'd discovered Nicholas's secret. She hadn't seen Nero since, either, and that saddened her. She knew it was silly, but would she ever see him again, her beloved Nero? To her, they were two very separate entities—her husband, and her pet. She simply couldn't think of them as one. Reminiscing, she sighed, and shut her eyes.

She had nearly dozed when Mrs. Bromley entered. The housekeeper made a beeline for the silver server, and lifted the lid.

"Aw, now"—she clicked her tongue—"how are ya ever goin' ta get your strength back eatin' like a bird?"

"I'll do better tomorrow," said Sara. "Dr. Breeden is going to let me up out of this bed for a bit in the morning."

"Then ya should have put this inta ya tonight," the house-keeper scolded. "Cook is goin' ta throw a fit. Ya hardly touched a bite."

"Tell Cook I'll eat a big breakfast," Sara said. "I'm too ex-cited about getting up again to eat now . . . it would only up-set my stomach."

"All right, my lady," said the housekeeper, taking up the tray. "I'll just bring this down, and I'll be right back with your herbal tea. You will drink that?"

"I will, Mrs. Bromley. I promise."

The housekeeper waddled into the foyer, tray in hand. When she opened the door, a scream poured from her throat, for the hulking shape of a shaggy black wolf crashed through, knocking the tray from her hands and sending it into the hallway in a clattering racket of metal and china and glass, as the beast bounded past her into the bedchamber.

"*Mrs. Bromley?*" Sara shrilled, but the woman's desperate screams were receding along the corridor.

Before Sara could blink the wolf leaped upon the bed, looming over her, its lips curled back, baring fangs. Drool dripped from its tongue and jowls. Its fur, wet with the eve-ning mist, smelled fetid, of death and decay, especially in the matted area of the wound on its foreleg. It began to growl. Sara scarcely breathed. It prowled closer, puffing foul breath in her face, pinning her beneath the counterpane. She couldn't move—wouldn't have, even if she could. Its dilated eyes were full of menace. It was about to spring.

Moments passed that seemed like hours before Nicholas charged through the door. Dr. Breeden was right behind him. Nicholas waved the physician back.

"No!" he said. "Leave this to me. Fetch Mills. Tell him to bring his pistols and keep the others out."

"My lord . . ."

"Do as I've said and close that door behind you, he doesn't leave this room alive!"

"Nicholas!" Sara cried.

"Shhh, don't move," her husband cautioned in a voice she couldn't recognize. It was more bark than voice, something dredged from the finite edge of man and beast. It ran her through with cold chills. "Whatever happens, do not move!" She couldn't; the animal was practically atop her.

Nicholas pulled off his boots and stockings, then his waistcoat, pantaloons, and shirt, throwing them on the floor. He stripped off his drawers and tossed them down as well.

Sara gasped. "Nicholas, *no!*"

"It's the only way," he said. "He's caught us off guard."

"The pocket pistol!" Sara cried. "It's in the sitting room table drawer."

Nicholas shook his head. "I won't chance hitting you," he said. "He's gone mad, Sara. I've got to get him off that bed. I cannot do that in human form . . . but Nero *can*."

"And if he bites you?"

"He isn't rabid. It's the wound that's driven him mad. It was never treated. That's probably why he hasn't changed back. He cannot give me what I have already, but he can give it to you. You must do exactly as I say!"

"Mills is coming!" Sara cried. "Please, Nicholas, wait for Mills!"

"If I can't get a clear shot, how will he? No! Not while you're in that bed! Are you well enough to get out of it?"

"I-if I must . . . Oh, Nicholas!"

"Then do it the minute I get him off you, and get out of this room!"

Before she could protest further, a blur of flesh and fur and sinew streaked through the air, like a flash of molten silver, and slammed against the wolf broadside with such an impact Sara could scarcely tell them apart. They collided hard, but not hard enough to take the contest to the floor, and she drew her knees up out of the way as the two animals engaged in battle at the foot of the four-poster.

She inched to the side of the bed. No longer pinned beneath the counterpane, she slid her feet over the edge. Vertigo starred her vision with pinpoints of white light, and the room swam around her. Behind, the growling snarling ball of tooth and muscle locked together had finally taken the battle off the bed. Blood-speckled drool spattered the linens, and the counterpane was torn. The pillows were leaking feathers. Those floated in the air like snow around the two wolves, who were dancing on their hind legs, locked in mortal combat.

Sara couldn't tell one from the other. If only they weren't moving so fast. If only she weren't so dizzy. On her feet now, she reeled toward the vacant hearth and grabbed a poker. She would not leave the room as Nicholas had ordered. If Nero needed her help, she would be there to give it—but which one was Nero? Both their coats were wet with drool and streaked with blood. She could no longer tell which had the injured leg for the slime that painted them head to toe. Both their eyes were glowing red in the candleshine. Both their fangs were bared, and neither would give quarter.

The dull ache in her shoulder had become a sharp pain again. It didn't matter. Nothing did but making an end to the nightmare once and for all, and she staggered toward them, dragging the poker. It was too heavy to carry.

"*Nero!*" she cried, trying to force recognition, but it was Mills who replied. She hadn't even heard him enter.

"Stand where you are, my lady," he said, his pistol aimed, his free hand supporting his injured elbow. "Do not move from that spot. Do not draw its eyes. Let me handle this."

"They're killing each other!" she shrilled. "What if you shoot the wrong wolf?"

"Trust me, my lady. I will not."

Sara stood her ground, but it was too late. She had already attracted one wolf's attention. He prowled closer, and the other turned and lunged at her, driving her down on the carpet out of harm's way.

Mills raised his pistol.

"*No!*" she cried. "Don't shoot! It's Nero!"

If ever there was a human look of desperation in an animal's face, she saw it then in Nero's eyes. He was trying to shove her out of the way of danger, but it put him off guard, and the other wolf jumped on his back.

Rolling on her side, Sara covered her ears in a desperate attempt to shut out the howling, snarling pandemonium of sound reverberating off the walls—the floor—the ceiling.

"Are you all right, my lady?" Mills called over the racket.

"Y-yes . . . just winded," she responded. "Don't shoot! My God! You nearly killed him!"

"Trust me not to do that, my lady," said the valet. "Please now . . . stand out of the way! You are in my line of fire! I am at a disadvantage with this deuced arm here."

One of the wolves was down, but which one? The Aubusson carpet was fouled with blood and foam and clumps of fur. Sara staggered closer, raising the poker, despite Mill's warning. Both wolves were on their feet again. They had squared off, feet apart, heads down, their bloodied fangs bared. Leaking deep, guttural growls, they circled each other. Then one bit the other's heel and they joined in another whirl of fighting frenzy, coming closer and closer to Sara with each revolution.

She hefted the poker.

"Which one? My God, Mills . . . *which one?*"

The valet raised his fingers to his lips. A piercing whistle ripped the air—the same whistle she'd heard on the strand before Nero disappeared and she lost consciousness.

"Nero!" Mills thundered in a voice so loud it reverberated through her body.

One of the wolves responded—a hitch in his stride, a half-turn of his tousled head; a gleam of recognition in the dilated, bloodshot eyes blind with battle madness. The other lunged at Sara, and Nero sprang between, diverting its attention. It was a costly move. The other creature sank its teeth into Nero's neck, driving him down on the carpet.

Nero's agonized yowl rang out in concert with Sara's scream. Pinned down by the other's jaws, Nero couldn't right himself, and she raised the poker and swung it with all her strength at the wolf that had him in a death grip. It hit between the eyes. Stunned, the animal staggered, shook its head, and let Nero go, only to turn on her again. Sara screamed. Its bloody jaws clamped shut on her nightdress, just missing her thigh as she reeled away, taking another swing with the poker. She was tiring. This time, her balance was untrue, and she missed. Loosing a bloodcurdling snarl, Nero scrabbled to his feet and sprang at the creature's back. A shot rang out. One of the wolves fell at Sara's feet. The other howled and whirled and fell to its knees panting, before it sprang through the air and surged to full human height.

Nicholas stood naked before her, his wet skin running with blood—so much blood, she couldn't tell which was his, and which belonged to the twitching animal breathing its last on the carpet. Sara dropped the poker, and went into his arms.

"Your gown is torn!" he panted. "Tell me he hasn't bitten you, Sara!"

"N-no . . . he hasn't, Nicholas," she murmured. His eyes

were wild and terrible, searching her face—her body—again and again, as though he didn't trust her.

"I'm just . . . overextended," she murmured, forcing a smile. He crushed her close in a smothering embrace.

"Here," said Mills, thrusting Nicholas's clothes toward him. Shouts from the corridor and frantic pounding on the door could no longer be ignored. "There'll be time enough for that later, my lord. Let me help you. This is not over yet."

"I'll do that in the dressing room," said Nicholas, snatching the clothes. He led Sara to the lounge. "Have Dr. Breeden come at once," he said to Mills. "Tell the others that we have shot the wolf that killed Nell. Bring them in and let them see—*now*, Mills! Before it dies, or they will likely see something else lying there!"

"Are you sure you're all right?" Sara begged, taking his measure. "There's so much blood . . . !"

"It's not all mine," he murmured. "Dr. Breeden will tend me later. Do as Mills says, until I return."

The next few minutes were a blur of gasps and sobs and milling voices, as Smythe, Mrs. Bromley, footmen, and all poked their heads in to view the fallen animal. In the midst of the inspection, it wasn't Nicholas, but *Nero* who pranced through the dressing room door and a collective gasp filled the room. It was a brief appearance. Sara's jaw fell slack, as he padded to her side, wagging his tail and offering her his paw. Then, trotting about the room, he stopped and nuzzled Mills's hand before he bounded back through the dressing room door as though nothing untoward had occurred.

"There now, do you see?" said Mills, triumphant. "*Two* dogs, not one—and you lot had all condemned poor Nero. 'Twas Nero who helped me put that creature down."

Minutes later, dressed, the wounds in his arms and shoulders hidden beneath his shirt and waistcoat, his face splashed with water from the dressing room pitcher, Nicholas emerged and sent all but Mills and Dr. Breeden from the room.

The doctor knelt beside the wolf, probing its neck and body through the fur. "It's dead," he said, getting to his feet on stiff, unsteady legs.

"What now?" said Mills.

"We wait," said the doctor.

"What are we waiting for?" Sara murmured.

Mills had stripped the bed, and made it with fresh linens. Nicholas lifted Sara off the lounge and laid her down, propped against what remained of the pillows. He tucked the fresh counterpane around her. Then sitting beside her, he gathered her close in his arms. They were strong and warm, and she went into them murmuring his name.

"We are waiting to see if he changes back," he told her.

It wasn't a long wait. All at once, the blood-matted fur began to melt away before their eyes. The barrel-chested wolf profile shifted, lengthened, and took another form—one that scarcely resembled the Alexander Mallory Sara remembered. He was thinner, wizened. Deep shadow stains wreathed his eye sockets. His festered arm was black and swollen with gangrene, and the mark left by the poker dented his brow.

"Oh, my God, Alex . . ." Nicholas moaned. Sara turned her eyes away from the anguish in his staring down at the barely recognizable remains of what had once been his steward and his friend, and Mills threw the soiled counterpane over the body.

"We cannot show this to the guards," said Dr. Breeden, nodding toward the corpse. "How would we ever explain it?"

"We don't have to," said Nicholas, struggling for composure. "That's why I had you bring the staff in, why Nero made an appearance. They all saw two animals, and they all think I sacked Alex long ago. As soon as you're sure none of them are still lurking about, we'll take him down the back stairs and bury him in the graveyard. I shan't have Mills brought up on charges over this. Consider what has just occurred here a duel, because that is just exactly what it was."

"The bullet didn't kill him," the doctor flashed. "It was the blow to the head that did it. That's why he took so long to die. He hemorrhaged to death. Look at the body." He threw off the counterpane. "The pistol ball is lodged in his hip, hardly a mortal wound. That's twice my lady's saved your life, my lord. I think it's safe to say you owe her that life now . . . and all her heart's desires."

Nicholas folded Sara closer in his arms and she met the promise in his hooded gaze with breath suspended.

"Forever," he murmured, sealing the vow with a lingering kiss, soulful and deep.

Sara's heart quickened. Something was different, and she surrendered to the silken fire it ignited at her very core. It was a provocative foretaste of what was to come.

Epilogue

Spring came soft with rain again along the coast. Sara lay cocooned in her husband's strong arms, listening to the ebb and flow of the sea on the strand below in the darkness before dawn. It was hard to believe nearly a year had passed since the post chaise carried her up the treacherous incline to Ravencliff. So much had happened since.

She no longer occupied the tapestry suite. Now, her rooms were situated on the newly renovated third floor, nearby the master suite, in apartments once occupied by Nicholas's mother. Adjoining was a bright and cheerful chamber that had served as Nicholas's nursery. Another baby occupied it now. Theodore Arthur Michael Pembroke Walraven, such a daunting name for a child only two months old. Sara smiled each time she thought of it. They called him Ted, a beautiful boy, with hair as black as a raven's wing and eyes the color of blue seawater.

Nicholas reached for her breast. His lips were warm on hers. It was a brief, tantalizing kiss that promised so much more. He pulled her closer still, nuzzling against the hollow of her throat.

"You have given me happiness beyond belief," he murmured. "Beyond imagining."

"Not without a struggle," she murmured, through a playful chuckle, and a hug to match.

"We still don't know," Nicholas said, clouding up. "And we won't until he reaches puberty. . . ."

Sara laid a finger over his lips. "If needs must, we will deal with it together . . . and so will he, just as you have done, my love," she said. "But there is one thing . . ."

"Yes?"

"Isn't it time you introduced our son to Nero?" she said. "Either way, he needs to get to know him, don't you think? And I miss him so."

Nicholas laughed. "I still think you love that scruffy old wolf more than you love me," he complained.

Sara smiled. "I think I did love him first . . . because of your stubbornness," she said. "But you should be flattered that I fell in love with a part of you that all else shunned. I want our son to fall in love with that part also."

"And so he shall," said Nicholas. "But not tonight. There is so little left of it." He reached for her breast again, and the lips that took hers now were hungry, searching, drawing her closer to the promise of ecstasy.

Sara opened to him happily. Then she took him deep inside her, riding the white-hot surges that sparked and flared and flamed between them . . . and that always would.

TIGER EYE

MARJORIE M. LIU

He looks completely out of place in Dela Reese's Beijing hotel room—like the tragic hero of some epic tale, exotic and poignant. He is like nothing from her world, neither his variegated hair nor his feline yellow eyes. Yet Dela has danced through the echo of his soul, and she knows this warrior would obey.

Hari has been used and abused for millennia; he is jaded, dull, tired. But upon his release from the riddle box, Hari sees his new mistress is different. In Dela's eyes he sees a hidden power. This woman is the key. If only he dares protect, where before he has savaged; love, where before he's known hate. For Dela, he will dare all.

Blood Moon
✝ ✝ ✝
Dawn Thompson

Jon Hyde-White is changed. Soon he will cease to be an earl's
second son and become a ravening monster. Already lust
grows, begging him to drink blood—and the blood of his
fiancée Cassandra Thorpe will be sweetest of all. Is that not
why the blasphemous creature Sebastian bursts upon them
from the London shadows? But Sebastian's evil task remains
incomplete, and neither Jon nor Cassandra is beyond hope.
One chance remains—in faraway Moldavia, in a secret brotherhood, in an ancient ritual and in the power of love.

ISBN 10: 0-505-52713-8
ISBN 13: 978-0-505-52713-4

- -

The Marsh Hawk

Dawn MacTavish

Was Lady Jenna Hollingsworth's new husband the same man who had killed her father? After one night of passion, she begins to wonder. The jarring aroma of leather, tobacco and recently drunk wine drift toward her on the breeze—she remembers it so well, as well as the tall, muscular shape beneath the multi-caped greatcoat and those eyes of blue fire through the holes in his mask. Oh yes, she remembers that man with whom she shares a secret past. He is the highwayman known as the Marsh Hawk.

ISBN 10: 0-8439-5934-7
ISBN 13: 978-0-8439-5934-5 $6.99 US/$8.99 CAN

CHRISTINE FEEHAN
DARK DESTINY

Her childhood had been a nightmare of violence and pain until she heard his voice calling out to her. Golden and seductive. The voice of an angel.

He has shown her how to survive, taught her to use her unique gifts, trained her in the ancient art of hunting the vampire. Yet he cannot bend her to his will. He cannot summon her to him, no matter how great his power.

As she battles centuries-old evil in a glittering labyrinth of caverns and crystals, he whispers in her mind, forging an unbreakable bond of trust and need. Only with him can she find the courage to embrace the seductive promise of her . . . *Dark Destiny*.

CHRISTINE FEEHAN

DARK MELODY

Lead guitarist of the Dark Troubadours, Dayan is renowned for his mesmerizing performances. His melodies still crowds, beckon seduce, tempt. And always, he calls to *her*. His lover. His lifemate. He calls to her to complete him. To give him the emotions that have faded from his existence, leaving him an empty shell of growing darkness. *Save me. Come to me.*

Corinne Wentworth stands at the vortex of a gathering storm. Pursued by the same fanatics who'd murdered her husband, she risks her life by keeping more than one secret. Fragile, delicate, vulnerable, she has an indomitable faith that makes her fiery sur-render to Dayan all the more powerful.

ISBN 10: 0-8439-5049-8
ISBN 13: 978-0-8439-5049-6
